The Champion

Tim Binding was born in Germany in 1947. He is the author of *In the Kingdom of Air, A Perfect Execution, Island Madness, On Ilkley Moor, Anthem* and *Man Overboard*. He lives in Kent with his wife and daughter.

'*The Champion* is another nationally anatomical narrative in the manner of Binding's earlier works and of Alan Hollinghurst's *The Line of Beauty* and Philip Hensher's *The Northern Clemency* . . . Befitting his surname, Binding proves deft, as in his earlier novels, at tying together the personal and the political.'

Mark Lawson, *Guardian*

'An achingly poignant, thoughtful, and involving satire. Everybody is flawed: and yet, somehow, it isn't bleak, ending with a beautifully judged lament at the passing ways of tradition and class . . . Binding's talent for such nuances makes this one of the finest novels in an already promising year.' *Tablet*

'A bit like Martin Amis strained through Leonard Rossiter . . . Very, very intelligent' Pat Kane, *Saturday Review*

'Binding's expansive portrait of life in the orbital South East is lit up with passages of real descriptive power and dark comedy . . . It's an engaging and gutsy novel that reminds us that boom and bust is a story that never goes away.' *Lady*

'Tim Binding's . . . portrait of nihilistic excess feels as relevant as Martin Amis's *Money*, although Binding's neat satire is to swap the City for the provinces, where the most forceful personality is only as big as his small-town horizons.' *Metro*, Fiction of the Week

'A very readable, hugely enjoyable novel.'

^^^^^^^'s *Books Quarterly*

Also by Tim Binding

In the Kingdom of Air

A Perfect Execution

Island Madness

On Ilkley Moor

Anthem

Man Overboard

Tim Binding

The Champion

PICADOR

First published 2011 in paperback by Picador

This edition published 2012 by Picador
an imprint of Pan Macmillan, a division of Macmillan Publishers Limited
Pan Macmillan, 20 New Wharf Road, London N1 9RR
Basingstoke and Oxford
Associated companies throughout the world
www.panmacmillan.com

ISBN 978-0-330-51380-7

1 3 5 7 9 8 6 4 2

A CIP catalogue record for this book is available from
the British Library.

Typeset by SetSystems Ltd, Saffron Walden, Essex
Printed and bound by CPI Group (UK) Ltd, Croydon, CR0 4YY

FT
Pbk

For Celia

One

We knew he'd make it, and when he did, we drank to our own success as much as his. He'd done it in all our names, and though we understood he would be leaving, as leave he must, we bathed in the certain knowledge that he'd be carrying something of ourselves with him, just as there would be a trace of himself left behind. Like the scene of any crime.

As a boy he'd been something of a boxer, blond and broad, his flesh lying heavy on a frame made to take a man's blows, but blessed with that surprising agility that can sometimes be allied to weight. He danced through all his schooling like that, always quick, always sharp, eyes set to challenge, hands held down by his side, Muhammad Ali style, as if to prove his unbreakable confidence, his unnerving speed. In the ring, out of the ring, it was all the same to him, the space he governed, the room he made for himself, forcing his opponents back onto the ropes, into the corner, any place where they found no defence. There was nothing malicious in it. Power simply rested in his half-clenched hands, his watchful eyes. Girls, too, he treated to the same skill. One round, two, he'd have them flat on their backs by the third at the very latest, bells ringing in their ears. They couldn't get up even if they wanted to. Not with that weight on top of them. Large we called him, large as life, not solely on account of his size but also for the view he took of the world around him, its fruit, its pleasures, how it all seemed ordained to fall within his grasp. Large we called him, and Large he became, the name we wrote in our year books, the boy most likely to, the name that appeared under the newspaper photograph of his inter-county boxing champion-ship, the name that Sophie Marchand foolishly tattooed at the base of her spine in a vain attempt to make their connection permanent, as if even the most exquisite buttocks in town could keep him from his destiny.

I'd known him then, naturally, though not as well as I imagined others did. I wasn't on his register, that's what I put it down to then. I wasn't a rival, or someone he liked to fool about with in class, or later, in one of the pubs that were supposedly off-limits to us sixth-formers. Some obeyed, many didn't, but none held court in the back of the Merry Boys as he did, chewing his way through a plate of tomato sandwiches which Pat would make him for free, her husband dewy-eyed with the prospect of an evening in the company of this mag-netic young mauler, the crowd he could pull. Even at seven-teen, they'd come in to watch him drink and hold forth, dropping his aitches, munching his food, pouncing on any subject under the sun. How had he gained so much experience that he could hold forth on cars and women and the state of the nation with such confidence? Who had taught him all those worldly jokes, those quick asides, those half-believable tall stories which suggested an adult life way beyond his years? He'd stand there, his back leant against the bar, pint held in the crook of his arm, his hair gelled but left deliberately unkempt, flirting not so much with his audience, but at the very prospect of himself.

'Don't you ever use a mirror?' Pat once joked, as he took the proffered plate.

'What do I need of a mirror,' he told her. 'You're my mirror, Pat, every time I look at you,' and she fussed about with the bottles and glasses trying to hide her blushes. And we looked at him and wondered how it was that he should be such the red-hooded cockerel in the midst of such well-bred fowl.

We knew part of the reason – where he came from. London chuck-outs, we called them. They had estates built for them on the far edge of town, circles of semis, with concrete drives and built-in garages underneath the front of store, third bedroom, lying all lumped together brash and red-bricked, like sunburnt tourists herded onto a package-holiday beach. We didn't like it. Ours was a market town. It had settled ways. What industry it had once had (a goods yard, a farm-machinery plant) had long since closed; the yard morphed into the site for the monthly livestock auction, the factory bulldozed to make way for new council offices, in which my father once sat as a councillor, and for one long triumphal year, as mayor. Their arrival was sanctioned the year of his departure, the first estate built and occupied a year later. The notion that he had let the town down in its hour of need never left him. It was that which broke him, as much as later, more obvious events.

'Your grandfather had the right idea,' he would mutter. Back in the thirties, my grandfather Clarence and a group of like-minded householders had stolen out one evening armed with sand, cement and bricks, and built an eight-foot wall across their residential road in Oxford, thereby separating themselves from the newly built council houses on the other side. Their stand against planning laws, aesthetic balance and ordinary human decency sounded a chord which set the strings of middle-class Britain humming. They all wanted walls like that, thousands of them. The wall was torn down, but they had made their point. They didn't like it, integration, never would. My father was of the same mind, but had no course to mortar. So on they came, spilling into our lives, down the supermarket aisles, into the bars, swarming over the brand-new sports centre, with its pool and family crèche, that my father and his fellow councillors had envisaged for our exclusive use. That was not all. Suddenly we had a bowling alley, a video mart, a dingy nightclub with fights outside. Suddenly the town was not ours any longer. It was like one of those fifties science-fiction films that regularly surface on late-night television. Even when I see one now I am reminded of that sense of outlandish

3

intrusion hanging over the town like a poisonous cloud. An alien race had descended, their misshapen customs brought out at night from the boots of their cars like spores from another planet. In time we would all be infected. You only had to drive down one of their roads to know what we were in for; flash new motors, white vans and sightless rust-buckets up on breezeblocks: dodgy money, dodgy trade and a complete aesthetic bypass. The more they filled the streets, the emptier the town became; the more the shops multiplied, the less there seemed to be on offer. At Christmas time, though the lights shone ever brighter, never had the town's prospects appeared so dim. My father began to take my mother and me abroad, five days stuck in a succession of palm-strewn hotels which studiously ignored our Yuletide needs; Lake Como, Interlaken, once disastrously in Ireland, somewhere west of Skibbereen, where he regarded the black pudding sat upon the table with the eye of a surveyor who has discovered a seismic fault line running under the family home. He might not know when the catastrophe would strike, but come it would, tumbling about his ears. There was only one saving grace in all this mess. The schools. Though he could do nothing to save the town from its fall, at least the schools would keep their offspring safe.

There were two schools then; the minor public school, of which my father was a governor, with its fake motto and inflated history, and the comprehensive. No prizes for who went to which. Large was the exception, the boy who had rowed in from the other side of town on the raft of a sports scholarship. Not simply boxing, but hockey, judo and surprise, surprise, cricket.

We knew he was coming. I can't quite recall how, perhaps through Ben, whose father taught us history, that third eye which has been rendered sightless on every subsequent generation, but in the days leading up to that autumn term there was a good deal of discussion concerning his impending arrival. Not there was much debate about who this interloper would turn out to be; we knew that, someone thoroughly undernourished, a product of frozen pizzas and chip-fat culture. It was more a matter of the degree to which we would be prepared to accommodate such an imposition. A sports scholarship? We had our own champion, Tommy Nikolides, the Greek boy, who we called the Turk. His father, who, rumour had it, could barely read, owned the local hardware and garden shop. His wife had left him years back, and he'd had to work hard to keep his little family going. You'd see him standing behind the counter in what he took to be a suit, but was in fact a jacket and trousers of various shades of blue, running his thick, stubby fingers over catalogues and order books, his mouth labouring over the words. Mr Nikolides was acceptable, our pitied immigrant making good. We made fun of him behind Tommy's back, but we liked him and his industrious, respectful ways. We had all grown up with the Turk. The Turk was destined to become our hero, the boy who worked his way up, played by the rules, bearer of our democratic banner, the ambitions of our town personified. The Turk had a future. It was written on every hopeful mother's face, every disappointed father's too. He would play cricket for the county, perhaps beyond. He would become wealthy, mildly famous, rise through the housing ranks of the town. Why, he might even carry off Sophie Marchand. We all dreamt of carrying off Sophie Marchand, though most of us recognized that a dream was all it could ever be. Only the Turk had a chance. Only the Turk was given a chance. Until Large.

I remember that first time I saw him, the rest of us clustered round the desks in little groups, exchanging gossip, renewing rivalries, oblivious to the change that was about to be wrought upon us. I was talking to Sophie at the time, beautiful, dazzling Sophie, who with her blonde hair and her clear skin possessed an ease which rendered her intelligence almost invisible. She was describing a curious fish she had seen that holiday while diving off the Corsican coast. In those days I professed an interest in such things, though in truth I was more interested in the diver than the fish. Despite her status, Sophie had a soft spot for me, or so I believed. Perhaps she just felt sorry for me, or was paying the family back for the good turn we had done her. We had a lake at the back of the house, stocked with trout and tench, and the previous spring my father had given her a free run of it to study their breeding patterns. It was her thing, aquatic life, marine biology. Not surprising, really. Sophie was built for water. Contemporaries of mine might have fixed posters on their wall of bare-buttocked tennis players, but I simply closed my eyes and pictured Sophie diving off the jetty in the late afternoon, proud like a yacht with its full sails billowing. A truer sight you could never hope to see. That morning her hand was stretched out, demonstrating the shape of the creature's fins, its strange corkscrew motion as it swam along the sea floor, when she froze, the story draining from her lips. I turned. There he was, framed by the doorway studying us, both the portrait and the painter, Sophie struck momentarily dumb as she absorbed the tailored cut of his regulation-colour suit, the swaggered knot of his school tie and the sparkle of a gold wristwatch that hung loose over the swell of his hand. Even from a distance you could sense the power in those hands, their capability for destruction and other forms of distraction. Whether there was a smile on his face I cannot truthfully say, but certainly that is how I remember it, careless, quizzical, as if it was him about to take us into his fold, rather than the other way around.

He pushed himself off and ambled over. He had a kind of swing to him, as if walking to a rhythm that only he could hear, his head inclined a fraction, seemingly relaxed but listening out, assessing the hidden dangers, the sudden opportunities, his bulk nourished not simply on the fat of the land but by his place on it. He could have been in a Western. There was no hesitation, no embarrassment. He came up straight to the two of us, and stuck out his hand to the most accomplished, most assured, most unobtainable girl of her year.

'Clark, Clark Rossiter,' he said. 'Pleased to meet you.' He looked around. 'Tell me, which one of these fellas would be Tommy Nikolides.' He dropped his eyes onto me then back to her. 'Tell me it can't be him.'

Sophie laughed and pushed back her hair. 'This is Charles. Tommy's the one over there,' and she pointed across the room.

'That's more like it,' he said. He turned to me, amused by the prospect. 'If it had been you, I'd have asked for my money back.' He punched me lightly on the shoulder and without waiting for any further introduction, crossed the aisle.

'Did you hear that,' Sophie said. '*My* money?'

We watched as he singled the Turk out. Tommy was a good-looking lad, better looking than Large, olive-eyed, sculptured, with his curly black, devilish hair cut just a little too long; a body made for cling film, Sophie used to tease, but here he was up against someone who was carrying much more, an access to a world whose power and charm and love of danger we could only guess at. Tommy was the school's top sportsman, a fabulous player, football-mad long before the disease infected the whole country. He supported Luton, for reasons too arcane to remember, their success or lack of it weighing heavily on his mind. Large gave us a wink and stuck out his hand.

'I hear you're the man to know, when it comes to the football team. The thing is . . .' He dipped his hand into his jacket, brought out what looked like a book of tickets. 'Luton Town. Up to the end of the year. Complimentary, see?'

How he found out Tommy's name or what he looked like or who he supported no one knew, but there he was, squaring up to him with that dominant charm that was to become his trademark. He laid the tickets out on the adjacent desk, a pearl fished up from the deep. The Turk looked around, not knowing what to do. What was this, exactly? Some sort of cheap trick? A crude inducement to friendship?

'Are you trying to bribe me?' he demanded, his voice primed with indignation. The classroom went hollow. This boy had just crossed the threshold, and was trespassing on our hallowed soil. He laughed, a barrel of a thing with a touch of asthma about it.

'Why would I do that?'

'Because you aren't any good?'

Sophie's voice came through loud and clear, argumentative, protective. It was only a matter of time before she and Tommy made it official. We all waited. It was a good question. Was he any good? He didn't look like a footballer. He picked up the tickets and stuck them in Tommy's top pocket.

'You're right,' he said. 'I'm not. But I'm lucky to have around.'

Did he see it all then, who he would take as companions, who he would seduce, who were the also-rans? I think that must be so, for the swift have to move with assurance, and he possessed a superfluity of both those traits. Ben, Duncan, Laurie, how quickly he gathered them in, how quickly they became subordinate to his will. Paula, Rachael, the buck-toothed girl who died a year later of leukaemia, what could they do, confronted with such infectious insolence, such relentless patience, such huge demanding hands? One by one they toppled. It was all they had to offer this self-sufficient young man, or so it seemed, and they gave it up willingly enough. It didn't matter to them that it meant nothing to him, a dip in the sea, something bracing, something to leave feeling good, shaking the drops off. It was Large at play, transient, just like any other game (save boxing), and like all games had its rules, its customs, its fixed frame of time. Indeed his take-it-or-leave-it attitude made him all the more attractive, all the more of a challenge. They knew it. That was the whole point. Our very own rock star, in town for the taking for one night

8

only. And Sophie? He took one look at her that morning, her assured success as tantalizing as the fine hair on her sun-tanned arms, and wrote the time of her eventual bedding right there and then. He was in no hurry. As for the Turk, Large was games captain in all but name before the term was out and no one batted an eyelid, least of all Tommy. The Turk could play, the Turk could lead, but Large could inspire. He could trot onto a field, sniff the air, carve up the moment and hand it out like cake. He could twinkle his eyes, raise you up just by looking at you, the only man I've known to do that. That summer he'd stroll out onto the cricket pitch and stand at the wicket like a bullfighter in the ring, sideways on, inviting destruction. It was the stand of someone who cared but didn't care, who played by the rules yet broke them, who respected tradition yet cocked a snook at it. He broke three bats, and was bowled clean out more times than was deemed prudent, but we loved him for it. Or so we believed.

How can I convey it all, the whirlwind he brought into our lives, how caught up we became in his relentless energy, everything we had known or expected thrown into the air; how exciting he was, how fresh he smelt, the fun he was. That's what the year was all about as far as he was concerned, and we were like overeager TV contestants, throwing ourselves into a kind of prolonged game show, with him both the winner and the prize. Girls, drink, locker-room camaraderie, he was on a never-ending roll. In the classroom it was much the same. He was quick with figures, but that was about it; he worked hard enough but he was average, nothing more. It didn't matter. While others outshone him, myself included, such success no longer carried the same weight. He gave the impression that if he chose to, he could do it all, but as it was, academic success was simply loose change in his pocket. And thus, with one deprecating laugh, one shrug of the shoulders, one condescending clap on the back, he devalued the currency for all of us. When it came to university, he was equally dismissive. 'Them students haven't got a clue,' he announced one night in the Merry Boys, to a chorus of approval. 'They screw a few birds, take a few drugs, and think they're living. On a grant. Where's the sense in that? I'm going to screw a lot of birds, take a lot of drugs and make some serious money. Now whose round is it?'

Everyone liked him. Everyone had to. He wouldn't take no for an answer. He got that from his parents, and they in turn got it from him. He was an only child, after all. They had that loud familiarity that comes from living in a capital city, his mother, his father. They were from the north, Acton way, one of those faceless outposts with not even the dubious grace of the East End to save them, Carl, his old man, one-time foreman of a maintenance gang, working nights on London's underground, then a ducker-and-diver, a jack of all trades, a lathe operator, a butcher's van driver, even, Large told us once with a smattering of pride, a door-to-door salesman selling soft drinks to London housewives. He had that restless romance in him, the father, romance touched with violence. You could see it in the way he attacked the Merry Boys' piano, standing half bent over the keys, press-ganging all and sundry into the obligatory Friday-night sing-along. Before their arrival I don't think any of us understood what a sing-along was – fascism in its purest form. Never drunk anything but Guinness since he was twelve, that was Carl's boast. Rhoda, his wife was called, similarly boastful, a five-a-night brandy-and-soda woman. Before I saw her, I had always pictured her as someone rolling, voluptuous, with a girth broad enough to have produced such a tonnage of a son, but she was nothing like that, top-heavy maybe, but pert and wily, a harder-edged version of one of my father's favourite British comedy actresses, Liz Fraser. 'Pure shop-girl,' my father exclaimed, when she first appeared at one of the school carol concerts. Why they had left London was never clear, though something dark and cancerous had thrown its shadow over their departure. They hadn't come for the fresh air, that was clear. They had that indoor pasty look, brought about by years of game shows and instant gravy. They were serial smokers too. You could always tell when anyone had been over to his house; they came back reeking of it.

I was not a regular there, but I remember one time, the afternoon of the inter-school county boxing championship match. Large had made it to the final. He was famous by then. He'd forgotten part of his gear and asked me to go over, to pick up his spare trunks, his spare pair of gloves. I was grateful to be asked, a small satellite to his star. Rhoda answered the door. She had a towel on her head, her face hot as if fresh from a shower, and a kimono wrapped around an obviously bare body. It was half-past one on a Wednesday afternoon, and it unnerved me to see someone so undressed at such an hour. I introduced myself and blurted out my mission, conscious of the colour rushing to my face. I stood in the hall as she sashayed up the stairs to fetch the bag. There was a photograph on the wall of Large's father standing at the end of a pier holding a giant conger eel. Frank Sinatra was playing somewhere. Fly me to the moon. Carl was smiling, but it was the smile of a hard and unforgiving afternoon's work, barbed and steely, like the hook through the monster's jaws. A glass of half-drunk red stood balanced on the radiator, left over I presumed from the night before. Somewhere I imagined there'd be an overflowing ashtray or two. The house smelt of cigarette smoke and air-freshener and something else, a cloying thickness that gave the air a sour solidity. I thought it might be her cooking. It was only when she came back down that I realized what the smell was; Large, the work of his thick, oily body as it negotiated its way from one cramped space to another. Upward mobility, no wonder it loomed so prominently.

'So, Charles, you're a friend of Clark's?' she enquired, handing it over.

'Not really,' I stammered. 'Just doing him a favour.'

'That's our Clark, always getting someone else to do his dirty work.' She wagged a ringed finger at me. 'Stand up for yourself. Don't let him take you for granted.'

It sounded friendly enough, but it was a belittling remark. I knew what she saw when she opened her front door, an errand boy, doing her precious boy's bidding, a smile of satisfaction flitting across her face. I might have had the right start in life, but her son had me beat by a mile. Always would do.

'Will you be going this evening?' I enquired. I had been brought up to be polite, whatever the provocation.

'Me?' She poked a foot out from underneath the kimono and wriggled it up and down. Her toenails were painted in the school colours, egg, green and egg, my father called them. 'Take a wild guess.' She winked.

I left, angry, vowing never to be used like that again. Forty minutes later I was in the changing room, where Large had completed some essential pre-match preparation. He was sitting on the bench, soaked in sweat. Ben was kneading his shoulders.

'Charlie,' he said. 'My main man.' He threw a playful punch in my direction. 'Is that my gear?' He took the bag and checked the contents. 'Nice one. You got any change?'

'Change?'

'Yeah. Fifty-pence pieces. I need them for the machine. This side pocket is quite empty.'

'You shouldn't be smoking now, surely.'

Ben started to laugh. Large squeezed his nose between thumb and forefinger, holding his own back.

'Not that machine. The one next to it.'

I blushed and dug into my pocket. I had three fifty-pence pieces. He took them all.

The match took place in the new Pemberton Sports Centre. The Olympic-sized swimming pool had been boarded over, the ring erected, Large's father towelled up in a livid pea-green shellsuit, revelling in the prospect of a legalized punch-up.

The town was out in force, an uneasy mixture of bigotry and brass, both camps lorded over by the newly installed mayor and his lardy wife (herself a towering example of both qualities). My father had absented himself on the grounds of an upset bowel. The truth was he couldn't bear to see the project he had spent years nurturing and which was named after him being legitimized by the very people whose presence he resented so much. Relinquishing the mayoralty eighteen months before, he was still on the council, a force to be reckoned with. Any potholes in our road got mended double quick. So absence noted, there we sat, the town worthies, the school sixth-formers and their parents, to one side; the family's entourage, their fly London cousins, the estate, on the other. For the old town, those not in school uniform wore sports jackets, casual trousers, open-necked shirts; they wore suits to a man, dark and striped, their jackets hanging down like lengths of corrugated iron, their women decked out as if bound for some Las Vegas casino, all bosom and bangles, and slabs of raw meat. The mayor, seeking to satisfy both factions, hung his chain of office, with its gold links and moderately obscene pendulum, around Carl's neck, clutching his hands in the air in a manner he had doubtless seen on television, but which on him looked ridiculous. The cheering that greeted this flourish was as caustic as it was raucous, though the sarcasm was lost on him. Small wonder that come the council elections the following year he would lose, provoking a similar gesture from my father. All that though, even then, seemed rooted in the past. Here the future beckoned. This was what the world was waiting for now, boys like Large, and the men they would become. This is what counted now, the swagger, the upper cut, the quick careless laugh as you wiped the blood away. The lights dimmed, and on he strolled.

His opponent was from the coast, a freckled lad with red hair, a farmer's boy, heavy, cumbersome, slow to anger. His hands were made for felling rather than fighting, arms more suited for splitting logs than the flurries of activity he might expect in the ring. Before the match began, as they stood, heads bowed, listening to the referee, he leant across and whispered half a dozen words into Large's ear. It was reminiscent of that electric moment in Zaire when Ali told Foreman of his coming doom. Large had been given Mailer's book on it, *The Fight*, the paperback as often as not stuffed into his jacket pocket. When he'd had a few, he'd read passages out loud in the Merry Boys. It was one of his star turns, particularly the passage concerning the fifth round, where Ali sinks back on the ropes, inveigling Foreman to expend his fury. Sometimes Carl accompanied him on the piano, a regular music-hall double-act. Perhaps this lad had read Mailer's book too, or at least had heard of Large's affection for it. No matter his reasoning, he decided that what had worked for Ali would work for him. He licked his fleshy, dew-drop lips and said his piece, Large staring ahead, unblinking. Whatever the sentiment, it was not well chosen. For the next eighteen minutes Large laid siege to the boy, possessed by an indignation that could barely be assuaged, his face flushed, his fists heavy, the boards creaking under the weight. The freckled lad stood there, unable to comprehend the speed, the skill, the sheer cruelty that struck him from all sides, a beleaguered ox danced and jabbed at, confronted by his own gullibility, caught in the headlights of rage. Round upon round he rose slowly from his corner to face yet another bewildering assault, eyes blinking, arms moving first this way then that, in a fruitless attempt at protection, Large darting out from invisible alleyways, from unseen shadows, pounding, smothering, blocking his retreat, one arm locked around the boy's head while his mouth delivered his own half-spat taunts. Rounds two and three he worked on the body; rounds four and five he reserved for the face, opening up a cut over the left eye, which by the opening salvo of the sixth had the eyebrow practically hanging by a thread. Even then, when the referee stepped in, Large pushed him aside, for one more blow. It struck me then that I'd never seen Large angry before, barely in control, overwhelmed by a sentiment that for the most part he kept under lock and key. Here was an opponent, I thought, who when riled would give no quarter, who would hunt you down to the ends of the earth, drive a stake through your heart, bury you in an unmarked grave. That night, when he appeared at the Merry Boys, his hands were so swollen he could barely lift his pint. Sophie Marchand held his glass for him, nestled between her breasts. A cigar stuck out of his top pocket. The Turk was nowhere to be seen.

'Large,' I called out. 'Congratulations.'

'What?' He turned round. 'Charlie! My main man,' and feigned another blow.

'Let me buy you a drink,' I offered.

'Nah. This is on me.' He took out a roll of five-pound notes. 'Sophie, get the man a drink.'

Sophie turned to the bar. He looked at her rear end and winked.

'There's gold in them there hills, Charlie. Just needs some good spade work, wouldn't you say?' He kicked the bag at his feet and winked again. I was at a loss for words. She was well within our hearing. The trophy peeked out amongst his soiled clothing. It wasn't important to him any more. There were banknotes there too, lying carelessly at the bottom.

'Is that money?'

'Course it's money. Two hundred and fifty quid.'

'I didn't know there was a financial prize.'

'There wasn't. My old man laid some bets on. Round six I predicted, just like Ali used to do. This is my cut. He should have given me more, the cheapskate. I'm worth a lot more than this.'

'Still, it's a lot of money.'

'You hear that, Sophie. Charlie here thinks this is a lot of money. You know what I think?' He delved into the bag, pulled out a twenty-pound note and took a match to it. Then came the

15

cigar. It took time to light, Large inexperienced as to the vagaries of cigar-lighting. By the time it had taken, the note was ash on the floor.

'I've always wanted to do that,' he said. 'Looks like all my wishes are going to come true this evening.'

'What did he say?' I asked.

'Who?'

'Your opponent. What did he say?'

Large smiled. 'Something he shouldn't have.'

Sophie returned with my pint. I never liked the stuff much, but it's what we drank in those days. Large's glass was conspicuously empty.

'Aren't you having one?' I asked. He laughed.

'More than one, wouldn't you say, Soph?'

She punched his arm, a conspiratorial protest which brought a sudden blush to my cheeks. Large tapped her on either side of her head.

'You're going to have to do most of the work, though,' he added. 'Putting the glove on.'

I gradually edged my way out as others joined in the laughter. It wasn't so very bad, I suppose, but I was with my father on this one. I didn't like this new way of things, the ease with which such language unlocked such guarded doors. But that's how such things were going to be done in our town now; manners, propriety out of the window; everyone punched on the arm, press-ganged into having a good time. Mexican waves, sing-songs, package holidays. They all come from the same family tree.

So the school year ended. We had all made our plans. Voluntary work overseas, college, the armed services. I was going to Durham to read law, Sophie to Keele to study marine biology, the Turk to Exeter to read civil engineering. Most of us had something lined up. That's how it went. Except Large. Large took a job with the council, working for Parks and Maintenance. I'd see him behind one of those giant Atcos,

16

mowing verges, or bouncing on the back of the trailer amongst plants destined for the municipal gardens. Sometimes I'd wave, sometimes I would pretend not to have seen him. It depended on who I was with, what car I was in. I didn't want to embarrass him, or me. Then one morning I stepped outside the front drive and there he was, sitting by the side of his machine, having a smoke. It was about half eleven. I was on my way down to have coffee. Ben and one or two others would be there, maybe even Sophie. I was taken aback. I didn't know whether he knew where I lived. Certainly he'd never visited it.

In those days we lived in one of the larger houses on the south side of the town. Beyond us lay fields and farms and the beginnings of the small run of villages that led down to the sea. In one sense the house was nothing, just a collection of walls and stairs and draughty corridors; not a pretty house, not particularly comfortable. It was large, overbearing, built in the twenties I imagine, with a dark wood interior that lent gloom to the brightest of days, adding to the feeling of helplessness whenever my father felt that life had somehow taken a turn for the worse. But there were things about it that made it wonderful, almost magical, a house that suddenly, inexplicably came into its own, when days in it would somehow turn into drifting journeys, as if one was on one of those lovely old-fashioned boats you find in the south of France, idling on the still water, floating along on a dreamy summer's afternoon. There were attics and cellars, back stairs, front stairs, a landing with mullioned windows, a drawing room with French ones. There was a washroom, two cellars, an attic schoolroom for me, a room for my mother to paint her watercolours, another for my father to lock himself away and work his way through his recordings of Bach and Maria Callas. There was a huge kitchen that one walked down into, with a Welsh dresser and an antiquated Aga; there was a dining room with the Regency heirloom table, with chairs to match, and in the heyday of father's mayoral and business duties, company to sit round it.

Outside there was the lawn and behind it the sunken square of grass on which to play croquet; to one side of it lay an old rose garden suffused with blooms of red and white, on the other a small orchard of apple and plum; finally stood a walled kitchen garden and beyond, the lake. It had a finality to it, a beginning and an end. There were days when you felt you need never leave it, others when it held you within its walls, a prisoner. It was an English house of silences and depth, of umbrella stands and wet dogs and odd rooms with no visible point to them whatsoever apart from the ability to absorb junk. It was a house where one's future seemed laid out as clearly as the patterned tiles in the hall. It was our house. My house. And there he was, outside it.

'Large,' I called out. He looked up and waved.

'Charlie, my main man!'

I crossed the road. We made conversation. I inspected the machine, professed admiration in his ability to master its gears and levers. I thought of inviting him in. It was a hot day. Then I remembered my mother in her gardening clothes, my father fussing about the house with his papers, Callas's 1961 recording of *Norma* drifting down the corridor. I didn't want Large barging in, forcing them to have to confront the brute reality of their vanquished town.

'Could I get you something?' I asked. 'A glass of water or something.'

'Water?' he scoffed. I corrected myself.

'No, not water. A beer. A can of lager.'

'Can of lager.' He punched me on the arm. 'Now you're talking.'

He got up and without asking, walked across the road and into our drive. I followed, my equilibrium unsettled. I took him through the kitchen, drew out a couple of cans from the tall, twenty-year-old fridge and handed one over. We could have gone straight out the back door into the garden, but now he was here I wanted him to see it, the furniture, the pictures, the cabinets full of good glass. We walked down the corridor, past the open dining room and my father's closed study door, across the long drawing room, the fire as always laid for an unexpectedly cold night, out onto the flagstone terrace. We had one of those old-fashioned swing seats there, frowned on nowadays, too floral, too fussy, too like a drawing room, but I always liked its slow, cumbersome swing, its unapologetic ugliness. Large sat down and with his feet sticking out, started to rock back and forth as if he was on a playground swing. Beyond the lawn and curved flowerbeds at the entrance to the rose garden stood a wheelbarrow, half full of weeds.

'Do you do this all yourself?' he asked.

'How do you mean?'

'The lawns and flowers and that. Must take some doing. Them hedges, looks like they've just been to the barber's.'

'It's all my mother's doing really, apart from the lawn. My father does the mowing, when he's a mind to.'

'Got one of them ride-ons, I'll be bound. Got no stripes, though.'

'He doesn't like stripes. He thinks stripes are vulgar.'

'Does he?' He took a swig. 'Nice, though. I could live here. All it needs is a swimming pool.'

I bridled. 'This is south-east England, Large, not the Costa del Sol.'

'Ah, but think of the pulling power.' He waved the can at me. 'I'll tell you what would happen. In the afternoon, when it's hot, you'll be thinking, why doesn't she take her top off, there's no one about, but she won't, see, 'cause she knows that's what you're thinking. She'll just play with the straps and that and hang over you asking for a light. But come midnight, a nice warm evening, a bottle of wine, a bit of weed and she'll strip the lot off before you get time to work out the colour of it. Stick it over there, instead of that grass. What's that you got on there, croquet?' He snorted. 'They won't take them off for that, Charlie. Get your old man to stick a pool in. Tell him it's a necessary part of your education.'

I looked out at the garden, its deceptive simplicities, its unexpected splashes of colour, my mother's hat bobbing in the distance. She hadn't seen us, or was making it appear so. I tapped my watch.

'Don't want to rush you, but I'm due in town in a minute,' I said. 'Meeting Ben and the gang. Sophie said she might join us.'

'Is that right? Now, if you had a swimming pool you wouldn't have to go down town, hanging around in hope. She'd be up here, getting out of her togs day and night. You'd see as much of her as you want. And there's plenty worth looking at, I can tell you.' He chugged down his lager and burped. 'Best get back. It's a great responsibility, cutting the grass, trimming the verges, cleaning up the dog shit. I've a little bag for that you know, slung over the handle. Two or three a day I fill up, all these stuck-up ponces and their dogs. Don't get up. I'll see myself out.'

I waited until I heard the mower start up again and the whirr of its blades fade into the distance before moving. I was late for coffee. Sophie never showed.

My father took the family on holiday on the Isle of Wight, our traditional obeisance to the English summer and Britain's redolent past. It was the last one we ever had together. The Isle of Wight in the eighties was like Britain in the fifties. Shopkeepers still sold their goods in brown-paper bags. People rode around on bicycles with wicker baskets at the front. In one of the many second-hand bookshops I found an antiquarian oddity entitled *The Constituencies of the Fish*, with intricate engravings of bone structure and type definitions, perfect I thought for a late birthday present for Sophie's eighteenth. It cost me fourteen pounds. I returned two weeks later to the news that not only had Large taken a two-room flat above the town's only decent fish-and-chip shop, but that Sophie Marchand had moved in with him, three days after blowing the coming-of-age candles out. There'd been a scuffle between the two fathers on the pavement outside, Large piling down in his underwear to separate them.

My contemporaries couldn't get enough of it. To them it was everything they dreamt of, independence and defiance, glued together by a surfeit of brazen, profligate sex. Ben, Laura, Duncan, half the class, even Tommy, would troop round after the pubs closed, to watch Large and Sophie holding court, playing records, rolling joints, drinking, smoking, talking raucously into the night. Come one or two, when the drink had been drunk, and the drugs smoked, and Sophie had made sufficiently obvious eyes to her grinning trophy-holder, Large would shoo them out with a laugh and a wave and they'd wander home to their single bedrooms with their posters and record collections and shelves of childish artefacts and lie there, imagining their once-uniformed school friends, so nakedly entwined, not half a mile away. I was forbidden to go, my parents close friends of the Marchands. It confirmed all their worst fears. 'The ability of these people to corrupt,' my father pronounced, 'is infinite.' I half agreed. It was one thing to indulge in the quiet activities of which one's parents would not approve – but to flaunt it in their faces seemed wilful, ungrateful and, more importantly, unnecessary. It never occurred to me that she might be in love with him. It was an act of rebellion, I assumed, not romance.

But I did go there the once, after a desolate evening at the Merry Boys, walking along the High Street, the excuse for my visit still wrapped in its brown paper. I was conscious of what I was taking with me and what I could bring back. I saw myself rescuing her from her own folly, gaining the gratitude of both our parents and maybe, in later months, Sophie herself.

There was no one else about. It was about half eleven, the night warm, the town's nightlife for some reason suspended.

I'd drunk a little more than usual, but nothing to worry about. The chip shop had just closed, the heat from the ventilator set into the wall still seeping out into the night. The upstairs light was on, a thin yellow curtain stretched across the window. A bag of discarded chips lay strewn outside their door, a ribbed boot-print clearly visible across the squashed paste. I rang the bell. There was no reply. I rang again, longer this time, my finger pressed down on the buzzer. The door was pulled back abruptly, as if the doorframe was warped. Large stood bare-chested, slightly out of breath, a pair of baggy shorts pulled up over his stomach.

'Charlie Pemberton!' He looked out, half expecting to see the others behind me. 'What brings you here? All on your lonesome?' He settled back, full in the doorway, blocking the entrance.

'I was passing, as they say. Fancied some chips. But I seemed to have arrived at the wrong time.'

'You could say that. Monday is our quiet night. When we like to be alone. Most of the gang knows that, but as you're here.' He turned and shouted. 'Sophie. You got a visitor.'

There were sacks of potatoes in the hall, the smell of cooking oil hanging on the stairs. Sophie was sat up in a large double bed, plates of half-eaten toast and empty cigarettes packets strewn across the sheets. I shuffled in, willing my eyes still, trying not to register her naked shoulders, her naked, mussed-up hair and the stark outline of her naked, thick-nippled breasts, covered by a hastily gathered stretch of sheet.

'I'll just pop down the road for some more fags,' Large said. He grinned and looked at me. 'Got any change?'

I fumbled in my pockets.

'Not you, Nefertiti there.' He caught the look on my face. 'That's my new name for her. She was married to Akhenaten, you know.'

'Was she.'

'A bit of a boy in his day. Upset the order of things. I like that in a man.'

Sophie fished about in her bag before throwing him her purse.

'Put something on,' she said. 'You'll catch cold.'

He patted his paunch. 'Not with this I won't.' He turned to me. 'She's got to learn to love the fat, you all have. Fat is good for you. Fat feeds you, gives you a cushion. You got to be good and fat if you want to push your weight around. She tries to stop me eating chips, but she won't, will you, Nef, not if you promised me the Nile.'

We listened to the thump of his feet down the stairs.

'Well,' I said. 'This is a bit of a surprise.'

I looked about. A television with his silver boxing cup balanced on the top, a crimson bra hanging down its side; an expensive stereo deck, a rack of Sophie's clothes fixed between two walls where a bookcase had recently stood; that picture of a whale's tail on the wall above her head. In the far corner lay a loose scatter of coloured underwear, and by the bed a pack of lager and a stack of paperbacks on top of which stood a spotted mug, cigarette ends floating at the bottom. Wedged down the side, half opened, the unfamiliar packet of three, one of the foil wrappers torn open. It seemed to me even then such a loathsome object, revolting to handle, awkward to administer; demeaning and desperate. What could be more absurd than the little bulb at the end, ready to catch the futility of it all.

'You OK?' she asked. I swallowed and held out my parcel.

'I brought you a birthday present. I would have come earlier, but . . . It's a book. All about fish.'

I handed it over. She tore open the package and flipped through it like she might a fashion magazine at her local hairdresser's, idly, her mind on something else entirely.

'That's great, Charlie, thank you. Come here.'

Holding the sheet against her body with one hand she held

out her arm. I walked round, bent down and kissed her on the cheek, my hand resting on her shoulder. I could see down her length of back, below the press of a bare haunch. I stepped back, not knowing where to sit.

'Have you been in contact with your—?'

'No,' she interrupted. 'They had a fight, you know.'

'Yes, I heard.'

'Can you believe it? My dad and Carl. It's lucky they weren't arrested.'

'They're worried about you, Sophie. We all are.'

She stared at me. 'You think I'm here under duress?'

'No, but . . .'

'I'm misguided?'

'No.'

'Well, what, then?'

What could I say. Because you're being penetrated night and day by someone not of your class? Because you live above a fish-and-chip shop? Because your fingernails are dirty. Because you've gone against the rules. Because it's all so predictable, the world falling for this loud-mouthed charm. Because it's an affront to my eyes.

'I'm surprised, that's all. I mean it's one thing to . . . To go out with someone, it's another to set up shop so blatantly.'

'Set up shop? What year were you born in? What are you trying to say. That you disapprove?'

'No, of course not. It's great, but what about Keele, your career? Or is this your future now?'

It was the wrong thing to say. As soon as I said it I knew it was the wrong thing to say. And yet it was the right thing to say. What *was* to become of her? She looked at me again, a hardness creeping into her eyes. She was older than me. Always would be.

'I'll let you into a little secret. We're all going to be fucked by the Larges of this world one way or another. I thought I might as well get to the head of the queue.' She leant back a bit, her head to one side, and opened her legs under the sheet. I'd never seen anything so depraved in all my life.

'Isn't that right, Large?' He was standing in the door.

'What's that?' He threw the cigarettes at her and plumped down beside her.

'We're all going to be fucked by you.'

'I bloody hope so.' He put his hands behind his head and winked at me. The hair underneath his arms was ginger. I found the sight of it almost pornographic.

'You been trying to mend her ways?' he asked.

'Not exactly. I'm concerned, that's all. As a friend.'

'Ah, a friend.' He threw me a can. 'Go on, Nef, show him my birthday present.'

She wriggled round to face the wall, and with one hand across her breasts eased the sheet down. His name ran along the base of her spine in old-fashioned scripted letters, the kind you find on invitation cards, the capital L echoing the curve of her hips. Large ran his hand over it before giving it a seigniorial slap.

'Neat, eh,' he pronounced. 'I'm going to take a photograph of it and send to her folks, like a postcard. "Bet you wish I wasn't here." Drink your beer.'

I sat down on the edge of the bed and drank my beer. Neat? There was nothing neat about it. I could see the edges unravelling already. The two of them started to argue which late-night film to watch. It was as if I wasn't there. I drained the can as fast as I could.

'Finished?' Large said.

I nodded.

'Good. Now piss off out of it.'

*

How long it lasted I can't quite recall. Tommy maintains two months, I think it was a little shorter than that. It doesn't matter. What mattered was what came next, the news that he'd landed this job in the City. He'd gone up one day and talked his way in. Thirty grand a year, just for starters, just like that, the futures market, not that any of us, even my father, had any clear idea of what that entailed. It was like reading a history book about another age. There was something gladiatorial about it, something Roman; its decadence, its love of spectacle, its willingness to destroy. It took place in the heart of the City, fought out in an arena of temples; it was capricious and cruel, lacked all morality. Yet such was its coming power, the whole country lay at its mercy. Thumbs up, thumbs down, it was theirs to choose. A week later he was gone. His records, his silver cup, Sophie Marchand, all left behind. He had no need of them now. Sophie, Ben assured me, was inconsolable.

I went round. The lights were out, just the drape of the curtain, hanging half open to reveal the flesh of abandonment. I drove back through the pale one-way streets, past the pink bowling alley and the harshly lit video store, past the Pemberton Sports Centre, through the bus station towards the road that led out of town. Sophie was slumped on a bench outside, a sports bag by her feet, huddled in one of those quilted jackets that only covered three-quarters of what jackets were traditionally required to cover. I rolled down the window.

'Sophie. Where the hell are you going?'

She looked up. She seemed pleased to see me.

'Who cares? I can't go home,' she said. 'I simply can't.'

'Course you can.'

I got out of the car, picked up her bag and threw it in the back. It was fortunate that I was driving my father's car. It had that solid, reassuring look. It reminded her of the order of things, what was. A student runabout and she'd have been on the first coach out.

We drove back in silence. What was there to say? I followed her into the hall, and waited there as she walked into the living room, the L of his name peeking out over the belt of her jeans. I could hear them all talking inside, low, mannered voices, though whether in recrimination or reconciliation I couldn't say. What did it matter? I had brought her back.

'Who?' I heard the father say sharply.

'Charles,' Sophie whispered.

There was a silence and a snort of disapproval, though from which parent I could not determine.

'He's still here, I think.' There was almost laughter in her voice. Andrew Marchand came out, brushing his hands down the side of his corduroy jacket. He was a good-looking man, conscious of the blonde, slim, elegance he had bestowed onto his daughter. Men like him need all kinds of mirrors.

'Mr Marchand.'

'Andrew, please.' He held out his hand. 'It was very good of you, Charles. We were worried.' I shrugged off his thanks, unwilling to flesh out the details. He stood there, similarly stranded.

'University soon, isn't it?' he enquired.

'Durham.'

'Ah, Durham. It's very old, Durham.'

'Yes.'

'English?'

'Law.'

'Law. Of course. No time for any nonsense like this from you, then. Not with all those law books to contend with.'

'No.'

'And your father? Is he well? We seem to have lost touch. That's what happens when someone retires. They don't have any spare time any more. Tell him to get in touch when' – he waved behind him – 'all this is a bit more settled.'

'I will.'

'Good. Well, best get back. Fatted calf and all that.'

I walked back to the car and drove down to the Merry Boys. I took the stool in the corner and looked around. It was quiet, wonderfully empty just like it used to be. Pat was behind the bar.

'He's gone, then,' she said.

'So I hear.'

'Usual?'

I nearly fell right into it. Then I thought, no, I wouldn't have the usual. I didn't have to have the usual any more. I could sit there and drink what I pleased. I never had to join in, sing along, raise a laugh, ever again.

'No. I think I'll have a sherry, Pat. Nice and dry.'

Pat pulled a face and searched the shelves for a schooner.

'Place won't be the same without him,' she sighed, dusting it.

'Think of the advantages,' I said. 'It'll be yours again.'

She looked up, surprised. 'It was always mine, Charlie.'

'Charles,' I corrected. 'Charles.'

And Large? We'd hear occasional reports. Someone had seen him lounging outside one of those City bars at lunchtime, a flute of champagne in one hand, the bottle in the other, a crowd of six or seven of them, jackets slung over their shoulders, ties torn loose at the neck, their hair plastered back as if they'd just bathed in asses' milk. Cleopatra had nothing on them. He'd been thrown out of a lap-dancing club for urinating in an ornamental tub; he'd fallen asleep at his trading desk with a bid still open, lost the company millions. No, he *made* his first million, betting against the price of copper. No, not copper, wheat. And it wasn't Roman, this new age. It was English, Elizabethan to be exact – the time of the buccaneer come again. Those who took the plunge could expect only two things. Ignominy or wealth. Who else could seize this moment but the pirate, the young blood. My father? His son? What good would I have been in such cut-throat times? I'd been a moderately clever boy, taught as moderately clever boys had always been taught. I'd learnt our history in a linear fashion, from beginning to an end. I knew how our island story (and beyond) went, however one-sided that story might be. I knew about the Poor Laws and the Reformation, about the Thirty Years War, the Luddites, the Industrial Revolution, the two Cromwells, the Younger Pitt, Elizabeth's man Cecil. I'd been read to as a child, taken to the seaside and Twickenham. I'd learnt the names of our Test cricketers, knew my Latin declensions, was equipped with passable French. I'd read Chaucer and Shakespeare, Wordsworth and Kipling. I knew a Constable when I saw one, a Turner, even a Henry Moore. I'd believed it all, the set of backdrops that I would play my life out against. And then I discovered that none of it mattered. No one looked at those scenes any more. They were yesterday's production. They didn't mean anything, they'd been washed clean of resonance. What had it all been for, this learning of mine? It was all redundant, history, England, people like me. No one wanted to know.

I went to university, and took no drugs, slept with no one, and felt out of sorts every law-reading minute. This wasn't the place I thought it would be. For a month I couldn't quite work it out, and then it dawned on me. I missed home, not simply the house and my creature comforts, but the town itself. I wanted to know what was happening to it, fearful of what damage might be wrought in my absence. At least that's what I thought at first. Then it came to me, that unlike my father I was intrigued by the prospect. There was opportunity in the change, old businesses expanding, new ones starting up. Some would work, some would fail. Whatever, they'd all need accountants, accountants for their tax returns, accountants for the VAT, accountants for when their divorces started coming through. I could become a part of the town in a way my father never could, never wanted to. What Large had said in the Merry Boys applied even to the likes of me. I didn't need university either. For appearances' sake I stuck it out for a term before coming home. I knew my mind. I would study in London, become a chartered accountant. If I applied myself it would take three years. It took me two and a half. My father tried to swallow his disappointment, but every now and again it would rise abruptly in his gorge, like a persistent ulcer.

The week after I got my qualifications, he took me to his golf club down by the coast, for the member's lunch. I'd never been one for golf, though as a way of making business contacts I could see its advantages. I imagined he was going to suggest that I became a member, offer to pull a few strings, bump me up the waiting list. I was prepared to be grateful. We took the table by the window. The restaurant wasn't full. Outside, players were struggling against the stiff wind driving off the sea. A waitress, a middle-aged woman, grey spun hair, stout shoes, came and stood by the table.

'Five minutes,' he said, needlessly abrupt. Almost immediately he turned in his seat and beckoned over the younger, prettier uniform who was standing by the coffee machine. She skitted over with breezy familiarity. My father rubbed his hands in approval.

'And how are you, Bee Bee? You're looking very brown.'

She put her head on one side, pleased with the observation. 'Just got back from holiday, Mr Pemberton. Two weeks and a bikini.'

'That's the ticket.' He flicked his menu in my direction. 'This is my son, Charles. Trying to put him on the straight and narrow.'

'And you're just the man for that.'

My father nodded. 'And how *is* that boyfriend of yours, what's his name, Jerry, Jay?'

'He's in restaurant management now, Mr Pemberton. We're going to find a business together.'

'Good for you. And has he done the decent thing yet?'

She put her hand to her breast. 'I don't think he knows the meaning of the word, Mr Pemberton. Least not when he's in Fuengirola.'

My father roared with laughter. Bee Bee grinned back,

rubbing one foot against a black-stockinged calf. Catching sight of me, Father's face fell.

'Well. What'll you have? They do a fair lunch here, though the choice could be wider.'

I studied the menu. For starters there was a plate of smoked salmon or a corned-beef salad. He was quite wrong. The choice couldn't be much wider at all.

'I'll start with the smoked salmon,' I said. The girl pursed her lips, her pencil hung in the air. My father lowered his menu, gave her a wink.

'Shall you tell him or will I?' he said, mildly amused. 'That's for members only. That's why it has a little star against it. Guests have the salad. It's perfectly adequate. Off you pop, Bee Bee. We'll order the main course later.'

She turned and clipped her way across the wooden floor. I regarded the menu with increased respect. To carry snobbery so far, and with such aplomb, was quite something. My father waited until the girl had elbowed her way through the kitchen door, then picked up his napkin and shook out the folds.

'Pleasant little thing,' he acknowledged. 'Her beau got himself in a spot of trouble with the council. I helped sort it out. A bit of a wild card, but ambitious.'

'And the other one? The one you waved away?' He waved her away again.

'I haven't brought you here to talk about waitresses, Charles. Your mother tells me you've been looking over some premises. Above a shop.' He dabbed the edge of his lip, as if he'd tasted something unpleasant.

'Parson's, the outfitters. There's two rooms directly above, an inner and outer office, plus a storeroom and a loo. I'll put a part-time secretary in the smaller one and take the larger one for myself, overlooking the High Street. Come and see for yourself.'

He shook his head. 'With those narrow stairs? No, thank you. Overlooking the wrong end of the High Street too,' he added. 'They won't come beating down your door, you know. If it works at all, it'll be in a very limited form. Is that what you want?'

Before I could answer, the waitress reappeared bearing two plates. The smoked salmon was accompanied by two slices of brown bread, four spears of cold asparagus and a dollop of sour cream with chives; the corned beef boasted a quartered tomato and a spoonful of potato salad, tinned by the look of it. The girl set them down with exaggerated care. I could see the white of a shaved underarm through her short sleeve. She caught me looking.

'The usual bottle, Mr Pemberton?' she said, straightening up.

My father shook his head. 'Just two glasses of the club white, Bee Bee. Not too stingy, mind.'

'As if!'

Again we waited until she skipped out of earshot.

'I could have a word with someone at Graylings,' he continued. Graylings was a large accountancy firm in the City. 'They might have an opening, though you'd have to pass some sort of test. Still, my word does count for something there, I believe.'

I could just imagine their faces after the phone call. I turned him down as diplomatically as I could.

'It's a kind thought, but I'd rather see if I can make a go of it first.'

'But why? What's here for a man of your . . .' He couldn't bring himself to use the word talent. 'Facilities.'

'You're not being very loyal to the town, Dad.' He flinched. Dad was not a word we used.

'I am perfectly loyal to the town. I live there, don't I? However, there's no reason why you should.'

'It's growing every day,' I insisted. 'You've said so yourself.'

'But into what? Nothing's safe there any more, not even this place. We may be twenty miles away, but they'll even find

32

a way in here eventually, them and their lady wives. Bee Bee's all very well on the eye, but wait until her beau's ensconced this side of the counter. The town has had it, Charles. If it wasn't for your mother's garden . . .' He stared out of the window, unwilling to finish his sentence. 'Still, if you've made your mind up. Graylings probably wouldn't have suited. Competition's very fierce.' He turned back briskly, tapping the menu again. 'So what's it to be? And don't say the tournedos Rossini. It's got another of those stars against it, see?'

So that is what I became, an accountant, not especially good, not particularly bad. I got by. I found my clients among the shopkeepers and newly self-employed, a predictable group in the main enlivened by a couple of minor artists, a retired criminal and a once famous, now bitter playwright. I took the offices at the wrong end of the High Street and employed a middle-aged secretary, Betty, who, glad to have found work, fielded calls, sent out bills and made me think I was more successful than I was. Seeing my name engraved upon the glass of the upstairs office for the first time, I felt like a character out of an H. G. Wells novel, infused with the stirrings of small-town beginnings. My name had proclaimed itself. It looked to our civic boundaries for its welfare and place. My father was less pleased, regarding the frosted glass as some sort of usurpation. The news that I had reeled in one of his acquaintances would be met with the declaration, 'Just don't land them in it, that's all. I still have my reputation to consider.'

I thought no more of Large, or if I did it was only momentarily, when a name seemed to conjure up his bulky frame, his loud frisky voice. The Turk took his degree, crewed on a boat for a year, lost his arm, and came back to help out in his father's business. He was a town boy, as we'd known all along. Sophie Marchand got over her tattoo. She went to Keele, took a research fellowship in Berkeley, California. That was more like it. As for Large himself, the next time I saw him was at a distance. I'd been set up for a couple of years. His father had been killed in a car crash, coming back from a Euroshuttle booze run, his mother paralysed from the waist down. They had the funeral here, the huge hearse, the gaudy lettered wreaths, large florid men walking behind the coffin, hands in front of their genitals. No one walked behind coffins any more, except gypsies and Irish terrorists, certainly not in our town. Needless to say, I didn't attend. I stood behind my engraved windowpane, a present from my mother, Charles Douglas Pemberton, Chartered Accountant, and watched the procession make its over-theatrical way towards the crematorium, Large in Savile Row black, a tall, shapely girlfriend, unexpectedly aristocratic-looking, in her mid-twenties hanging on the crook of his arm, a host of others, presumably aunts, uncles, cousins, friends, all seemingly descended from worlds which were the stuff of second-rate film scripts. A week later I saw him outside the estate agent's office. He was moving his mother back to London, selling the council house they had bought eight years before. I ducked into the doorway, not wanting to see him, not wanting to have to commiserate over a family I was glad was going. I watched him as he stood there, a dark expensive overcoat slung over his shoulders, the cold wind whipping down the hall, tugging at the hem. He looked lost. We'll not be seeing you again, I said to myself.

How wrong I was.

Two

'If God had not meant for them to be sheared, he would not have made them sheep'

Ralph Hiscox, after Eli Wallah

The eighties came too late for my father. It was the time he had wanted, the time he and his kind had all been waiting for, but when they kicked off, he could only stand on the sidelines and watch them set forth. His ship had been beached long ago, her timbers too frail for such high rolling seas. And what seas, what voyages, what new territory claimed. We sailed upon the globe again, a player. We had oil, we had gas, we had money; we let the City rip, we put the miners in their place. And as for the uncouth, clamouring at the gates, wanting a slice of the action, well, that was the price you paid, rough edges of the new coin.

He found it impossible to keep away. Once a week he'd end the evening polishing up his brogues, his left hand tucked into the well of the shoe, his right obliterating any trace of provincialism. Upstairs would lie the pin-stripe, the shirt, the tie, and next to them the pocket diary, the names of whom he was to meet punctuated by a series of asterisks, the number depending on their rank, their usefulness, and for a few, their likeability. The next day he'd be up in town, sniffing out old haunts, visiting his stockbroker, lunching with members of the old shipping firm, rubbing shoulders with the new order lounging on the streets with their loud tongues and rapacious appetites. He did not admire them, and in public he would disparage their gratuitous lack of charm, but he envied them, with their unashamed whorehouse mentality, the wet of this fresh young sex glistening on their fingers.

My own business flourished, albeit spasmodically. I didn't earn a fortune, but enough to be comfortable. Trust breeds its own regularity, and that is what I became known for, a safe pair of hands. I was unadventurous, I suppose, but then I didn't want to be anything else. I didn't need the excitement that came with risk. For a time I took a partner, Rodney Wright. Rodney was ambitious, a briefcase bulging with plans. He described the town as 'wide open', a phrase I found erotically hypnotic. He talked of moving to better premises in the coming part of town, how our decor should match the aspirations of our new clients, how with drive and commitment we could in four, five, years become a county-wide business. To begin with I fell in with him, and spent long, self-delusionary evenings in the Indian across the road, talking of targets and outlay and minimalist furniture. The truth was I wanted none of it. I didn't want my aspirations to match my clients. I didn't want to move. I liked my creaking stairs and the view of the old timber-framed shop fronts from my half-frosted window. We parted within the year. He took his clients and moved to the flashier part of town. Betty and I stayed put. Within three years he had a staff of five and a second office down by the coast. The few times we met, he would look at me as a disappointed lover might, embarrassed, enquiring after my well-being with a mixture of pity and unashamed relief.

I found an upstairs flat in a solid, half-timbered house, built in the nineteen thirties, half a mile from the office, with a garden I could only look out on, and a hallway that smelt of cat. I furnished it with odds and sods found in the attic back home, added some touches of my own; a nineteen-twenties cocktail cabinet, an art-deco nude, a coffee machine which woke me every morning with its compelling burble. I'd walk to work and at the end of the day walk back again. Once a week I would go home, Sunday usually, sit with my mother in the kitchen while she prepared lunch, afterwards take the dog for a walk round the lake, or, if he was mindful, help my father dislodge the reeds that laid permanent siege to the little jetty. At lunch he'd bring out a bottle, and give us a lecture as to its provenance. Nothing top drawer, he'd tell us; our palates weren't up to it. Once a month he'd take worthier offerings down to the golf club, to share with his friends. It had become a regular fixture since his retirement, Pemberton's lunches. He'd come back satiated, his breath heavy, his voice slow and rich, the delivery driven not from drink, but from the reverential company he had corralled. The club secretary didn't approve but indulged him. My father was used to being indulged. It came with the territory.

Unexpectedly my mother had found his permanent presence much easier than she had ever imagined. The dread homecoming ritual, the meeting of the train, the barely sentient enquiries as to each other's day, the empty clatter of the evening meal, vanished in a puff of familiarity. There was an elasticity to their existence now. Things were spread out. For the first time in forty-five years she established a weight to her activities that matched his. It was a matter of timetables, room allocations, nothing as revolutionary as respect, but it worked well enough. In any event my father was not in the mood for argument. He'd done his duty by us, and now he wanted to be left in peace. Mother was of the same opinion. They were civil to each other, good company on occasions, but essentially they were guests in each other's house.

Theirs became a regular life. Only disease and death would change its course. They had weathered the seasons of marriage; they had weathered me, not that I had been much of a problem. I had been an undemonstrative child, but then I did not come from a demonstrative family. Man, woman, child, none of us had wanted to learn the other's language.

Consequently there was always something separate about us. Sitting with them, I would sometimes look across, and wonder how it was that we were ever related; what they were, my mother and father, and what I was to them: strangers, the three of us, divided by a common history.

*

It was Sophie's father, Andrew Marchand, himself a Name, who persuaded my father to put his money into Lloyd's. I'd been in business about a year. He rang him up out of the blue, keen as mustard for a round of golf. 'Exercise, Alex, I need the exercise.' My father was glad to hear from him again. The Marchands had been one of their fixtures in earlier times, but since my father's retirement they had dropped off the radar. 'Shouldn't you be working?' my father drawled, and they both laughed. Later, he would describe that afternoon as a walk in the Garden of Eden. Despite the still brilliance of the day, the long fairways were almost empty, stretching out to the promise of green arcadia upon green arcadia, wild orchids growing in the border grass, the scented air alive with bees, the flat line of the sea beyond glittering like a vein of running silver. He had played a seemingly effortless round, the spirit of the game clean upon him, the ball driven high and hard, rolling across the green as if guided by God's own hand. At the eleventh hole, Andrew Marchand had leant on his putter and said to his old friend, 'With luck like that, you should really think about becoming a Name.'

A Name. He had thought about it all along, of course. It just needed an Andrew Marchand to roll back the stone, to rub the lamp, have the genie come call. It wasn't greed that propelled him. Rather it was the sight of that artless golf ball rolling towards its destiny, the realization that what he knew he deserved could come true. It was his birthright to become a Name, his sword in the stone. He had earned it. He'd done with drudgery. Now it was time to sit back, let it drop in.

'Lloyd's?' he said, testing the name on his tongue.

'Lloyd's,' Andrew repeated. 'If you want, I could introduce you to Midas.'

Everyone had heard of Midas, Midas the bully, Midas the deformed, Midas the underwriter with the golden touch. His real name was Piers Winkler. He was forty-two. Midas made the papers, not only the financial pages, but the tabloids, the heavies, the Sunday supplements. Where rules of City etiquette prevailed, he professed not to know them. Informed, he professed not to care. Though good dress sense was obligatory at such institutions, Gieves and Hawkes suits, Turnbull and Asser shirts, Midas chose to clothe himself in polyester drip-dries and off-the-peg Burtons, his flapping pockets bulging with soiled scraps of paper, scribbled phone numbers, scrawled figures. His shoes were permanently scuffed from rubbing one impatient foot over another while interrogating pleading brokers. His fingers were stained with ink which leaked from his cracked fountain pen, a relic from the *Lusitania*. He revelled in knowing nothing, never reading the papers, never studying trends, avoiding the gossip and clusters of conversation that hung like barnacles in the surrounding bars and restaurants, following instead what he described as his nose for 'risk with cleavage'. According to one interviewer, he was 'impressively ugly', with the hands of a strangler, the eyes of a Mormon and the flesh of a baby, adding in a revealing aside that his back was as dense with hair as a gorilla's. He had a wife in Wiltshire, a mistress in London, and a boy in Cuernavaca, Mexico, who he visited three times a year. In June they took a month's holiday together in his pink stone villa above Cap Ferrat. Away from the underwriting room, at the dog track or the boxing ring, he would dress divinely, silk suits and hand-made shoes, a bee orchid in his lapel, and as often as not, an unashamed, high-class whore on his arm. To be introduced to Midas was to find the source of the Nile, split the atom, take that small step for man. He made everyone a fortune.

Andrew Marchand made good his promise. My father was duly summoned, bought a silk tie as fresh as a bride's underwear, boarded the ten-twenty, nervous, virginal, his love-sick heart hammering. He came back flushed, coy, unwilling to talk, his eyes fluttering from an awakened intimacy. I was waiting for him at the station with the car. There had been a spate of breathalysing. He got into the car and fiddled with his tie.

'Well, come on, say something. What was he like?'

'He has half a finger,' he said. 'He rubs it in the palm of his other hand as he speaks. He has a lisp.'

'What did he say, with his lisp?'

He pursed his lips together. 'He said, "I hope you're not in it for the money."'

'But aren't you?'

He looked across at me, exasperated. 'It was a joke, Charles. It's how things are done there. You don't talk about money to a man like Piers Winkler. You just let him get on with it.'

He saw his accountant, he did his sums, he became a Name, three-quarters of his shareholding sold to realize the capital. That was the beauty of Lloyd's. It worked your money twice; once on the interest on the deposit, and once again on the underwriting returns. June 1986 was the date he joined, '86 the year of the Big Bang, the deregulation of the money market, June the month after the new Lloyd's building burst upon the scene, the building itself turned inside-out, the innards lifted by a surgeon's hands, elevators, air-conditioning plants, pipes and cables grafted onto the exterior, wet and gleaming. Seen by day it was merely incongruous, seen by night, animal. It was both alien and ancient, the outside blowing its hot, infected breath over the Golden Mile, while within lay a cleansed castle, all detritus and distractions removed, with six towers at each skewered corner, the dark lords inside, contemplating the mastery of their universe. It was hypnotic, a conjurer's trick, the building a sleight of hand, the brash confidence of the exterior leading the eye away from what went on inside. It was the *White Album* building. The inside is out and the outside is in. The outside is in and the inside is out. 'Everybody's got something to hide, 'cept for me and my monkey.'

On the day of his formal induction, he took me up to town with him. Andrew Marchand would be there to meet us. I hadn't wanted to go; an unwanted intrusion into my burgeoning office life, but he insisted. We travelled first class, discounted because of the hour, but first class nevertheless. First class was still first class then. There were compartments, antimacassars, blinds, no special offers for those who couldn't afford it. He slid the door shut and turned on the little overhead light.

'Andrew's giving us lunch afterwards,' he said. 'Do you hear from Sophie ever?'

I hadn't heard from Sophie at all. The others surfaced regularly enough, Laurie, Ben, Rachael, eager to show off her pretty Senegalese boyfriend, but Sophie remained absent. She had appeared once, briefly, over Easter, but by the time it had become known, she'd already left for the snows of Austria.

'Sophie? Not often.'

'Pity. She liked the lake.'

At Charing Cross we took a taxi. He bundled me in, announcing our destination with gusto. He sat on the edge of his seat, his hurried eyes pointing out places he knew; Simpson's, Somerset House, the twisted lane that led to his old firm, the basement bar he had frequented, the jewellers where my mother's wedding-anniversary watch had been purchased; his life a series of small adventures. He was nervous, excited, the little boy in him awakening.

We were met in the Lloyd's reception area by one of Andrew's younger clerks. We had just under an hour to spare. He offered to take us to see the underwriting room. My father hesitated, but I accepted. 'Really, Charles?' my father complained as we were led through the security gates. 'Do you ask to be shown round a bank when you go and see the manager? I'm giving them my money, not selling their house.' We were still arguing when we found ourselves ushered along what turned out to be the first floor over to the landing on the broad curved staircase, from where we could look down upon the main underwriting room. It looked like the reading room in a well-heeled university library more than anything else, only with studious conversation permitted. The age range was not much different either; the bright young students, eager at their desks, the matured fellows leaning back, fingers poised, and behind them all the quietly flowing dons, taking everything in their stride. I had expected something altogether more intense, more nakedly commercial. There seemed no trick to it at all, no curious hand signals, no waving of papers, no cut, no thrust, just rows of double-sided desks and the underwriters seated at them, brokers striding purposefully in the aisles, papers in hand. It was relaxed and informed, the way businesses should be run, the way in time I would like to run mine, with civility and order and the minimum of fuss. How Britain had ruled the world. Below us a young man, not much older than me, was adding his signature to the broker's slip. For a moment I wished it was me at my desk, and my father up here, watching me unnoticed.

'The stock exchange could learn a thing or two from this lot,' he broke in, reluctantly impressed. 'They're animals over there. Bedlam in braces.'

Then it was time for him to appear before the Rota Committee. Every prospective Name had to go before them. We got into the glass lift and rocketed up the outside of the building, the cold shock of London's bottomless wealth dropping into the pit of our stomachs.

'God,' my father said, clutching the railing, turning round to face the lift door. 'Just thinking about it makes my eyes swim.'

We got out on the chairman's floor. Andrew Marchand was

there to greet us. He put a long manicured hand around my father's shoulder and propelled him forward, leaning into him like a prince might a peasant. We passed the foyer, a strangely emptied area, populated only by an empty desk and darkly laboured oils, one of the old underwriting room, all quills and top hats, another of the Queen opening Lloyd's previous incarnation, Catholic in its approach, the Queen as Pope, Churchill as cardinal.

'There's nothing to it, the interview,' Andrew explained. 'But we do insist upon it.'

It was noticed by both of us, that division. Before us stood a broad wooden door, different from the rest. Taller, older. Throwing it open he stood back. Another arcadia, more formal this time; walls of green and gold, decorative plaster ceilings, a row of tear-drop chandeliers and beneath it a long Regency leaf table. A painting of an old sailing boat stood above the fireplace. Plates of silver stood on small decorative tables.

'It's called the Adam Room, after the designer,' he said. 'Can you believe it?'

I could believe it. Another sleight of hand. Later I learnt that it was designed for the first Earl of Shelbourne at Bowood House, 1763. The Scottish architect had just returned from a trip to Rome, and was still swooning. By the nineteen-fifties it had fallen into rack and ruin. The chairman of Lloyd's heard about it and sent down a couple of his henchmen to buy the fireplace, to stick in his office. They returned having bought the whole room, and put it up, slightly shrunken, in what was then the new Lloyd's building in Lime Street, even found the plastering firm, who still had the original mouldings. Now, with more room to spare, it had been restored to its original proportions. There was, to be sure, an eighteenth-century sweetness about it, a rural tinge to its classical formality, but to my mind there was something degrading about this poor room, hoisted hundreds of feet up in the air, skirts flapping, to be plumped down and powdered up for another turn of heightened unreality. For all their shutters and ruched curtains, it was the windows that gave the game away, the orchards of steel and glass that flickered beyond, that and the lifeless brittle that lay underneath her skirts. Two men sat on the table's far side. They were dark-suited, with a surfeit of comfort sprouting out from their collars; pudding-eaters, the pair of them.

The men rose and shook our hands hand. Andrew made the introductions. Johnson and Hardy were their names. My father was wearing his best cufflinks.

'We have a table something like this,' he said, 'only not quite as . . .' He let his hand finish the sentence. The man on the right, Johnson, pursed his lips into a strained smile.

'Churchill dined on this one. And George VI.'

'They do say that the third Earl was conceived on it,' his companion added, 'though I have my doubts. No scratch marks.'

My father laughed.

'You're in with Piers I hear, Mr Pemberton.' Johnson folded his hands under his nose, due reverence shown.

'Yes.'

'Lucky man. Now.' He leant forward and placed both hands upon the table. 'We've looked at your application and I'm happy to tell you that everything seems in order. But there is one thing I must point out to you. It is of the utmost importance that you understand. When you are accepted into Lloyd's, you accept unlimited liability. You understand that. You can lose everything. Everything.'

'Yes, I understand.'

'It's important that we point this out, though' – he too wafted his hand to display the room – 'we do it as pleasantly as we can. And also I must remind you of our golden rule.'

'*Fidentia* – confidence?'

'No, that's our motto.'

My father covered his tracks, flustered to have failed the test. 'Yes, of course. I meant *Uberrima Fides* – utmost faith.'

'No, Mr Pemberton, that is our trading standard. Our golden rule is not even in Latin. If you lose, you pay up and shut up.'

Back outside we waited while Andrew and Johnson exchanged a few more words. I walked about the lifeless, empty floor. Through one massive window I could see the atrium high above while below lay the patterned marble floor where the underwriters walked. I stood alone, silent, not a sound coming from anywhere. I looked in vain for people. There was no one. What was it then, this Lloyd's? At its heart, there was nothing; no secretaries, no phones ringing, no purposeful strides. Like the building, like the Adam Room, Lloyd's was a chimera. It didn't exist. But it was an idea made concrete, made steel. Down the sides of the glass hollow, I could see into the rows of underwriters' offices, the antique desks, the swivel chairs, the Queen Anne tables set with decanters and cut glass. Was that brandy drunk? Did those windows open? Could the phone ring, the books open, or were they, too, Adam Rooms, versions of a reality that didn't exist?

Lunch took place in Leadenhall Market, another stage set, hatters and quill merchants jousting with butchers and game-dealers. Andrew Marchand led us to his table, raising his hand in greeting, whispering a favoured word, as he threaded his way through. As we sat down Father gave me a nudge.

'There he is, Charles. Midas.'

I looked across. A distracted-looking man was crumbling bread into a bowl of soup. He was small and fleshy, with wispy hair and dimpled cheeks and fat cherub lips. I could imagine him in the Adam Room, high up in a corner, blowing on a trumpet, looking down on ringlets of hair and plump pink breasts. He was dining alone, the table cleared of all other cutlery, just the bowl and the bread, and his thick knuckled hands, speckled with hair. People edged their way past, unwilling to meet his eye. My father started forward, to make himself known, but Andrew raised his hand, shaking his head. My father sat down.

'That reminds me, Andrew,' he said, lowering his voice, 'someone told me that I should take out a stop-loss policy. In case . . .' His voice trailed off, unwilling to complete the sentence.

Andrew Marchand looked round, to see if anyone had heard.

'It's your call, Alex, but I wouldn't recommend it.' He nodded in Winkler's direction. 'He wouldn't accept you if you did. He would take it as a reflection on his ability. Not that he would lose out. Everyone wants to be with Piers.'

My father tucked his napkin in, embarrassed. 'There's an end to it, then. Now tell me. How's that lovely daughter of yours?'

'Sophie? Didn't I tell you, we're all thrilled. She's engaged.'

'Engaged? Are you sure?' My father threw me a look of panic. Now I understood why he had invited me. It was too absurd for words.

Andrew Marchand was as taken aback as me. 'My dear Alex, of course I'm sure. He's a bowel-cancer specialist based in Santa Barbara. She's done very well for herself. He earns an absolute packet. We're thinking of following, our only offspring and all that. Now, what do you fancy? They do a superb shepherd's pie here.'

And so we returned home, my father a Name, invisible ermine lying upon his shoulders, coffers of gold to be carried into his tomb. He no longer bothered reading the financial pages, their prosaic tales of shares, directorships and take-overs. He didn't go to London much either. Travel was for dusty feet. Old friends, business colleagues took on a different hue; they had warts, disfigurements, were subject to waste and disease, they were mortal. Father had moved beyond that.

Prosperity and regard were now to be delivered to his door and he would wear them well. When the stock-market crash came, in the autumn of '87, the day after the great storm that swept across the corner of south-east England, he found no need to disguise his pleasure.

'What did I tell you?' he said, holding the paper as if he'd just won the Derby. 'It's a matter of breeding.'

The hurricane was a different matter. Much of my mother's patient skill had been overthrown that night. The croquet lawn lay in ruins, its surface pitted with the spread of an uprooted willow, the pergola had been ripped from the ground, and both our apple trees had been toppled. Most distressing of all was the loss of her Victorian greenhouse, prim and stately like a lady-in-waiting, spirited clean away, only fragments of shattered glass embedded in a holm oak, standing some forty yards away. In the following weeks, when the roads were finally cleared, they spent days driving to reclamation yards and builders' yards, seeking a replacement. They would come back flushed with an intimacy that took them both by surprise, some sapling they had bought instead sticking out the back of the Rover, father's red cashmere scarf tied around its young root. Love, or what passed for it, had been a restrained, formal thing, worn discreetly; now it was set loose again, flapping on the wind. For a time it gave them an energy that had them setting off every other morning in their determined search, an open map on my mother's knee, a thermos of Earl Grey and a Tupperware of egg-and-cress sandwiches wedged by her feet. Kent, East Sussex, even across to Hampshire they drove, once staying overnight in Winchester, scene of their first encounter at his cousin's twenty-first. They found their greenhouse too, a little larger than the original, had it dismantled and transported the seventy miles within the month. When it arrived, he tried to inveigle the men from Parks and Recreation to erect it, but was warned off; interference with their proper duties, he was told; Pemberton's writ was running out. It was the Turk who came to our rescue, or rather the Turk's father, my mother one of his best customers. He turned up one Sunday morning, a white collarless shirt and thick flannel trousers, the Turk in attendance. He looked good, Tommy, despite his one arm, with his strong left hand and his clean working clothes. We held the frame steady, while old Nikolides bedded it in. We'd never been close, the Turk and me, even though I'd often met up with him, by his shop, on our way to school.

'Half of Kent's gone,' I said. 'Terrible mess it's made.'

'Terrible,' Tommy agreed, grinning from ear to ear. 'The strain on our tills.'

A couple of weeks later, with the greenhouse finally ready, my father held an inauguration ceremony to celebrate, the Turk and Mr Nikolides his only guests, a bottle of Laurent Perrier balanced on the stone mushroom that guarded its entrance, a red ribbon stretched across the door frame, and a cushion with a pair of secateurs upon it placed across his open hands. It was how the municipal mind celebrated things; with ribbons and champagne and formal declarations.

'You have to name it, Meredith,' he told her, easing off the bottle's wire restraint.

'Name it? Alex, I can't.'

'But you must,' he insisted. 'You may not enter until you comply.'

'Well, then.' She hesitated, unused to such formal responsibility. 'Well, then, I shall call it the Ark, harbinger of new life, coming to rest on its mount,' and she kissed him, a girlish thing, up on her heels with her arms round his neck and a blush to her cheeks that I would not have believed possible. Even he was taken by surprise.

'Meredith, please. You'll have the cork flying God knows where. We can't afford another one, you know,' and he smiled, a complacent, knowing smile. Of course we could.

'Theo says I'll be able to grow twice as much in this one, though I don't know if I have the energy any more. If you weren't retired, I might have asked you to come and help me, Theo, be my Noah once a week, for a cup of tea and a slice of home-made cake.'

Nikolides bowed. It would be an honour, he said, to work alongside someone with as much skill and knowledge as Mrs Pemberton. Though he didn't know what use he would be. He was such a clumsy brute.

'Nonsense,' she demurred. 'You have the true gardener's touch. Remember I have seen your garden, seen you at work.'

The Ark. We all had a hand in its fulfilment, painting the frame, cleaning the glass, making up the new benches for the seeds and plants to be housed there. It stood, like the old one, to one side of the croquet lawn, rising up behind its protective hedge like a liner on a maiden voyage, sparkling, proud, full of promise. The Ark. Mother had chosen a good name. There'd she be, out amongst its cargo, sailing into the spring. The alchemy of change had turned her earlier despondency into workmanlike enthusiasm. She didn't call on Nikolides. She didn't need to. She was possessed of a new proselytizing energy. Beds were re-shaped, the pergola extended; a small fruit garden was added, raspberry canes, black- and redcurrant bushes. Those were hard-working days for all of us, fallen trees to cut up, logs to store, the wounded areas nursed back to health. Even my father helped, re-turfing the croquet lawn. But by the start of next spring, it seemed that order had been restored. The right order, the wrong order? It was order, and that was enough.

The garden recovered. My parents grew older, more content. The first year the cheque came through, he reduced the mortgage on my flat. That July we ate our first summer pudding made from the berries in our new fruit garden. We settled into being as a new sort of family, the restrictions of the past worn away. I felt happier about going back. I could walk into the house without them looking at me as if I were the cuckoo in the nest; I could put my arm around my mother's waist and let her teach me the names of plants I could never remember. I could open the door to my father's study, where he would turn down the music and enquire after my business. I invited him to the office. He came two weeks later (booked well in advance), coming up the stairs with the measured tread of a visiting dignitary. I introduced him to Betty, who had put on her most startling lipstick for the occasion. He handed her his coat and walked through, rubbing his hands in anticipation.

'Not bad,' he said looking round. 'But a better desk, perhaps. Clients like good furniture. Let me buy something for you.'

'There's no need.'

'No, I'd like to. We could go to the auction rooms together. Find something with a little more gravitas. Mmm?'

'Well, if you want to.'

'Good. That's settled, then.' He turned and closed the door. 'And Betty. Is she trustworthy?'

'Of course. Why?'

'I couldn't help noticing, she's quite attractive in an older, best-sail-to-the-wind sort of way. She's never tried anything on, has she? A woman past her prime, on the lookout for prospects . . . She could do worse. It's very easy to get ensnared if you're not used to it.'

'Please. We shouldn't be having this sort of conversation.'

'I'm not prying, Charles, believe me. But I do wonder sometimes whether that side of life interests you at all. Your mother's getting on, you know. You know what women are. Or perhaps you don't. Tell me, do you find them attractive at all? When you were at university, didn't you ever come across one that appealed in a basic, trouser sort of way?'

'I can't say that I did.'

'Well, law is a very intensive course,' he blundered on. 'How about here? I know the town's going a bit downhill, but if you only looked around, put yourself about a bit more, the tennis club, the Conservative Association, you might give yourself a chance of meeting someone. God, I was handed a Labour Party leaflet by an absolute cracker the other day. I wouldn't even mind you joining up with the socialists if it meant . . . It's not the other thing, is it? I mean we did go to the trouble of sending you to a mixed school.'

I hastened him out of the office. We did not go to the auction together, but he bought me a desk. It was too big, laden with drawers that were too small and inkwells that I had no use for. I had to hold my breath just to squeeze past it. Within a month I'd torn open my best jacket's pockets on a corner. I got rid of it and brought back the old one, which Betty and I had jammed into the store room. When my father came round next time on some pretext or other, he didn't seem to notice. Just tipped his hat and winked to Betty on his way out.

The second year, 1990, he took my mother for a fortnight on the Isle of Capri, accompanied by a new five-piece luggage set, ostentatious leather items bought from Harrods. I house-sat for them, the first time I had ever truly been alone in our home. Even the dog had gone, buried behind the summer house. One night, I sought out one of his better wines, tucked away behind the racks, something I knew he wouldn't find. I bought some fish and chips from the chippy below Large's old flat, went back, pulled the cork and drank it all, didn't even let it breathe, just ran it under the hot tap for a couple of minutes and drank it, quickly, compulsively, with greasy fingers and a greasy mouth. It stayed with me for a long time, those tastes, the ruby depth cutting through the cheap fat, the wine a little too cold, the chips a little too raw, the fish simply delicious. I longed to do it again, fantasized about consuming his wine stock like some alcoholic death-watch beetle, his cellar three-quarters devoured before he even noticed. Months later, he visited my office for the third time, his tread hurried on the stairs. From the way he barged in, I thought my secret was out.

'God, Charles, have you heard?' He looked around, his face pale and blotchy, his eyes bulging. 'Haven't you got a radio in here? Every office should have a radio.'

His fingers fumbled in his pocket, searching. It wasn't the wine. Some calamity had befallen the town, I guessed, the old corporation stuffing knocked out of him, a fire on the new industrial estate, a death in the sports centre carrying his name.

'What's happened, Dad?'

'She's resigned,' he said, angry that I didn't know. 'They've done for her.'

I knew at once who he meant. There was only one She in this world, a Rider Haggard warrior, with her steely bosom and her handbag shield and her spear of confrontation stuck in the flames. He pulled out his blue rosette, the one he'd worn for the last council elections, screwed it in his fist.

'Knifed in the back,' he said, letting it fall to the floor. 'Do you know the date? November the twenty-second. Can you believe it?'

He waited. It meant nothing to me. His expression changed from one of irritation to disappointment, a familiar progression.

'November the twenty-second, Charles, nineteen sixty-three.' I still didn't get it. He exploded with frustration. 'God, didn't they teach you anything in that school? November the twenty-second, the day they shot Kennedy, and now this, the two greatest leaders of the free world both assassinated on the same day and by the same hand. The enemy within, Charles, the enemy within. God knows what's going to happen to us now.'

'They're not quite the same, surely?'

'What do you know? You belong to a generation where politics has no meaning. For us, politics was half the battle. Even my opponents believed that. Kennedy was where it started. He probably wouldn't have been that good in the long run, but we thought the world of him then. How could we not,

52

from this distance. Mac liked him too, which helped. For all that Camelot baloney, Kennedy knew how to stand up square when it counted, just like she did. I met her once.'

'I know. I was there, Dad, remember?'

'I know that. What I meant was . . .'

I knew what he meant. Standing in the school line, shirt ironed, shoes polished, my hair cut specially for the occasion, he had introduced me not so much as his only son but as a true believer's gift, a father's own flesh and blood produced solely for the purpose of keeping her legacy alive. There was something mystical in that afternoon presentation, the nervous dancing of his feet, the formality of her stoop, the hooded majesty of her eyes looking at me through a sort of eugenic haze as she shook my hand and enquired as to my age and prospects. I had my reply well prepared.

'An engineer,' my father had instructed me. 'If she asks you, tell her you want to be an engineer – an engineer or a geologist, something practical. Whatever you do, don't say television or the media.'

'Why should I say that? I don't want to go into television or the media.'

'Don't be obtuse, Charles. Just make sure you say something appropriate.'

I had conjured up appropriate answers all that preceding week. Miner was the first occupation that sprang to mind, though I abandoned it as too obviously contentious. Tap-dancer held sway for a time, but poet was what I eventually selected, a word sufficiently ambiguous to distract her for a short time. She might not have a lot of time for poets as such, but didn't she go for Kipling in rather a big way? And so she came and my father, using as always the trappings of his office to his own advantage, ignored the other boys and guided her straight towards me.

'This is my son, Charles,' he announced. 'He's a great admirer of yours.'

53

He hadn't told me he was going to say that, but it didn't bother me. I did rather admire her. She beamed.

'I'm honoured,' she said. 'And when you leave school, have you any idea what you might want to do?'

I gulped. 'Engineering. I want to be an engineer.' She patted my arm and moved on.

'Of course,' my father was saying, 'it'll all go to pot now, whoever takes her place. No backbone the lot of them, not like her. Can you appreciate, Charles, as a man, how marvellous it has been to be ruled by a woman who told us all what to do? Not there, there. Yes, that's it, that's how I like it, like that. And she thrilled to our touch, Charles, when we did it right, positively thrilled to it. Drank whisky late at night, after it was all over. Very post-coital.'

I looked through the open door, to where Betty sat, head down, pretending not to hear.

'Have you been drinking, Dad?'

'Not a lot. I've rung up the council, talked to Bill, the chief exec. I told him every member of staff should write and say how sorry they are.'

'You can't ask them to do that.'

'Why ever not? They're working for the council, aren't they, an elected Conservative council? They should do as they're bloody well told. It's the least they can do. Bill put up all sorts of ridiculous objections. I'm off now to make him see sense.'

He left. Bill held his ground. So he wrote the letter himself, resigned from the party in protest, Pemberton Sports Centre or no, went out with her, made the papers like her, defiant like her. It all seemed perfectly normal. Even with our little upheavals, we were a settled family now.

Then it all changed.

We should have seen it coming. The years after her departure had been marked by any number of financial upsets, peppering the face of ruddy capitalism like a series of unwanted rashes – as if those gorged upon it had been infected with a ravaging disease, similar to the one that had sent our poor cows mad, their sanity and balance all undone. First, in nineteen ninety-two, came the Czech.

The weekend before that story broke, my father and I had gone to Twickenham to see the World Cup Final, England versus Australia. It was all we had in common, rugby, cricket, the Five Nations Cup, the Ashes, the County Championship; sporting events that were governed by a sense of privilege. That and the fact they weren't football. My father had been in ebullient mood. The tickets had come via Piers Winkler, pressed into my father's hand, a gift.

'No one gets a gift from Piers,' he'd boasted. 'The man's renowned for his tight fist. But we were talking of the match, how I'd tried to get tickets too late, and he just stuffed his hand into his pocket, brought out this great bundle of untidy papers and plucked them free. "Take them," he said. "I was going to take my mistress, but it's not good for her to see all those young men. Not good for me either, the way her expectations are raised." The man's quite brazen, pressed them into my hand. "Are you rich enough yet?" he asked. I told him, "No, that's why I joined up with you." "Neither am I," he said. "Neither are any of us." Said this was a good time to invest more. A very good time. Put my assets to work.'

I was an accountant, but to hear this coming from my father was something new. 'Assets?'

'All this. We've stuff lying around here doing nothing but gathering dust,' he said. 'I've a good mind to sell the lot.'

'What would Mum say?'

'Charles. Where money is concerned, one must make decisions oneself, unencumbered by sentiment, womanly nervousness, and false affection.'

The match proved to be a thrilling, stupendous, even epic affair. England led by Will Carling, the lover it was rumoured of Princess Diana, Australia led by Farr-Jones, one of the greatest captains the game had seen. Although England had won their place via testing matches in both Paris and Edinburgh, it had been Australia's season, marked particularly by an almost superhuman composure under pressure, that and the freedom they gave to David Campese, their fleet-footed wing, who could run the field it seemed almost at will. They had been an awesome team to watch that tournament, mounting a winning attack against Ireland in Dublin with only minutes to spare, toiling furiously against Western Samoa in the driving Welsh rain before disposing of the All Blacks with an ease that bordered on blasphemy. At Twickenham, with the sweet chariot of patriotism swinging as low and as loudly against them as we could muster, England ran at them time after time, but no one could get through. Territorial advantage, greater possession, the cries of fifty thousand English supporters, counted for naught when confronted by their uncanny ability to read our game, Farr-Jones and his fellow halfback Lynagh in particular implacable. Sitting in the stalls, it was like watching a modern version of the Charge of the Light Brigade, magnificent, glorious but comprehensively futile, and, in the way of these grand gestures, barely rugby, more an act of reckless defiance. The match notwithstanding, there was the added frisson of seeing Will Carling both in his physical prime and a third undressed, the third that the future Queen of England was reputed to come to grips with at every opportunity. Seeing those sturdy thighs and clutched buttocks throwing themselves upon the nation's foes, it was hard not to imagine them on top of our glamorous royal, working away with equal enthusiasm.

'Carling played well, I thought,' my father said on the train back and I nodded, trying not to laugh. He hadn't been able to take his eyes off him either.

The match had reverberated in my head for days afterwards. Father and I relived it over the following Sunday lunch; Monday and Tuesday, all business had to be preceded by a lively appreciation of how the game had played. It was in our blood still, the way we went down. It was Wednesday's head-lines which finally drove it from our minds, with the news that Robert Maxwell, proprietor of the *Daily Mirror*, had fallen off his yacht and had been found floating in the sea dead as a lost whale. It sounded fishy from the start, the calm Atlantic waters, the early morning hour, the waist-high brass railings that ran the circumference of the ship. Maxwell had the voice of a snake-oil merchant; insincerity simply oozed out of him. We knew he was a crook just by looking at him, the brazen smile, the booming voice, his card-sharper's skill at hiding his tricks up his sleeve. Here was another sleight of hand. It took, what, five, six days, to discover what he'd done, stolen his employees' pension money, bamboozled all his fellow directors to get the big man out of debt, five hundred million pounds' worth, with not a thought to those he left bereft, little men the lot of them. Though his sons tried to save his reputation, it didn't cut any ice. 'Look at that,' my father said, coming in again, waving a paper. 'They're asking for breathing space, see if they can talk themselves out of trouble.' He tapped the newspaper. 'See that? Twenty-second of. Another one. It's not a date for the faint-hearted.'

They hadn't all been crooks like Maxwell, R. They weren't all dishonest. Pride, greed, incompetence, bad judgement all played their part, but underpinning it was the rationale that gambling with money, our money, your money, my money (rarely theirs), was what it took, the roll of the dice. They were high on a prospector's adrenalin; there were rivers to pan, partners to fleece, whores to bed; the mother lode lay somewhere out on that trading floor, slippery with blood and champagne. Bet on the beast! And what a beautiful, capricious beast it was, wholly sensual in its smell and colour and shim-mering shape. Norman Lamont was more teddy than bear, fool rather than fraud, and yet when it happened, and Britain was thrown out of the ERM, he was not ashamed, nor even contrite. He'd gambled. He'd lost. It was as simple as that. I remember him standing outside the Treasury the year after Maxwell, brushing the hair from his forehead, blinking into the flashing lights, hands behind his back, the future leader of the country hovering behind with sheaves of paper barely enough to accommodate all the nation's noughts he'd squandered that afternoon.

'Today has been an extremely difficult and turbulent day,' Lamont began. 'Massive speculative flows . . .'

'Look at him,' my father spat. 'Reminds me of that ghastly comedian.'

'What ghastly comedian?'

'Charlie Drake,' he explained. ' "Hello, my darlings." That was his catchphrase. Can't you see it? You know what happened to him? He crashed out of his career too, live on television. Just like this one.'

I didn't know who he meant. I watched Lamont squirm. One of the great offices of state, with all that care, all that fiscal responsibility, reduced to this shuffling apologist, who later boasted *Je ne regrette rien*, recalling the French singer Edith Piaf, who had been brought up in a brothel, which in essence was what the money market was, full of pimps and whores and punters. We'd all known that Major had set the rate against the Deutschmark too high, a prickly and conceited novice at the poker table, absurdly confident with his inflated hand, remembered too his Mansion House speech a few weeks before, that resolute piece of conceited hubris. And here was Lamont picking his way through the rubble. Ten billion had been spent that afternoon, and two interest-rate hikes, forty per cent of our nation's reserves, *forty per cent*, as Norman and his merry men chucked million after million out of the Treasury window, while financiers the world over stood stuffing the windfall into sacks.

'The Krauts didn't lift a finger,' my father spluttered. 'Sat on their fat haunches, snapped their braces and gloated.'

58

'Can you blame them?' my mother replied. 'With that parvenu in charge.' Mother, like the rest of them, believed in the quality of stock.

Worse was to come.

We had lamb that day, lamb bred on the salt marshes, stuck with rosemary and garlic. My father had asked for it particularly. We knew something was in the air. He had demanded the works, the Spode dinner service, the cut crystal, the silver coasters, even the bishop's candlesticks. He'd been in town the previous Thursday and according to my mother had come back strangely ebullient. I had speculated on a Harley Street specialist, a terminal illness diagnosed which he would announce with fatalistic aplomb. I even envisaged a manly reconciliation, the solemn transference of familial responsibility. He had asked for the table to be set for four, but come the hour, there were only the three of us, the two of them at either end and me in the middle, facing the empty setting.

Mother and I sat in expectation as he drew the scene out, fussing about the sideboard, sharpening the knife on the old bone-handled steel with exaggerated efficiency, carving slow, deliberate cuts of the pink meat, each slice laid out upon the plate with a surgeon's precision. The bottle stood in its place, next to the decanter, cork by its side. He poured the wine slowly.

'This,' he intoned, 'is a very good bottle.'

'Special occasion?' my mother asked.

'You might say that.'

She nodded in the direction of the empty chair.

'Who was it, then, who was coming?'

'My little joke,' he said, sitting down, fussing with his napkin. 'The spectre at the feast.'

She took a tentative sip and settled the glass down.

'It's a little too heavy for my liking,' she said.

He scowled with irritation. 'It's called depth,' he said.

We ate. Despite the warm June weather he wore his heaviest tweed jacket, a yellow Vyella shirt, and a thick woollen tie tight around the collar. He worked his way through the meal with studied compulsion, the meat, the potatoes, the buttered carrots all treated to the same furious mastication.

'Those roast potatoes are quite excellent, Meredith,' he pronounced, halfway through. 'What are they?'

'Maris Piper.' She was almost afraid to speak.

'Piper! Maris Piper! Foodstuff for an oil rig. How very apt.' His neck began to glow, beads of sweat collecting on the rim of his collar. It must be the drugs, I thought. The drugs and the drink. Eventually he pushed his plate aside, and drinking heavily from his glass, put his hand into his inside jacket pocket.

'I have an announcement to make. I've had a communication.' He waved a letter over the table. 'Have you heard of asbestos?'

Of course we had heard of asbestos. So I was right, then. Asbestos had got to his lungs.

'It seems a lot of Americans are not very well, thanks to all the asbestos fibres they've been inhaling.'

My mother looked at me for reassurance. I could give her none.

'I don't understand, Alex.'

'Emphysema, cancer, all manner of complaints. Not that they're inhaling it now. We're talking thirty, forty years ago. But now, they're dropping like flies. And they want compensation.'

My relief was tempered by a sudden rush of unexpected pleasure. My father wasn't dying. He'd screwed up! And now he was going to confess it. Mother was still in the dark.

'What's this got to do with us, dear?'

He swirled the glass, breathing deeply, taking his time.

'Lloyd's,' he said, dabbing at his mouth. 'That's what it's got do with us. Apparently I owe them just over five hundred thousand pounds. And that's just for starters. There's more in the pipeline – next year, the year after that, who knows when it will end.' He poured another splash into his glass and held it to the light. 'There've been some rich goings on,' he said, 'right under my nose.'

'Five hundred thousand pounds?' My mother repeated the words if they were in a foreign language. 'Don't be so silly, Alex. There must be some sort of mistake.'

'The only mistake is mine, trusting those bastards.' He banged his fist down, sending the cutlery scuttling across the table. 'They saw it coming!' he shouted. 'Years ago. Not just asbestos, but pollution and God knows what else. Know what they did?' He caught my mother's uncomprehending face. 'Oh, it's too complicated to go into, Meredith. You wouldn't under-stand.'

'Try me,' she said quietly. 'Just for once in your life.'

So he told her. He hadn't understood himself, but he had learnt. In the past few days, oh how he had learnt, amazed, incredulous, the fraudulent magician's trick laid bare.

To understand the catastrophe he was facing, you have to understand a little about Lloyd's. Lloyd's Names participate in one-year venture syndicates. The underwriters in the syndi-cates choose the policies on their clients' behalf. Each Name pledges his entire personal wealth to back up his share in the syndicate's policies. The syndicate trades for one year only, then allows two more years for claims to come in and be settled, a throwback to the days of the old shipping industry. After three years, each syndicate closes its year of account and winds up its affairs. However, if there are claims not settled by the end of three years the account remains open. That was fine to begin with, but as business became more complicated, staying open delayed distributions of profit. The solution was to have each closing syndicate pass on its entire portfolio of business and reserves for any future claims to its immediate successor syndicate. They called it Reinsurance to Close.

This RITC transaction occurred at the end of the closing syndicate's third year; its immediate successor was in its second year. This second syndicate now assumed all the liabilities of its predecessor. This process was repeated year after year, so that the assumed liabilities included not only the ones attributable to the closing syndicate's policies written in its own first year, but all the other liabilities lying latent in the daisy chain of policies handed down. A pretty necklace to hang around any neck.

In order to carve out a share of the US insurance market, between the nineteen-thirties and fifties, syndicates at Lloyd's issued a great many low-priced, loosely worded policies without monetary limits. By the seventies these over-generous terms were looming up on the horizon, long-range missiles aimed at Lloyd's seemingly impenetrable hull. It was clear to those in the know that claims due to asbestos, pollution and other health hazards were ripening into full-bodied lawsuits. Millions of Americans had been exposed to asbestos over the years and thousands of them were filing claims against policies written ten, twenty, sometimes fifty years earlier. Some of these policies had lain dormant for so long that the original reserves had been paid out as profits, or eroded away by inflation. Thousands of claimants would soon be asking for billions of dollars, and Lloyd's had to find a way of paying.

Their answer was a process called recruit to dilute. In the seventies and eighties Lloyd's invited thousands of new Names aboard. They lowered the price of admission. They recruited sportsmen, politicians, women, foreigners too. Well why not, they were *all* foreigners, this new intake. There were 6,001 Names in 1970. By 1988, two years after my father joined, the number had risen to 32,433. Two-thirds of the old Names left quietly, while none of the new names were told of the billions of losses moving steadily towards them.

There was a further complication. With the growth of new Names, the capacity for new business increased dramatically, but it was difficult for the agents to meet demand. So they started to insure themselves, in what became known as the

Excess of Loss Spiral. One syndicate insured another syndicate against its own excessive losses. The second syndicate then obtained reinsurance on that reinsurance from another syndicate, who in turn then did the same, and so on and so forth, the twists and turns of the spiral focusing back on the same Names time and time again, concentrating instead of spreading their vulnerability. Now, seven years after he had joined, the Lloyd's ship had been holed. The water was beginning to swirl around my father's feet.

'And you didn't you know anything about this? You handed over our money, our house, everything, without knowing what they were doing, without even *asking*.' There was armour in her voice.

'That's the whole point of Lloyd's, Meredith. You don't have to do or know anything. You just sit back and let it drop through the letterbox. I thought I was dealing with gentlemen. I would never have done the dirty like this, not to anyone.'

'What about Andrew? Have you spoken to him?'

'Andrew? He's flown the coop, remember, sunning himself in sunny California. He's probably laughing at us right now.' He turned on me. 'If you hadn't been sweet on his daughter, I might not have gone along with it.'

'Alex!'

'Well, it's true, Meredith. The times I heard you say that girl could be the making of him. She might have had the morals of an alley cat, but she wouldn't have been content with a two-room office above a clothes shop. When I think of her father that day, her father and Mr Winkler. I trusted him. I trusted them all. Confidence! Utmost faith! They were their watch-words.'

My mother rose to her feet and stretching across, wrapped her hand around the neck of the claret. We watched as she filled her glass almost to the brim.

'Do we have it, then,' she said, raising it to her lips, spilling not a drop, 'the five hundred thousand?'

'Just about, what with the house, the furniture . . .' He pointed to the bottle. 'That.'

'There must be some way out. Have you talked to your business friends?'

'Somewhat thin on the ground now. I'm an embarrassment to them. Heaven forbid I might start asking them for money. We have to face it, Meredith, we're cleaned out.' He waved a hand around the room. 'Take a good look. It'll all be gone within six months. The moment I was put on those syndicates, we were well and truly . . . I don't like to use the word, Meredith, but you know what I mean.'

'You mean fucked.'

He laughed.

'Yes, my dear. That's exactly what I mean. Well and truly fucked.'

My mother straightened her unused cutlery.

'And you think *me* ignorant of the ways of the world. What if I'd done something similar, given the house, all we had, to the first smooth-talking salesman that appeared on the doorstep. You'd have had one of your golfing chums to certify me within the hour! Oh, Alex, how could you! Our home! Our life! Everything we've worked for!'

And so we finished our meal, contemplating our absent guest, Lloyd's of London. Lloyd's of London had come to our dining table. Lloyd's of London was going to eat us out of house and home.

*

It took seven months to sort it all out. Piers Winkler had put my father on four of the heaviest-losing syndicates. In total he owed £585,675. Other Names took to the press, briefed lawyers, joined protest groups, but he could not bear the indignity of such exposure. He obeyed the maxim. He would shut up. He would pay up. He would take his punishment, go to the wall un-blindfolded. The furniture, the glass, the wine were to be sold at auction, the house put on the market. He found a bungalow to rent, across from the sports centre, the Ponderosa he called it, the property hemmed in by a bare wooden fence, the flat ochre yellow of the swimming-pool roof just visible above a cluster of young trees.

As the weeks for the move advanced, my father began to shed layers of his old skin. He became restless, energetic, almost rebellious, not to the company that had thrown his life over, but to the life it had caused him to lead. He sold his golf clubs. He drove round to the clubhouse and harangued the club secretary to give him a rebate on his membership and after that morning's work he drove back and put the car in the local paper. He bought a drop-handled, fourteen-gear bicycle. I would see him about the town, his trousers tucked into his socks, a silver bullet-shaped helmet perched upon his head, sucking from water from a bottle. At least I presumed it was water. Judging by his behaviour, it could well have been some kind of hooch. To my mother's fury, he insisted on doing the weekly shopping, spending hours in the supermarket hunting down the special offers. He took her to the cinema one afternoon and held her hand. It was an inconsistency that troubled us both.

One morning he appeared in the office and, putting his finger to his nose, beckoned me down the stairs. I followed him out the back, where in the little alleyway old Nikolides stood beside his green Bedford, the back doors swung open. Wedged in beside rolls of fruit netting, bamboo canes and bags of fertilizer stood a stack of wooden crates, their provenance stencilled on the front.

'Six of the best,' my father whispered. 'I thought your storeroom would be safest, until it all blows over.'

'Dad, I don't know if I ought to. Is it legal?'

'It's seventy-two bottles, Charles, that's what it is. If I ration myself to one a month, they'll last me six years.'

We carried them up, one crate at a time, my father acting

the anxious smuggler every time a bottle clinked. When we were done, he pulled his bike out of Nikolides' van and offered him five pounds. The old man shook his head sadly and drove away. Betty was looking out of the back window. I tried not to show it, but I wished I hadn't been involved.

'How's it going?' It was a week or so before the move. He drank greedily from his water bottle. I shouldn't have let him exert himself upon those stairs.

'I'm looking forward to it. We should all live in one-storey buildings. Keeps your feet on the ground.' He took another gulp, water trickling down his chin. He hadn't shaved properly, I noticed. 'You could fetch one of those bottles over every month if you like, drink it with me. Two, when I get back in.'

'Get back in?

'I'm thinking of standing for the council again. Independent this time. You'd vote for me, wouldn't you?'

*

Lloyd's hired an outside firm to oversee the removal of our effects. The best stuff was destined for Bonham's, the remainder was going to the local auctioneers. They came, a small army of grey overalls, moving through the house with exaggerated politeness, sheets and stacks of newspaper at the ready. We stood and watched the experts dismantle the table, barely aware of the reality, each section wrapped in soft grey blankets before being carried away, like an injured racehorse. The chairs followed. Then the glass, each piece lifted and stored, a little light going out of our lives. How could this be happening? What had we done? My mother disappeared upstairs, for some last-minute packing, while my father retired to the kitchen table. Below we could hear the bottles being loaded up. He tapped one as I walked down.

'See, Charles. I'm taking a leaf out of your book.'
'Sorry?'

'This bottle, Charles, is the brother of that Talbot you drank when we were on holiday, remember? Thought I wouldn't notice. There were two of them, you know, put by for a special occasion. What was yours? A girl? Was that it? You had a girl around?'

'No, there was no one else. Look, Dad, I know I shouldn't have. I thought . . .'

'What glass did you use? Did you decant it, give it time? I would this, but I haven't got time, have I?'

'No, it was like this, I just . . .'

'What, you just *drank* it?'

'I had a little meal.'

'A little meal.' He pushed the bottle into the centre of the table. A tic started to develop in the corner of his mouth. 'Which reminds me. Whatever happened to that desk I bought you? You sold it, I suppose.'

'Oh, Dad. Why now? Yes, I put it back in the auction, yes. It was too big.'

'What did you get for it?'

'I forget. A hundred?'

'A hundred? It cost me two fifty.'

'Well, I must have picked a bad day.'

'I don't know, Charles. You steal my wine. Sell my presents.' He paused, eyes glaring, breath coming in starts. 'What did you eat with it?'

'Eat?'

'With the Talbot. Your little meal. What was it? Beef? Pheasant?'

'Fish and chips.'

'Fish and chips! God, not even a decent steak. Not even a girl. Why did I ever bother.' He waved me away. 'Go on, see to your mother. I'm worried about her. She's taking this better than I thought.'

I went upstairs. She was in her dressing room, sorting

through clothes. There wasn't the room in the bungalow for all of them. She stood folding cardigans and tops into a hatbox. She looked beautiful, composed and strong.

'I've been singing that song, you know.'

'What song?'

'They can't take that away from me. I suppose he was right really. At the end, memories are all you have.' She held up a green wrap-around. 'Shall I keep this?' she asked me. 'I bought it in Ventnor. That last holiday, remember?'

I remembered. I remembered what I had bought too. I wondered what had happened to it. Probably never made it out of the chip shop.

'We're having a little housewarming tonight,' she announced. 'Your father insists on cooking sausages on the little barbecue they've got out on the terrace, despite its being February. I'm going to make some punch, so we don't both freeze to death. Do you think you'll come.'

'Of course.'

'It could be quite a pretty garden, really,' she said, 'though it lacks privacy. Still, in a couple of springs, with a few hedges . . .' She turned, spinning on her heels. 'Oh, but I loved this house. Didn't you?'

'You know I did.'

'You never brought anyone home, though, to lunch or supper, or asked them round for a game of badminton. Never once.'

'I'm sure I must have.'

'I don't remember anyone. You should have introduced me to your friends, Charlie.'

'I don't think I had that many.'

'There was Sophie. Such a nice girl. Such a pity . . .' She slammed the case shut. 'I don't know what I'm going to do without this house. It's been my life. And my garden, Charlie. My garden!'

She began to cry, soft little murmurings, like a spring from a deep well. She would call on it every day now, fresh tears from its depths. I tried to reassure her.

'It won't be so bad. It was getting too big for you anyway. You'd have had to sell it some time.'

'It gave us room, Charlie, room to put up with each other. But a bungalow. Can you imagine living with your father in a bungalow? Can you? He thought he was so clever. We had the money, Charlie, we had the house. Even if we'd lost it all on the stock market, we'd still have had the house to sell. We could have bought somewhere decent, somewhere in the country, with a little garden. Not a rented bungalow. I could kill him! I really could!' She straightened up, pushing the case away with her foot. 'Come on. One more turn outside.'

Downstairs the kitchen was empty. We could hear footsteps in the cellar, my father taking one last lingering look. We walked out to the lake. It was cold and wintry, the reeds dark and spindly, the water grey and ruffled. I remembered all the times I had spent upon it, sitting on the jetty, rowing in our little boat, idle afternoons, remembered too Sophie Marchand, standing there, the haze of the summer burning off her skin. How she had folded into the water, how she'd risen up out of it, streams of the future cascading off her like falling stars. How wonderful it would have been if we had married, if I had inherited this house. We wouldn't have had to go anywhere, do anything. We would just have taken over, slotted in place. Trouble was, Britain wasn't like that any more. No wanted their place any more. They wanted someone else's. What would Sophie want with this when she could have California? Why would she want an accountant when she could have a bowel-cancer specialist?

We wandered back through the rose garden, past the little seat where my mother used to sit and look out on her handi-work. I made to sit down, but she pulled me up, shaking her head. Coming down through the croquet lawn, she noticed the games box, still under the bench on the summer-house veranda.

'I'm taking that,' my mother announced. 'It's a tiny lawn, but we could manage a hoop or two. Quick, Charles, before they nab it.'

I crossed over. As I bent down to pick it up, a glint caught my eye, light flicking on and off from the greenhouse opposite, like the flash on a mirror. The sun was shining through the greenhouse, something blocking the rays. I knew what it was the moment I saw the shape. I ran across. He'd hung himself in the greenhouse, looped a rope over the central beam and launched himself off from one of the benches. Though his face was misshapen, his neck swollen, his face blotched, his tongue hanging out, dark and red, the air redolent from the fumes of wine and his soiled trousers, he looked almost reproachful, as if we had brought him to this indignity, our demands for his eternal probity. By the bench, almost touching his hand, stood the wine glass, fully drained. I turned to stop her, but my mother was standing only a few feet away. She looked at me and then up to my father's face, then back down again. My face, his face, my face, his face, my face, my face, his face, his face. And then she did not return.

*

Broken times; not just for our family. Broken times had busted out all over. The whole nation had the rug pulled under their feet, left with nothing. Remember those resources we had, oil, gas, coal, where did it all go, our wealth from it, on what was it spent? The unemployed? What all of it? What did we have to show for it in the end; our trains defunct, our hospitals closed, school playing fields sold off, homeless teenagers dossing down in shop doorways, local police stations closed, their houses sold, post offices shut down, unemployment shooting up, families destitute, rickets reappearing, the miners dispossessed, their union destroyed, their pits filled in, the very substance itself an affront; its weight and dirt a reminder of the industrial power we no longer possessed. It was an East European commodity now.

Was that it? Was that the mark of it, my father hanging on the end of a rope, others taking a similar way out – not just by rope: shotgun in the mouth, exhaust fumes hosed into a car's interior, a bath with a bottle of paracetamol and a packet of old-fashioned razor blades – was that the final confirmation that things weren't right and hadn't been right for some time; negative equity, brown envelopes full of cash, everything we thought was there, jobs for life, unions, decent pension schemes, railways, enough schools, enough houses, all blown away. We were never the land of plenty, but this! Nothing! Nothing? After we had won a war, beaten the Argentines, hand-bagged the French, gone to war with Ronald Reagan. Nothing?

And then it all seemed to come right again, balance restored. We had new leaders, new looks; minimum wages, uncouth rock stars again, ones who knew their place. Money was making a comeback too, money maybe on an ever-grander scale, but it had a conscience now. My business was growing too.

Things happened fast after that. It was the time of things happening fast, change. There was spirit abroad, and even though you didn't believe in it (and there weren't many of those) you knew it was all for the good. Everything was all for the good. The good age was upon us.

Three

It was three years later, July 3rd, the day before American Independence Day. For some reason I always envied the Americans and their Independence Day. It seemed such an unlikely thing to be able to do, celebrate one's independence. I'd got in the habit of taking the day off myself, an act of envy almost (for when was I ever going to be independent of anything?), doing something I imagined an American might do, drive to an out-of-town shopping mall, buy myself a checked shirt, eat a burger, indulge myself in pointless frivolity. I rarely wore the shirts I bought, and I didn't care for burgers much, but that was hardly the point. It was being someone else, someone even more anonymous than my habitual self that thrilled. To give it all some anchor, some spurious sense of purpose, I'd buy a new fountain pen too (I had four now), then later take a taxi to one of the bogus bars in town that had sprung up, where I would sit on a stool and order a martini, eschewing conversation but mildly enjoying the stares – the accountant as enigma. I was looking forward to them, my childish pleasures, but then, what are Americans save overgrown children? The pursuit of happiness indeed.

That year, July the 3rd fell on the Thursday. The Turk and I would meet most Thursdays, half twelve at the Merry Boys. Though not legally binding, they'd become pretty much obligatory over the years. The Merry Boys had gone downhill since Large's day. Pat had lost interest. She'd done with bar-room banter. The less company she kept, the better she liked it. So, in true management parlance, for us, the pub's weakness was

72

its strength; no music, no slot machines and precious little of the new clientele. It was a slice of the old cake, turned slightly mouldy.

Out of all of us, the dim-witted, the clever, the plain unlucky, he and I were the only ones left, though for Tommy staying put had worked better than most. Tommy was becoming a rich man now. I knew how rich. His father might not have been able to read much more than his name but his son's ability went far beyond the letters on a page. He could read the future, and the future for a retail outlet such as theirs lay in garden centres. When he returned home, Tommy had changed the direction of the business overnight. Unlike most uneducated men faced with a son more prescient than themselves, old Nikolides showed no resistance at all. On the contrary, he took a fatherly pride in Tommy's far-sighted anticipation, and in those weeks of change I'd see him hard at work, hammering the store into its new shape with those constant peasant hands, his eyes flushed with an innocent optimism that only the immigrant can embrace. Out went the screws and hammers and that beguiling smell of linseed oil, in came bedding plants, climbing roses, wicker furniture, hoses, sprinklers and all the composts, feeds and sprays the modern garden craves. It took off from the very start, and when he was sure of it, Tommy put his account my way. The Turk had suffered under Large's reign too, and it had pleased him, I think, to rope another outsider alongside.

That Thursday, the bar was empty save for the Turk, tucked in the corner window, working on one of his quiz books. He was proud of his education, was Tommy, what he had learnt. Historical dates, chemical compounds, the different parts of a volcano, his was a diligent, workmanlike memory. He was like his father that way, storing knowledge up slowly, carefully, noting it all down in his big ledger of a brain. He hadn't lost his looks. Still the dark seductive hair, the hot afternoon eyes, the figure for such activity too, despite the

73

missing arm. The trouble was, Tommy looked a part he wasn't willing to fill. In time people found out that the Turk was as solid as a rock, but he had that slick, waiter-boy lover look about him that had led to all sorts of misunderstandings. The years had eroded some of that brilliantine shine, but there were times, when he was holding open a door, checking his watch, or simply standing in his store, his eye roving from customer to customer, when he looked as if he should have been standing on the edge of a dance floor, ready with his chat-up line.

I studied the menu board, though I knew perfectly well what would be on offer. Still, it was a relief to see it. Ever since the golf club I'd taken a perverse pleasure in all things corned beef.

'Pat. A little damp this morning.'

'Something to warm you up, then. The usual?'

'Please. And the Turk too?'

She nodded and setting a schooner down, fixed me with a hard look.

'You should know, Charles, you and Tommy. We're selling up, me and Pete. Moving back to Ireland.'

It wasn't a complete surprise. Pete had wanted to return ever since I'd known him.

'But what about us?' I protested. 'You can't leave us in the lurch. There's nowhere else for us to go.'

'You'll find somewhere. We all have to find our place, Charles, and we've found ours.'

She smiled, a full-bodied smile that broke through the wear and tear of life behind the bar. Pete had never played the role of landlord with any degree of conviction. The Merry Boys had always been Pat's. Now she was going to be free of it. She handed me my sherry, age cascading off her face at the very prospect. I raised the glass and took a sip.

'Well, good for you, Pat. We must give you a proper send-off.'

Pat shook her head. 'No, nothing like that. The last few years, they've been nothing to shout about, have they? Best we just slip away one day. It won't be just yet, any road. We have to find a buyer first.'

I carried my drink to the table. The Turk stuck out a leg and waggled his foot. He had a thing for needlessly expensive shoes, even when traipsing about in compost. It was his trademark. He'd read somewhere that Freddie Mercury only wore a pair of shoes once, and while he couldn't emulate such extravagance, he did the best he could. Shoes were Tommy's stab at a decadence he otherwise deplored. These were the colour of Moorish sand, soft strips of tawny leather layered across the width, with a brass bumper around the tip. They sat on his feet like little turbaned princes.

'Lovely hooves today,' I told him. 'Kick this one around. Pat's selling up.'

He took up his pint of Guinness and sighed.

'It was just a matter of time,' he said. 'Well, that'll be the end of this place, then.'

We fell silent. We were fond of the Merry Boys, despite its shortcomings. The Merry Boys had seen our future settle into substance. Here was where we'd celebrated Ben's eighteenth, when he'd admitted to Laura that he was gay. Over the door was the mange-ridden fox's head that Tommy had once tied to the bonnet of Duncan's car. Up there, on the corner where the bar flap could be raised, was where Sophie Marchand had stood holding Large's victory pint. Had there ever been a more potent sight than that, seeing that hand wrapped round that glass pressed to those breasts? Flesh and drink and the future. What had become of her? What had become of the whole family? We never heard from them any more.

'Only you and me left,' the Turk said, unnecessarily.

I protested. 'Not quite. Ben's within spitting distance.'

'We're too conventional for Ben. Only you and me, Charles. The last of the Merry Boys.'

Then I saw it, like a spring morning over the lake, the mist rising, revealing the expanse of it all. It shimmered in front of me. I jumped in, there and then.

'Why don't you buy it, Tommy? You could raise the capital, no problem. We could write off part of the investment. God knows we don't want one those chains ruining it.'

Pat came out and set our food down. I waited but Tommy said nothing. She hovered over the table, expecting some suitably sympathetic observation, but he simply stared back, trying to read the story in her eyes. Then it struck me. He'd already thought of it. He'd been turning it over the moment the news had dropped out of my mouth. She wasn't good old Pat any more. She was the vendor, the opposition. He wasn't going to show his hand to her. Sympathy, interest? He'd rather let her stew. He waited until she disappeared into the other bar.

'I don't know, Charles. I'm thinking of buying Fletcher's. One supermarket, another on the way, they'll be out of business within three months. I could start up an antiques section, wrought-iron gazebos, sundials, that sort of stuff. It would be a quality addition to the business. But a pub?'

He sat back. That foot came out again, willing me to egg him on.

'You can do that any time, Tommy,' I argued. 'This is too good an opportunity to miss. In the right hands, this place could be a gold mine.'

'You said it. In the right hands. Shouldn't I stick to what I know? Pubs are all sorts of mayhem. And then there's the hours. I don't think Lyn would approve.'

He'd already made up his mind, but people like Tommy like being argued into what they already know. I did the best I could. He wouldn't have to be there much. He'd get a husband-and-wife team in, develop the food side. That's where the money lay. Everybody knew that.

'I know what places like this can earn, Tommy, believe me. I might even be able to put a bit of capital in myself.'

'Really?' Tommy affected surprise. That's the trouble with self-made men. They never lose an opportunity to remind you how much they have in their back pocket, how little's in yours.

'Not a lot. Perhaps if I did the books gratis, that could be factored in.'

He picked a forkful of food and swallowed hard. Pat had a way with corned beef that would put the navy to shame.

'OK. Make some enquiries for me. Be discreet. Come round tomorrow after work and let's see how the land lies. I'll get Lyn to knock up some pasta. One thing, though.' He tapped his plate. 'Whoever we get, Prue Leith, the Roux brothers, this will be our signature dish.'

I nodded seriously, without thinking, and he burst out laughing. He'd caught me out, in a typical Turk way. He was testing me, to see how keen I was, and I'd fallen at the first hurdle. I laughed back, happy in my eager foolishness. I felt so content then, so reassured. I could feel a different future within my grasp. I was reaching out, digging my fingers into the fabric of the town. I felt like Pat, the years of self-imposed drudgery running off my back. I would find out everything about running a pub. I would surprise Tommy with my knowledge, my logic, my dedication. I would watch the books like a hawk. And if we made a real go of it, I would develop an indulgence of my own to rival his.

'You're on,' I said. 'If this comes off, we'll have corned-beef hash once a year, at this very table, on this very day, made especially and only for us. Deal?'

I put my hand out. The Turk grinned and wiped his palm clean. For a short moment I was his equal.

'Deal.'

I went back to the office. I made some calls. I talked to the one of the local estate agents, Steve Tanner. I was as discreet as I could be, but he had a pretty good idea. We all knew each other too well. A hundred and fifty thousand was the asking price. They'd probably get it too. It was in a good location. It had a weed-choked pond that could make a pleasant setting for a beer garden, a generous parking space and a back room that could be converted into a dining area. It had potential, and ours was a town that was addicted to the stuff.

It had been raining on and off all day, hot, violent splashes of summer squalls. Under any other circumstances, what with the thunderous rain, and the thoughts of a part ownership in the Merry Boys rolling in my head, I would have found it impossible to concentrate, but that morning I'd been mulling over the accounts of a new client with business interests in Russia, and I still had some work to do. He'd landed a refurbishment contract, to 'tart up the Kremlin', as he'd put it. He'd spoken the words with such a barefaced gleam in his eye that at the time I'd wondered whether he wasn't some sort of financial fantasist (and we have plenty of those wafting through our doors), but running through the figures, he appeared to have some hold on reality. It wasn't the Kremlin, however, rather some official building round the corner devoted to the management of the country's natural resources. How he had struck this particular little gold mine I'd no idea, and he wasn't the sort to hand out confidences, however tall the tale. Castle was his name, Haydn Castle; an implausible kind of entrepreneur, small head, large black-rimmed glasses, with a rented out-of-town house bereft of furniture, a wife who looked like an undernourished cabin boy, and a unnerving habit of his very own of talking to you while looking over his left shoulder, as if waiting for the bailiffs to march in and take what little was left.

Yes, of course the set-up was suspect, but in my line of work a twitchy balance sheet nestling amongst the dullards is something of a prerequisite, if for no other reason than to reassure yourself that you still have blood in your veins. I've always admired the slightly crooked. It amuses me to see the way they keep a straight face while pushing their books across the desk. I like the way they can't help giving themselves away – the surprised inflection in their voice, the heavy dependence on jewellery, absurd personalized number plates, the way they cross their legs back and forth in front of you, like a man with a nervous bladder. It's a game we play, keeping the fraudulent shuttlecock in the air, sailing back and forth over the tax net. I like the thought of the tax man standing on the sidelines, eyes swivelling from side to side, hoping somehow that the net will snare them, that one time, one of us will play a bad shot or a sudden unpacked gust of wind will blow the feathered bag of lies clean off course and land at his feet. As long as I'm not asked to put myself in jeopardy, I find it hugely relaxing, to drive out to their places of residence, sit on their fake furniture, cross my ankles and look up to the ceiling, knowing that maybe under the floorboards above our heads great packets of illegal wedge lie crammed together side by side.

Looking at the amount of money washing into Haydn's business account, the explosively expensive tat he was proposing to saddle them with, it was obvious that he was either a negotiator of extraordinarily hypnotic dimensions or something more prosaic, more akin to the immediate neighbourhood. But as long as the figures didn't start to haemorrhage over my cufflinks, I could see a mildly entertaining future in Mr Castle. I wondered how long it would take for the VAT inspectors to call, as call they would, unannounced no doubt, nice and early in the morning. That would be a very merry show, everyone tripping over each other in exaggerated politeness, and Haydn Castle the man to outfox them all.

I'd been so absorbed in the naked absurdity of the enterprise that I only became aware of the commotion being enacted in the outer office when it was almost over, Betty's protesting shrill washed away by a cocksure laugh that pulled me out of it, like a blow to the head. The door was flung open, and a voice bounded across the narrow space.

'Charlie! My main man!'

He stood there, rain running off his gelled hair like a well-fed mallard's, his dark blue raincoat swung open, streams of rainwater forming puddles on my floor. He'd filled out, more slack to his jowl, more pork to his belly, but the swagger remained and the muscle which propelled it. His face was bright pink, his eyes a mite watery. He was not as fit as he had been, but it didn't matter. Success oozed out from every scrubbed pore. Even the sharpness of breath that the flight of stairs had occasioned had a positive resonance. That was the price a man like him had to pay. He puffed himself out, slapped his paunch in self-congratulation. Take a look at that, Charlie boy. It's what you'll never have.

I sprang up from behind my desk, a move I regretted the moment it was completed.

'Large. This is a bolt from the blue.' He took my hand and grasped it with the lightest of touches. I was surprised. I'd expected one of those power squeezes, but it was elusive, without substance, as a concert pianist might respond, afraid of bruising the means of his livelihood. It was damp too, not from the weather, but from a life spent sweating on uncertainties. Would Sophie have tolerated clammy hands wandering all over her? It didn't seem likely.

'You're soaked through,' I observed. 'Lost your umbrella?'

'Umbrellas! Poking people's eyes out is all they're good for. What's wrong with getting wet?' He slapped his stomach again, looking around. 'So this is where you've been hiding all these years. I couldn't believe it when I saw the name up on the glass. Charlie Pemberton. Fancy you, an accountant.'

It was said jovially enough, but there was no hiding the contempt with which he held my profession. We were drones, unable to handle money the way money was meant to be handled, with flair and daring. I was back on his mother's doorstep, staring down at her painted toenails.

'I'd have thought you would have known,' I said evenly. 'The school grapevine.'

He batted the prospect aside. 'Never comes to anything, does it, all that "we must keep in touch" bollocks. I didn't bother. Then after Dad . . .'

'Yes. I was sorry to hear that. And your mother, Rhoda, how's she?'

The bravado fell from his face. 'Never forgave herself for what happened,' he said. 'They were arguing. Will never say about what. It's too painful.'

He was gratified that I'd remembered her name. She'd had a tough time apparently, six months of operations, much pain, her effervescent life stilled. There was no excuse for it, but I felt almost pleased. I could imagine her, wedged in a wheel-chair, making the best of it. The spirit of the Blitz.

'She's doing great, though. We moved in together. I got the first floor, she got the ground. A pit-bull on wheels, she is. Nothing gets past her.'

He patted his raincoat and pulled out a bottle of wine.

'Thought we might celebrate our reunion. Something special, see?' He held the bottle out in the palm of his hand. It had been a while since I'd seen such a bottle, let alone tasted one. Château d'Armailhac. Too young, anyway. I remembered my father saying that good Pauillac shouldn't be drunk for at least ten years. And here it was, jiggling against his leg like a schoolboy's bottle of pop.

'It's a bit early . . .' I trailed off. He wagged a finger at me.

'You always was a bit of an old woman, Charlie. Come on, live a little, this afternoon at least. What you got to lose. Got a corkscrew?'

I hadn't. He smiled and pulled one out of his other pocket.

'I knew you wouldn't. There's two things a man should have in his office, Charlie. One's a corkscrew, the other's a couch. And you haven't got either. I can see I came back just in the nick of time.' He caught my look. 'Ah, you picked up on that quick enough. Yeah. I'm back, Charlie, for good. I'm retiring. Not bad, eh, for a man of my age. Was you younger than me or older? I can't quite remember. Matter of fact, I can't remember you having a birthday at all.'

'I was the same age,' I told him evenly. 'I still am.'

'Course you are. You was in my year, wasn't you? You was sweet on, what's her name, the girl what tattooed her bum?'

'You mean Sophie? I wouldn't say that exactly.'

'No? Must have been the only c. that wasn't. Whatever happened to her?'

'No idea. We lost touch.'

'See what I mean? Great arse, though. Glasses?' He didn't wait for an answer. Throwing his raincoat into a heap in the corner, he fished out two wine glasses, one from each inside jacket pocket, delighting in his theatrics. The cork went off like a starter's gun. I wondered what sort of race I was in.

'Here,' he said, slurping it out like petrol from a jerry can. 'Take a whiff of that.' He settled himself in the chair opposite and swirled the colour round.

'The thing is, Charlie, I'm glad I've found you, 'cause that's what I'm looking for, someone a bit old-fashioned like you, someone I can trust. I've left the City, chucked it, before it chucks me. I'm too common for them. Can you believe it, in this day and age? Glass ceiling, my agitated arse. It's a class ceiling, Charlie, the way I talk, where I come from. No one gets on the board by saying "was you" instead of—'

'Were you.'

'See? I know that, but I can't say it. Doesn't sound right. To my mind, it's "was you", always will be. But they don't like it, not in the boardroom. They don't mind it on the floor, in fact it's pretty much the order of things, on the floor, but the only time you'll hear it in the boardroom is if you're on your hands and knees, cleaning it. So I'm getting out, six hundred K in the bank and a new life. I'm a business man now.'

'Six?'

'You expected more, I know. You don't save, living that life, Charlie, not when you're twenty-five. You spend it, throw it up in the air and stand under it stark bollock naked. I've had a good time, Charlie, believe me; eaten in some of the finest restaurants in the world, stayed in the best hotels, screwed some of the most beautiful women you'd ever lay eyes on, Brazilian, Jamaican, French. You name the country, I've sampled their wares. But it doesn't half burn you out, all that wheeling and dealing, living in fifth gear. I mean it takes it out of you, you and your bank balance. A weekend in Paris, a flight down to Rio, suddenly you're fifteen grand short and only a runny nose and a dose of something nasty to show for it. So I'm out of it, before I crash out. I've bought a business, Charlie, right here in town. Guess what? Guess what I'm going into?'

I was at a loss to know what to say. All I could think of was the shop down below. They were on their last legs.

'Menswear?' I suggested.

'Menswear! What do you take me for? Care homes, Charlie. Residential care homes.' He leant across the desk. 'When I was sorting out Mum, everyone expected me to put her away. "You're a young man," they'd say. "Got your whole life ahead of you. You can afford it." It got me thinking. People don't want their folks around any more. They want to be shot of them at the earliest opportunity. Mother losing her marbles? Stick her in a home. Dad got a bladder problem? In he goes. Old age? We hate the sight of it. Not in our house, not in our spare bedroom, thank you very much. Care homes, residential homes, we can't have enough of them. They're like motorways. The more you build, the quicker they get filled up. I've got the first one lined up already. Monkton's. You heard of it? It's a bit run-down, but I can sort that out.'

Heard of it? My mother was a resident. It was the only one we could afford. I took another sip of wine, slower this time, trying to keep my voice as level as I could.

'My mother's there, as a matter of fact. After her stroke, I couldn't look after her and work here.'

Large leant over and patted me on the shoulder. 'Course

you couldn't. I'm not saying sometimes you don't have to. Course you do. I'm sure they're looking after her splendid. What was her name?'

'Meredith.'

'Course it is. And your dad was called Alexander. One of the old school, Mum always said.'

I didn't know she'd ever met him, but I kept quiet.

'The point is, Charlie, I need someone I can trust to run it, to look after the books. I don't want to do that. I'm fed up with that side of money. I hate the bloody stuff, VAT, tax, all that shit, I hate it. I want someone to see the books done regular. But not just that. Reading the runes, that's what I'm good at. Costings, stock, depreciations, assets, I need it all laid out in front of me, week after week, so I can see how the business is doing, plan ahead, expand. Don't talk to me about the other stuff, it's a rip-off. I need someone to make sure that I'm pulling in as much as I can. So, I saw your name, up on the glass, couldn't believe it.'

'Why shouldn't you believe it?' I was cold at the prospect. A clear rebuff and perhaps he would vanish.

'Don't get me wrong. It couldn't be better. It's just I always thought, being a bit of a clever-clogs, you'd have been a professor or something. What you do at university?'

'I gave it up.'

'Why was that, then?'

'It didn't suit.'

'No? I'd have thought a brainy chap like you, it would have been just the job. So you haven't got those things after your name.'

'I couldn't see the point. I didn't belong, all that idle time. I wanted to set up on my own. So I do have things after my name, the things I want.'

'See, I like that. A dark horse, Charlie Pemberton, never ran with the crowd, did you? We always thought it was because you was stuck up, but we was wrong. You're your own man, like me. So, what do you say? Interested? I'll make it worth your while.'

I hesitated. I wanted to say no, but I could see he was going to break back into my life, one way or another. More income would give me greater leverage with the Turk. I could outstrip Rodney yet.

'There's only me here, Large,' I warned him. 'There's bigger outfits I could point you to.'

'I know that. Don't you think I don't know that? They'd do all right at first, say all the right things, but in a year's time? They'd charge me the hours but eventually cut corners. They're businessmen like me.'

'And me? What am I?'

'You?' He ran his finger along the edge of the desk. 'You're an honest man. You believe in doing right. You'll just put your head down, do the work and more, and send in the bill, worrying that you've charged too much.' He picked up the bottle and topped my glass up. I'd hardly touched it.

'This is just the start, Charlie. There's all sorts of opportunities in this town. Not just care homes. Hairdressing, restaurants, wine bars. A wine bar would be nice.' He splayed his fingers out. They still had that fat, greasy look. 'The thing about a wine bar, pub, any sort of shop really, there's cash going in, cash going out. Open to interpretation, from what I understand.'

'If you mean . . .'

'I don't mean anything, Charlie. Just an observation, that's all.'

'I'm not the man for that, Large, truly I am not. I'm thorough but not . . .' I let the sentence fall.

'I know you're not. That's what I wanted to hear. So, what's it to be? Come on, don't tell me I bought this bottle for nothing.' His eyes flirted with me, half teasing, half goading. He'd snared me, and he knew it.

'No, Large. Not for nothing.' My hand reached out again,

the second time in a day that I'd shaken on a deal, although there was no semblance of equality here.

'Only one thing, Charlie. It's Clark now. There's only one person allowed to call me Large and you haven't got the legs.' He leant back on his chair and with an outstretched arm pulled open the door.

'Meet the wife,' he said and there she stood. Sophie Marchand.

I've only been winded once, falling on the terrace's flagstones bringing some lemonade out to my mother, my life knocked clean out of me. I remember lying there, unable to move, unable to register who I was, what I had done. It was if someone had stuck his foot down on me, as if I was a ball in a croquet match, and sent my life inside hurtling away, a sledgehammer to my heart. It was like that then. I sat there pole-axed, unable to grasp what stood before my eyes. Sophie? Sophie Marchand? It didn't seem right, that she should be here, in this cramped place, out of the rain, her arms folded, that glossy hair, that unattainable shape, soft like a pencil drawing, angled in the doorframe, heavy bangles on her wrist, high heels on her feet, a white summer two-piece, the jacket, bordered with black, buttoned low. Was she posing? Yes, of course she was. Was she smiling? Yes, a smile of victory, a smile of constant ageless conquest. Had they rehearsed this, argued over it, when would be the best moment of entry, what she should wear? Had they planned it the night before, ways to wind old Charlie up, ways to get his breath banged clean out his body? What was the point of it, this little play, to prove the low value of my currency, lead to their gold? The look on my face, would that be tonight's entertainment?

'Well, say something,' Large declared.

I struggled to my feet. She ran over to my side of the desk. There was a pair of sunglasses perched on the top of her head. I was disappointed. Sunglasses on the top of the head was what my father used to call 'a very bad sign'. She flung her arms around me and kissed me. I can feel it now, the awkward stiffness that seemed to seize my body, as she pressed herself unnecessarily close.

'Sophie. My, this is a day of surprises. So, did I hear right? You two are married?'

'That's right. Only seeing you, I'm thinking of getting a divorce.'

*

They had met in Barbados, she on holiday with her surgeon husband, Large with his fiancée.

'We'd been going steady for over a year, me and Tiffany,' he explained. 'I'd bought the engagement ring two weeks previous. Eight grand it cost me. Looked lovely on her, that ring. She was a good-looking girl.'

'She was gorgeous,' Sophie insisted. 'She could have been on the cover of *Elle*.'

'She had it up here too. Worked at Christie's. Rare wine was her speciality. That's where I got a taste for this . . .' He tapped the bottle. 'She tried to interest me but I didn't have the patience. Don't get me wrong, I like a nice drop, but I'm not going back to school over it. Your dad was a bit of a wine buff, wasn't he?'

'A bit.'

'That's what Mum said.'

There it was again. The shop-girl and my father.

'Anyway, we was sitting there, in the early evening, having a couple of margaritas. We'd been scuba-diving. I was into diving in a big way by then. Wonderful what you can see down there, all them fishes and colours. We was wondering where to go and eat, when who should walk in, hair all piled up like she'd just stepped off Cleopatra's barge, but . . .' He laid his hand out.

'We'd been snorkelling too.'

'Yeah, they'd been snorkelling too, only he didn't like it as much as you, did he, Nef?'

'He liked it well enough.' She spoke quietly, a hint of what, regret in her voice. The story hung in the air.

'So what happened?' I asked. Large jumped back in.

'We hit it off straight away, all of us, me, him, her, Tiff. He was a nice guy, Wallace, quick, funny, and Tiff, she could give as good as she got. We started hanging out together, spent the mornings diving off this boat I'd hired, see the turtles and seahorses. Magic, them seahorses, the way they swim along, like on a bit of string. Tiffany wore bikinis, she had a whole suitcase full of them, but Nef here, every day she'd be wearing the same black one-piece, classy, not too low at the front but with a nice slice out the back.'

'Well, I wasn't going to compete with her figure. Of course I wore a swimsuit.'

'The thing was, Charlie, we'd be in and out the water all morning, sitting having a drink, diving and talking and all the time I'd be wondering . . . you remember?'

'The tattoo.'

'The tattoo. Was it still there? Had she got rid of it? Had she got rid of me? I couldn't ask Tiff to take a look. We was practically on our honeymoon.'

'They didn't know about . . .'

'No, we just said we'd known each other at school. It seemed simpler that way. But it got to me, day after day, looking at her. The evenings were no better. She'd turn up in some backless outfit, and we'd dance and I'd try to feel for it, but it wasn't written in Braille and fair's fair, her husband's looking on.'

'Didn't you ask her? On the privacy of the dance floor?'

'I was shy, Charlie. Can you believe it? Me, shy? I felt like a schoolboy with a great gobstopper in my mouth. I wanted to but the words wouldn't come out. I was all seahorses inside, bobbing around, making my eyes swim. It was driving me mad! Sometimes she'd sit there and squirm in her seat, like she knew exactly what I was thinking.'

'I did.'

'See, she admits it. But would she help me out?'

He told it so well, how he had told all his tales, as if the whole world was in the room. He had that ability of throwing you into the swim of it, the ebb and flow swirling around your feet. You felt near to a life you wished you could live yourself. Sophie watched him intently, her lips moving with his, like a prompter concealed on stage. She'd heard this story many times and she liked the telling of it. It was her story, after all. Occasionally, as he lost himself in its bravado, she'd turn and smile quickly at me, a conspiratorial link that seemed to snap me as close to her as to him. Weren't we from the same stock? Didn't we recognize Large for what he was, what he would always be? His was such a beguiling combination, this warmth, this childlike frankness, this brash naivety, coupled with the deft dealer, the rough-cut swaggerer, the hard diamond on which would snag her skin, and scar her reputation. Those edges would never be smoothed, nor did they want them to be. Polished, perhaps. Her proximity would do that. And me, what was I? The appraiser, the one with the glass stuck in my eye? That afternoon, the world seemed to close around us, Large and Sophie Marchand and me. They had come to me; they were sitting in my office, in my town. I felt older than them, that my narrowed horizons provided me with a stability that they lacked, for all their air miles. What was this story but a tale of one unable to control his feelings. No different from the stag coming down from the hills, spraying on his territory. We were back in the Merry Boys, celebrating his masculine foolishness, his engaging virility.

'One evening I even tried to bribe one of the waiters to chuck a lobster claw or something down there, so that we'd all have to rush round and dig it out. A hundred dollars I offered him, but he wouldn't. It got so bad I couldn't think of anything else Night after night, I'd lie awake, thinking of it. Poor old Tiff, she didn't half get put through her paces. I had to take my mind off it, somehow. There I was, on a tropical island with my beautiful fiancée, lobsters, caviar, champagne, the lot, and all I could think of was that tattoo. It was sheer bloody torture every day.'

There was a coral reef about two miles out that both Sophie and Large wanted to explore. Their partners weren't keen. They decided to go shopping instead. I couldn't help thinking back to that first time I had seen him, how he took us all in, there and then. Is that what he'd done there, bided his time, had the other two in and out of the water, day in day out, until they could take it no more? Was his insistent joviality nothing more than a ploy to lead them to exhaustion, exasperation and inevitable defeat? I could imagine his straight face when they persuaded the two of them to go ahead alone. I could see it, that look of innocent surprise, agreeing only after patient re-assurance.

'It was weird. All them mornings, nothing, and then on this, the last day but one, she slips out of her jeans, and underneath she's got this new costume on, white, holes everywhere, across the stomach, on the shoulders, and when she turned round, in the small of her back, where it counted. And you know what?'

'What?' My heart sinking. She'd kept it!

'It weren't there! She'd had it rubbed it out! My name! I was outraged. Outraged! If she'd kept it, I don't know, I wouldn't have done nothing, but seeing it not there, it got me going. How dare she! Had she forgotten what we was like?' He laughed. 'I was thinking, I'll show you, girl. You can't rub me out just like that. God, I got a nerve, haven't I? I didn't say nothing. We just got togged up and jumped in, right into a shoal of, what was they, Nef?'

'Fish.'

'Very funny. Thousands of them there were, all darting about like little pixies. Ugly, all eyes. There was a picture book I had as a kid, when Noddy were kidnapped and taken to the forest by these goblins, and I felt like that was happening to me, dragged down into a green underworld. We was trying to swim down, and they were busy all around us, you could feel them, darting in and out your legs and then, all of a sudden, they was gone, and there we were, floating along above this reef. It wasn't like them others. It was long and ghostly, kind of bleached, all white and lumpy, like you was wandering around the back of your head. Nef were swimming a little below me, a little ahead of me too; and I was looking at her, thinking what I shouldn't, when I saw it as clear as daylight, my name. I don't know how. The water must have brought the colour lying underneath the skin back up or something, but I could it see again, I swear to God, like it had just been written, and I thought, no, it hasn't gone away, not really, even though she thinks it has, and I haven't gone away either. I tugged on her leg and pointed, like I needed to go up quick, and we surfaced in the middle of this flat, fucking blue, and I pulled off her facemask and kissed her, right there in the middle of the ocean. That's how it started, wasn't it, Nef?'

'That's how it started.'

Again, the pause.

'So what, you ran off together?'

'No, course not. What do you take us for? Tiffany was a nice girl. It wasn't her fault. No, we said our goodbyes, exchanged phone numbers. I thought, well that was a bit silly, good job she's six thousand miles away. But when I got back I couldn't think of nothing else. It was Nef what I wanted. Know what I did?'

I shook my head.

'Tell him, Nef.'

Sophie walked across and tilted my empty glass in her

direction. I nodded. She filled it half full, swirled it twice and took a sip. I wondered why they hadn't brought three glasses. For us to sip the same cup, bring me in to this conspiracy.

'He started phoning, said we should start up again. I told him not to be so stupid. He said if this was being stupid he was going to remain stupid the rest of his life, that we should all have the courage to be stupid once in our life. I said, well, that's OK, then, I've already done my quota. I had the scar to prove it. He said I was wrong. I'd been sensible then. Now it was time to be stupid. Being sensible would be to stay where I was. To be stupid I had to come back with him, to another flat, maybe above another chip shop. Didn't I remember how it was, how we loved the smell of it, even in the morning? I said tastes had changed. I preferred cranberry juice and the smell of the ocean now. This went on for months, and I put him off and I put him off and I put him off. Then one morning, I look out of my window after Wally's gone to work, and there he is, standing on the grass, with this rolled-up newspaper in his hand.'

'I'd been standing there fifteen minutes before she noticed me. And I'd been casing the joint for three days, getting the time right.'

'Casing the joint! Stalking me, you mean, standing there in your winter overcoat, beckoning me to come down.'

'And you did.'

'And I did. All ready to be angry. And as I walked towards him, he unwrapped the newspaper. And you know what was in it?'

I knew what was in it.

'No?'

'Fish and chips! Real English fish and chips with proper batter and vinegar and salt. I'll never forget it as long as I live.'

'In California? They couldn't have been the real thing.'

'Course they were.' Large butted in, indignant. 'I flew this Freddy guy out on Concord, who ran a chippy in Holloway. He had the cod in one of them cold bags, the right potatoes too. Flew to LA, borrowed this duplex in Venice from a trader I knew, used his kitchen. English cod, English spuds and English newspaper.'

'Listen to him. I tell you, though, Charlie, it worked. We sat there, eating greasy fish and chips at half nine in the morning. I didn't think you could eat fish at that time of day and survive. It was the most wonderful meal I'd ever had in my life. After we'd finished, he rolled up the newspaper, stuck it in his pocket and said, "I'm taking you home now," and by one o'clock we were on the plane back to England.'

'How long ago was this?'

'Two years.'

'And you never came down here?'

'No, Charlie, I never came down here.'

'What did your parents think?'

'Oh, Charlie! They thought what parents always think. I'm messing up my life, throwing everything away, a good husband, a good job, a wonderful house, a family any day now. A family!'

Large wagged a finger at her. 'Don't knock it, girl. There was nothing wrong with all that.'

'No?' Sophie swirled the wine and emptied the glass. 'Who's being sensible now?'

Four

My mother would be a falconress
And I her gay falcon, treading her wrist

Robert Duncan

It didn't happen straight away. They had things to do; a home to find, a mother to re-house, a family to placate. When they left that afternoon I could do nothing. The office seemed empty, devoid of purpose. The life had gone out of it. Haydn Castle would have to wait. The Fourth of July notwithstanding, I put my head round to Betty and told her I would be out for the rest of the day. I stuffed my hat upon my head and ran down the steps, glad to be outside, the wine still burning in my cheeks. I wasn't used to three glasses of wine in the afternoon, particularly after a schooner of sherry and a belly full of corned beef.

I needed to walk it off. The rain had stopped, wet heat rising off the pavement. I started to make my way through the town, seeing it not in the present, as I usually did then, my eye attuned to new businesses opening, how my current clients were faring, trying to gauge the economic health of the town, but drawn to those sights that reflected my own hesitant past, the bowling alley which I had loathed to enter (the very idea, wearing those communal, sweat-stained shoes), the square-box council offices and the ugly fish-tank window at the top that was once my father's domain, and then, a little further up, the bus station, with its little concrete islands and four-legged shelters, two girls fighting over a teen magazine on the slatted bench where Sophie had once slumped, so resigned to her fate. I watched them with their boisterous humour, not knowing quite what to do next, but the talk of old people's homes must have prompted me, for then a bus pulled up, with the name Monkton's on the scroll above the driver's seat, and before I knew it I had a ticket in my hand and was making my way down towards the back seat, like a schoolboy on his way home. I sat down and wiped the window clean. They were still there, giggling, bashing each other over the head, their skirts rucked up. What if I hadn't taken Sophie home that night? What if I'd sat beside her, driven her out to the country, given her a shoulder to cry on, taken her back to their flat, put her up in our guest room, done *something*, other than refer her to a higher authority? What if I'd shown her there was spirit in me too? A thankful touch, a grateful kiss, a fleeting moment of intensity, what might it had done, if not to us, then to me? Outside one of the girls stuck her tongue out at me and called me a name which luckily I couldn't hear, though the accompanying gesture provided a clue. The doors hissed and we eased out into the ring road.

Ours was an ugly town. It still is. My father used to say that it had always been an ugly town, trying to excuse his predecessors from their more inane blunders, but if you looked close enough you could see vestiges of its former self, a cobbled alleyway that now led to a clutch of Portakabins, a gabled town-house caught between a cut-price carpet centre and an abandoned Chinese takeaway. These clues notwithstanding, it was a mess, everywhere you looked, roads cut off in their prime like hastily amputated limbs, residential enclaves stranded in between a pair of dual-carriageways, a blotch of retail businesses stuck hither and thither as the fancy and the backhanders took them, and yet I couldn't help liking it all. Crass, crude, not up to aesthetic scratch, it wasn't here to be admired, written up. It was here to be used by men like Large and Tommy, even by men like me. My father hadn't used it, he'd lorded over it. Perhaps one day we would put our capital into it, as well as our interest, turn it into a town which called upon our pride as well as our pockets. Perhaps that's why I looked forward to the Fourth of July. Wasn't their Independence Day to do with that too, raising towns in their own image?

We drove out, past the Asda, past the Kwik-Fit and the Matalan and the TK Maxx, out along the new private housing estate, with its gated Ruritanian battlements and mock heraldic flag, out along the dual-carriageway towards the common, where the town's married homosexuals relieved each other in their dainty tasselled shoes. It had been my mother, years before while Sammy was still alive, who had twigged the gay fraternity. Out one afternoon, for a family walk upon the common, me thirteen years old, my father fulsome in his Bank Holiday break, stretching Easter Monday another two days, we had come across a steady stream of them, solitary men tripping back along the muddy path towards the car park, picking their polished leather over the puddled mud that the spring sun had not yet hardened, the cut of their clothes, the button-down Brooks Bros. shirts, the natty ties, as incongruous amongst the gorse and bracken as the meticulous partings in their hair.

'It's Wednesday afternoon,' my father declared, as the fourth passed us, car keys in his hand, eyes locked on the trail ahead. 'What on earth's going on?'

'Oh, don't be so naive, Alex. What do you think's going on? If you come here alone, bring the dog, that's my advice, and don't wear too much after-shave. Not unless you're prepared for a big surprise.'

The bus filled with passengers, a smattering of carrier-bag-laden shoppers, an underage mother and child, a compulsive cougher, but in the main they were going where I was going, to the nursing home where my mother now lived: Monkton's. It was not the best nursing home in the area, and it was not the worst, but my heart sank every time I passed the brick pillars and walked down the unkempt drive to its red-brick sprawl. It had been an orphanage once, for railway workers' children, farm labourers', the fishing communities from Deal and Hastings, dangerous industries to be born into, machinery and the elements surrounding them taking away the men, childbirth and general squalor the women, chiselled Portland stone above the two side entrances, *Boys* to the right, *Girls* the left, and above the main entrance the exhortation *May Them Oppress No More*. By the mid-sixties, the goods yard closing, the fleets shrinking, the willingness of mothers to run to five, six, seven children declining, it was turned into a young offenders' institution, bars placed on the windows, a bristling wire fence ringing the premises, hooked inwards at the top, like a World War Two prison camp. Youth was the enemy now. I remember going for school runs across the common, seeing them in their grey shirts and dark-blue trousers, working in the grounds, wheeling barrows, digging trenches, hoeing the ground, how they would turn and hurl abuse at us as we ran along a bridle path not fifteen yards away, how virulent, how messianic the hatred they voiced. We never shouted back, we understood the risk. The fence hadn't been built to contain that rage once ignited; they'd have torn it down with their bare hands to get to us, and though none of us would admit it, we knew what the outcome of that confrontation would be. So we ran on, fascinated by them, drawn to their danger, fearful of confronting it, Tommy, Duncan, Ed, the straggling lot of us, self-conscious, nervous, eyes straight ahead, not cowards exactly but running away nevertheless. By the time Large arrived, our regular Wednesday appearance had become something of a matinee performance, their reception orchestrated by a stunted, putty-faced lad who we nicknamed Napoleon. He'd post a lookout, and the moment we popped up over the rise we'd hear the cry go up as they hurled down their spades and forks and raced down to the edge of the perimeter, stones and clumps of earth, occasionally a fresh bundle of excrement wrapped in cabbage leaves, at the ready. We'd warned Large about them, or rather Tommy had, as soon as he saw him emerge from the changing room in pristine ironed shorts and brand-new trainers, but Large had said nothing, merely closed one eye and tapped his heart, a typical Large gesture that we came to understand as signifying an understanding of the world, and of the human nature that rolled within it, that we collectively lacked. He could take care of that, as he could take care of everything.

Off we set. He was a solid, determined runner, his boxing training saw to that, pounding the path rather than running over it, beating it into submission, with enough stamina in his legs to carry his heavy fleshed frame. The school had been built as a reflection of its psyche, a short distance from the town's commercial heart but still close enough for everyone, parents, pupils, teachers, to feel the bind of those vulgar ties, and though in the preceding decade it had seen that measured isolation relentlessly encroached upon, it still did not take long to leave it behind and find oneself in what still passed for the country in the south-east of England, across the playing fields, down one of the Victorian back roads, past rows of tall gabled houses, stone-stepped and yew-hedged, then mostly cheap flats and medical surgeries (one dental, one ophthalmic, one veterinarian), save for the last, a mission house of some indeterminate closed-door faith, before coming out alongside Stan Colley's turf farm and thence onto the common itself.

Almost at once the heckling began, cat-calls, wolf-whistles, the fence shaking as they leaped up, jeering and shouting obscenities, clumps of earth and half bricks flying over to greet us. We ran as we always ran, steadily, looking ahead, each of us trying not to invite further derision by stumbling or appearing not up to the task, Tommy, Duncan, in the lead, the rest of us strung out, as runners are. Large had been up at the front, but as we neared the fence and the taunts grew louder, the obscenities more elaborate, he slowed down, letting the rest of us pass, before he came to a halt and left the path altogether, pushing his way through the bracken to where they stood, temporarily silenced, Napoleon at their head, his arms hung down by his side, as if he had a pair of holstered guns on his hips.

Standing at an angle of forty-five degrees to them, his actions visible to both us and them, Large unzipped his fly and tucking in his right hand, pulled out his cock, holding it pink and fleshy in his hand, almost as if for examination. He stretched it once, and settling his feet and knees like a golfer might, began to urinate, a long thick stream which arced into the air with the force of an unblocked hosepipe. We could hear it twenty yards away, where we were nervously gathered, hear it as it hit the ground and began to run down the dried muddy bank into the ditch at the bottom. He stood there looking down, hardly bothering to hold it at all, his left hand on his hip, his right holding back the cotton fold of his fly, his penis long and thick and boldly circumcised, so even in its flaccid state it looked tumescent, potent, ready to joust with life. On it gushed, a torrent of yellow, steaming urine, one minute, two, it seemed to go on for ever, splashing and foaming onto the dry earth, the jet constant, the same volume, the same consistency, a production line of piss, industrial in strength, no jerks or pauses, just a seemingly endless flow, pouring onto the hardened ground. It was more like a cork being pulled from a beer barrel than a bladder being emptied, such was the energy that piss possessed. You could have sung a Bach cantata, played a Chopin étude at the onset and he would have still been pissing after the last note had been sounded. No one said anything. No one moved. Finally, when our ears seemed to be filled with nothing else save this flood, it came to a stop; a pause while he studied the ground, followed by a twenty-second spurt, equally ferocious, followed by another pause, and a second onslaught, this time of around ten seconds, again with equal force. It was like one of those scenes in British war films, the Nazi standing with his legs apart, pouring machine-gun burst after machine-gun burst into the bodies of his fallen victims. One more came, like an afterthought, then it was over. He was finished. There was no more. He shook himself once and stood there, looking up, his penis hanging out still, as if cooling, in want of air. He dug his hands into his pocket and pulled out a packet of cigarettes. He shook it and took one out, using his mouth alone, lit it, his hand cupped round the flame in a manner which established years of familiarity. He inhaled, two deep, unhurried lungfuls, zipped himself back in and strolled up to the fence, shaking the packet once more, so that the remaining cigarettes fanned out in that organ-pipe row before offering them up to their pasty-faced emperor. Napoleon, his head held high, his eyes looking down his nose, studied the packet for a minute without moving.

'Cunt.'

'Cunts can't piss like that,' we heard him reply. 'Cunts ain't got the bladder for it. Only men can piss like that.' He shook the packet again. 'I ain't touched them. You'll get no piss from me, so let's be having none from you.'

He offered them up once more. Napoleon wiped his hand and took one. Large presented his lit cigarette through the fence. The lad lit his own, handed it back. He said something we couldn't hear.

'You must be fucking joking,' we heard Large reply. 'Bedford Park?' and then his voice lowered.

'What's he saying?' Duncan asked. Tommy punched him on the shoulder to silence him, but Duncan was right. What *was* he saying? They batted back and forth, Napoleon's short staccato tempered by Large's slower delivery. Then a short laugh, and Large tossed the packet over and running his fingers round the elastic of his shorts, walked up to where we stood.

'They're all right,' he said, as he re-joined us. 'They just can't stand the sight of you.'

'What did you say?' Duncan asked again.

'Me? I said I couldn't either,' and he set off again.

We looked forward to more – a new association. We understood that Large could be the key to many things beyond our experience, and this could be one of them; after all, somewhere down the line, wasn't he descended from the same stock, couldn't he give us an introduction to a different breed of youth, who stole cars, burgled houses, stabbed and fought and pissed in the open air, for whom nothing, not least life and liberty, was sacred? We had too many things that were deemed sacred; their rampant atheism could only be of benefit. But it never happened. Before we knew it, the place had been closed down. It was pressure from the school governors, from councillors like my father that put an end to it, that and the homosexual connection that had surfaced, a town scandal that never made the newspapers, the boys doing favours through the fence in return for cigarettes, alcohol and money, some of them demanding similarly oral favours of their own, one of their supervisors, Stuart Lee, married to one of our English teachers, father of ten-year-old twins, wicket-keeper for the Sunday team cricket club, a participant both sides of the wire. They were gone, the four of them within the month, the home closed down after six, reappearing a year and a half later as what it remains, a residential home for the elderly. Only the middle-aged have escaped its clutches.

In some ways my mother had changed dramatically, in others not at all. She was still my mother, still looked at me with that questioning eye, searching for signs of an attachment. It was she who had goaded me, sent me out, helped me set up on my own, but though I could fly hither and thither, she still expected me one day to return, feathers puffed up, my trophy fresh in my mouth, a bride-to-be, plump and ripe, and though not virginal, at least full of tender, sweet flesh that I could lay at her feet. And I knew who she wanted, who she had always wanted, for hadn't I wanted her too? God, how foolish could a mother be, imagining she could will such desire into reality. Yes, she was my falconress, yet tied now to her own perch, yet my wilful misuse of my freedom still tore at her wrist. My mother would be a falconress and I . . . I wished for no wings at all.

It had been a bloody time, my father's death, his body dominating the next two months. I watched him being cut down, laid out and wrapped up in a roll of blue polythene, his face pressed against the opaque surface, as if he had risen up from the bottom of the lake, the men from Bonham's standing around, not knowing whether to carry on or to quietly fade into the background. They had their work to do.

'Let them get on with it,' my mother had insisted, 'nothing belongs to me now, not even him,' and by the mid-afternoon, once the police were satisfied, my father and his worldly goods were loaded up into their respective removal vans and driven away, black suits for him, brown overalls for the effects.

There was an inquest, naturally, exceptionally well attended, for by that time the whole town had learned of the notoriety of our circumstance. My father's downfall had been common knowledge amongst the town cognoscenti long before, the talk of the club and committee rooms of which he once was master, but with his suicide we became a more public property. His death was the lead item on that evening's local television news, a film of my mother shielding her face while being driven away repeated long into the weekend. The following day his inauguration photograph, complete with mayoral chain and self-important smile, reappeared on the front page of the *Gazette*, underneath the headline, "Ex-mayor commits suicide. Wife blames Lloyd's", which she most certainly did not. It was more personal than that. She blamed him. The press was wholly sympathetic, the publicity for Lloyd's wholly bad. The funeral, three weeks later, was well attended, councillors, officials, secretaries, golfing partners, fellow members of the Conservative Association, friends of the family, the former colleagues of his old shipping firm filling an entire first-class carriage with their black ties and double brandies. The road to St Saviour's was roped off, the local MP read a psalm, the mayor's chambers given over to the reception afterwards, the funeral meats furnished out of his hospitality fund, his own portrait witness to the corporation's meticulous generosity. Outside the emblazoned doors they lined up to greet my mother, kiss her veiled cheek, clasp her laced hand (she had insisted on the whole black embroidered thing), but they were nothing more than pressed flowers in a forgotten book, pristine in their shape, but sterile in their intent.

Her stroke came within the year. That too was laid at my father's doorstep, but I was not convinced. Once gone, I don't think she suffered on that account. Widows are like that. They find they don't need men much, especially when we're not there. It's something they've always known, something we've always known too. It was other deprivations that pressed in upon her, that suffocating bungalow, with its cramped quarters and its flimsy doors, no room to paint, no garden to walk around, nothing to see but Pemberton's civic sports centre, hanging over her like a cloud of mustard gas, squeezing the air from her lungs. Alone in our old house, or in another, smaller one of her own choosing, she might have flourished, but there, stubborn to the last,there was only one option available – and that was for her to dig her way out. All that that damp spring, that cold summer, she was out there, dragging out the bindweed entrails by the handful, pulling up clumps of obstinate nettle roots, tugging and tearing at that stony, stubborn soil, which was where she was found, face down, her mouth half buried when she had tried to call for help. And thus, she came to Monkton's, paid partly by the state, partly by what little money she had in her own name that Lloyd's could not touch.

She didn't have to think of money, anyway. I looked after all that, took power of attorney, looked after her bank account, her finances. She was happy at Monkton's. It reminded her of home. It had corridors and staircases and big draughty rooms; it had that welcoming glow of gloom that comes with excess space. When we went for drives, she would me ask me to take her past the old house, and I obliged, knowing that though it gave her pain, it was pain she wanted, pain to see it, pain to remember it, pain to know it lost.

There was no one at the reception desk, but they knew me well enough. I walked down the corridor. There was a trolley ahead, already full of dinners.

'Bit early, isn't it?' I said in passing. The woman, Katie she was called, tall, boyish, with dark eyelashes and a young, sug-gestive mouth, too pretty for that job, shrugged her shoulders. She hadn't been there long.

'New rules,' she said, rattling the metal covers.

My mother had a room on the ground floor, standard furnishings save for a few things we'd salvaged for the bunga-low: a painting of the Needles, a favourite of hers, her walnut bedside table with its marble top and pretty glass lamp, the Iranian carpet from the living room. Its main advantage, apart from the light from the tall window that ran almost floor to ceiling at the front, was its proximity to the side entrance and the neglected grounds beyond. I had visited her the day before, so she wasn't expecting me. I knocked and swung the door open. She was seated in the armchair by the window. Drawn up alongside her was old man Nikolides, pointing to the sketch pad balanced on her lap. I had no idea he was a caller. She looked up, annoyed at being disturbed.

'Charles. What are you doing here?' She spoke out of the right side of her mouth, the left side of her body, particularly the arm, set asunder, the left foot dragging slightly, helped by a walking stick.

'Just at a loose end. Thought I'd pop by.' I stepped in.

Nikolides had got to his feet, knitting his fingers awkwardly. He looked old. You didn't see him in their store much these days.

'Mr Nikolides. I saw Tommy for lunch today. Business thriving, I'm glad to say.'

'Ah, Tommy,' he blustered. 'He never stops. Never. Like his father, only he has it up here,' he tapped his head, 'while I, only here.' He banged his heart and showed us his crooked teeth. Nikolides, ever the professional peasant. I marvelled at his theatrics.

'Not just there. You have it here too,' and my mother reached out and touched his hand. I pretended not to notice.

'Mr Nikolides and I have been plotting,' she continued, as he pulled his hand gently away. 'I'm in the . . . what is it, Theo?'

'The takeover business,' he said quietly. He was plainly embarrassed.

'That's it. I've commandeered the garden. We're going to work it properly this spring, starting with the vegetable patch.'

'What about . . . ?' I nodded my head, indicating the powers that be. 'Are they happy with it?'

My mother waved my question away with her good hand. 'Why shouldn't they be? They can use the produce in the kitchens. It'll cut their bills and be healthier.'

'She should ask for something in return. Free meals. A new television,' Nikolides put in, suddenly expansive. He put his hand across his waist and bowed. 'I take my leave. Mrs Pemberton. Charles. My good intentions to you both.'

We watched as he walked down the drive, small, bobbing strides, as if he were astride a donkey. Halfway down he placed a finger against one nostril and blew a stream of phlegm out onto the verge. It was a wonder that there were people like Nikolides still allowed.

'You never told me about him,' I said as he disappeared round the corner. 'What is he, a regular visitor?'

'He walks all the way,' she said, her voice glowing with admiration. 'There and back. Keeps him in trim, he says. I like him coming. We speak the same language, Theo and I. He's as much at a loose end as I am. It'll give us something to do.' She patted her book. 'I've got it all planned out here. There's a disused . . .' she gathered herself up, then jumped the word clear, 'greenhouse facing south, which would be ideal for tomatoes.'

'All the same, you'd better check. You know this place has changed hands. Large has bought it, you remember, the boy who caused such a fuss with Sophie, who then dumped her and went off to the City? He's back. And guess who with?'

She couldn't guess. She didn't want to. Even when I repeated the name, it didn't seem to register. The outside world was holding less and less interest for her now, even the small plot inhabited by her son. It was not until I added her surname, Marchand, that she took any notice. Then she sat up, nervous, as if an intruder were about to break in.

'Andrew Marchand? He's not involved, is he? I couldn't stay here if he was. I'd rather be thrown out on the streets than stay under his roof.' Through the defiance I could see that she was frightened, alarmed at the thought of another upheaval.

'It's all right, Mum. They're still in California, as far as I know.'

She sat back, smoothing down the front of her dress, still unsettled. 'You still haven't told me why you're here. You come in unannounced, and all you've done is upset me.'

'I thought I'd come and see you, that's all.'

'Why?'

'Why ever not?'

'Because you never do, that's why not. Not unless you've made an appointment. You're like your father, writing it all down in that little book of yours. I've seen you do it. "Mum, Wednesday, six o'clock." Every week you write it.'

'I'm busy,' I remonstrated. 'I just don't want to forget.'

'Wednesday! Six o'clock!' she scorned. 'Your own mother!'

'As a matter of fact,' I said, making it up as I went along, 'the reason I came, is as it's Independence Day tomorrow, I thought we might go out and celebrate.'

'Celebrate what?' She wriggled impatiently in her seat.

'The Fourth of July. American Independence Day.'

'What's that got to do with me?'

'Nothing, it's just—'

She cut me short. 'I've never heard anything so silly in all my life. Anyway, I can't. Theo's coming round, first thing. We're making a start.'

So I had the Fourth of July to myself. I did what I always did. I rang Betty, told her I wasn't coming in. I put on a pair of stone-washed jeans and an open-neck shirt, walked to the baker's, bought a couple of doughnuts, and back at the flat, read *Time* magazine, while dipping them in my coffee. Breakfast completed I drove round to the car wash round the back of the garage, sat amongst the suds before lighting out for the new territory, the out-of-town shopping centre just opened off the M25, the day as all Fourth of Julys should be, flapping in the summer breeze, bright and sparkling, like a star-spangled banner.

The place was heaving. It had been built by an international consortium, Dutch, Belgians, Russians too. It hadn't been open six months but it was as if it had been there since shopping began, hewn out of rock, built upon the bones of apes. It was moon-scaped, set down in a crater, a sprawl of steel and glass: it had north entrances and south entrances, it had east and west wings; it had three car parks, a dozen silver-studded walkways, cameras at every corner, yet despite it all there was something undeniably transitory about its appearance, as if it were held there solely by some sort of gravitational defiance. Circling down the slip road towards it, I felt as if it could vanish at any moment, lift off without warning, suck everything and everyone in it into the blackest ether. It wasn't real, it wasn't fake, it was something in between, outside society, outside the family, the workplace, even the high street, set down in no-man's-land, all normal laws suspended. There was a madness to it. You could imagine disaster happening.

I took a map from one of the floor guides and headed for those stores whose names smacked of hoe-down wear. I was not disappointed. An hour later I had bought two checked shirts, a leather belt and a pair of cowboy boots. I was doing well. I began to wander, the sales bags swinging in my hand, shop after shop after shop, trying on business suits, business suits, fingering rolls of curtain material with impunity, discussing with the shop assistant the necessities of adaptable shower heads, all the while thinking about Sophie and Large. What were they doing back here? What was *she* doing back here? What was it about Large and residential homes and this overburdened corner of south-east England that outstripped California and the Pacific Ocean and that surgeon husband? What was it about attraction, how did it work exactly? Was I attracted to her? Was I attracted to anything? Shop after shop after shop.

The aisles were filling up; it became harder to walk freely. Time for lunch. I'd noticed a diner on the second floor, griddled steaks and hamburgers, pancakes and maple syrup. As I came up out onto the floor, a jacket caught my eye in the window opposite, black, with a silky sheen to its folds. It reeked of freedom, of a life beyond mine. It hung there with a kind of insouciant arrogance. It said, 'I will look good on anyone, even you.'

I went in. The assistant sniffed, took it down reluctantly. As he held it open the lining dazzled my eyes – a flash of gaudy midnight-blue and white stripes, with little silver stars running down the inside of the sleeves. It was like putting on Captain America. The moment it settled on my shoulders, I could feel it, great and expansive on me, as if I had gained miraculous powers. It cost three hundred pounds, but with an interior like that, how could I refuse? I paid up without a moment's hesitation, and walked out, triumphant. The diner stood a matter of yards away. I queued up, ordered a hot dog with French fries and onions, and took them and a proper bottle of Coke to a table with high stools near the exit. I put the bottle to my lips, almost choking on the pleasure of it all. Across the table opposite sat the young woman from Monkton's, the girl pushing the trolley. She wore a checked shirt and a buckskin jacket with fringed sleeves, like the buggy in *Oklahoma!*. She was drinking a strawberry milkshake. She was even paler than I remembered, her dark hair fuller. One of the tassels on her sleeve had caught in her drink and she was sucking it clean. She caught me looking at her.

'It's Katie, isn't it? You look after my mother, Mrs Pemberton. I saw you there yesterday afternoon, serving some very early dinners.'

'High tea, they call it. They get sandwiches later.'

I nodded, wondering what to say next. 'I hope my mother doesn't give you too much trouble. She can be quite demanding.'

'Oh, she's one of the easy ones.'

'I brought her up properly, then.'

She laughed, the fierceness in her face suddenly gone.

'Have you worked there long?'

'Not long.'

'Enjoy it?'

She gave an equivocal frown. 'It's a bit unsettled at the moment. We've got a new owner.'

'I know. You met him yet?'

'Two days ago. There was a special staff meeting.'

'What was he like?'

'OK. He's got plans, that's what he said.'

'That sounds like Large. I went to school with him, you know.'

'Did you?' She bent her head round as if looking for

someone. This was where it usually ended for me, running out of things to say. What was there *to* say? But that day I felt emboldened. I could find out more about Large from her, about how the place was run, about how he treated them all. He wouldn't tell me everything. It wasn't in his nature. But she might. Besides, I had checked shirts in my bag, cowboy boots.

'May I ask you an impertinent question? That jacket. Are you wearing it deliberately?'

She glanced down at it. 'How do you mean?'

'I know it sounds a little bizarre but on the Fourth of July I go a bit American.' I opened my bag. 'Checked shirts, boots, this hot dog. Given the jacket of yours, I was wondering if you did the same.'

She shrugged her shoulders. She had lived there, just over a year, she told me, Fort Worth. It was where the jacket came from. The recollection of buying it caused her mouth to curl. She touched it almost affectionately. I could feel myself intruding on the memory. I tried to imagine it, what she could have done there.

'So what's it to you, then,' she asked, 'the Fourth of July? You're not from there, are you?'

I shook my head. 'It's a day of exhortation. It's saying, "Go on, you can do it." '

'And can you?'

'For today I can, yes.'

She nodded, studying me in a disarmingly unashamed manner. For all her paleness there seemed to be a deep intensity within her, a core of hot concentration that lay like fuel rods in a reactor. She spoke again, carefully, as if her lips were unused to words, wary of the power they could unleash.

'So, after the checked shirts and the cowboy boots and the hot dog, comes . . . ?'

'I buy a new pen. Nothing to do with Independence Day, I know. That's my reality check. The shirts say, "Freedom!"

The pen says, "Back to work!" What made you come back to work here? Didn't you like Texas? Too right-wing?'

'No, I *loved* Texas. I'm quite right-wing myself. No, it was the heat. I just couldn't take it. This pen obsession of yours. Are you a writer?'

She liked the word obsession I could tell by the way she licked the sibilants, liked the idea of being obsessed, of succumbing to a manic need. It had caught her attention, my Fourth of July nonsense. I had done something I had never done before. Aroused a woman's interest. I wondered what it was, that she might be obsessed about.

'Not me. I just like them, they way they feel. Come, I'll show you. You can help me choose this year's. Tell me what an American might like.'

She took it in good spirit. She slid off her stool. She was half a head taller than me. I didn't mind, in fact I liked it. That mouth seemed to stare at me without even trying. In the store I went straight for the Conway Stewarts. They fit comfortably in the crook of the hand. For all the razzamatazz I find Mont Blancs too fat. They had a nice one in tortoiseshell blue, for just under a hundred. I dipped it in the complimentary ink and ran my name out over the paper, wrote it several times over. It flowed beautifully. She looked on, bemused.

'Here, see for yourself, how different it feels.'

I held the pen out, the back of my hand brushing against her fingers as she took it. They were cold, yet the touch seared my skin. I could feel proximity shimmering like heat rising off a tarred road, the little drama we were skipping round, the burning fact of it. I hadn't been this close in years. She placed her right elbow on the counter and wrote. Katie Jinks, she was called. She was left-handed. Her mouth was hard. Her tongue poked out between her lips. She had better handwriting than me.

'It's lovely.' She made to hand it back.

'No, go on, have a proper go.' She wrote something else. I couldn't see what.

'It's weird,' she said, her face hidden from view. 'It gives you time to think.'

'Not just that,' I beamed, almost proud of her observation. 'It *helps* you think. What did you write?'

'I don't think I should tell you.' She straightened up.

'Why not? Go on.'

'Oh, all right.' She cleared her throat. '"I am wearing my cowboy jacket and standing here with a man I do not know, who is obsessed by the Fourth of July. Is this wise?"'

'And is it?'

'I don't know yet.' She handed the pen back. 'Are you going to buy it, then?'

I hesitated. It seemed the wrong thing to do, to spend all that money in front of her. 'Maybe later.'

'Don't worry on my account,' she said, suddenly fierce again. 'If I had a spare hundred, I'd probably buy one too. It might help.'

'Help how?'

'It's not important. Go on, indulge yourself. It's your big day, remember. You must obey your own rules.'

I did as I was told. Back outside we stood, both of us unwilling to go our separate ways.

'Is that it, then?' she asked. 'Are the fireworks over now?'

'Not quite. There's one more thing.' She put her hand to her mouth and straightened her face. She was enjoying it, my day out.

'It's just, to round the day off, in the evening I go to a bar, have a martini, watch the world go by. You're welcome to join me, if you like. We could go somewhere on the way back. I've got my car.'

She looked at me. She couldn't have been much older than twenty-two.

'You asking me out?'

'If you've got nothing better to do.'

'Does it have to be a martini?'

Her voice was serious. It was an important question.

'Well, it is the Fourth of July.' She looked back, turning it over.

'I haven't finished here yet.'

'I wouldn't mind tagging along.'

'I would. Bras and stuff.'

'Ah.' I tried not to blush. There was a long silence, thoughts of here and now flying into the unknown.

'You know the Hacienda?'

I knew the Hacienda: a straw roof above a bottle-dangling bar, large hats on the wall, a pervading inbuilt Hopper loneliness, despite its garishness I couldn't have chosen better myself. There was a giddiness in my head. Everything was picking up speed. Pat going, Sophie and Large turning up, the Merry Boys up for sale. My life was rattling over a new set of points onto a new set of tracks. I could feel the shudder of it.

'Seven o'clock, then,' she said.

The traffic was bad going back, an accident outside Maidstone. Back at the flat I showered and shaved, and in a panic thought it necessary to polish my shoes. I ironed my grey and green striped shirt, put on a fresh pair of jeans and to give myself courage took my new black jacket out from its bag. Halfway through drying my hair I had a moment of inspiration. I locked the door and hurried over to the office. Betty had left me a list of callers. Haydn Castle, Steve Tanner, a couple of names I didn't know and underneath them all, Miss Sophie Marchand. No message. I picked up what I wanted and walked over. The Hacienda was part of an old converted warehouse not far from the cattle market. Katie Jinks was already sat at the bar, a light green dress against white legs and white arms, green fingernails picking at peanuts. She looked thinner than before, a creature of the cold. I could imagine her lips blue, her teeth chattering, her white arms covered in goose-bumps. When she saw me she threw a peanut up in the air and caught it in her mouth. She had a long white neck.

'Sorry I'm late,' I said, 'but I had to get Uncle Sam to sew on this.' I opened up the jacket. 'Stars and stripes, see? Stripes, anyway. The stars are down the arm. The day's not over yet, you see.'

I ordered our martinis. She approved of the jacket, approved of the fact that I was prepared to look ridiculous in my quest. I asked her, wildly bold, if the rest of her shopping trip had been successful, whether she had got back all right, whether she had been caught in the traffic jam. We batted back and forth trying to latch on to similarities, connections. By the second martini she had asked me about my mother, how long she had been a guest at Monkton's. I told her the whole story, about me, about my family, our highs, our hardships. I made myself a more active participant than I had been, more affected by it. It was a good story, I knew. I was like everyone else, wishing there was more to me than there really was. Isn't that what we want? For us to be more? Strangely, she knew none of it, despite having lived here when it happened. Her father laid pipes. Texas was all about cattle, she explained, not oil. Round 'em up, brand them, cut them loose, that was their philosophy.

'When I was buying the pen, you said, if you had the money you'd get one too. You wouldn't say why.'

She blushed, the first time I had seen colour on her. I had touched her somewhere, that hot core, perhaps, that lay under the still surface.

'I shouldn't have said anything. If you must know, I'm trying to write a story – about somewhere like Monkton's. There's a lot that goes on, in a place like that, feelings, memories. No one hears them, though. All the books I read are all about young people. I thought I might write about old people. But it's not as easy as I thought.'

'Maybe this will help.' I took out the pen I'd brought from the office. She thought she recognized it.

'No, Charles, I couldn't.'

'Don't worry. It's not the one I bought today. It's one of my old ones, one I don't use much any more. It takes cartridges, but if you want my advice, use bottled ink. There's a ritual to using a pen, like the Japanese tea ceremony. Unscrewing the bottle, smelling the ink, wiping the nib clean after you've filled it up, it all adds up to the moment of writing. And don't forget the paper. You want good quality paper, smooth to the touch.'

'Smooth like silk,' she said and reaching in, rubbed the lining between her fingers. Then her arm slipped round and she was kissing me on the mouth, on a bar stool, in public, on the Fourth of July. She wiped her lips.

'Let's have another of those,' she said. 'It's Friday night, after all.'

We waited until the drinks were stood in front of us before speaking again. It came harder now. Her fingers lay on the counter, close to mine. I wanted to touch them. It was all I could think about. I began to stumble, lose the thread of what I was saying, what she was saying. Something had crept in, we both knew it. She cut it short.

'Where do you live, then? Not with your mum, eh?'

'No.'

'You got any brothers?'

'No. No sisters either.'

'I know *that*. A lot of blokes do, you know, live with their mum.'

'It's an expensive business, setting up on your own.'

'You share a flat?'

'With myself. The non-Fourth of July one.'

'Would I like it?'

'Depends which one of me is in.'

*

We took a taxi back. She followed me up the stairs. I switched on the light. It looked bare, unaccommodating. It didn't even have a sofa. She wandered round, not knowing where to sit, opening the cocktail cabinet, looking at the photo of my mother and father squinting in the Isle of Wight sun, finally alighting on the ebony nude. She picked it up, turning it in her hands.

'You show this to all the girls?'

'You're the first one who's ever seen it.'

'Perhaps that's why it's here. It's horrible.' She handed it over. 'Put it away. Somewhere where I can't see it.'

I stuffed it in the cocktail cabinet and closed the lid. She was standing in the room, watching me.

'You haven't got a clue, what to do now, have you? Put on a record, lower the lights, pin me to the wall, you haven't got a clue.'

'I hadn't really thought of it like that. My breakfast things are still in the sink.'

'But the bed's made, I bet. You like things tidy.'

'Yes. I do. I'm very boring, really. Shall I make some coffee, then?'

She looked out of the window, to the garden below. 'If I stay, what will happen next time?'

'Next time?'

'Next time you visit your mum. Will you blank me, blush with embarrassment, or what? I bet management have rules for this sort of thing.'

'What sort of thing?'

'This sort of thing,' and she pulled me close again and kissed me, her hands behind my head. I stood there, still unsure.

'Turn off the light,' she said, breaking off. 'And take that bloody jacket off. Show me the stars.'

I turned out the light. I took the jacket off. There were no stars, no room either, just an empty space and me loosened from my moorings. Then somehow we were in the bedroom and without fuss she was stepping out of her dress. Her skin was white, luminescent. I had never seen such white. She got into bed, long and sinewy, pale and white and yet very dark. I started to undress with my back to her.

'Your mother's quite grand, isn't she?' she said.

'Is she? It never struck me.'

'She orders you about, without ordering you about, if you know what I mean. Like I'm going to do to you.'

She pulled me down. She pulled me down and I didn't mind, didn't mind at all. She wrapped her arms about me and brought an end to it. My Independence Day.

Five

Halfway through, in the dead of night, I had to say it, get it straight.

'I went to school with him, your new boss, Clark.'

'So you said.'

'Did I? Did I tell you what I do?'

She kissed me, as if it was the most natural thing in the world.

'You're an accountant. You got a little office above that gents' shop. You're very correct. Even this thing has manners.' She giggled, busy with her fingers. I held her still.

'Listen for a minute, Katie. Did I tell you, did I make it clear that I might be working for him, your new boss. Looking after his accounts.'

She sat up, sobered.

'No, you didn't tell me that. Is this why I'm here?'

'No, of course not.'

'So why not tell me?'

''Cause you would have stopped it. You would have done, wouldn't you?'

'I might have.'

'I didn't want you to stop it. I mean I've only just started.'

'Only just started? What am I, a practice run?'

'You know what I mean. I didn't mean that. I meant you and me. Out of the mouths of virgins.'

She laughed into my neck. 'Oh, you lovely man.'

And I was, for a moment, a lovely man. And she didn't mind at all.

Six

I hardly dared catch myself in the mirror the next few days, such a change had come upon me. Facing Betty, my clients, it seemed as though my thoughts must be plastered on my forehead, so made flesh had they become. I found it difficult to sit at my desk, the chair constricting, my pen uneasy in my hand. I stood staring out of the window, thinking of that Friday and the weekend, the ease with which she had slipped into my life, how natural it felt, and yet how bizarre. There were things that had taken place that weekend, things of sight and sound, of smell and touch, things that I would not have believed possible, not in my flat, and yet, there they were, running riot before my eyes. Friday night had become Saturday morning, and Saturday morning had become the afternoon, Katie sitting alongside me as we drove down to Deal, a walk along the concrete pier, a bag of cherries to pit along the seafront, a turn on a fairground whirligig, the centrifugal force pressing her body uncomfortably close to mine, as if we were unable to be free of each other, then a drive back to town, her hand on my knee, and the bus stop where I left her, so that she could go home to change into some fresh clothes that 'didn't smell of us so'. When we met later that evening, a quiet drink she insisted, nothing more, and I moved to kiss her, she turned her face away.

'No, don't. My face is all sore. You need a shave.'

'I'll go and shave, then. I can't not kiss you.'

So we went back to the flat, but I didn't shave. If anything it was she who was hurried this time, as if time was running out. We talked and then we stopped talking. We started to eat and then stopped eating. I played her my favourite Hot Club of France album and she sprawled in the one comfortable chair, loose and redolent of what had gone before, what was to come, and I forgot what it was I wanted her to listen to. I didn't know who I was any more, what I was doing. I had a strange being in my flat, making strange noises, moving in strange ways. When I woke up, she was by the foot of the bed, pulling on her jeans. Light was streaming in over her skin. I'd forgotten to draw the curtains.

'You going?' I said, surprised. I was almost getting used to her.

'I have to get changed,' she said, drawing in her stomach as she zipped them up.

'For work? I thought you said you had the weekend off,' suddenly remembering the Saturday visit to my mother that I hadn't made.

'I do. It's Sunday, Charles. Church.'

'Church?' I laughed. She turned, the fierceness upon her again, her breasts swinging, such extraordinary things. I tried not to stare, but the Church and her nakedness were difficult images to reconcile.

'What's so funny? Anything wrong with that? Throw me my bra, would you?'

I leant across and flicked it over. 'No, it's just, I didn't expect it, that's all.'

'Christians have sex too,' she said, fastening the clasp at the back, 'even unmarried ones, and with the most unlikely of people. It's the missionary in us.'

'You're a regular church-goer, then?'

'Looks like it, doesn't it?'

I nodded, feeling the confusion rise up. 'Any particular sort?'

'My mum's C of E. I'm a lot more muscular.' She didn't expand on how. 'The world's in a mess, Charles. We need to turn back to God.' She stopped dressing for a moment, that core inside her, burning. 'Too heavy for you, a Christian girlfriend?' She pulled the short-sleeved jersey over her head and combed her hair with her fingers.

'Is that what you are?'

'I just told you. I believe in God, in the Bible. We all should.'

'No, I mean girlfriend.'

'Oh, that. Don't look so frightened, Charles. No, you're right. I'm not a girlfriend, not yet, anyway. A lover, though? Would that be OK? A God-fearing, God-worshipping, God-loving lover?'

'Katie . . .'

'That's settled, then. It's nothing to worry about, Charles. No prayers before bedtime. And if it's all too much for you, don't worry, you've just had a weekend's fucking.' She bent down and kissed me. 'Call me if you want to, yes? I've written my number down on an envelope in the kitchen. God bless.'

And she was gone, the flat suddenly empty. I tidied the place up, washed the glasses, changed the sheets, put the furniture back in place (the armchair pushed halfway across the room from our Saturday evening exertions), that last phrase, *a weekend's fucking*, ringing in my head. Not a weekend fucking, but a weekend's fucking, as if there was a measurable totality to it. A kind of alien contamination clung to everything. The flat hardly seemed mine any more. The more I thought about it, what had happened, *how* it had happened, I began to wonder as to her motives. It couldn't be simply me she was after, surely? What was I then, part of a recruitment drive? Wasn't that how the more disreputable faiths enticed new recruits, with a hefty dollop of sex to swallow the taste of religion down? What better place to snare the next victim than in that temple of Mammon? And Katie, was she really as funny and intelligent and attractive as I imagined, or was it simply the novelty of being with a woman that was so beguiling, the intoxicating power of it?

The phone rang. I picked it up, hoping it was her.

'Charlie! My main man!'

'Large.' How he had got my number I had no idea.

'I should have called you sooner. Bet you thought me and Nef was some horrible nightmare, come back to haunt you.'

'No, I . . .'

'Sorry to disappoint. We're back all right, flesh and blood. I've got the flesh, she's got the blood. How are you fixed this week?'

'I'm not absolutely . . .'

'What about tomorrow? No, tomorrow's no good. Tuesday, then, no, Wednesday. What about Wednesday? In your office. Late afternoon. We need to talk things through. Has Nef rung you?'

'Sophie? Not that I know of, no.' My first lie. I don't know why I did it. His use of that name, I supposed.

'She said she would. Fix up a dinner for the three of us. Four, if you've got someone special in tow. Have you got some-one special in tow, Charlie?'

'Not really.'

'That's a shame. We should all have someone special in tow, even if it doesn't last. Do you like curry?'

'Not particularly.'

'Scrub the poppadoms, then. What about that restaurant out of town, the one with the chef taught by what's-his-face?'

'The Five Maidens.' Father had been fond of the Five Maidens. He'd steered through the planning permission for them to extend out the back, came back with a bottle of Armagnac after every subsequent visit. I still took Mother there on her birthday. We got a complimentary glass of champagne.

'What about there? You and I could meet up first at your office and go on after. I'll get a taxi so we don't have to worry about the vino. I could bring someone along for you, if you like, someone who's willing to sing for her supper. Them girls know how to keep their mouths shut. Know how to keep them open too, when it's called for.'

'Really, Large, I don't think that's quite . . .'

'Just pulling your leg, Charlie. And it's Clark. Try and remember that.'

He hung up. I eased the ebony nude from out of the cocktail cabinet, set it back on the coffee table. There were patterns forming here, triangles, that I was not entirely comfortable with, Large and Mother and Katie Jinks – with me firmly in the middle – Sophie, Tommy and me, old loyalties and town friendships. I remembered my mother taking me, a reluctant schoolboy, to the National Gallery, sitting me before Seurat's *The Bathers* while she explained, with that over-the-top enthusiasm of hers that I had found so embarrassing, all the triangles that gave the painting its peculiar symmetry – the boys on the bank, the boats on the water, the formation of the trees. The more I looked, the more there were, and I wondered how many more there would be here, some close, some distant – symmetrical like them, but none of them, I feared, as tranquil.

*

Monday, Steve Tanner rang me, a follow-up call I presumed concerning the Merry Boys. I found it reassuring, to be back on familiar ground.

'Guess who popped his head around Saturday?'

I'd forgotten, Steve's father had been one of the part-time coaches at Large's old boxing club. 'You mean Large? Looking for a house, I suppose.'

'Made me go through every property I had on the books. He's married, did you know?'

'He was never one to do things by halves.'

I didn't want to talk about Large, not to Steve, not to people who didn't know me well. 'The Merry Boys, Steve. I was wondering if you could ask Pat if I could come round and pick up the books for a couple of days.'

I went round that lunchtime. The pub was empty. Pat showed me into the room at the back. Pete was sitting at the bare table, sewing a button on his half-open shirt. His chest was heavy, covered in silky grey hairs. He'd been a boxer himself in his day. You could hear it in the concentrated breath in his nostrils, see it by the carry of his piston arms.

'I never thought the day would come when I'd be glad to see you go, Pat, but, to be honest, if it means that I might end up owning the Merry Boys myself . . .'

Pat smiled, the smile of the younger woman within her, a smile that believed in the future.

'That was nicely put, Charles. It does appeal, selling it to one of the old crowd. But I can't allow sentiment to get in the way of business. You understand that, don't you?'

'We understand it perfectly.'

'We?'

I hesitated. 'I might not be doing this entirely on my own, Pat.'

'Is it Tommy, then?'

'I can't say. Not yet.' She nodded. She knew it was Tommy. She was glad it was Tommy.

'I'm not selling it cheap,' she insisted. 'A fair price, that's all I'm asking. We want to enjoy ourselves. Pete's going to buy a boat. He's been stuck in one place too long. Did you know Large is back?'

'I did.'

'With that girl, Sophie Marchand. They're married this time. He hasn't seen fit to show his face here yet.'

Pat's own face wrinkled, a mixture of disappointment and distaste. Large's return she had always looked forward to, the tales of adventures he would bring, but Sophie Marchand? Sophie should have known better. Like the pub she had run for thirty years with its public and saloon, like my father's trust in Lloyd's, like my grandfather's overnight wall, Pat believed in divisions.

I spent that night poring over the accounts. The following evening I drove over to Tommy's and sitting at the kitchen table went through them again, a bottle of red wine between us, Lyn, his wife, busying back and forth, listening discreetly. Lyn was one of those stylish, good-looking women, with faded jeans and expensive haircuts, who looked as though they were capable of changing the Volvo's flat tyre, baking a kid's birthday cake, and being stupendous in bed all on the same day. They'd seen what had happened to their mothers. They weren't going to make the same mistake. They were still young. Forty, fifty, sixty, they were always going to be still young. They had to work at it, that's all, just like they worked at everything. Halfway through she placed a bowl of pasta down.

'What's it like?' she asked, leaning over, doling it out with a big steel spoon.

'Dead in the water. A few years' time they'd have had to sell it anyway. But with the right amount of investment, some changes . . .'

She slapped an extra dollop on my plate. Lyn had been a sales rep for a garden-furniture manufacturer. They'd met at an Ideal Home Exhibition in Earls Court. Tommy had just started out and had asked her to come down, take a look at the place, see what she thought he needed. He didn't order a thing, had no intention of doing so. What he'd wanted delivered was her.

'It was the arm that did it,' he confided to me once. 'Curiosity, see what a one-armed man would be like, physically. It made me stand out.'

'You stand out anyway, Tommy. You always stood out.'

'Not enough for some.' We'd both known who he was talking about.

In the early days she had helped out behind the till, but twins, a burgeoning bank balance and a devastating, straight-down-the-line backhand had put a stop to all that. Lyn Nikolides had become part of the town's new aristocracy, part of the breed who could build walls all of their own. They had a culture too of a kind, not an atrophied one like my father's, clinging to bits of inherited chain and old-school cloisters, but one spanking new, bought and paid for over the counter. They knew about thrift, about cutting one's cloth; they knew about clearance sales, loss-leaders, the spice of competition, winners, losers and those in between. They were saleswomen, personal assistants, team leaders; they'd all worked, many of them still did. They knew the business of womanhood; anyway hadn't the foundations been laid by one of their own, a shopkeeper's daughter? They didn't waste their time running charity shops or meeting every month for a fund-raising lunch and an illuminating talk. They could lunch on their own, illuminate their own lives. They weren't going to cross the road for anyone. That generation, where money had brought with it responsibility, my mother's generation, had been, or were in the process of being, quietly put out to grass. Money didn't bring responsibilities any more. Money *was* the responsibility. The age of the new kitchen was about to break upon us.

'I'm warning you, Charles,' Lyn said, stretching out, her hand on my hair, 'if you turn him into a pub landlord, I'll sue you for all you've got, just after I divorce him.' Tommy wrapped his good hand high up her leg. She always stood, I realized, on his good side.

'Don't divorce me,' he said, 'just chop the other arm off. I'd be irresistible again.' He twisted his hand so it rode a little higher, another display for my benefit.

It didn't take Tommy and me long to work out what could be done. I did the books for three pubs now, and it was easy to see where the money was being made. Food and wine. Identify your clientele, give them a good, reliable menu, and away you went. We knew the kind of thing we wanted too. No TV, no games, no music. There was an intimacy in our deliberations, a shared experience, touched by the fact that we were investing in a part of our history. We knew the walls and doors, the outside loo, the draughty games room, knew how it *could* look, what could be done. We could imagine ourselves walking into that space, making it our own. Tommy rolled a pencil through his fingers, listening to my enthusiasm. I could raise ten thousand, I told him, fifteen if the bank went for it, ten per cent of the asking price. If I did the books too, I could be looking at what, a fifteen per cent stake? Tommy motioned to Lyn.

'Check on the twins would you, Lyn. I thought I heard them.'

He waited until we heard her reach the top of the stairs, calling softly. I hadn't heard the twins, neither had he. But she had to run with the pretence, even if it meant waking them. He re-filled my glass, pushed it closer.

'Fifteen per cent? It's just a pub, Charles. The accounts won't take that much of your time. We'll have to spend at least another thirty on refurbishing, maybe more. Managers don't grow on trees, either.' He stared at me hard, flickers of impatience touching the corners of his mouth. There was no equality now.

'Seven per cent, Charles, that's it. I'm letting you in on the ground floor here. I don't have to, you know.'

'Well, if you don't want to . . .'

'I didn't say that. You do a lot for this town. But a pub. If I needed a business partner I'd find someone who knew about running one.'

'But I know them inside out.'

'You know about the books, Charles. It's not the same. Why, Lyn would know more than you.'

'Lyn hates pubs.'

'But she's good with people. She knows what they want.'

'And I don't?'

He picked up the plates, took them to the dishwasher, spoke with his back to me.

'You're not a mixer, Charles, you never have been. Who were your friends at school? Who are your friends now? How often do you go out with them? Do you think you really know what customers want, what drinkers want, what diners want, families, lovers, wives, girlfriends?'

'I can't help being a bit of a loner.'

'You're an outsider, not a loner.'

'The difference being?'

'A loner is someone who's made a choice. An outsider is someone who has no choice. The very idea of get-togethers, having a good time, has you twitching like you had a skin complaint. Even at the Merry Boys, any sign of something going on and you'd take yourself off to the saloon.'

'Once or twice I did that.'

'More than once. We all saw it. You only really liked it when it got quiet, when he left. Well, I don't want it quiet any more. I want it to make money.'

He turned, leant against the loading door. I hadn't told him about Large's return, Sophie, the handshake. Truth was I felt slightly ashamed by what I had agreed to, an accomplice in an act of disloyalty, not solely to Tommy, but who we were, what we wanted the town to be. It struck me as strange, though, that Large hadn't come to see him, hadn't let him know that his old rival was back in town, with the girl he stole now the wife on his arm. Perhaps Sophie had held him back, embarrassed the same way as I was, at what she had done.

'Seven point five,' Tommy was saying, 'that's the best I'm prepared to do. If you're happy with that, I'll have the papers drawn up. Have you talked to your bank yet?'

'Tomorrow.'

'And the price? How much do you think they'll come down?'

'Not a lot. It's not a bad asking price. Someone will pay it.'

Tommy shook his head. 'Pat's in a hurry, I saw it in her eyes. All she can see now is Irish mist. It'll cloud her judgement. Get a surveyor in quick. Let's see if we can't wrap it up before the week's out. If we offer cash in hand we could knock twenty grand off it.'

I saw the bank. I was good for fifteen if I wanted, twenty when he heard who I was going in with. I declined. Tommy wasn't going to give me a better percentage, whatever I could raise. I called in a favour and persuaded the local surveyor to give it the once-over the next day. I was all set.

I drove to Monkton's to tell Mum the news, a half-bottle of champagne tucked in amongst the magazines I usually brought along. I was going to be a property owner, a businessman, a man of substance. And I wouldn't lose it like my father had. I'd build on it. Tommy might imagine I was the most junior of partners, but the business interested me way beyond Tommy, who simply saw it as an investment. Tommy was wrong about me. I knew how pubs worked, what people liked. I dropped into enough, on my rounds visiting clients. I knew a good atmosphere when I saw it, what a nice cut of ham tasted like, how an open fire and someone pleasant behind the bar had them rolling in. I knew the margins too, knew how to read them. I could read the runes, just like Large. He was in for a surprise, Tommy. Mum too.

It was only when I crossed the Monkton threshold that I realized who else I might bump into. In my enthusiasm I'd barely remembered her working here. That was quite a different Katie to the one who played so fresh in my mind. I suddenly realized that I didn't want the embarrassment of meeting her there, especially in front of my mother, having to pretend we'd never met, or worse, giving the game away. The idea of introducing her as a girlfriend was out of the question. I hurried down the thankfully empty corridor.

My mother was sitting in her chair, doing nothing much at all. It's what I suppose most of us end up doing, sitting in a chair, doing nothing much, but it's not very encouraging to look at. I raised the carrier bag in greeting. I didn't tell her right away what I had in it. She'd had enough financial surprises in her life. I kissed her on the cheek. One when I arrived, one when I left, that was our arrangement. Neither of us wanted more. She settled back in her seat, preliminaries over, while I set out the magazines on the table, asked after her health. She had a sore throat and a swollen ankle.

'I know how you got those,' I said reprovingly. 'How's it coming along?'

'The vegetable garden? We've made a start. Theo is such a workhorse. A man of his age.' She looked me up and down. 'You should try and get some exercise, Charles. Sitting in that office all day, lounging about that flat of yours every evening. What exercise do you get.'

Last weekend, more than you imagine, I thought.

'And they're happy with what you're doing, Mum, Mrs Lambert and the management?'

'Mrs Lambert isn't happy at all, but not because of that. I don't think Mrs Lambert is long for this place.'

'Oh?'

'Changes, Charles. New style. The new meals. They come very early these days. Still, we get a snack later, if we want it.'

'That's something to look forward to,' I said, anxious to get to the meat of my coming. 'I've got some good news, Mum. Brought some champagne to celebrate. Look.'

I brought the bottle out the bag. Her eyes were bright.

'Don't tell me.' She clapped her hands together. 'You've got a girlfriend, someone serious.'

'No, nothing like that.' I tried to suppress my irritation. She wasn't a girlfriend. She'd said as much. I took a deep breath. 'I'm thinking of going into business, Mum. With Tommy.'

'Tommy? Tommy Nikolides?'

'Yes. Anything wrong with that?'

'You don't want to be led into something you might regret later.'

'It was my idea, Mum, not Tommy's.'

'Does his father know?'

'I don't think so, no. Why?'

'Because he's his father, that's why.'

'He's a grown man, Mum. Like me. We can make our own decisions.' She fussed with her newspaper, trying to marshal her thoughts.

'It's a pity your father isn't here. He could advise you.'

'I don't need advice. It's all quite straightforward.'

'That's what your father thought. Look where it got him.'

'Perhaps it's fortunate that I don't have to listen to him, then.'

'Charles!'

A knock and the door opened. Katie stood there, tray balanced in her hand, a white plate with a grey metal cover, a white pudding bowl and tumbler of orange juice. She stood there, staring at my mother, without a muscle in her face moving.

'Come in, come in,' my mother urged. 'You'll let the draught in.'

Katie advanced. She moved differently from when I last saw her, that fluid authority gone. She had her hair tied back again, thick stockings on her legs, everything pressed in. Her mouth seemed even bigger than I remembered, swollen with everything I wanted kept quiet. 'Throw me my bra,' she had said, one of the last thing she had said to me. She was a Christian. She'd been to bed with me. Joked about my mother. I could feel my face burn. I turned to the window, unable to look at her. I should have called her, found out about her times, made arrangements. It was too late now.

'This is Katie, Charles. She only just started a week or so ago. Isn't that right, Katie?' I turned back.

'That's right.' She gave me a moment's glance.

'That's right, *Mrs Pemberton*,' my mother corrected. 'It's

131

nice to hear one's name every now and again. This is my son, Charles. He visits me twice a week.'

'That must be nice.'

Mother sniffed. 'Katie's been all over. India, Australia, even lived in America. Where was it?'

'Texas.'

'Texas.' She repeated the word with exaggerated triumph. 'Charles has barely been out the front door. He's a terrible stick in the mud. Look at that suit! I've been telling him, he'll never get a girlfriend dressed like that, not in this day and age. His father was quite the man about town in his day.'

'Perhaps he should go to that new out-of-town shopping centre, Mrs Pemberton. They have all the designer labels there.'

She placed the tray on the table straddling my mother's lap, her eyes lowered.

'Hear that, Charles? The out-of-town shopping centre. That's where you should have gone. He wanted to take me out last week, Katie, Independence Day or some such twaddle. Perhaps I should have accepted, taken him there.'

'Oh, I am sure he can shop for himself, Mrs Pemberton.'

'In a pig's eye he can.' She turned back to me. 'And what happened to you on Saturday, Charles? I waited all day for you. What do you think of that, Katie? Too busy to come round to see his mother for an hour or so.'

Katie fussed with the bedclothes.

'I'm sure he had good cause, Mrs Pemberton.'

'Do you? Did you have good cause, Charles? Business, I'll be bound. He works too hard, just like his father. He needs someone like you, Katie, to take him in hand.' She pulled the tray towards her. 'Will you be coming round to collect it?'

'No. I'm off in half an hour. Eric's on duty.' She stood up, looked me in the eye. Mother removed the lid to the plate, keen to see what lay underneath.

'Oh, I like Eric. He makes me laugh. He's very camp. You can go now.'

She waved her away. We watched her walk across the room, close the door behind her. I hadn't said a word.

'Chicken Kiev,' my mother announced. She hunched over the plate and began eating in hurried snatches. Bits of food fell out of the side of her mouth. I could hear the trolley being pushed back along the corridor.

'Pale little effort,' my mother was saying. 'There's a bitterness there, don't you think, roughness round the edges, but nice enough, considering.'

'Considering what, Mum?'

'Where she's from, the estate. Wild family, the Jinkses, the older brother's a troublesome character by all accounts.'

'When did she tell you all this?'

'She didn't tell me anything, but they're terrible gossips, the staff. Nothing they like better than telling you their own and everybody else's troubles. After all, they have to listen to ours often enough.' She pushed her pudding away. 'I don't want this. Go and give it to Mr Glover next door. He eats all my puddings.'

I picked it up and took it out into the corridor. There was no sign of Katie or the trolley. Mr Glover was standing across the way, waiting in the open doorway.

'Which did she choose?' he demanded. 'The rice pudding or the cherry tart?'

'The rice.'

He screwed up his nose and held out his hand.

'I had a cherry orchard, you know. Three different varieties. People would come for miles around. They don't feed you enough in here. My father's it was. When I was a kiddie he used to have me walk around, banging a stick against a tin. All day I did that. Wasn't allowed to go to school, not when the cherries were plumping up. You're new here, aren't you?'

'I'm visiting. My mother, Mrs Pemberton.'

'My son lived in Cambridge. He died last year. Skiing accident. Last of the line. Tell her, next time I'd prefer the tart.' And he shut the door.

I turned. Katie had reappeared at the far end, hands crossed in front of her pale blue uniform. There was something of the nun about her, something cloying, oppressive, something I wished I'd never given myself to, something that pulled me towards her still.

'Charles,' I heard my mother shout. 'You've left the door open. I'm not on public display, you know.'

I fled back into her room.

*

I waited a good hour before leaving. My mother didn't want the champagne, neither did I. It lay in its wrapper on the front seat as I drove away. Katie was leaning up against the brick wall outside, her bag slung over the railing. She'd changed into jeans. I wound the window down.

'Katie. I was hoping you'd wait.' She came up to the driver's window, her face even paler than in the moonless night. The engine idled. I wanted to get away but couldn't.

'How was church?' I said. Her face screwed up into something like contempt.

'Church! Is that the best you can do? You blanked me, Charles. Church was marvellous, thank you, Charles. I had a simply wonderful time.'

A black P-reg Merc turned into the drive, forcing her to jump closer. Large was behind the wheel, the right arm hanging out of the open window, what sounded like the Rhine-maidens blaring through the speakers.

'Charlie! You never told me you was coming today.' He looked us up and down, sensing the awkwardness. 'Everything all right?'

'We were just talking about Mrs Pemberton,' Katie offered,

the over-bright confidence in her voice confirmation that we were talking about anything but. 'She's got a bit of a cough.'

Large obliged, and followed the false tale. 'Nothing serious?' he asked.

'No. I was just telling Mr Pemberton that we had it well in hand.'

'Good girl. It's Katie, isn't it, Katie . . .'

'Jinks. Yes.'

'Katie's new here, just like me, isn't that right, Katie?'

'Not quite like you.'

She stood her ground, wondering what came next. No one wanted to say anything, betray what they knew, what they felt. Many years ago there'd been a girl from Ashlyns, the state school on the other side of town, who I'd rather liked. My parents, like those of my friends, hadn't approved of such associations. A temple to mediocrity, my father used to say of the place, though there was nothing mediocre about Susan Ashley. She'd beaten me at chess in the sixth-form inter-school tournament and for a heady term I used to meet her after school and walk her back home. Nothing came of it, of course. It needed bolder material than me to win her heart, but I remember, walking through the town, how terrified I was that my mother would see us together and later demand an explanation. I felt like that now. Large came to the rescue.

'Well, don't hang about, girl. Get off home. Enjoy yourself. The night is young.'

We watched her as she crossed the road, bag swinging against her hip.

'Not bad,' Large said, that wide grin on his face. 'Fancy her, do you?'

'Don't be ridiculous.'

'Never a good idea, Charlie, knocking off the staff. You'd be better off with one of the old dears. Now turn that heap around and take me to meet your mum. After that I'll give you a guided tour, all the rat holes you can hope to find. She OK, your mum, got a decent room? Telly big enough, bed nice and comfy? You're one of the family now, Charlie. We'll see her all right.'

Mother, *Dictionary of Plants* on her knee, was annoyed to see me again. Large soon changed her mood, patting her hand, engaging her with that mixture of courtly deference and out-right flirtation that older women seem to thrive on. What did she think of the wallpaper, wasn't that cupboard in the corner a bit big for the room, a bit blooming ugly ('I mean what you got in there, Mrs Pemberton, Harrods?'), how the light from the big window complemented her complexion. Then he stood back and admired her taste, what she'd brought in; the inlaid card table, the shepherdess and her swain on her sideboard, locked in a Dresden embrace, even got the age of the French clock within the decade, charming the room as if it had a personality all of its own, mother sitting by the window lapping it up. As for the garden:

'Mrs Lambert's told me what you've been up to,' he said, pulling the guest chair up close, 'tell you what. I'll give you a free hand. You make it so everyone can sit out there when the weather suits, flowers and stuff, and we'll knock it off your monthly bill. Work out the hours, and I'll give you a rebate. What do you say to that. Is that fair or is that fair?'

'That's more than fair, Mr . . .' Her hand clasped the air. She remembered his name well enough.

'Clark. Call me Clark. Course, the rates are going up a bit.'

'They are?'

'Have to, Mrs P. Frankly, I want to attract a better sort of client, one that people like yourself feel more comfortable with. There's probably one or two here who are not quite for you, to be honest.'

'I wouldn't go as far as that,' she said, masking her own snobbery with the lightest of disguises.

'Nevertheless, it's nicer to be amongst your own. You're paying for it, after all.'

'Well, there's that.'

He patted her hand. 'Course there is. Now if you'll excuse us, me and your son have business to attend to. I'm going to have to watch him, though. Should have seen him chatting up an auxiliary just now.'

She looked at me, a mixture of relief and distaste. 'I can't keep track of him these days,' she complained. 'Doesn't even come to see me when he says. Too busy with Tommy and this madcap scheme of theirs.'

'Oh?' Large's radar popped up. 'What madcap scheme would this be?'

I jumped in before she could say any more. 'Mother's getting ahead of herself. It's nothing definite. I can't really talk about it.' I gave Mother an unmistakable look and hustled Large out of the door.

*

We started off, Large rattling off Monkton's facts and figures; twenty-six residents paying from £700 to £1250 a month, £24,000 a month coming in, staff of eleven, one manager, two cooks, five help, unqualified, three nurses, and a part-time handyman. Wages approximately £10,500 a month. Then there was food, just under £3000 a month, heating which fluctuated between £1500 and £5000, plus admin, electricity, upkeep, say £21,500 in all, £5,500 before tax. The margins weren't good enough. He needed more residents, the food was second-rate, the cook (an ex-P&O employee) too wasteful. The manageress, Mrs Lambert, had no sense of purpose, no get-up-and-go, the whole place was dead from the feet up. We went through room by room, dining room, recreation room, kitchens, Large in turns defensive, argumentative, apologetic, throwing open doors, decrying not so much the place, rather the money it wasn't making. The bedrooms got the same treatment whether occupied or not, Large introducing himself to the startled inmate ('For the third time, Charlie, the third time,' he'd tell me, sotto voce), explaining the changes he was going to bring into their lives, not fully appreciating that change perhaps was the last thing on their wish list. 'You won't recognize the place,' he promised to their upturned eyes, 'quiz nights, weekend entertainments, I'll have you all dancing on the tables before the year's out,' leaving them bewildered, exhausted, alarmed. Room after room we invaded, each one crammed with the artefacts of memory, photographs, knick-knacks, the women decked out in oddly formal dresses, outsize pieces of jewellery hanging round their wrinkled necks. I'd never thought of the other residents much before, my mother had never seemed much bothered by them, and yet here they were, a whole parade of them, no different from any other residential home but bizarre in its rich, forgotten mix. Large remembered all their histories, talking to me in front of them as a consultant might talk to one of his interns on their hospital rounds, his assured bedside manner tempered by the eye on the fiscal clock. I was overwhelmed. It seemed impossible that these near-motionless beings had led such active, intelligent lives, bursting with muscle and brain and emotion. A driller from the North Sea oil rigs, the Catholic father of seven, none of whom he'd seen for twenty years, the one-time PA for the managing director of Will's tobacco factory down in Bristol, whose own daughter piloted 737s for Qantas. Across the hall from her, in adjoining rooms, lived Veronica and Beatrice Galloway, who'd spent their lives on a coffee plantation in Kenya, and whose husbands, themselves brothers, had both burnt to death in a Kitare brothel – an event which they retold with ghoulish, scabrous relish. And then there was Lilly Martin. I recognized the name right away, a television star from the black-and-white era, a singer-dancer of limited though attractive talent, a breezy occupant of the late-fifties hit parade, who had a regular high-kicking, song-belting spot on one of those cheery variety programmes that were still going in the late sixties, and who later had traded in her suspect youth for a part in one of the new soap operas, as the put-upon wife of an alcoholic bank embezzler. How had she ended up here, with her fur stole, and her lacquered candy-floss hair, and her silver-framed promotional photo, a bare, twenty-five-year-old left corker slinking out of the split sequinned dress in time-honoured, Raymond Revue-bar fashion? She was still startlingly beautiful in a cracked, angular sort of way; alert, sardonic, heavy pancake make-up presiding over a hefty bosom; a dedicated smoker who looked at Large with bemused detachment.

'My dad had a thing for her,' he said as he closed the door. 'Tonsils-on-legs, that's what he called her. "Tulip Time", that was one of hers. Remember? Dad used to play it all the time down the Merry Boys.'

I nodded. I didn't remember it at all.

'If we got a piano in here, perhaps she'd sing it for the old dears. She was a real trouper, Dad said. Three husbands she had, mostly for show. Set up shop with some woman tennis star when it was safe to admit it. Her son chucked himself out of a New York hotel. She's seen it all.'

I nodded again, though in truth, they'd all seen it all, Monkton's residents. Their cups had runneth over, all the stuff you could think of. And yet this was where they had ended, boxed away in an ex-boys' reformatory just off the A20, a rusty no-man's-land between it and the out-of-town twelve-screen multiplex. Was this what our condition led to, all its hopes and mysteries, its seventy-odd years of living reduced to a forty-watt bulb flickering through yellowing lampshades, the cloying smell of defeat and incontinence hanging on the walls? Guilt flooded over me. That my mother should be living out her days in such a place, when she had lived in a house such as ours. What was it about the old that we had to squeeze all the useful

139

life out of them so ruthlessly? Upstairs, on the third floor, the last room was empty save a single bed, the thin striped mattress rolled up on the bare springs. Large, sensing my unease, fell silent.

'This was a Mr Bernstein's room,' he said eventually. 'Died a month ago. Polish. One of them camp victims; I forget which.'

We stood and stared. I bet he hadn't.

'This was where Napoleon posted his lookout. Look, you can see the track clear as a bell. Do you think they run it still?' Large's voice gathered strength. 'Eight beds.'

I didn't answer.

'It's crying out for a facelift. Know what I'm going to do, Charlie? I'm going to tart the whole place up, from the bottom up, en-suite toilets and sit-in baths. Where I can I'll divide the rooms, double the income.'

I took in the room. It was about a quarter of the size of my parents' old drawing room. 'My mother's room is bigger than this,' I objected. He clapped me on the back.

'And as long as she's in it, it'll stay that way.'

That night we went to the Five Maidens, him and me and Sophie, the first of many. We had a taxi as promised, the driver Brendon, one of the gold-earringed brigade, while the three of us sat in the back, me in a little jump seat, facing the two of them.

'Brendon's going to be my regular driver, just like you're going to be my regular accountant,' Large announced, rubbing his hands. 'Only one difference. He doesn't drink, do you, Brendon?'

'Not since I was ten.'

'You told me fifteen.'

'I don't like to boast.'

'It's a very long-term decision for a ten-year-old to make,' Sophie put in. 'Any particular reason?'

'People look horrible when they've had a drink. Mum, Dad, uncles, aunts, everybody.'

'What about me?' Sophie demanded.

'You and all your kind in particular, madam. I'm with Saudi Arabia on this one. Shouldn't be behind the wheel, and shouldn't be in front of a bottle. If I was in charge I'd pass a law against women and drinking.'

Sophie squealed with delight. 'I *love* it. The Saudis don't let anyone drink, Brendon. Perhaps you should up sticks and live there.'

'I did live there. All the women behind the front door, waiting to do as they're told in a sober world. Show me a better way.'

Sophie clapped her hands. 'And the hair? Have you worn your hair like that since you were ten? It is hair, isn't it, and not a by-product of oil, asbestos or something?'

Asbestos. There it was, corroding her memory too. I looked over to her, wondering how many times that word had cropped up over family lunches, on the phone with her father, wondering whether she had any inkling of what it meant it to me. Could she be that guileless? She sank back in her seat, smiling at her seductive brio. Large hadn't bothered to change, unlike me, but Sophie had gone to some trouble, a low-necked black outfit that seemed to accentuate the effortless strength lying within it, the sleek muscularity in her legs, her broad, powerful shoulders, the sexual dip of her bared bones. She wore ear-rings too, more elaborate than Brendon in front, who she continued to goad with flirtatious, over-familiar conversation, balancing one hand upon my knee as she leant across, enquiring after the nature of the tattoo on the back of his neck, the astringency of his aftershave, the tanned gloves he wore, despite the warmth of the evening, Brendon turning his bullet-shaped head, giving as good as he got. Large seemed to think it great fun. They all did.

It wasn't much good, the Five Maidens, but it was the nearest thing east Kent had to haute cuisine: over-elaborate dishes, overfamiliar service and overpriced bills – the three hallmarks of the provincial restaurant. It was run by a Geoffrey Price, the type of man who'd tried any variety of careers and failed at all of them. This was his last throw. Large had clearly made his presence felt several times before, for a bottle of Taittinger stood waiting in its silver bucket on the one good table by the window. Large ordered the beef Wellington, Sophie the sole meunière. I stuck with chicken. They chose a burgundy and a white Bordeaux, Sophie dismissing my protests by topping up my champagne glass to an unnecessarily difficult level. They were drinkers, both of them, that was clear. Large always had been, but Sophie, Sophie had become one. In the car coming over I thought I'd detected that sharp cut of vodka on her breath. Now I could see it lying deep in the sparkle of her eyes, the drinker's bottomless pool. She was excited, flushed, both of them were, but she more than he. I wondered what else they were on.

'So,' I said, 'have you found somewhere to live yet?'

Sophie gave him a quick look and tore her bread roll in half. Large popped an olive into his mouth.

'Not as yet. We're renting that bungalow we used to run past, the other side of Stan Colley's farm, that his ex lived in. She had that hammock slung between two apple trees, remember? I always fancied that hammock. And what was lying inside. Good-looking woman, Stan's wife. Must have been fifty if she was a day.' He gulped his fizz down.

'You fancy anything that isn't yours,' Sophie said. 'Once you've got it, it's a different story.' She upended the bottle, then waved it the air. The waiter hurried away to get another. Enlivened, Sophie continued. 'He's bought a mountain bike, Charles, did you know that, a mountain bike and a snazzy helmet and some stupid leotard thing that makes him look like a weightlifter. Jumped out the garage a couple of days ago when I was getting the car out. Frightened the life out of me.'

Large slapped his stomach. 'Got to keep in trim. There's a thin line between fat and flab.'

Sophie continued talking as if he hadn't spoken. 'He won't do it, Charles, believe me. It'll sit there, cluttering the place up, along with the archery set and his fishing rod. Know what else he's bought? You won't believe this.'

'She's talking about the golf clubs. You a member?' I shook my head.

'I'm not talking about the golf clubs. He's bought a shotgun, Charles, though he's nowhere to keep it. A shotgun. What's he going to shoot? Monkton residents who fall behind on their payments?'

'Rabbits,' Large replied, his voice suddenly argumentative. It was obvious they'd had this conversation before. 'Rabbits and pheasants and what-not. Snipe.'

'You can't shoot snipe! There's nothing on them.'

'You know what I mean. Those things in the heather. We're living in the proper country now, Nef. Country pursuits. You should take a cookery course. Cordon bleu.'

Sophie looked down at the swell of her cleavage, as if to reassure herself of her provenance. She attempted to brush a crumb from its pressing fold, but it rolled in ever deeper, such rich soil on which to scatter seed.

'I've always lived in the country, Large. It's you who doesn't know one end of a cow from the other. Ah, about time.'

Another bottle of champagne was opened. The banter went back and forth, for my benefit, for theirs, it was hard to work out whose. What were they saying here exactly, that theirs was a dynamic marriage full of spit and spirit, or that buried underneath this mutual attraction lay the fault lines of contempt and loathing, she for his brash money, his guileless philistine ways, his rude chip-fat physique, he for the very thing that attracted him in the first place, her carefree manners, her languid breeding, that pedigree poise pumping day and night round that body of hers: a little class war with a little wall building up in between, all of their own. Why *was* she here? I still couldn't work it out.

The first course finished, indifferent pâté on my part, Large tilted back his chair, and put his hands behind his head. It only needed the radiator and the tall, tiled surround of the window and we could have been back in class.

'Well, Charlie, this afternoon. What did you think of it?' His face was expressionless, as if we'd seen nothing.

What did I think? I thought it should be burnt down. 'It's more run-down than I expected,' I said. 'My mother's room's OK, but some of the others—'

'Your mother's at Monkton's?' Sophie broke in, turning to me in surprise. I felt my face flare.

'Yes. Didn't he tell you?'

'Large! Tell me things? What happened?'

I told her the story, trying to see behind her look of concern. Did she really not know, my father's fall, his suicide? Had her father not told her, hadn't Large? It was hard to relate what had happened and not hang some sort of noose around Andrew Marchand's neck, though for the sake of the evening and my future employment, I kept his involvement to a minimum. Still, family culpability lurked in there somewhere. It was impossible to keep it out, with his hand on my father's shoulder, guiding the story to its grim conclusion. I didn't blame her for it, how could I, and yet I could sense her father's genes flushing through those veins, those little flickers of superiority flashing through the cheek muscle, the suppression of what – amusement, satisfaction? She'd known, all right. I could almost taste it.

'We're lucky that she can afford it at all,' I concluded. 'If she hadn't had a bit of money of her own . . .'

'Lucky. Call that lucky!' Large threw down his napkin. 'You know what you saw this afternoon? Our civilization, that's what, how we see it, what we want to do with it. Take the rest room downstairs we saw, half of them sitting there, playing cards, having a chat, watching the telly. They weren't infirm, not as such, just a bit old, a bit creaky round the edges, a bit cranky in the mouth. What's wrong with that? The truth is we don't want our old any more. There's too many of them, they're everywhere cluttering up the place. "Thank you very much, Mum and Dad, but kindly fuck off." And you know what? Our kids will do exactly the same to us, 'cause they've seen us do it to ours. Their dear old gran lives two hundred miles away up the M40, their grandpa is pegging out his emphysema some-where north of the Humber. We're making our own future, and bloody horrible it is.'

'What are we supposed to do?' Sophie put in. 'Unless they both pop off at the same time, we have no choice. No one wants their parent to die alone.'

'And they don't want them living with them, neither. Do you want yours? Course you don't. The very thought of it makes your face go sour.' He pushed his plate aside, laid his arms out on the table. Here we go, I thought. The Gospel according to Large. 'Twenty years ago, thirty, you go down the street where my dad lived, and Gran lived upstairs or some-where nearby, Gran or Grandpa, depends how it worked out. Whatever, they was around, in the spare room if you had one, and if you didn't, and your kids were already doubled up two, three to a room, then bang went the front parlour. And yes, it was bloody awful, your smelly old aunty with her thick stock-ings and false teeth warbling on about the war and how you should chew your food three hundred times, but you didn't pack her off somewhere. You brought her in, made the best of it. There was a thread to it, who you were, where you came from, who mattered in the world. Not just our street, the armpit of London, or working-class Liverpool or backstreet Glasgow. Your middle-class suburbs, they looked after their own once. But then they started to have aspirations. It was them what started all this, what with their drinks and dinner parties, afraid of what people would find once they came through the front door, Dad honking in the fireplace, Mum putting her foot in it with the wrong accent, the wrong word. Wanted them well out the way. Nowadays we all do it, not the class thing any more, just that we don't want them there. Life's better off without them. We don't even think about it no more. We're so well trained we do it to ourselves, volunteer. Come sixty-five, seventy, it clocks in like a bleeding egg-timer. "Don't want to be a burden on you," we say. "You have your own life to live," and off we trot. Really? Your own life? What's that, then, your own life, if it isn't to do with what gave you life in the first place, who brought you up, right or wrong.'

I sat listening, bemused by his rosy remembrances of the non-existent past, astonished at his galloping insensitivity. Didn't he think I'd have done better if we'd had the money? Did he imagine she'd be there at all if Sophie's father hadn't fattened my father up like a Christmas turkey?

'Are you saying that I've neglected my duties?' I bridled.

He looked affronted. 'Of course you haven't. Circumstances have made it difficult for you, I know that. If your dad was still alive, if things hadn't turned out the way they did, they'd probably be still in that house of yours. I'm not saying there's no place for places like Monkton's. Of course there is. But it's the norm now, Charlie. It's what happens. The moment you can't live on your own, off you go, onto the communal scrap heap. I mean, be honest, there's no reason why you couldn't have found a flat that could have accommodated you and your mum, but neither of you ever gave it a moment's thought. It isn't what your culture wants.'

'It's your culture too.'

'Not if I can help it, it isn't.'

He changed the subject. Did I see any of the old crowd? What was Ben doing now, Duncan?

'I thought you didn't believe in that we-must-keep-up non-sense,' I said, still smarting.

'I don't. As long as I'm not there, they don't exist, right?' He leant forward. 'It's different now. I'm back.'

Sophie excused herself. Large waited until she had left the room, then he sat back, and let out a huge sigh.

'It's good to be back, Charlie, good to be working with you, someone from the old days. We had some fun then, didn't we?'

'We were never that close, Large.'

He nodded the observation away. 'Not close, no, but sort of aware of each other, you holding back, me holding forth. Sophie liked you. That helped.'

'She didn't like me much that time I came around with her birthday present. You weren't too pleased to see me either.'

'Can you blame me? You'd touched a nerve, Charlie, pointed to something she didn't want to see, that *I* didn't want her to see. You were right. She was risking it all. I mean, I wouldn't want my daughter shacking up with the likes of me. I wanted her for all the wrong reasons. Take her away from that stuck-up little c. of a Greek for starters.'

'Tommy? Tommy's not stuck up.'

'No? Thought he was some sort of god fresh out the temple. Thought he'd captured the golden snatch. I put my oar in there, didn't I?'

'I always thought you and Tommy got on.'

'He couldn't stand me. I was everything he wasn't – harder, quicker, cleverer and with a bigger set of balls. All Tommy could do was suck up to the town's elders and betters in the hope they'd lay him a golden turd or two. Whereas I was going to fuck the town and leave it smiling. Everyone knew that. That was what they wanted.' He leant forward again. 'I'll let you into a little secret, Charlie. People like being fucked. They bend over backwards for it.'

'But, Sophie,' glancing over my shoulder to see if she was coming back, 'surely you must have had some feeling for her.'

He winced at the memory. 'Her old man was just as bad. Treated my dad like a piece of shit, made fun of him at one of those school concerts we had to go to, when he mispronounced

147

some French piece Sophie was playing. Making fun of him, and there was my dad who could play anything you threw at him. Anything. And he ... I thought there and then, right, mate, I am going to give your daughter an elocution lesson you won't forget, get her tongue wrapped around a few words she's really never used before.'

'But now, Large,' I persisted. 'You're back together now, for different reasons, surely?'

'Now. Yes, of course now. And then too. I mean, who wouldn't. But there're rules, Charlie. I'm in charge of everything, see. What we do, where we do it, when we do it. "Fetch us a towel, Nef," and off she bloody well trots. It's the Brendon in me.'

He poured himself another glass. He was grinning, but there was a sombre quality to his smile, a reminder of something lost, or never gained. Sophie returned. She came up behind him and placed her lips on the thick swell of his neck, a pliant, elongated thing, suggestively oral.

'What have you two been talking about?' she asked, sitting down.

'The state of your fabulous arse,' Large replied. 'What else?'

'Very funny.'

'Honest to God. I was telling Charlie that first time round, my intentions were entirely dishonourable.'

'Thank the Lord.'

'Someone to whet my appetite, amongst other things.'

'Don't be crude, Large. I don't like it. Neither does Charles. He gets like this,' she told me, 'when he's had a few.'

Large shrugged his shoulders. 'I was just telling him like it was. I wanted you. You wanted me. And both for the same reason. To get back at them all. This fucking town. True?'

She stared at him, then turned to me, smiling. 'To get back at this one, at least.'

I tried to laugh.

'You don't know the half of it,' Large added. 'Every time we did it, you know what she said?'

'Large! Stop it!' She threw a napkin at him. Large threw it back. It was a game they played for their public. I was keen to change the subject.

'So why have you come back, to this . . . effing town.'

'Fucking town, Charles. Don't be afraid to say it. It had a taste of me once. I fucked it and left it wanting more. Well, now they'll get more. Me and Nef are going to fuck it until it doesn't know what day of the week it is. Isn't that right, Nef? Are we going to fuck this town or are we going to fuck this town?'

Sophie raised her glass, her breasts glowing, swollen by a luscious contempt. The room seemed to fold around her, the sparkling chandelier above, the white-linen tablecloth stretching out before her, crumpled like a bed. Her voice rang out across the room.

'We are going to fuck this town, sweetie. Fuck this town and every soul in it.'

'That a girl.' Large wiggled the bottle, looking round. 'Where's the help? This bastard's empty. Go and get another one, Nef. Tell Fred to shove the red. Just bubbles tonight. Chop, chop.'

Sophie pushed her chair back and left without a word.

'See what I mean?' he said, giving me a wink. 'Better than Cruft's.'

*

I spent the next three days looking over the accounts with him, in my office, in his, a nasty little room at the back of Monkton's. I didn't tell my mother I was there, and I made sure that I didn't see Katie. I knew I would have to confront her some time, but this was more important. He was paying me well and he was right. There were plenty of savings to be made at the home, rationalizations to be done, tax advantages to take. Large was looking over another property as well, six miles away, an old Georgian workhouse which had since served as a cottage hospital, announced by a rather splendid arch and set in a solid, two-storey square.

'I could get thirty in here,' he said, striding over the concrete and pigeon droppings. 'Thirty of them shelling out two and half grand a month.' He held up his arms, and started to swing them out, as if back in training. 'We got to get moving, Charlie, before the powers that be fuck it up. As soon as they twig someone's making money out of it, out comes the regulation book. Nothing they like better than poking a finger in the eye of success.'

He had a surveyor round. It proved too expensive to convert, but that didn't stop him looking. All the time he was looking. Loans, mortgages, builders, buildings, he was in and out of my office every day. I wasn't merely an accountant. I was a confederate, flattered, cajoled, put upon, demanded of, goaded, pushed this way and that according to his mood, his need. I dreaded hearing his footfall on the stairs and yet when he plonked himself down I was glad that he was there. I got caught up in it, the way he did things, the way he stabbed the air with his fingers, the way he picked up the phone, paced the room, drummed his fingers against the windowpane, hard, impatiently, as if he wanted to break through. He'd leave with papers littered with his doodles of three-cornered hats and spectacle-covered sphinxes, the surface of the desk sticky with sugar fallen from the apple doughnuts he'd bring, one for Betty, always one for Betty. Why, he couldn't even open a newspaper without shaking crackles of electricity from its pages, everything he did imbued with this restless, probing energy. And me, I had to be right there with him, field his impatience, temper his frustration, see the town as he saw it, not as I had done, see it for the cracks in its edifice, its points of weakness, see others as rivals, contestants in an as yet unannounced battle, ready to see his problem, ready to follow it through, ready to come up with the answer. He needed simple language, a language made of yes and no, black and white, can and can't. He was testing, demanding, expecting knowledge, clarity, decision. I had to brush up my tax law, write-offs, grants, loans, he wanted to know every loophole, every advantage going. I hadn't had to work so hard in years.

'Wait till we close some deals,' he said, after one particularly long day, too much doughnut, too much coffee sitting in my stomach. 'It's like screwing all night or doing six rounds in the ring. Your knees might have turned to shit, but after a shower and a fresh shirt, you're on top of the fucking world.'

I didn't feel like it then. I'd seen other clients, even driven out to hear Haydn Castle's latest fairy tale and a promise to meet his Russian partner, but for the most part I'd been with Large cheek by jowl for half my working hours, sweating every night so that I could impress him the next morning with my hold on his figures, trying to match his quick, mercurial mind. He found another property, a run-down hotel on the outskirts of Folkestone that had been on the market for six months; twenty-five bedrooms and planning permission for a ten-room extension. Property was cheap in Folkestone. He was all for raising the capital and snapping it up right away, but I signalled caution. I'd seen too many people over-extend themselves in bursts of similar enthusiasm. Servicing debt is always more problematic than it appears. Though he chided me, he liked me for that, liked it if for no other reason than it gave him something to rub up against. 'That's why I hired you,' he said, 'for the old woman in you. All you need is one of them bicycles with a wicker basket in front and you'd be made. Dame Charlie Pemberton. The widow of the Weald.' It was not an unattractive form of flattery.

I wasn't in contact with Tommy much. While negotiations were going on we thought it better to keep out of the Merry Boys, and without it, there seemed no place for us to meet. He hadn't invited me over to his house again. My flat? Another pub? They wouldn't have been appropriate. He could have come into my office, I could have gone to the garden centre, but something prevented us doing either, a belief in the integrity of our own territory. We'd put our first offer in, which they had refused, followed by another, which they'd turned down with equal conviction. A week later, and one tense telephone conversation between us, Tommy half intimating that he wished he hadn't bothered, or more particularly he hadn't bothered with me, we upped it by eight grand. *His* eight grand, he took pains to point out. Tommy had been surprised at their intransigence, but I wasn't. Seeing Pete sewing that button on his shirt had given me an insight into their solid imperturbability, his thick patient fingers slowly working the fine needle through. They weren't going to be hurried, pushed off course, not even by the garden king.

Three weeks' work and I was exhausted. I'd had enough. It was the Saturday, two months after Large had shown up. I'd neglected everything and everyone, the flat, my office, Tommy, Betty, Mother too. I went over to Monkton's, determined to make amends. Old Nikolides was back in my mother's room. Large had been as good as his word and had replaced the heavy wardrobe at the back with something off-white that sank into the colour of the wall. My mother pretended to be pleased to see me.

'Charles. We're just taking coffee. Theo and I have done a really good morning's work. We're early risers, both of us.' Nikolides got to his feet, his hands as grubby as his trousers.

'Next year we'll have a proper vegetable garden,' he boasted, shaking my hand with unnecessary vigour. 'Fresh produce on the table every day. That is if you're still here.'

'Theo,' she scolded. 'You shouldn't say things like that.' She smacked the back of his leg, delighted, a very un-Mother-like thing to do. I'd never imagined she'd greet the prospect of her death with such frivolity. After her stroke, we'd gone through her burial requirements with a fine but solemn tooth-comb.

As always Nikolides scurried off at the earliest opportunity. My mother retired to the bathroom. There were flowers on her table, big things, like daisies.

'He's bringing you flowers now is he, Theo?' I called out.

'Management,' she said. 'We all get them, once a fortnight.' Needless expenditure I thought, and not at all in line with what Large had been banging on about. She emerged from her bathroom, rubbing skin-cream into her hands. She was looking more like her old self. Mother and her garden. She just had to dip her toes in soil and she turned a different colour. She was gaining strength, putting on a bit of weight, coming back to life again.

'Why don't we go somewhere this weekend?' I suggested.

'How do you mean?'

'We could drive down to the coast, further if you want. Take an overnight bag.'

'What is this? It's not my birthday. Nor yours.'

'I need a break, Mum. Thought you might like one too.' She took up her propelling pencil and sat down with the crossword folded on her knee.

'It's not right, Charles,' she said, without looking up. 'A single man taking his mother away for the weekend. You should be taking someone your own age.'

'You mean like Tommy?'

She huffed in her chair. 'You know perfectly well what I mean. You're getting on, Charles. Where were you thinking of taking me?'

'Dorset, Hampshire; how about the Isle of Wight? You used to like it there.'

'I don't know. I'm quite happy here, really. Go on your own.'

I left, another offering rejected. In the hall Katie was

sticking flowers in a vase, poking the long stems in one by one, as if the place depended on them. I'd seen her in town a few days before, walking along the High Street, and a jolt had run through me, remembering the pleasure she had taken in my nervous, clumsy ways. She'd been with another man, taller, older than her, but with the same sense of purpose, the same unforgiving length to his stride. They were handing out leaflets, stuffing them through business letterboxes, fanning out to clusters of youths sitting on a bench, before bracing a pair of pram-pushing mothers. They wouldn't get many takers, not with that approach. I'd stepped up to the window to follow the two of them more closely, to see how close they were, but had been forced to jump back when she'd glanced up at the window, scared and thrilled that she'd done it, the realization that my name was scratched on her skin, as hers was on mine.

Another flower purposefully placed. I hurried towards her.

'Katie.'

'What do you want?' She turned, her lips full of blood. Memory flooded back, the colour of them in the dark, the words they'd formed around me. 'You lovely man,' she had said, and stretched out her arms. Who had ever stretched out their arms to me before? Who had ever wanted to?

'Katie,' I implored. 'Look at me.'

'I am looking at you.'

'You know what I mean.' I stayed her hand. 'I meant to call. But it was so complicated. You being here. My mother.'

'I can't help working here. It's my job.'

'My mother says you're very good at it, very caring.'

'Well, that's all right, then.' She pushed past me. 'Can you let me finish, please?'

I stood aside. She plucked a flower from out of the jug of water. Her hands were wet. Her lips moved as she slid the stem in amongst the others.

'Katie,' I admonished. 'Couldn't we give it another go? I'm not used to all this. I'm . . .'

'A bit of a mummy's boy. I know. You blanked me, Charles. After you promised.'

'It wasn't easy, you bursting in like that, waiting on her. I didn't know what to do. I still don't.'

'You could have told her that we'd bumped into each other at the shopping centre. I wasn't asking you to tell her you'd had your thing inside me for three-quarters of the weekend.'

'Katie. Don't talk like that.'

'Well, it's true.'

'Not three-quarters. Three-eighths, maybe.'

Her face tightened, trying not to smile.

'You know what I did when I left you?' she said.

'You waited for me. I couldn't talk then, not with . . .'

'I meant that Sunday morning, after we'd fucked all night.'

'Katie! Don't talk like that, please. You make it sound so . . . You went to church.'

'I went home and washed our sins away, so I could go to church, pray to my Lord without the stink of us all upon me. That's what I'd done with you, Charles. Sinned, hour upon hour, with my eyes wide open. Because of you. Don't you see that? And the next time you saw me you turned your face away, as if you were ashamed.'

'It wasn't you, Katie. It was never you. It was her. She frightens me, Katie, what she thinks, what she says, what she thinks of me, what she'll say of me. I was frightened of her knowing what I'd done, of her seeing me in that light. I still am. I'm not expressing myself very well.'

'You're doing all right.' She paused. 'Like a kid with a new bicycle, you were.'

She was staring at me, watching me blush.

'Do you really think it's a sin?'

'Of course it's a sin. Doesn't make me not want it. Doesn't stop me from succumbing. I'm human, Charles. We're made to sin. Don't you look at the people around you in this town and think what terrible lives they must lead, the thieving, the whoring, the everyday cruelty? Don't you see it stamped on their skulls like they was branded, on their kids' faces too, all pinched and grown up before their time.'

I nodded. I thought exactly that, almost every day.

'That's not sin, exactly, is it?'

'Not exactly. Maybe ours isn't exactly.'

She was staring, that pale intensity shining out.

'Are you free this weekend at all?' I said.

'Does it look like it?'

'I mean afterwards. I was thinking of driving somewhere. Dorset. Hampshire, maybe the Isle of Wight. Would you like to come?'

'I'm on late shift on Sunday.'

'Call in sick.'

She shook her head. 'It's not fair on the others.'

'It doesn't have to be the Isle of Wight,' I persisted. 'We could drive down to the coast. Brighton, for instance.'

'I've never been to Brighton.'

'We could come back early Sunday morning, if you need to be back for church.'

'They have churches in Brighton, Charles. Besides, I won't be dragged down to hell if I miss one Sunday.'

'Are you saying yes, then?'

'Depends.'

'On what?'

'If you can persuade me. Right here. Right now.'

I looked down the corridor. There was no one about. I stepped forward, kissed her on the lips. She wiped it away contemptuously.

'That won't get me there. For fuck's sake, Charles. Lose it, will you?'

I stood, a blankness come over me.

'The reserve, the politeness. Loosen up, Charles. Do it like you mean it, like you don't care. Get a little uncultivated. Grab hold of me. Put your hand under my skirt, break a button or

156

two. Aren't you angry with me at all? Don't you want more of it, come what may? It's my fault what you've become.'

I pushed her against the table, her hands going back, crushing the heads on the flowers. The kiss was cavernous, thick. She stuck her hand into the jug, slopped water over my face, a sea raging below. 'Down, boy.' She held me off.

'I'm off in an hour. Pick me up at half two, by the shopping arcade.' Her hand went down. 'I suppose you'll want to fuck me on the way down.'

'Katie.'

'Just make sure the car's clean. I can't stand a dirty car.'

*

I drove down to the garage, to find the car wash closed. The woman behind the counter directed me round the back of the new industrial estate that had sprung up on the edge of the one-way system, not far from the warehouse where Haydn Castle stored his merchandise. He'd told me about the place too, where a couple of ex-squaddies cleaned your car armed with rubber mops and air-pressured nozzles. Better than those nylon brushes, Haydn had told me, although his own car, an old-fashioned Citroën, was permanently layered with the wash of the road. I did as suggested, driving through a part of the town that seemed to me to presage its economic future, an outcrop of small, barely noticed businesses, each employing three or four workers, a dozen at the most, selling, fixing, manufacturing; small stuff, VAT-registered, no-frills establishments – a classic car-repair shop, a pottery seconds concession, a carpenter's workshop, bare, flat-roofed near-windowless buildings, a two-car parking bay outside the one-room, one-filing-cabinet office. I drove along, the detritus of light industry lining the route, lengths of piping, tyre stacks, rolls of black plastic, busted crates, trying to follow the haphazard, arrow-head cardboard signs along the increasingly constricted, pot-holed roads. There were buildings here too, but boarded up, derelict, monuments to times passed and failed. It was a wonder anyone found the place at all, and who would go there, who would take the risk? Then the last sign came up, bolder than the rest, as if a reward for making it this far – Car Wash Fifty Yards. I rounded the corner. Four silver metallic Mercedes were parked up in front of a greasy washing bay, three radial-spoked four-wheel-drives, one spanking new convertible, light tan upholstery, top down, not a spot of dirt visible on any of them. Leant up against the three four-wheelers, a row of baseball-capped young men, bull necks, white T-shirts, faded jeans, pristine sneakers, none of them a day over twenty-five, gold bracelets on their wrists, mobile phones clamped to their ears. From out of the convertible a short-skirted young woman was swivelled round in the front seat, the door open, her right leg stretched out as she leant down to paint her toenails, short, muscular legs verging on fat. As I pulled up, the men turned towards me, their eyes wreathed in suspicion. I had broken in on something private, something their own. This was a place of business, a place of deals, decisions, everything on the hoof. They didn't go in for paper trails, these boys. Not yet anyway. Give them five years and too much loose money in some garage lock-up and it would be a different story. Not that I would handle any of them. Rival Rodney was carving out a niche for himself in that area, I had heard.

I switched off the engine and got out. A man I hadn't noticed pushed himself from the far wall, bare-headed, a black leather jacket over his T-shirt, mobile dangling from a leather loop on his wrist, a gold cross on a gold chain around his neck. He was leaner than the others, his blond hair a little longer, his skin a little more tanned. He looked quicker, cleverer, the one who made the running.

'Marty,' he called out. 'Give this unbeliever's car a wash and send him on his way. Japanese? It's an affront to my fucking contact lenses.'

The laughter came like gunfire, explosive, spluttering. They killed their calls and closed in, ready for the kill. A man in overalls stepped out of the bay and beckoned me forward.

'Take no notice, mate,' he said, kicking a hosepipe out of the way, 'Jay's just being his usual bastard self. Drive it in.'

I shook my head. 'I don't want to jump the queue.'

'Yes, you do,' the man called Jay said. 'Here, I'll do it myself.'

He pushed past me and before I could stop him, had jumped in, jammed his foot down, and with the door hanging open and wheels squealing had skidded the car into place.

'Now strut your stuff, Marty,' he said getting out, 'and be quick about it.' He tossed me the keys. 'Impressive. Nought to sixty in what, three and a half rice bowls?'

He went back to his phone, shaking his head. Marty and his chum got to work. I stood by, nervously proprietorial. For a time, the way Jay looked at the car, at me, I thought he might be talking about me. Too late to cut and run now, but that's what I wanted to do. Half ten in the morning and I was on an alien planet. There was no way out. I could hear the grind of the one-way system not a hundred yards away, but it might as well have been on the moon. Emboldened by my obvious discomfort, Jay's friends crowded round, dodging the sprays of water, tiptoeing through the soapsuds to peer through, make derogatory remarks about the interior, the plastic mould of the dashboard, the checked upholstery, even the wheel lock that I kept on the passenger floor had them in fits. It reminded me of being forced to get undressed in the school changing rooms, that feeling of being naked, vulnerable, emasculated. So this is what the wrong car can do, deplete your psyche, hold you accountable, whether you like it or not. I stood there shrivelling while Marty and his chum hosed it down, dried it with hot air, swabbed it with wax.

'That do you?' Marty asked when they had finished, wiping his hands.

I nodded, grateful it was over. Jay flicked his phone shut, strolled back into the arena.

'What I want to know is why anyone should want to waste fifteen quid washing crap like that? Must be a big occasion, squire. What is it? Shopping at Tesco's? Taking your mum out for a spot of ram-raiding?'

I still don't know what prompted me. Simple irritation, the smell of Katie Jinks hanging in my nostrils, or the realization that the only way of getting out of here unscathed was to cut a way through. Whatever, the wimp struck back.

'As a matter of fact, I *am* taking my mother out, though to the coast rather than the nearest cash-point. Nothing wrong with that, is there?'

There was a pause. They were weighing it up, what it meant, how to take it. They looked to their leader for guidance.

'That'll teach you to be so fucking rude, Jay.'

It was the woman who spoke. She had finished with her toes and was busy with her cigarette lighter. Her voice was warmer than I had imagined. She turned her face to me. 'Do me a favour and take his as well. We need a break.'

Thankful for her intervention, I spoke as graciously as possible.

'I think one mother is all I could handle.'

'Ah, but she wouldn't be your mother, would she?' she pointed out, amused by her observation. 'You could do what you like with Jay's as far as I'm concerned. Leave her on the beach. She's half barnacle as it is.' She waved the smoke away from her face. I couldn't help but smile.

'I think most mothers are half barnacle.'

'I'm not.'

'You're not a mother.' Jay jumped back in. The tone was as forceful, but the mood had changed.

'I could be, if yours weren't round every bloody night.' The others laughed, clearly familiar with the complaint. 'It's no joke, I tell you. You don't have to put up with her every Saturday night.'

'I'm her only son. She loves me.'

'Well, do something special with her, so she'll leave us alone for a bit. I mean, you never take her to the seaside.'

'There's no point, is there, if Nissan man here is going to do it for me.' He took another squint inside, shielding his eyes, gold bracelets clanking down his wrist. 'Don't know if Mum would fit in, though. That's the trouble with Japanese motors. They're built for Japanese.' He straightened up, looked me straight in the eye. He'd thrown me a lifeline, given me a chance to return to the living.

'She can sit in the front if you like,' I told him. 'My mother's quite small. Besides, there's nothing she likes better than back-seat driving.' It wasn't true, but it was the right thing to say. We both had mothers.

'I would appreciate that.' He stuck out his hand. It was the size of a small frying pan. 'Apologies. Shouldn't knock a man who takes his mother out. It's worse than driving in Spain. Where are you taking her? If mine's going too, I ought to know.'

'I'm not absolutely sure. I thought we might make the weekend of it. Drive over to the Isle of Wight.'

'She'd like that. She's never been there. Dad has, of course.' He turned, his audience snorting with laughter. It took me a while to work it out. 'So, it's a date, is it? I'll get her to pack her cossy.'

'And I better go and break the news to mine, ask her to cut a few extra ham sandwiches.' I dug in my back pocket for my wallet.

'No, no, it's on the house,' Jay insisted.

'I couldn't let you do that.'

He placed his hand on the bonnet. 'Yes, you could. And don't come here again, not on Saturday mornings. It's private.'

'Private my arse.' The woman butted in again. 'He can come here whenever he wants. It's Charles Pemberton, isn't it? Remember me?'

I looked at her again, more fully this time. I hadn't thought it wise to inspect her too closely earlier. I didn't remember her at all. But then she put her head to one side, and I remembered completely. The girl from the golf club. The one my father couldn't take his eyes off.

'Bee Bee, isn't it?'

'Yes. I was hoping I'd bump into you one day, tell you how sorry I was.'

She skipped up out of the car, hugging me if I was a long-lost friend, clouds of perfume swirling around my head. She held me at arm's length.

'He was special, your dad.'

'Thank you.'

'If it hadn't been for him, heaven knows where Jay would be. Or me. I wanted to go to the funeral but couldn't get the time off. And then, you know how it is. But when Mr Rossiter said you'd be looking after the accounts, it all came back, what your dad had done for us.'

'Mr Rossiter? Clark? You're working for him?'

'We're going to be his right-hand man, me and Jay. Up front. Keeping the customers happy, making sure no one's got their fingers in the till. Beats working.'

I had no idea what she was talking about. She tapped her foot.

'The bar,' she said defiantly. 'He's putting us in charge.'

'I didn't know Monkton's had a bar.'

'Who's talking about Monkton's. He's bought that run-down old pub, the Merry Boys. Didn't you know?'

*

I drove home, put a call through to Monkton's to tell Katie that I couldn't make it after all. I wrote a letter to the bank, cancelling my loan, thanking them for their cooperation, hoping they would be so understanding if the occasion arose again. Then I rang Tommy. Lyn answered. She could tell by the tone in my voice that the news wasn't good. Tommy took it like I knew he would, the shrug of his shoulders coming over the line by his understated delivery.

'Well, that's the way it goes. Do you know who bought it,' he asked, a throw-away line which I took up with some reluctance.

'Yes. You're not going to like it.'

There was quiet on the line. I could picture him standing there, Lyn to one side, head inclined, hand on hip, questioning. I started in on the tale, Large's arrival that overcast Thursday, the raincoat with wine in its pocket, the proposition, Sophie springing up from behind the door, like a Playboy rabbit out of a hat. There came an intake of breath on that, suppressed but audible all the same, Lyn asking, 'Tommy, what is it?' in response. I dug my way further in, a mole blind in the dark of his story, hacking my way around the obstacles that loomed up: why I hadn't rung him up that day? Why had I kept the fact that I was working for Large from him for so long, not told him that Sophie was back in town and married to him? What had I done? Nothing much it seemed, just plied my furtive trade on behalf of one amongst many others, but somewhere in this now accountable transaction I had managed to cross a threshold – a threshold of gain and loss. As I dug my way free of the take, stood once more in relative light, trying to shake free of it, it was clear that I had come out upon a different, less hospitable, landscape.

There was no immediate reaction. I couldn't even hear him breathing.

'Tommy?' I said. 'Are you all right? Say something.'

He cleared his throat. 'You know what Large used to say about you, Charles? Back in the good old days?'

'I didn't know he said anything about me.'

'He said things about everybody, me, Duncan, Rachael, everybody, some true, some not so. But you, you he got right on the button. "There is only one thing Charlie dreads more than being given the cold shoulder," he said.'

'And what was that?'

'Friendship.' And he hung up.

I put on a jacket and walked down through the town. It was half one. I could have been in the car with Katie driving down to Brighton. I could have rung Tommy from Brighton, let Katie soothe the blow. The High Street was full of its Saturday market stall largesse, cut-price tat, dodgy screwdriver sets and second-hand videos, and pale, pregnant mothers strutting past clumps of emaciated disaffected young men in amongst grease in the air from burger stalls and hair lotion, my town in all its tawdry glory. I ducked into the old alleyway behind the new police station and the library, into one of the bent forgotten streets, where the Merry Boys stood, huddled at the end of the road. I wanted to confront Pat with what she'd done. We'd been such loyal customers, Tommy and me. Large was sitting on a stool, a till-roll in his hand. He sprang up.

'Charlie! My main man! Have I got a surprise for you!'

'I've just heard. Congratulations.'

'You know?'

'I just met your new manager. Bee Bee someone. She used to work up at the golf club.'

'Bee Bee Conley. I used to go out with her when I wasn't dating all them posh birds at school. Her family came down from the smoke same time as ours. She lived two doors down.' He dropped his voice, though no one else was there. 'Matter of fact she was the first I ever . . . She was barely out of her pram but you wouldn't have known it. We couldn't get enough, after school, up in her bedroom, when her mum was working. Better than homework, I can tell you. She's been to cookery school, you know.'

'I don't know anything about her at all.'

'You will, though. A real live wire.' He rubbed his hands. 'Charlie Pemberton. My first customer! What's it to be? You'll have to pay, though. This place isn't taking any money at all.'

'I just came to see Pat. Wish her all the best.'

'Shove her down the cellar head-first, more like. You was after it, wasn't you?'

I shrugged my shoulders, as if it no longer mattered. Large showed me his hands. They were fat and pink as always, as if they'd been just been scrubbed.

'I couldn't tell you, Charlie, could I?' he pleaded. 'We was rivals.' He sat back on his stool, changed tack, took the ground to the real enemy. 'What was you in for, as a matter of interest? Ten per cent?'

'I don't think I should tell you that.'

'Less, then. You should have come to me, Charlie. I'd have given you ten. Hardly worth bothering with, anything less. What was it, eight?' He caught my face. 'Less than eight. That's a shopkeeper for you.'

I felt obliged to defend him, even though my heart wasn't it. 'It was a fair offer.'

'Was it? Who had the idea, Charlie? You or Tommy? You, wasn't it? Course it was. Tommy can't see beyond the next pile of horse manure. Now, if I wanted to, I could give you that ten per cent, let you in on it. Why shouldn't I? It's your town. You'd help to make a go of it, turn it into something. But I'm not going to. Know why? 'Cause it'll teach you not to go behind my back, not where that little c. is concerned. I'm the one who's going to fuck this town, Charlie, not you, not Tommy, not all them farts licking each other's arse in the Chamber of Commerce, but me. Right?'

'Right.'

'Course you and Tommy would have kept it like it is now, a few hunting prints on the walls, better furniture, maybe someone who knows how to cook a decent shepherd's pie, but basically, you'd have kept it like it is now, half asleep, out for the count. You want to see what a place like this really can do? Come back in six months. Now bite your lip and buy me a drink. Take it like a man.'

I bit my lip. I bought him a drink. I took it like a man.

Seven

So, Large bought the Merry Boys, not me, not Tommy, his second purchase of the town, cash on the nail, one lump sum, six thousand more than we offered. The night before Pat and Pete left, he held a party for them. They hadn't wanted it, but Large insisted, all the old crowd invited, the out-of-towners put up at the Post House at his expense, the boys he'd once ruled over, the girls he'd once sampled. They all came, Ian, Ben with his partner Andy who worked for Channel 4, Rachael, who'd replaced the Senegalese boyfriend with a Nigerian planning officer and their two-year-old son, Laura, now a dental hygienist in Southampton, resolutely single and affecting a jolly lesbianism that wasn't wholly convincing, Large the generous host, grabbing them as they ducked in through the doorway, Sophie by his side, more dollar to the cut than the rest of the frocks put together, Large sweating in a bright blue suede jacket that she'd bought him, she boasted, in the bordello back streets of Rome. They'd been drinking, the two of them, way before the kick-off. They had that hard-liquor glitter to them, brittle astringency to their cut and thrust, Sophie taking every opportunity to garner her old town friendships around her, flaunting Large's undying incongruity, his misplaced confidence that wasn't. 'I bought him for the bad taste, darling,' that was her motif, that and the pearl necklace that hung around her proffered neck, and yes, we all recognized the symbolism in *that*. And me? I was the guest on hors d'oeuvres duty. As they trooped through, the Rachaels, the Bens, it was clear they were surprised to see me so clearly part of his entourage, that out of all of them, Large had chosen me as his side-kick. It was there in the uncertain clap on the shoulder, the too-eagerly proffered cheek, unasked questions hanging in their eyes. I didn't blame them. I couldn't quite believe it either.

The place filled up rapidly: the old boys who'd sung songs with Carl, pleased to see Rhoda back in the fold, her wheel-chair tucked into the little alcove beside the bar flap; the new manageress Bee Bee dressed in cheap designer wear, a pack of near-indecent girlfriends forming a scrum around the bar; her husband Jay, and his 4x4 mates, trying to engage at every opportunity – the place hadn't seen so much bare flesh in years. Brendon, his scalp freshly shaved, had been sent up to London to fetch a trio from Large's trading days, leaner, chip-per versions of the man himself, fast-talking, watch-flashing, quick-footed boys, buzzing with that relentless, no-quarter-given jollity that was their trademark. 'Flies on shit,' Brendon murmured as I handed him his orange juice, and he wasn't wide of the mark. A party it may have been, but Large had insisted on a paying bar, the price of beer and spirits knocked down to what it had been more than ten years before. I'd have preferred wine, but there was no wine. We hadn't drunk wine back then. No matter. We were mostly happy to pay, to take part in his little charade, re-live the time when he had ruled the roost, reprise the old dawn.

They were in top form, Large, his mother, his friends, Jay's buddies chatting up Laura and Paula and the married Rachael, the girls enjoying their cheeky audacity. Did I say charade? There was no pretence here. He'd done it again. He'd hadn't been back two months and here they were, back on track, dancing to his tune, frivolous when he wanted to be frivolous, loud when he wanted to be loud, crude when he wanted to be crude, games, jokes, songs, arguments, everything and every-one on tap, Large, elbow on the bar, orchestrating his own amusement. 'Do that Elvis number, Mickey,' he demanded and

Mickey swept back his hair and launched into 'Heartbreak Hotel'. They were like children again, Large and Sophie, the top couple at school, bursting with promiscuous promise, tanked up on copped feels in the corridor and the hip flask full of whisky, diving off the cusp now, aping what they took to be adult behaviour, a mixture of sex and sophistication, the blow job and the bow tie. They wanted to be – what, naughty, descendants from another careless age, Large dressed up in his circus-ring clothes, Sophie adulterously slinky, underwear, judging by the stretch of her plain light-grey dress, abandoned. That's what this was all about, throwing it all off, what had been, the slights, the worries, the fear of failure that we would never hear about. Here they could be anything they wanted. 'Show them where you put your fist of a night, Bee Bee,' he demanded, and Bee Bee opened her mouth and stuck it right in, working her wrist back and forth over her lips, revelling in the obscenity. I turned away to find Rhoda had wheeled her away across, and was sitting right under me.

'No shame, that girl. Never had. God knows what she gets up to in here when I'm not around. Still, best to be broad-minded in this day and age.'

I regarded her coldly. We'd met any number of times since they'd come back, but it was always under sufferance, the boy cap in hand, running errands. I had a plate of vol-au-vents in my hand.

'Is it?'

'That's our Charlie. Never one to swing with the times. Do you remember that day when you came around and I was painting my toenails in the school colours, egg, green and egg.' I nodded, relieved to be leaving the present.

'Yes, of course I remember. Large's boxing triumph.'

'Quite a day to remember all round, what with a Pemberton coming to call.'

'A Pemberton running errands,' I corrected her.

'I wasn't expecting visitors,' Rhoda said, shamelessly coy,

'the state I was in.' She shifted, willing me to look down upon the remnants of her bosom. I held my eyes steady.

'I didn't mean to embarrass you.'

'You didn't embarrass me, Charlie, I was long past that. You embarrassed yourself. You're still embarrassed.' She rearranged herself. 'It's the way you was brought up. A boy like you is always careful with his manners. Not like mine. Look at him. The cat who's got the cream.'

I looked across. Sophie was up at the bar, her position unnervingly familiar, not a foot away from where she had stood the night of Large's victory, another beer balanced against her breast. Large had his arm round her, tugging at her while she was trying to chat to Ben and his spiky-haired, alternative boyfriend. She was doing her best to ignore him, shoving his hand away only to have it snake right back. Her years of independence, it seemed, had taught her nothing.

'He has got the cream.'

'Cream curdles,' she said. 'How's your mother?'

My mother? What did she know of my mother? 'She's well, thank you. She keeps herself busy with Monkton's garden.'

Rhoda nodded. 'Quite the thing with her, wasn't it, gardening. Don't see the point of it myself, all them weeds. I mean you can buy flowers in a shop. How does she find my boy?'

'Large? Fascinating.'

'What, like a strange breed?'

'Well, he makes a change from her son.'

She patted my leg in agreement. 'And your poor father, Charlie. Who'd have thought it, you and Large losing their fathers.'

'Not exactly in the same circumstances,' I pointed out. 'My father left his family out of choice. And not at a wholly appropriate time.'

She waved a finger at me. 'You're too hard on him,' she admonished. 'It was a car crash, just like Carl's, everything closing in so fast. Life just smashed him to pieces. Your mother and me, we walked away from it. Well, she walked away from it. Me, I'm stuck here with two useless pins, though no one's told my toes. But them two, your dad and my Carl, their injuries were fatal. Did you ever think to look at it like that?' She wheeled herself off.

'Charles. Didn't think I'd find you here.' Rachael had come over. In the race for sexual ascendancy, she'd been Sophie's most serious competition, a Sophie manqué, the girl with the second-best looks, the second-best lines, the second-best opportunities waiting for her outside the school gates, but a girl who despite her best efforts had seen her rival increase her lead with every closing term, until that last summer, when Sophie had lapped her with a palpable, contemptuous ease. She was more subdued than I remembered, as if this reunion had only served to remind her of that year of disappointment. Rachael had been the first of Large's school conquests. She'd been foolishly proud of it at the time. I'd never liked her much after that.

'I live here, Rachael,' I said. 'I've always lived here.'

'No, I mean here,' she said. 'Part of his merry band.'

'He's a client, Rachael. Why does everyone think something else?'

'Cause you're handing out the canapés, the only one wearing a suit. You look official. Where's the Turk? Is Tommy coming?'

Is Tommy coming? It was the question all the old friends asked me. Since his return, Large and Tommy hadn't met yet, everybody knew it, the old despised grapevine at work, I supposed. They all remembered that first encounter, that blitzkrieg, that seizure of Tommy's long-held territory, and had come here in anticipation of this, the re-match. It had been Tommy's town before Large had appeared and Tommy had been handed it back when Large had decamped. We all knew what was at stake. It lay there waiting, like my untouched pint up at the bar.

They arrived a good hour after everyone else, both of them looking as if they'd dressed up for a dinner dance, deliberately out of place, Tommy wearing patent-leather pumps and an elegantly cut DJ, Lyn in something long and equally formal. Tommy had a white scarf wrapped around his neck, as if to emphasize the superiority of their position, the transitory nature of their appearance decreed solely by an unbending regard for etiquette; this was business politics, small-town courtesy. Large moved towards them with the speed of a shark.

'Well, well, Tommy. Here we are, back at the old corral.' He wrapped both his arms around him, hands digging into Tommy's shoulder blades, that old boxer's hold, keeping your opponent in check, the two-handed clinch a reminder of what he possessed and Tommy did not – not simply the girl and the goods, but the limbs to hold them fast. Tommy twisted himself free.

'I hear you've got rid of your old name,' Tommy said quickly. 'What was it, the outside world cut you down to size?'

Large took a bow. That was *exactly* why. 'It's hard to get rid of it, with you lot around. Perhaps I should let it go back to what it was.'

Tommy pulled at his nose, showing off his gold cufflinks. 'You know what they say,' he said. 'Never go back. Nothing's like you thought it was. It all changes. Even the past.'

He looked up at the moth-eared fox, still hanging above the door. I was struck with a bitter flash of knowledge. This would be the last time Tommy ever came here. It was over, what had taken place over the years in our quiet lunchtimes, my steady elevation in this town, my position of slowly rising regard. The town was soon to be plugged into a different energy supply, too much voltage for discreet, unobserved growth such as I had been cultivating. I'd blown it.

'Well, this one hasn't changed much, has she?'

Large propelled Sophie forward on her high heels. She put her hand to Tommy's face, held his cheek while she kissed him lightly to the side of his mouth, a shade too lightly for mere reunion, catching him quite deliberately on the corner of his lips, suggesting there was something else she wanted to pass on here, something open, fluid, something he could barely resist. Then she patted his shoulder, feeling down the upper arm to where the prosthetic took over. Lyn stiffened.

'At the bottom of the sea, Charlie said,' Sophie purred, running her hand down the length of it. 'You should have written to me, Tommy. I'd have gone down for it. It had your ring on it, didn't it, your grandfather's, the one from the old country? It meant a lot to you, that ring. You hardly ever took it off, remember?'

The ring. We all remembered the ring. There'd been something of a kerfuffle over it, not the first time in our school there'd been trouble over jewellery, earrings, dating rings, those vain attempts at singularity, but the first time it had revolved around someone in long trousers. His father had taken the Turk to Greece that winter to see his grandfather stretched out on what was soon to be his deathbed. To hear Tommy tell of it, it was like something out of Gogol, the dark, low-ceilinged room crowded out by this high, feather-mattres- sed affair, some sort of animal skin laid on top of it, the old man propped up with cushions, with dark-suited men and shawl-clad women trooping in and out, bare wood to sit on; not English, not even twentieth century; something biblical, peasant, full of blood and myth and family. Four days they had of it, black-hooded priests waving their beards and crosses over him, and still the old man hadn't died by the time the morning came for father and son to return home. Outside Tommy had found his father sitting by the big table under the cypress tree, his eyes blinking back the tears. 'It's OK, Papa,' Tommy had reassured him, 'we can stay longer.' Theo had gripped his son hard with his big bony hands (they had peasant hands, all of them, even Tommy with his matinee-idol looks couldn't mask the rough width of his own), and with his lips pressed to Tommy's ear, lest anyone else should overhear, whispered vehemently, 'The shop, Tommy, the shop. He doesn't need us now. The shop does.' So Tommy had gone back to say his goodbyes, and was standing there looking down at his grandfather, with his long black eyelashes and his bare feet poking out the end, when the old man had jerked up, as if a catch on a spring had been freed, and starting pulling off this ring on his finger, an ugly lump of gnarled silver that spread like a wart over the whole of the back of his hand. It took him a full twenty minutes to get it off, yanking it back and forth over his oversized chicken-wing-skinned fingers, pausing every now and again to get what little breath was left in his body back, his body bent double over the goat-skin or whatever it was, Tommy starting anxiously forward in a vain attempt to help, only to be waved angrily away before the old man returned to the task. Finally he pulled it off and grabbing hold of Tommy's hand, rammed the ring down the index finger of the Turk's right hand, imploring him never to remove it, even if his life depended on it. This ring was history. This ring was family, honour, bloodline. Tommy kissed his grandfather on the forehead and promised on his life, on his life, that he would not. The man sank back on his pillow, exhausted, content, satisfied. Tommy and his father flew back that afternoon. Forty-eight hours later, three hours into the first day of the spring term, Tommy was told by Ed's father, who had spotted it while handing out new work sheets, to take it off. Tommy refused as politely as he could muster, for we all liked Ed and felt for his dilemma. Marched into the office of his house-master, Tommy was told to take it off again, that it was against school policy, for safety reasons rather than any aesthetic concern, and again he refused, only more stubbornly this time, and (and here was his Greek blood giving notice) without giving any adequate explanation as to why. After the third confrontation, which took place in Godly the headmaster's office, he was sent home with the instruction not to return until he obeyed the school's injunction, a ruling which occasioned the only time his father shut up shop on a Monday afternoon. Marching into school house in his ill-fitting suit (held up, Sophie had exclaimed at the time, her voice rising in excitement, *with a piece of string*), Theo Nikolides thumped the headmaster's table and the headmaster's conscience into submission, calling upon history (the headmaster's own subject), honour (he was also a Scout) and the fact that the grandfather in question had died two days before, as his witnesses. The headmaster relented. Tommy and the ring returned the following day. Thanks to Duncan, whose mother was account manager for the local rag, the story even made the local newspaper with a picture of Tommy, the ring on his finger, and in his other hand, a blurred photo of the deceased, standing outside what looked like a cowshed, but was in fact his home. *On for life*, read the caption. That was the whole point. Tommy never took the ring off. And now Sophie was saying, what, that he *had* taken it off, and in her company? Suddenly the realization of what the circumstance might be, what young intimacy might have provided the circumstance, what precious folds of delicacy its crude and cumbersome angles might tear and bruise, became all too apparent. He took it off for that, so his fingers might . . . ? Tommy's face flared for a moment like the heat from an oven.

Sophie touched him again.

'Do you miss it?'

'The ring?'

'Your arm, silly.'

'It's been a long time gone, Sophie.'

'Funny to think of it, all nibbled away by crabs and turtles.' She turned. 'And you must be Tommy's wife. I'm Sophie.'

'So you are,' Lyn said. 'There was a time when Tommy talked of no one else.'

'And when was that?' Sophie tried not to look pleased.

'Just before he met me.' Tommy smiled at his shoes.

'So, Clark,' Tommy said, lifting his eyes. 'Any more surprises planned?'

Large rubbed his hands together. 'I thought I might buy a football club. Still support that team of yours?'

Tommy nodded. 'I do more than that. ' He slipped his good hand into his tuxedo. 'Season tickets. Hospitality suite. I'm a director now.'

He pushed the fold into Large's top pocket, then dug his fingers into his pocket again.

'Time to return these too. Remember, you gave them to me when we first met? I didn't want them then. I don't need them now.'

He stuck it in with the others. I was open-mouthed. Ten years the Turk had waited, and here it was, his counter-punch to Large's embrace. I'd never see him so calm.

Large took his time, moved back on his heels. He hadn't been prepared for this. Yet he was in better shape than Tommy. This was Tommy's only moment, Large back on the ropes, off balance. For Large it was simply a matter of absorbing the blows.

He lifted the bundle out, ruffled the blue perforated paper against his fingers, then slid them into a side pocket, already discarded.

'Don't know if I'll find the time, Tommy. Too much to do. Businesses to develop. A house to find. Big enough for the brood.'

'You're starting a family?' Tommy's eyes flicked over Sophie's figure in alarm. No one had ever contemplated Large's spawning anything but a series of red-faced bastards, but here the possibility of a dynasty was being offered up. Sophie tried to put his mind at rest.

'Chance would be a fine thing,' she drawled. 'He's too busy stroking his old biddies for anything like that.'

'Remember that flat you had above the chippy,' Ben broke in, trying to break the ice. 'Christ, we were jealous. Who'd have thought it, you and Large the first to set up together, and here you are, together all these years later.'

'I landed a few fish in between,' Sophie admitted, 'some of them could even speak the Queen's English.'

Large grinned, but he didn't like it. 'We might have been the first,' he countered, 'but Christ we paid the price. All we wanted was nights of passion and all we got was you lot coming round to smoke dope and listen to the stereo. By the time you'd gone we was too whacked to do anything about it.'

'Nights of passion,' Sophie declared. 'Whatever happened to them?'

'Late-night snooker,' Large joked.

Sophie turned a shoulder away. 'He thinks it's funny. Are you a fan, Tommy? Tell me you're not.' She opened her eyes, the closest she could come to stripping without taking off her clothes.

'Not much.'

'Lucky Lyn. Large can watch it all night, can't you, darling?'

'We can't swing from chandeliers all the time, Nef.'

'We didn't have chandeliers, sweetheart. We had youth. Youth *is* the chandelier.' She ran her fingers up Tommy's lapel. 'Look at that stitching. Gieves and Hawkes, isn't it? They never go out of fashion, do they, whatever the style. But there was no need to dress up, Tommy. You and Charles are the only ones all formal. What, are you two, some sort of double act now?'

Tommy and I looked at each other. A letter each way was the only communication we'd had since that telephone call. Tommy shook his head.

'Lyn and I have a dinner date. We can't stay long.'

'When you come to us, you must wear nothing more formal than jeans, the both of you. I bet Lyn looks fabulous in jeans. The drink will be better than wherever you're going too. Large is building up a formidable wine cellar, though he knows fuck all about it, don't you sweetheart.'

177

'I know fuck all about fuck all. You know that.'

'Course I do. It's what attracted me to you in the first place. They say knowledge is power, Tommy, but thanks to Large I have come to understand that an ignorance like his knows no boundaries. It simply crashes through regardless. And how's your father, Tommy?'

'Not bad. And yours?'

She shrugged. 'He should have settled on the east coast, Boston or down in the Savannahs, somewhere where his kind still have a place. Unfortunately for my mother, out on the west coast he's discovered that his English accent is a fantastically efficient knicker-remover. God, Tommy, parents. They still manage to embarrass us way beyond their years. Remember that frightful suit your dad used to wear in the shop?'

'He wears it still.'

'He's never serving? Or do you stand in for him nowadays, Lyn? You were a sales rep for a fertilizer firm when you two first met, is that that right? So romantic!'

'Garden furniture, actually.'

'Cutting down the rainforests. And why not, if it makes for better garden furniture. Large loves a barbecue. Beef, chicken, lobster, he's out there with his little fork every weekend, rain or shine. God, I think he'd even barbecue my tits if he could, the way he prods them about.' She laughed, though no one else did. It was only then I realized how far gone she was. We waited until it fell to the floor. Large lit a cigarette, let the smoke curl into his eyes.

'Your business must be doing well, Tommy. Quite a transformation I saw.'

'Careful planning, that's what it took. Not rushing things.'

Large nodded. 'Still, retail, it comes and goes, don't it? Half the shops I knew when I was at school have gone, and what's left look on their last legs. Too many charity shops, Tommy, not enough businesses, not enough investment, not enough risk. Where's the decent deli? Where's the decent wine bar?

It's a fucking desert, 'scuse my French, Lyn. Look around you, what you got, a crap this, a crap that. I mean where's the proper—' He stopped himself, tapped Tommy on the chest. 'Shouldn't be telling you this. You probably got your eye on a few opportunities yourself. You and my trusty accountant here.'

'No, I—'

Large stopped him.

'Don't come that with me, Tommy. Businessman like you. Course you do, just like me. That veg shop that no one goes into any more, not far from you, Fletcher's. Bet you got your eye on that. You could do something there.' Tommy glanced over at me. I shook my head. 'So could I. Not the same as you, but I could, prime spot like that. Menswear for instance, designer clothes, something for the under-seventies. Or a tapas bar, lively music, lively staff charging fifteen quid for a two-pound bottle of plonk.'

'He means lively young women,' Sophie added. 'He can still look, if nothing else.'

'Do I? What about a top-class hairdressers then, all them poofters chatting up your wives once a fortnight? Nef here has to go into town, thanks to the wallies you got down here. Where's the sense in that? Where's the vision? What did you have planned for it, Tommy? Don't tell me. Something plant-related. I know, a hospital for sick plants. Poorly Petals you could call it. How about that?'

'I'll think about it.'

'No you won't. You'll go into that estate agency first thing tomorrow morning and make them an offer. You'll be lying awake tonight, saying, "He's not getting his hands on Fletcher's. Hairdressers! Tapas bar! Not in my town."' He punched him on the arm. 'You got competition, mate. Better recognize it.'

'Nothing wrong with competition.'

'We can still be chums, though. Like we was.'

'I don't see why not.'

'Wait till I set up a garden centre, then you'll see why not.' Tommy's face froze. 'Only kidding, Tommy. We'll need some help, mind, when we get set up, garden-wise.'

'We'd be very happy to help. Lyn here's a garden designer. She went to college.'

It was the wrong thing to say. Large held up his hands as if to ward off the word before it came within striking distance. He'd batted away accountant in a similar manner too. Those meagre job descriptions, those bourgeois aspirations. He despised them all.

'Is that right? Gardening college? One of the things I know fuck all about, gardens. Don't mind sitting on one, looking out onto a nice bit of lawn, watching Nef here doing her yoga, but all them weeds and hardy perennials, forget it. Low-maintenance, that's what we'll need. Decking. Rockeries. You can help with all that?'

'We can do it all.'

'Done. And you must come here regular, you and Lyn, make it your local again.'

Tommy shrugged. I hadn't told Large about our Thursdays. 'We'll see. We're not one for drinking out much.'

'No? Good job you didn't buy this, then.' And he walked off, like he always walked off, when his moment had reached its peak. Exits, entrances, his life was measured by them.

The room broke into predictable groups; the old school friends, Large's City buddies, Bee Bee and her crowd. I hovered on the edge of all of them, unwilling or unable to join in, ever the town accountant dressed in his dark suit and his careful manner, still somehow an observer rather than a participant. Tommy didn't help, either. Every time I came within ten feet of him he'd move away.

I couldn't stand it any longer. I pushed my way through to the snug, helped myself to an outsize gin and sat down, overwhelmed by a feeling of loss, belches of laughter coming from the other side of the partition. The time I had spent here, what I had imagined I was becoming, was evaporating before my eyes. I helped myself to another drink. The door opened. Tommy's wife, Lyn. She looked as fed up as me. Half an hour ago she'd been part of the town's royalty. Now it wasn't even clear if she'd remain a member of its aristocracy.

'Is he always like this?' she said. She let the door swing behind her. She had a little silver bag in her hand, no drink.

'No, he's usually a bit over the top.' I tipped the drink back. She tried to smile, plonked herself down beside me.

'And you, Charles. Are you all right?'

'Not a hundred per cent.'

'You mind, losing this?'

'Doesn't Tommy?'

'More than I imagined.'

'Large will ruin it, sure as eggs is eggs. It wasn't all my fault, Lyn, despite what Tommy thinks.'

'It was stupid of you, not to tell him.' She smoothed down her dress. 'Maybe there'll be something else.'

'Not like this, not that me and Tommy could have done together.' I lowered my voice. 'He's left me, did he tell you? Gone to Rodney Wright.'

'Yes, I'm sorry, Charles. I couldn't talk him out of it.'

'Rodney won't give him what I did, Lyn.'

'He knows that. But then, Rodney won't let him down like you did, will he?'

There was nothing I could say to that, or indeed beyond it. We'd reached an impasse. Tommy banged open the door.

'There you are. Come on, we're going.' He moved in, handing her the small black shawl she'd brought with her. 'Charles.'

I got to my feet. 'Tommy. I was hoping we could talk sometime.'

'About . . . ?'

'This. You've got it all wrong. It was my idea, remember? Why would I want to scupper it?'

'A better percentage?'

'Tommy. I've told you, he didn't offer me anything. I was as surprised as you were. You know what he's like.'

His laugh was short, contemptuous, spiked with anger. 'I know, all right. Large rides back in town and you roll over, you of all people. I was one of the first to put work your way, Charles, and this is how you repay me.'

'Tommy.' I was getting angry now. 'I'm not rolling over for anyone. I'm running a business, same as you, same as him. I can't turn away clients just because you don't like them.'

'Don't like who?' Large stood leaning in on the doorway. 'What are you two up to, plotting another takeover?'

He stepped in. It was a small room, no bigger than a boxing ring, and he could sense it, the skirmish that had taken place. He was in between us now, a referee. Tommy shifted his shoulders, settling back.

'We have to go, Large. We're late as it is. Enjoy your evening. And good luck with the Merry Boys. The old place deserves it.'

He held out his good left hand. Large took it with his own. They stood there, testing each other's grip. It reminded me of the Low cartoon showing Hitler and Stalin shaking hands, with my body standing in for Czechoslovakia. Then Tommy let go, beckoning to his wife.

We followed them into the saloon, Tommy holding the pub door open as Lyn swept out. He took one final look and ducked out after her. Large grabbed my shoulder, speaking quickly, making sure no one could hear.

'Monday morning, Charlie, get on the blower. Find out about Fletcher's, what they're up to, if it's for sale.'

'It isn't.'

'It's just a matter of time. Tommy knows that, it's in his eyes. Ask them, discreet like, what their plans are. Say you know an interested party, but he doesn't want to make a move quite yet. Say he might even give them something every week, so they can hold off for a while, a couple of hundred a week, something like that.'

He stopped my protests in mid-air. Pete came through the kitchen door pushing a trolley of food, smoked-salmon rolls, spicy chicken wings, Pat following with a plate piled up with his favourite tomato sandwiches. Large wrenched it from her, holding it high above her head, Tommy quite forgotten.

'Look at these!' he exclaimed. 'I mean, look at them, Mickey. Did you ever see such things from such a woman?'

'They're just sandwiches, you big baboon,' Pat scolded, blushing, still in thrall. 'Anybody can make sandwiches.'

'Not without your Irish fingers, they can't. If they can do that to a loaf of bread, think what they could do to a man!' He twisted round behind her, grabbed her by the waist. 'Go on, Pat, take me with you. You got the money now. We could run off together, leave Pete in the lurch. Mum can look after here, can't you, Mum?'

Rhoda beamed, back in the fray again. 'I could if I could reach the optics.'

'Bee Bee will do all that. A bar stool is her second favourite thing to sit on. Charlie here will make sure she's not fiddling the till, won't you, Charlie?'

Everyone turned to me. They'd been quite happy for me to stand on the poolside, watching them all enjoying themselves, splashing about. Now I'd been thrown in at the deep end. Bee Bee dropped her cigarette into the ashtray and slid off her seat. She was quite drunk.

'Charlie,' she pouted. 'Charlie tight-arsed Pemberton.' She tripped over and draped her arms around my neck. 'Your dad was real proud of you, did you know?'

'I didn't as a matter of fact, no.'

'He was good to me. You'll be good to me too, won't you? I'll make it worth your while.'

She stood on her toes and kissed me to a crescendo of cheers, her open mouth sour with nicotine and vodka, her breasts pressed full against me, soft and sticky like a shop bun. I was rooted to the spot, unable to move or speak. She stepped back, fingered my tie.

'No need to fret, Charlie. Look at it this way. The more I nick from him, the nicer I'll have to be to you. And I can be very nice when I have to be, believe me.' She put her head to one side, rubbed one foot against her calf. I could feel my father's eyes on her still.

'Now there's an offer, Charlie,' someone called out, 'what do you say?'

There were cat-calls, whistles. Large hadn't been here two months and they were calling me Charlie again. I looked around. Sophie stood with her arms folded, savouring my embarrassment; Jay, talking to a woman with her back to me, gave me the thumbs up; one of the City boys blew a smoke ring into the air and rested his arm on a willing knee; Ben was up in the corner, whispering, Rachael, her son in her arms, laughing his joke into the sleeve of her jacket. Large took a pull of his pint and gave Rhoda a wink. She winked back, wriggled her toes.

The phrase fluttered into my head, the phrase she had used, not forty minutes beforehand. Egg, green and egg. Only one person I knew had ever named our school colours so, a typical off-the-cuff remark of his, economic, accurate, disparaging, but served with a notion of humour. The first time he had used it, I'd been standing in the hall in my brand-new uniform, showing it off to him before he left for work. He'd grunted and pulled my tie loose, hitching up the new knot tight round my neck. 'You would have thought,' he'd murmured, 'they could have dreamt up a better colour scheme than this. Egg, green and egg. Looks like some jumped-up African dictatorship.' He'd said it again, pleased with his little phrase, at dinner time later that evening. My mother had scolded him. 'Don't make fun of the boy, Alex, not on his first day,' but it was too late by then. Egg, green and egg it was, and egg, green and egg it stayed. Had he used the term so liberally that it had passed into common town parlance, or had it passed from him to Rhoda under more specific circumstances? At a school concert? A sports day? I doubted it. My father was not for mingling, and besides, he would not have made fun of it at a public event like that. Backstage sneering, that's what he enjoyed. I stood there, Bee Bee with a finger to her pursed lips, a tableau of stilled faces staring at me as I recalled every detail of that afternoon, the way Rhoda had stood in that ghastly hall. It wasn't hard. It hadn't been many years ago. There were the stairs and Frank Sinatra playing. There was the picture of the conger eel, stretched and bloodied, like his adversary; there was Rhoda, loose under her kimono and behind her, balanced uneasily on the radiator, there was the glass of red, the glass of wine that might have been Carl's, who'd never drunk any-thing but Guinness since the age of twelve or which could have been Rhoda's, the five-a-night brandy-and-soda woman, Rhoda, her forehead spotted not with water beads from a recent shower, but with pustules of sweat as she laced up the ends of her silk belt. I recognized that configuration now, that flush of flesh recovering from the longueurs of orgasm.

I felt faint, as if I was going to be sick. I pushed my way to the toilets, hoping to find relief in the colder air. I wondered whether it could be true. I knew my father, his enjoyment of women's company, their physical presence. I'd seen how he'd tipped his hat to Betty, how his eyes had followed Bee Bee at the golf club, even the manner in which he'd shift in his train seat whenever an attractive young woman came down the aisle, but this? My father and that woman?

'Charles. Are you all right?'

Katie Jinks stood in front me.

'Katie! What are you doing here?' I straightened up, brushed my hair with my hand. I hadn't seen her for ages.

'I saw you dash out. Are you all right?'

'Something I ate. You shouldn't be in here.' I led her out. Barry and his chums were doing Madness impressions.

'I didn't know you'd been invited.' I had to raise my voice.

She shouted into my ear. 'I haven't. I had a message to give my brother.' She pointed. Jay was lifting Bee Bee onto the bar.

'Jay's your brother?'

'Anything wrong with that?' I shook my head, looked about. Bee Bee had been joined on the counter by two of her bare-legged friends, the three of them doing some sort of synchronized hand jive. Katie stood there, jiggling her foot.

'Can you stay a moment?' I said.

'Not really.'

'Just for a minute, Katie.'

I took her arm and edged my way to the table in the far corner, where the dart board had once hung. Across the room Rachael shifted her boy to get a better look.

'You look terrible,' Katie said, sitting down. 'Your hands are shaking.'

'It's seeing you here. I feel ashamed, the way I've neglected you.'

'Happens all the time, men letting you down. Didn't you know?' Her face was set firm.

'I didn't want to let you down. Sometimes it simply doesn't go according to plan. But I've been thinking about you. What you were talking about last time.'

'You mean Brighton?'

'Not that. What we did that first weekend.' She withdrew her hands. 'No, listen. I believe what you were saying now. The price you were prepared to pay for it. The price you did pay for it. It's almost physical isn't it, sin? You can almost see it, feel it, know when it's in the room.'

'Sometimes.' She was guarded.

'Here, for instance. This place is stuffed full of it. They're all full of it, aren't they, greed, lust, the whole shooting match.

Born in sin, that's what the Church says, isn't it? I realize that now. That's why our night together was so special, why it made such an impression on me.' She shifted. Her mouth, usually so hard and uncompromising, looked amused.

'It made an impression on you, Charles, because it was your first time.' She caught my look. 'Don't worry. I won't tell any of your friends here.'

'They're not my friends.'

'No? You seemed very chummy just now. Quite the party animal.'

'You're making fun of me.'

'It's not the worst thing, being made fun of. Waiting outside the shopping arcade for an hour and a half with an overnight bag destined for Brighton is a lot worse.'

'I can explain all that. Seeing you here, I feel emboldened, as if you were meant to come, tonight of all nights. I saw you the other day, you know, from my office window, handing out leaflets with a man.'

'Jacob. He's one of our pastors.'

'I thought as much. I could hardly bear it, thinking of him so close to you. I wanted to run down, grab hold of you, take you from him, possess you. I know that's an unfashionable term to use these days, but that's what it felt like. A need to possess you. Like I feel now.'

'Like you feel now?' She took a step towards me. For the first time I took note of what she was wearing, her jeans and scruffy burgundy coloured top, old school sweatshirt judging by the emblem above her left breast, gloriously out of place.

'I don't mind you wanting to possess me,' she said. 'We're all possessed by something. You're just starting on the path. Are you going to buy me a drink?' I ignored her.

'I want to understand the state of sin in which we exist, Katie, embrace it. I want to be aware, to know when I *have* sinned, when I want to, need to.'

'Need to?'

'Yes. Isn't that the crux of it? That we need to. I feel I'm going to sin, Katie, in a big way.' I wiped my forehead. I was burning like Moses' bush. 'Will you come back with me, tonight, right now?'

'Charles! Calm down. You can't just drag me off like that.'

'Don't you want to?'

'Why should I? You're not very reliable.'

'I let you down, I know. You can punish me if you want.'

Her face lightened. 'Punish you, how?'

'I don't know. Yes I do. You can cut off the sleeves of that jacket I bought. Dance on the lining.'

'There's no call for that. Lovers need jackets, even errant ones.'

'Is that what I am?'

'It's what you might have been, before you stood me up.'

'I didn't mean to. It was all because of this place. I was trying to buy it. Large got there first.'

'You were trying to buy it?'

'There's no need to look so surprised. I had a friend. He was putting up most of the money. It fell through that very afternoon. I couldn't go to Brighton with you, Katie, not after that. I felt so deflated. I had such hopes.'

'Why didn't you tell me? We could have gone some other time. Or done something else, something to take you out of it. That's what you do if you're with someone, Charles, help them through things. You don't have to pretend that everything's always marvellous. That isn't how it works.'

'It does for the first few weeks, surely.'

'Oh, Charles. You're not on a timetable here. Anyway, that was a month ago.' She nodded in the direction of the bar. 'From what I saw, you seemed to have recovered all right.'

'That thing with Bee Bee? That's what made me feel sick. I mean, look at her. Do you think she's damned?'

'Bee Bee? More than likely.' She spoke calmly, in all seriousness.

'Really? That she'll be dragged down to hell for all eternity? Seems a bit severe, doesn't it?'

'If there's a heaven, Charles, there has to be a hell. And if there's a hell, someone has to go there. I mean it's not going to lie empty, is it. Think of the upkeep expense.'

'You're making fun of me again.'

'A little bit.' She patted my hand. 'There is a hell, and yes, if Bee Bee keeps on going the way she's set out, she has a very good chance of getting there. My brother has an even better one. If not hell then at least a good long spell in purgatory. But then you and I will have to make a couple of pit stops there too. Especially if I come back with you tonight.'

She stared at me with a face without guile or seeming complexity. It was all so matter-of-fact. We could have been discussing our trip to the south coast.

'That's the difference, you see. You are aware of what you do, its consequences, in a way that Bee Bee isn't, in a way that I wasn't. But when you are, it brings something extra to it all, doesn't it? I should have known it at the time. When you lay next to me that night, every time you moved your breasts burnt into me, like . . . like branding irons.'

She looked down at herself. 'They've never been called that before. How much have you had to drink?'

'Hardly anything. Two gins.'

'And the rest. You're not driving, are you?'

'Of course not.'

'And if I come back, tomorrow morning, after I put my branding irons away, will you come to church with me?' She took me hand. 'Have you got rid of that statue yet? No, don't tell me. It's back on the table. And your mother, Charles? Are you going to blank me again?'

*

Katie was delightful, surprisingly warm and generous, despite it all. We could have been together for months, years, such was her easy familiarity. God hadn't left us, though. If anything, His presence was even stronger.

'It's so lovely fucking,' she said, halfway through. 'But it isn't just you that's makes me feel like this. It's God. He swells my breast.'

'Sorry?'

'It's Handel, don't you know. *Solomon*. I feel God, he swells my breast? Can't you feel me, all swollen, filled with God?'

Despite it all, I couldn't help thinking of Tommy, the tickets stuck in that top pocket. That he should have kept them all those years, kept them after he'd moved out of his father's flat above the shop (where Nikolides still lived, despite Tommy's entreaties to take up residence in the bungalow that he'd built for him in his grounds), kept them in a desk or an old shoebox, wedged amongst school reports and old photographs, kept them while moving into his first marital home and then his second, with his trophy wife and his trophy twins and his trophy garden centre, ringing with cash, the talk of the business community, kept those scraps of paper for what, in case of Large's return, so that he'd have them to hand, to fling back in his old adversary's face? And he'd never made a sound about them at the time, pushed off his perch, relegated to number two, never uttered a word, all the while we'd been there, not when he'd been knocked off the rugger captaincy or lost out with Sophie, never. If anyone could have resisted then, it would have been Tommy. And yet he had chosen tonight, when all his old friends had been present, to act. To what end? It wasn't as if he had won.

When I woke up, the bed was empty. Broad strips of sunlight fell across the length of the room. Katie was standing in the doorway quite naked. Anyone across the road could have seen her quite clearly.

'I've been looking through your bookcase,' she said, crossing over. She sat on the edge of my bed, stroked my hair. 'You don't have a Bible.'

'I don't?'

'All those other fancy books, and not the one that really matters. Why is that?'

'I suppose this is Church time, no?'

'Not quite.' She lay up against me, the cotton sheet between us. 'Let's pretend we've gone to Brighton after all. Here we are in a guesthouse overlooking the sea. Below the landlady waits, listening to our every move. But all we can hear are the waves washing in and out, in and out. And . . . what's that smell? Something salty?' I could smell nothing but the weight of her. She touched my nose with hers.

'I know what it is. It's the breakfast waiting for you downstairs. Everything you like and a big pot of coffee to wash it all down. What would you like to do after that, Charles Pemberton? After you've eaten your fill, after you've been to church?'

'A walk on the pier would be nice,' I said, happy to play along. 'Perhaps some oysters afterwards. A pint of Guinness.'

She made a face. 'I thought you didn't like beer.'

'Guinness isn't beer,' I told her.

'OK. A walk on the pier, oysters and a pint of Guinness. And before all that? Any ideas?' She eased up on her elbows. I placed my hands behind my neck. I had never felt so complete a man in my life.

'Not a clue.'

She prodded the sheet.

'Evidence would suggest the contrary.'

She sat back up, cross-legged on the bed. Unimaginable intimacy.

'I've got a surprise for you. Close your eyes.'

I closed my eyes. I could feel the mattress tilt as she bent down over the bed, reaching for something on the floor. When I opened my eyes she had a Bible in her hand.

'Where did you get that?'

'From my bag. I always carry a Bible. Everyone should.' She opened it. 'When did you last read it?'

'I don't think I ever read it. I had it read to me every now and again, in chapel.'

'Chapel?' She was suddenly aggressive.

'It's what we called church at school. When we were in the sixth form we had to take turns in reading bits out loud. No one took any notice.'

She sank back, relieved.

'Well, take notice now. I'm going to read it to you properly, as it should be read, by someone who believes every word. Listen to it, Charles, listen to it as a man should, as God demands he should. Listen how God spoke to Adam, how he speaks to you. You're a grown man, Charles. Your sperm is on the sheets here, on me too. Think of what we've done, will do again. Take on the responsibility. Listen to it as if it's the first time you've heard it. Try and see the sense in it.'

She began to read. The Book of Genesis. She read it to me like a mother might read to her child, with strong inflections and widening eyes, looks of encouragement thrown in my direction, delight and adventure on her face. For her the Book of Genesis was a wonderful, captivating story and she wanted it to be a wonderful, captivating story for me as well. I had a naked woman on my bed sitting in easy familiarity, curls of her pubic hair peeking over the sacred pages. No coincidence there. This was where I was, where I wanted to be, in close proximity to the Garden of Eden, where we had eaten of its forbidden fruit all night. I listened to her, attentive, not to the words but the mouth that shaped them, the throat that spoke them, the lungs that rose and fell while giving them breath. I listened to the making of the world and the darkness and the light. I listened to the story of the sun and the moon and the making of the oceans. And I listened to how man came from dust and how God blew into his nostrils and he became a living soul, and how God planted a garden where every tree that is pleasant grew and every thing that was good for food and that in the middle of the garden stood the tree of the knowledge of good and evil, which God forbade him to eat for should the day come whereof he would eat it he should surely die. And I heard how God did not want Adam to be alone and first formed all the beasts of the field and every fowl of the air and brought them to Adam so that he might name them, and yet he was still alone. And I heard how God fashioned Eve from Adam's rib and how they were both naked and not ashamed. And I listened as Katie told the story of the serpent, more subtle than any other animal, and how he persuaded Eve to eat the apple from the tree of knowledge and how she picked it and ate it and gave it also to her husband and how he did eat it too. And how both their eyes were opened and they saw themselves naked. And how they were driven out of the Garden of Eden. I saw as she was reading it, how she believed it, and how too, it excited her, this story of corruption, how her fingers ran over the words, how her lips spoke them, eagerly as she reached the point of knowing sin, knowing nakedness, how she touched her breast quickly, or held the flat of her stomach, as if her insides were tumbling with the thought of it all. And when she finished her face was flushed. I thought of the sin I would commit with her again. For the first time in my life, I understood the meaning and power of eroticism. She was possessed.

'Well?' She leant back, swollen.

'You don't believe all that, surely?'

She put her hand out, touched the black binding. 'Who do you think I would rather believe, Charles? All those scientists or the one God. Who knows more? Who sees more?' She leant forward. 'Who's done more?'

'But you can't think that God made the world in seven days, surely?'

'No. I think he made it in six. ' She moved again to lie down beside me. 'Do you know, I've started writing.'

'With my pen?' I spoke eagerly, glad to be moving away from this turn of conversation.

She put a finger to my mouth. 'With my pen.'

'Your pen,' I agreed. 'And?'

'It's harder than it looks. The words just get in the way. But it's taught me the miracle of creation, how difficult it is, even with something as simple as a story, how complicated it is to make something out of nothing. That's what this world is, Charles. And they dare to call it an accident.'

'I don't think they say it's an accident, Katie. They say it's a process of adaptation, selecting, a progression through trial and error.'

'It's still an accident, sort of, like an elephant painting a Picasso, or a monkey writing Shakespeare. That's what they say isn't it, that if you gave a monkey a typewriter, enough paper and eternity, eventually he'd write the complete works of Shakespeare. It's not true. What about all the other writers. Is this monkey going to write all them too. Only Shakespeare can write Shakespeare, only Beethoven can write Beethoven. Man can do a lot of things but he can't create a whole world, only bits in it. Only God can be God. Forget the voyage of the *Beagle*, Charles. Follow the journey the Bible takes.'

I shrugged. 'You're free to believe what you like, I suppose.'

'Free! We believe in freedom, the same way our forefathers believed the world was flat. Man is God now, man the Maker, man the master, free to do whatever he wants. It's fool's gold. It doesn't exist. It never has. Discipline, acknowledgement of a higher authority, that's what gives us freedom. Tell me. Don't you feel freer than ever before?'

I put my hand out, ran my finger on the ridge of her calf.

'You know I do,' I said, hardly daring to look up.

'You know why? Because for the time being, you're worshipping something, my body. You have never experienced such a power before. You can think of nothing else. It tells you what you think, how you feel, where you go. It is not a particularly good body, though you imagine it is. That's because mine's the first one you've had. It is not me that enthrals you. It's the altar of my flesh. I'm OK with that. I know there are greater things to worship than flesh, mine or anybody else's. I'm not saying you shouldn't worship my body. I like it. I worship yours, sort of. But though it seems that I give myself to you completely, it isn't really so. I worship God, not you. That's what makes me free. Worship, adoration, unquestioning obedience.'

She threw the sheet to one side, lay back half on top of me, her lips on my neck, her hand touching my face.

'I've had other men before you, Charles. I'll have other men after you. I like what they do, the way they touch me. You included. But no lover can surpass what God's hands can do. All a lover really does is add to His glory. There is a little bit of God in all of us, in everything, don't you know that? Have you never felt that moment, that something other than you was stirring inside you, something so huge, that you felt all giddy with it, like you've just stepped off a roundabout? That's what our world gives us, small ways of glimpsing into God. Now let's have another stab at it, shall we? Then we'll go and find those oysters.'

'No we won't.' I held her down by her shoulders. 'I'll go see my mother. Tell her all about you.'

I showered and shaved, put on a white shirt, maroon tie. I dropped Katie at the bus station and drove over, my eyes gritty from the lack of sleep, Katie's presence, her voice, the things she'd said shifting in and out of my vision, my mind running on sin and flesh, how they went hand in hand. 'I could come back tonight if you want,' she said before she got out, 'no Bible, just a change of clothes and those oysters.' 'Oysters,' I questioned, 'on a Sunday?' She knew a place that sold them, six quid a dozen. 'That's three for me and nine for you, if you want to finish the weekend how you started,' and we smiled between us, the meaning crystal-clear. I don't know what it was, the turn of my mouth, the turn of hers, the way her eyebrows lifted, the way mine flickered, but I could feel my father's face blossoming within me, feel my muscles settling into that irritating flirtatious expression of his, feel flickers of him invade my bones. I thought of him and that chirpy little waitress at the golf club. Was she one of his conquests too? Was that how she had repaid the favour? It wouldn't have meant very much for her. It wouldn't have meant very much to either of them, just a transaction carried through, two parties each with something to offer. And Rhoda, what did she have to offer? 'Pure shop-girl', that had been his judgement, not a description of denigration as I had imagined, but a compliment disguised as such, a contemplation of what he liked and where he liked it, the scales of sex and power rising and falling over the counter.

Monkton's hall smelt of lunch being prepared. There was no one about but I could hear plates being clattered in the kitchens. I walked down the corridor, oddly invigorated, conscious of how different I felt, the energy surrounding me, the strength in my lungs as if I was breathing in fresh mountain air. Katie's body had done that, I supposed, not just the fact of it, the physical exercise demanded, but the knowledge, the presence of it. She was right. I was held in her thrall and felt the better for it. 'I'll have the oysters afterwards,' I'd said to her, a sentence coming from my lips, so bold, so forthright, it surprised both of us. 'After *what*?' she grinned, adding, 'Well, you'd better not start thinking about that now, or she'll know exactly what you've been up to.'

I knocked on her door, thinking so what, why bother to hide it? How could I hide it? Hadn't she seen it, experienced it herself? Above, a trolley was being trundled along the first floor. My mother was at her chair, fountain pen in her hand. She looked surprised to see me.

'Charles. This is very timely.' She pointed to the bed. 'I have something to tell you. Sit down.'

I kept on my feet. This was no time to be on the same level.

'It's funny you should say that. As a matter of fact . . .'

'Theo has asked me to marry him.'

She sat there, arms folded into her lap, more the picture of a sedentary aunt than a mother, triumphant, immovable, a kind of implacable rigidity to her, impervious to criticism. She raised herself up out of her seat and crossed to the large window, dragging her left leg against her walking stick. She stared down the gravel driveway, the sun pale on her silvery hair. For a moment I thought she was watching for him, expecting to see him tramping down the drive, on his way to ask me for my mother's hand, but her hand went to her mouth and I realized she was thinking of the sadness of it all, that it had come to this. She turned to me, her eyes flicking over to the rosewood writing table we'd manage to salvage from the Lloyd's shipwreck, on it a letter, written in her post-stroke hand. There were tears in her eyes.

'Keep it simple, whatever you're saying,' I said. 'The rumour at school was he couldn't read.'

'It's not his to read, Charles. It's to here. I'm leaving in two months. I think they may make me pay for a full six. Perhaps you could do something about that.' She paused, exasperation filling her voice. 'Look at you standing there, unable to know what to say. For Heaven's sake, Charles, what is it? You think I'm too old to marry again?'

Of course she was too old to marry again. She was my mother, a widow recovering from a stroke, living in reduced circumstances. I'd just got used to that. It gave me a certain amount of control, a certain amount of stability.

'Not at all. But Nikolides. He's nice enough, but, marriage? That's very different. The demands made.'

'What do you know of demands, Charles, in marriage or anywhere else for that matter? It's not a sexual thing, if that's what you're worried about, though there's no reason why it shouldn't be, if that's what we both wanted. As it happens it isn't. Oh, look at yourself. You should be pleased for me. Do you want your mother to stay here for the rest of her days?'

Did I? I suppose I did.

'I know here isn't ideal, but you have your own things. I visit regularly. If it's company you wanted . . .' I felt the words coming up that would drag me down . . . 'we could always look at finding somewhere together, a little annexe for you, a flat for me.' She dismissed the suggestion with a little explosion of air though her lips.

'Don't be ridiculous. First you invite me for a weekend in Brighton, now you ask me to move in with you. I don't want your company, Charles. I want Theo's. He's had an extraordinary life. Did you know he was born in a room with mud on the floor, and never wore shoes until he was seven? He's a marvellous talker, chatters away about this and that, stories and people, something your father never did, a trait you've inherited from him, I'm sad to say. Look at it this way. Now you won't have to come round like this twice a week. Theo and I will be quite happy with our own company.'

'If you think I'll be an intrusion . . .'

'I didn't say that. Now I've got my life back, you should feel free to concentrate on yours. Let's face it, they're never very successful, these visits.'

'You don't like them?'

'Charles.' She patted my hand. 'You're a dutiful boy, but great company you're not. Getting you to talk about anything is like trying to open an oyster with a soup spoon. You should learn to talk more. People would find you much more interesting if you did.'

'People?'

'Girls, then.'

I took a deep breath. If I was going to talk her out of it, I had to be rational, calm.

'That's all very well, Mother, the way he chatters away, telling you stories, but a basis for marriage?'

'Why not? We share the same interests. He loves hellebores almost as much as me. And he wants to take care of me. That's quite a comforting thought. And I can take care of him. Have you seen the buttons on his shirts?'

'You can't marry a man because you want to sew buttons on his shirts.'

'I can marry for any damn reason I want. And there's an end to it.'

The conversation shuddered to a halt. In the corner of the room I noticed a cardboard box full of her pictures. Mother'd already started packing. Seeing them gone, I suddenly realized there was no photograph of me here, never had been.

'Where will you live? Not above the shop, surely.'

'You sound more like your father every day. It's quite a nice flat, as a matter of fact. He took me there only the other day, unchaperoned. Scandalous, isn't it? No, not the shop. Too many stairs. We thought we might take the bungalow Tommy built for him. It has its own separate drive, its own garden. Just the right size for us. Nice and near for his grandchildren.'

'What does Tommy think of all this?'

'I haven't asked him. I thought I should tell you first.'

'He won't like it much. We fell out, you know. That business of the pub.'

She nodded. She already knew. From my future step-father, I supposed.

'I knew you shouldn't have gone in with him. But would you listen? I should have got Clark to intervene. I told him I thought it wasn't a good idea, but he said it wasn't his place to interfere.' She said it without a flicker of guilt on her face. I was astonished.

'You told Large about it?'

'I was worried, Charles.'

'But he didn't know about the Merry Boys before that. It was a secret, Mother. If you hadn't told him, we might . . . Oh, Mother!'

'What?'

'Nothing. It doesn't matter now. So . . .' I tried to correct myself. 'When are you moving?'

'After the wedding.'

'You're having a proper wedding?'

'Registry office. As soon as we can. I thought you might like to give me away.'

Eight

I went to Fletcher's as Large asked, not that following Monday, but about a month later, when the proprietor had got back from the north, after tending to and finally burying her elder brother, wondering, as I walked through the open doorway, whether this would provide him with another opportunity as dramatic. He had bought the Merry Boys in cash, a wholly unnecessary method of transaction, but something he insisted on doing, taking the money over personally, bundles of rubber-banded hundreds stuffed in an old sports bag, marching through the town centre with the loot swinging on his arm, Jay and his bare arm tattoos trotting at a safe distance behind. At the Merry Boys the papers had been laid out on the bar, Pat and Pete and their solicitor on one side, Large and Sophie and their man from Tunbridge Wells on the other, the zipped-up holdall lying at Large's feet, bringing as he joked 'a little old-fashioned lawlessness into the town', as if we needed any. 'Why the money thing?' Sophie asked me once, 'Why the cash?' and I had no ready answer for her then. 'Swagger?' I'd suggested, and she'd been in the mood to agree. Once the papers had been signed, he'd hefted the bag onto the counter and stood back, arms folded as George Russell, a town factotum like me, and unused to such practices, counted out the bundles with a shaking hand. Outside two uniformed security men had stood waiting for the signal to come in and drive the money to Pat's bank.

'What will I do with it?' Pat had asked, when it all been counted and repacked. Large hadn't understood at first.

'Do what you want, Pat. Paper the walls with it if you like. It's your money now.'

She'd shaken her head. 'I meant the holdall.'

'Oh that!' He'd patted its stomach. 'I want that back. We go back a long way, me and that glory hole. You recognize it, Pat, surely? I had that cup in it, what I won that night, that and my sweaty trunks. You must remember my sweaty trunks. Nef does, don't you, nugget?'

The bag said it all – the school sports bag with the first eleven stripe down the side, the bag that had taken his gloves and his contraceptives to the Pemberton Sports Centre and thence to the Merry Boys, the bag which carried the means of both his conquests that night. Possession, that's what they'd been dragged into seeing that morning, Large buying the Merry Boys over the counter, stuffing it into his back pocket – but it came to me that morning, seeing him standing at the top of the stairs, legs apart, arms akimbo, that it was neither the Merry Boys' business prospects nor its function as a private club that had goaded him into the purchase, rather it was the location that mattered, the Merry Boys as history, site of his triumphant past, where he had first dazzled, made real his teenage promise, won the trophy and bagged Sophie Marchand, the town's prize livestock, from under our eyes, raised her up in his London-chuck-out, muscle-aching arms, carried her away. Perhaps, I thought, seeing him standing there, determination animating his frame, perhaps his time in London had not been the wild success we were meant to believe. He hadn't made *that* much money – just enough to make a difference here. Was that why he had returned, to re-claim the only territory that he had ever truly dominated?

To tell the truth I'd forgotten about Fletcher's and only went there halfway through that Monday, after a Saturday night, Large telephone prompting. They all knew me there, Marjorie Fletcher in particular – one of those decent hardworking women whose face told it all: up well before dawn to the drive to Covent Garden, back by seven to load up the shop, working through the day until half five, later on Thursdays – she never stopped. My mother had shopped there regularly. In the holidays when I was a boy I used to stand beside her, holding her shopping bag open as Marjorie dropped in the vegetables, while my mother ran her finger down the open notebook, checking off the list. Fridays we would go, and as often as not Marjorie would place an apple in my hand as Mother extracted the money from her purse, remarking on what a fine specimen of a son I must be, to help his mother out, but how, and this was her little joke, it would come to an end quick enough when the girls started showing an interest. I felt obliged to shuffle my feet as my mother agreed, but we both knew that would never happen. Nor did it, but I stopped going just the same. Now twenty years later Marjorie looked much as she did then, the same worn, pre-occupied face, the same bare arms, the same big, capable, red hands. The shop hadn't changed either, the wooden boxes racked at angles for the fruit, the tubs of different-coloured potatoes, the same set of scales with its dull coloured weights and the scooped pan the size of a small rowing boat. The only difference was the customers. Apart from me and one other, there weren't any. And on closer examination, Marjorie looked older, tireder than I remembered, as if the life had been pressed out of her. Some of her vegetables looked in a similar condition. I hadn't bought anything in Fletcher's the whole time I'd done my own shopping. I wondered when my mother had deserted her. Before her stroke, I'd be bound. Before Lloyd's, after? Those vegetables at that last lunch, those Maris Pipers that he had commented on so favourably, where had they come from? Here, or the supermarket? I stepped further in, wishing I had never come.

'Mrs Fletcher? You remember me?'

She nodded. 'Meredith Pemberton's boy. The apple-eater.' She stood there waiting.

'I'm an accountant now. Down the other end?'

She nodded. 'I saw the window go up. And your mother? She's not too well, I hear.'

'On the contrary. She's getting married again.'

She smiled, genuinely pleased, a different face emerging, another woman, the woman she might have been, perhaps was, when not bound to the shop's strictures. 'Good for her. Anyone I know?'

I turned my head, ignoring the question. 'Business seems quiet.'

'Tell me about it.'

'Only we were wondering.'

'We?'

'A business associate and myself. I'm not allowed to divulge who. We were wondering if you had any plans to put the premises on the market. You hold the freehold, I believe.' Now she ignored mine.

'Is this Tommy we're talking about?'

'I'm not obliged to say, Mrs Fletcher. The point is, at this moment in time, my client is not quite in a position to make an offer. But, to show his good intentions, he would be prepared to make a weekly contribution to your overheads and expenses, up to such time as he is. Then he would make you an offer based on the current market value, which of course you would be free to accept or refuse as you wished. However, it would be understood that in the interim, (a) you would not put the shop on the market, (b) nor make known your intention to sell to any third party, and (c) when the time came for my client to make an offer, you would not seek a third party's involvement until all options for a sale between you and my client had been exhausted.' I thought I'd covered it rather well.

'You mean he wants to buy it.'

'I mean my client is interested in buying the property at a fair and equitable price.'

'But not just yet.'

'Not just yet.'

'And if someone comes along and makes me an offer now I'm to say . . .'

'That you are not interested. Until he's ready.'

'That's a bit of a tall order, isn't it? What's Tommy going to use it for? Not a veg shop, I'll be bound.' She put her head to one side, as if asking me to share my secret with her. It struck me that there was an opportunity here. While I couldn't actively mislead her, it would be no bad thing if I let this wrong assumption of hers run its full course. I chose my words carefully.

'I believe that if Mr Nikolides bought it he'd move into the antiques market, garden furniture in the main. It would complement his current outlet. Not that I am saying my client is Mr Nikolides, you understand.' She ignored my qualification. People hear what they want to hear all the time.

'That makes sense. If Tommy wants to buy it why doesn't he just come and say so?'

'I am acting under instructions, Mrs Fletcher.'

'You're not his lawyer, are you?'

'I am not anybody's lawyer. I am acting for my client in a financial capacity. It's a sensitive time, Mrs Fletcher. My client is worried that if someone gets to hear of your future intentions . . .' I let the sentence drift. Another customer came in. I waited while Marjorie served her, feeling exposed. She came back to me, wiping her hands down the side of her dress.

'I'd like to sell it to Tommy. How much?'

'For the premises?'

'To pay me. To keep going on a bit.'

'My client was thinking of something in the region of two hundred and fifty pounds a week.'

'Five would be more appropriate.'

'Five is quite a high premium, Mrs Fletcher.'

'Not if I'm not selling to anyone else it isn't.'

'There may be no other buyers, Mrs Fletcher.'

'In this location? Pull the other one. Five hundred. End of the year, no longer.'

'I'll relay your response to my client.' I looked around. There was only one appropriate exit. 'Now that that's over, I'd like to buy some apples. Those Coxes look good.'

'There's no need for that.'

'No, I insist. I should eat more fruit. At least that's what my girlfriend tells me.'

'It's the only time men eat healthy, when their women tell them to. A pound, then?'

'Two, I think.' She handled the apples into the scoop, brown-bagged them.

'A local girl, is she?'

'It's early days, Mrs Fletcher. Maybe I should have some greens. To show her I've been paying attention.' We looked across at the unappetising displays

'What about some spinach?' she suggested. 'We got some lovely spinach in this week. You look as if you need a bit of iron.'

I walked back with a carrier bag full: spinach, a dark-ribbed cabbage, two pounds of Coxes, a bunch of bananas, a lettuce, an avocado, all topped with a punnet of strawberries. Large took the bag from me and followed me into the office.

'How'd it go?' he asked. I told him, the little trick I'd managed to play.

'You're a devious little runt, aren't you, Charlie.' He looked at me, something like admiration on his face. He helped himself to a strawberry. 'Give it to her,' he said. 'It's worth the money just to stop Tommy in his tracks.' He took another one, twisting the stalk out. 'Anyway I haven't come here to talk about Fletcher's.' He threw the strawberry in the air, caught it in his mouth. 'I'm taking you to lunch, knock the stuffing out of you.'

I looked at my watch, an unnecessary procrastination as I

was perfectly aware of the time. I could smell Betty preparing our mid-morning coffee.

'It's half eleven, Clark.'

'So? You're eating early.'

'No one serves lunch at half eleven.'

'Better tell Mum she's been wasting her time making us her special steak and kidney pie, then. '

We drove down to the Merry Boys. Only it wasn't called the Merry Boys any more. It was true what Large had said. Tommy and I would have put hunting prints on the wall, served up a decent shepherd's pie. Now there was a new sign, Rameses, the town's latest wine bar, not quite finished yet, but with a bright new bar in place, smoked glass and steel, stiletto-heeled stools to match, the bar girls wearing headbands and heavy make up, all eyeshadow and severe haircuts and tops that clutched at the neck. Through the door at the back in what used to be the snug was what he later christened the Tomb, huge leather armchairs, newspapers and magazines flung across the low tables, palm trees, and the odd incongruous lampstand looking over your shoulder, one of the old tills from the Merry Boys standing on a new teak counter, not that any money seemed to change hands in that room. It was all settled afterwards, or put on the slate. That morning the place was empty. A radio was playing in the kitchen in the back, one of Bee Bee's friends was putting on her eyelashes and mascara in the mirror behind the bar. The glass table in the corner, placed where Tommy and I used to sit, was set for two, a bottle of red on the table. Large put a hand to my back and guided me over, pushing the bottle in my direction as we sat down.

'Large, you know I don't drink at lunchtime.'

'It isn't lunchtime. You just said so.' He filled my glass, waved the bottle about.

'What do you think, then?'

'Distinctive.'

'You don't like it. I know. I'll make a fucking mint. Good name, don't you think, Rameses, a bit exotic, a bit me. 'Cause that's what I am destined to be, you know, round here, a bit of a king.' He poured his own glass, knocking half back in one gulp.

'I needed that,' he said, wiping his mouth. 'I got the colly-wobbles, like I was sweet on you and this was our first time out.' He filled the glass and looked at me. 'Tell me, before we go any further, do you fuck on the first date?'

I waited for his laugh to subside. 'Large. What's all this about?'

'An idea, Charlie. One of the big ones. I never thought it would be so easy, but it just popped into my head watching TV with Nef last night. It was when one of them adverts for those timeshare villas in Spain came on – you know the sort of thing. Buy your slice of paradise for a quarter of the price by sharing it with a bunch of similarly sorry Herberts. And it came to me, like a bolt from the blue, clear as daylight. I could do the same for residential homes, let people buy cheap in advance what they'll need to pay more for in the future. I'll have to think of a slogan for that. Anyway, here's the gist of it. Most people know that some time they'll probably need to go into a residential home. There's the state ones but who wants to crap out the rest of his life in one of those? Where you want to end up in is a place like Monkton's, or like what it's going to be in three months' time, all clean and fresh, with flowers in the hall and the staff all dressed up like you was in a little hotel that had known you for years. But how do you make sure that when the time comes, you've not only got the money, but there's a place suitable? Eh? Maybe it's not for you. Maybe it's for your old mum, no offence meant, Charlie. Whoever it's for, your mum, your dad, your wife, your husband, it's got to be done. We're all living longer, and it's all costing us more, that's the problem. How do we deal with that.'

The food came. He pushed his plate to one side, drew his

chair closer to the table. He hadn't shaved and there was a sort of red-eyed, gold-rush fever to his look.

'So, here's the thing. We set up this scheme, see, where you can pay up in front and buy your way in. The more you pay in advance, the greater the discount you get when you get there. Pay the top rate and after a certain number of years, you can come in inflation-free. No increase for the rest of your natural. We also set a minimum rate you have to put in, which, say after nine months of payments, guarantees you a place in one of the homes, no matter what. I'm going to set up a residential home in every town in the area, Charlie, a bloody chain of them, same decor, same little uniforms for the staff, same price, everything standardized, with a couple of people-carriers that can ferry them around, our name on the side. Say you put in three hundred a month, that's nearly four grand a year. If you don't go in for six years that's over twenty-one thousand I got in the kitty, and that's from just one of you, and no bloody outlay. Just money in the bank. Say I had a thousand of you. Say I had two. It's a bloody gold mine, Charlie. I was up all night working on the figures.'

He pushed a sheaf of paper over, leafing through it, stabbing at the jumble of figures with one hand, forking in great mouthfuls of pie with the other: take-up projections, capital expenditure, cash flows, scrawl upon scrawl. I could barely read a line or follow what he was saying. It was his look I was hooked upon, the glaze on his face, the intensity, the burning conviction, the *excitement* it displayed. He went back and forth, his mouth on overdrive, food stuffed in, ideas bubbling out, Large turning the pages halfway round to remind himself what he had written, turning them back again, pushing my plate aside to spread them out before me all the better; target markets, year-one forecast, year two, a business plan that offered immediate profitability to investors, his tongue running up and down his lips like a lizard in search of sun, the final page a series of underlined exclamation marks, the future foretold as punctuation. This was what he had come back for, to find this rainbow, this pot of gold that lay in every such town as ours, that had lain there for years, ignored by the Pembertons, and Marchands, and yes, even the Nikolideses, waiting for Large and his ilk to come and sniff them out.

'Well, what do you think?'

What was I to say? 'What does Sophie think?' I said to gain time.

He was scornful. 'Do you think I've told her.'

'She's cleverer than she thinks.'

'I know that. Do you think I don't know that? As a matter of fact I did tell her. I couldn't sleep, my heart was banging that much.'

'And?'

'She said to ask you. Looks like I'm going round in fucking circles. She'll be along in a minute. Come on, Charlie. Give it to me straight.'

'Three hundred a month is a lot. A lot of people couldn't afford that.'

'I know that. Don't you think I don't know that? That would be just the top rate. We can make it cheaper than that. Much cheaper. We'll have thousands of takers, Charlie, thousands and thousands. With all the money coming in we can afford to keep costs down, buy more homes, expand, dominate the market. There's been lots of chains, Charlie, shoe shops, kiddies' toys, estate agents, but not residential homes, not like this, of the same standard and the same staff and the same look, like a Hilton or what-not. Pyramid Homes, the McDonald's of the care-home business.' He tapped the side of his plate. 'Good grub, eh?'

I nodded. I hadn't noticed but the bar was starting to fill up. We were the only ones having steak and kidney pie, made especially I realized, but there were other offerings, lighter lunchtime stuff, chicken and salads, rice dishes, salamis, a good-looking cheeseboard. The place was livelier than it had been for some time.

'Pyramid Homes?'

Large looked embarrassed. 'I was coming to that. Here's Nef. Over here, nugget!'

Sophie came and stood over us, expensive white jeans, expensive white bag, those sunglasses back on her head. Large patted her bottom. The jeans had little golden notes on.

'Hungry?'

She shook her head and sat down. 'He's been telling you about it, then?'

I nodded. 'But Pyramid Homes,' I said, returning to the last point. 'It has unwelcome financial connotations, that word.'

Sophie poked him in the arm. 'What did I tell you? And you're meant to know about these things.'

'Well, we got to call it something special. I fancy Egyptian. They venerated the old, the Pharaohs and all them mummies. We'll be doing the same, venerating the old, restoring the balance. I mean this is social as well as commercial. It has ramifications. It could revolutionize how things are done, like when the Co-Op started. It could become a brand name, like Hoover or Marks and Spencers.'

'In that case you should call it Rossiter Homes.'

He shook his head at her. 'Doesn't have the proper ring to it, does it? Anyway, to get back. The thing is, Charlie, you're going to have your work cut out, looking after the books, 'cause I'm going to be moving on this one. No hanging about. Think you can handle it?'

Here I was, back in what used to be the Merry Boys, sitting where Tommy and I used to sit, being offered another foot on the town ladder. Town ladder? This had county rungs. I'd done the right thing after all. I tried not to look too excited, my insides dancing around just at the thought of it. It was all there again, a man with an income, a share in the profit, for doing what? I could overtake Tommy on this one, just glide past him on the outside lane. And in the balance between my mother's marriage and his father's, in whose favour would the scales rise then? Play my cards right, I wouldn't have to work for anyone, ever again.

'What's in it for me?'

'In it for you? He's changed, hasn't he, Nef? What do you mean? Like a company accountant? A director?'

'Something like that perhaps, yes.'

'Could be, could be? Why not, if it all goes to plan, if you help make it work.'

'I'll help make it work.'

He leant over, shook me by the shoulders. 'What did I tell you, nugget? Charlie's my main man!'

We had another bottle, though Large drank most of it, going back over the ground, this time talking about investors, bank investors, City investors, private investors. I kept glancing over at Sophie, but she seemed as enthralled by him as me, the first time I'd seen her look at him with any expression other than disdain. Perhaps that was what she had been waiting for. Perhaps this was why they had come down, why they had to come down, to this wide-open territory on which he could be let loose. By the end of the second bottle, he was running out of steam.

'Tell me,' I said, trying to impress him with my grasp, 'what if they die before they can take advantage of this scheme. Give the money back?'

Large exploded. 'This is a business, not a fucking charity. Of course they'll die, or re-marry or something. That's how these things work, on the backs of the people who don't take it up. Like insurance. What will we do? We'll keep two-thirds, administrative costs, keeping the room free et cetera et cetera, and give a third back, without interest.'

'They might kick up a fuss,' I objected.

He started to laugh. 'They could try, but they'll be dead, remember. Charlie Pemberton, you crack me up, you do.'

He put his hands behind his head, stretched his legs. 'Fetch us another drink, Nef, all this talking's made me thirsty. A large Courvoisier this time. Bee Bee knows what bottle. Charlie?'

I shook my head. I'd drunk quite enough. Sophie pushed her chair back, walked away. Large sighed. He was exhausted. He'd been talking at full throttle for the best part of two hours. He ran his hand over his face,

'I don't know, Charlie. It's beginning to get to me, all this old-people stuff. Do you worry about getting old?'

'Not a lot.'

'I do. All the time. I know it's stupid, but looking at them old biddies every day, I can't help it. It all seems so bloody pointless, going what we go through, getting married, having kids, working like a stiff prick in a brothel, to end up like that. Your mum's got the right idea. Not giving up.'

My mother. She'd been impossible the last week, endless speculations as to where Theo should take her for a honeymoon. I found the whole idea inherently distasteful.

'I'm not so sure. From what I've seen, for a lot of them, when they get there, they don't mind so much.'

'Bollocks. They fucking hate it.'

'They might say that, but in reality? It's a relief, not having to worry about the cleaning and washing and the endless cooking. Not to mention families. They're done with all that. Anyway, you change, chemically as well as physically. Like the dying. You must have noticed? When they know they're on the way out, they don't mind.'

'I'd bloody mind.'

'You say that now, but when you're over ninety?'

'Whether you make the best of it or not, it's a bastard. Tell me.' He lowered his voice. 'Do you think, if I had a stroke or something, incapacitated, do you think Nef would . . .' He looked across. Sophie was up at the counter talking to Bee Bee, a certain frigidity between them. 'It's all a game to her. It's what I am, what Wallace was, what we all are. She still fancies him, you know.'

'Wallace?'

'Tommy.'

'Don't be ridiculous.'

'On my dad's grave. I just have to mention his name and she goes all bandy at the knees. Sometimes I wonder if we should have come back at all. '

'I've often wondered why you did myself. It's not as if you have real roots.'

'No? I'll let you into a little secret, Charlie, seeing as we're going to be working even closer. I've come to make my money respectable, give it a bit of breeding. When people ask me what I did, I'm embarrassed to tell them, you know that, bawling down the blower like a cunt fourteen hours a day, shouting the odds. People like me can't get respectability easy. We've too much of that shit on our clothes. It gets up people's noses. It does that anyway, smell. Did you know that? I read a book by one of them Great Train Robbers once, how they had all this money stashed in their house, how it stank the place out. Every time they opened the door the pong hit them in the face, like they had a stiff under the floorboards. It's funny stuff, money, makes you do funny things. You know what I did with my first bonus? It weren't much, twenty grand. You know what I did with it?'

'Please, do we have to hear that again?' Sophie had returned, sat his drink down.

'Took it out the bank, every last cent of it, took it home, spread it out on the bed, and, 'scuse my French, had Tiff toss me off all over it.'

'Disgusting,' Sophie commented.

'We fucked on it afterwards, Nef. We were in the mood. You'd have done the same. It were exciting, all them fifties sticking to her back like she were a billboard, wiping ourselves on them when we were done.'

'And he wants to be civilized,' she murmured.

Large turned. 'So? What's wrong with that? She doesn't understand, Charlie, what it was like, what you had to be. Before Nef, my life was unbelievable, Charlie. Unbelievable. Top flat in Canary Wharf, a view across the Thames to impress the birds when you're trying to prise their knickers off. Not that they ever needed much prising. One look at the Rolex and off they came. But the expense. I mean a flat in Canary Wharf. Where was the sense in that? Tiff and me had to change it every six months it got so boring. Not just the colour, but everything, what we dressed in, what we ate, what we sat on. One month it would be Chinese, silk wallpaper and kimonos with fiery dragons on, six months later we'd be living in fifties retro, Formica tops, a little bar with cocktail shakers, Tiff in proper nylons sitting on a stool too small for her arse. We had a twenties look, a minimalist look, even a country peasant look, with one of them dressers we had to saw in half just to get it in the lift. The worst one we had was when we went swinging sixties, lava lamps and those big scooped chairs, where the seat comes to a sort of point at the end – I mean what did they think you'd turned into, a fucking wasp? We had that black-and-white op-art wallpaper too, gave you vertigo every time you walked into the room. Tiff went the whole hog on that one, dyed her pubes, shaved them to look like the Ban the Bomb sign, but she got it wrong somehow and it ended up looking like she was radioactive. Probably just as well. I mean she was lethal down there, no offence, nugget. But that was the thing, Charlie. It gave us a buzz, all these new looks, got us going, gave us a new reason to have a bit of a fling. It was all we wanted to do, Charlie, all we could do. The change sent us a bit wild, you know, the taste of money, like the taste of cunt does. Wouldn't you agree, Nef?'

'Stop it, Large. You're embarrassing him.' She looked at me, her eyes unnaturally wide and calm.

Large put his arm around me. He smelt of body wash. 'Am I embarrassing you, Charlie?'

'Nothing I can't handle.'

'See, Nef. Pyramid Homes, the taste of cunt, the double-entry method, there's nothing he can't handle.'

'Well, you're embarrassing me. These tales of Dockland debauchery, they do me no good at all. All this boasting and swearing.'

'When do I ever swear?'

'You've just used the c-word twice, darling.'

'But it wasn't swearing, was it? It was an observation. I don't swear. It's a weakness. I didn't do it even in the City.'

Sophie leant forward. 'Perhaps that's why you didn't make us enough money.'

'Yeah and what have you missed out on?' He stood up. 'I'm going to get a drink.'

'I've just brought you one. Haven't you had enough?'

'No.' He picked it up and knocked it back. He stomped off. Sophie pushed her glasses further back on her head.

'See what I have to put up with? I didn't get a wink of sleep last night. Pyramid Homes!'

It was a complaint, but not one made with any conviction. She was pleased really, Large asserting himself. No, more than pleased, thrilled. She reached for my glass.

'May I?' She took a sip, before sitting back, taking the glass with her. 'You've changed, Charlie.'

'Charles,' I corrected.

'Charles, Charlie, I don't know which is right any more.' She ran her finger slowly round the rim. 'This idea, it hasn't fazed you at all, has it?'

'Why should it?'

'Something's happened to you. You're hungrier . . . more . . .' She leant forward, tapped me on the knee. 'I know! You're seeing someone!'

'Sophie. I'm far to busy for anything like that.'

'Well, something's got your testosterone level up. Whatever it is, Charlie, you're almost becoming attractive.'

'Sophie, please. Stop trying to flatter me.'

'I said almost, didn't I?' She took another sip, looking at me over the rim of the glass. 'Well, what do you think? This scheme of his. Will it work?'

Would it work? What did I care? What did any of us care? He was doing what he always did. The spectacle was enough. He came bursting back, fiddling with his flies.

'If there's enough money coming in,' I told her glibly, 'almost anything works. And by the way, I've just thought of the name. Golden Years.'

Nine

The wedding took place in the register office in the council building, the staircase to my father's old quarters just visible from the waiting room, where we sat on leather chairs lining the walls, Mother, Nikolides, Tommy, Lyn, and the twins. I thought of him, staring blankly from the wall, wondering what he would make of this, that last happy trip the two of them had made in the old Rover, her girlish enthusiasm, his sudden rediscovery of his gentlemanly charm, what it seemed to do for them, all wiped clean away. That's what Nikolides was himself, of course, a charmer, of the earthenware variety rather than the silver-cup effort that my father once possessed, presented with thicker, more hesitant hands, but charm nevertheless. He wore a suit of heavy brown which permeated the room with a smell of dried lavender that everyone, save my mother, affected not to notice. In his top pocket peered an embroidered handkerchief, the red tie underneath his chin sprouting like a forced greenhouse bloom, the white collar stiff around his neck. His hands were unnaturally clean, his hair freshly barbered, and planted firmly on the floor were a pair of stout leather shoes that must have walked halfway across Europe. He was nervous, fussy. Sitting there, waiting for the call, he discovered a grease spot on the sleeve of his jacket and began wiping at it with the other cuff. Only my mother's hand stayed him. She was dressed in something altogether more glamorous, an old Norman Hartnell dress that she had first worn, she informed us with some pride, over twenty-five years ago. She didn't say where and certainly I had no memory of it.

'I've had to let it out,' she confessed, 'but only by that much.' She held a proud inch of air between thumb and forefinger. It was made out of rustling black silk, her bosom accentuated by black of a different material, diamanté sequins patterned around the waist. I thought it more suitable for a ballroom than for a register office, for an evening event, rather than the eleven o'clock production line that she was now taking part in.

'I thought you said she'd told you she wasn't going to wear anything special,' Lyn whispered to me, put out that she had turned up in a less than celebratory pair of designer cords.

My mother turned, her hearing as good as ever. Had they ever met before? I didn't think so.

'If I'd told him that,' she said, 'you'd have dressed your boys up, and then they'd would have started off hating me, wouldn't you, boys,' and she winked at them.

For a moment I thought it must have been a muscle spasm, something to do with her stroke, but then the twins laughed and she sat back, pleased at her little coup, the wink quite deliberate, as if she was as young at heart as they were, as if she understood the innate indignity that such an occasion held for them. She had never winked at me, nor I at her. I didn't believe she was even capable of such a thing. Now it seemed both my parents retained this capacity. Was it buried somewhere in me too, this cheap attempt at camaraderie? Did it come on in life only when one had reached a kind of complicit maturity, like a dog starting to lift its leg? Would I suddenly start winking to all and sundry, to Betty, to clients like Haydn Castle, to Katie?

Katie wasn't there. As far as that gathering was concerned, Katie barely existed, and for now, that was fine by both of us. When I'd seen her the evening of my mother's announcement, and told her why I'd been unable to speak of her yet again, she'd laughed, her mouth set in a moue of contemptuous excitement, a confirmation of something she had known all along.

'See?' she'd said. 'They're doing the right thing. Not like us. We're never going to get married, are we, Charles? Never,' and she'd pulled me to her. 'I don't want you to tell her any more,' she urged. 'It makes it more exciting for you, doesn't it, if you don't tell her, if you see her with me on you everywhere, your face, your fingers, *this*.'

It was true. Keeping Katie a secret did make it more exciting. She'd begun to stay over regularly. I'd given her a spare key. If she was on a normal shift she'd phone to check in and I'd just sit in the front room watching aimless television, waiting for the sound of her boots on the stairs. If she was on a late shift, I'd park the car in the lay-by down the road, watching for her in the rear-view mirror. When she was working nights, she'd slip into the bed at around half six, smelling of disinfectant and skin cream. Saturday mornings, if she wasn't working at Monkton's, she'd be out on the streets, handing out leaflets, or back at the mission house, attending Bible-study sessions. In the afternoon she'd be home with her mum, who as far as I could work out knew as much about me as my mother knew about her. Saturday nights she'd be back with me, so I suppose her mother must have known something. We'd go out, a bar, a restaurant, the cinema once, but neither of us liked that much. Staring ahead in the dark, concentrating on something else, was not what we wanted. We wanted build up, talk, playful argument, it didn't matter what, as long we could see the shape of each other's mouths and the thoughts inside them. And on Sunday, that seventh day, she would do what my mother had never done, sit me down for Sunday school; morning, afternoon, late evening, it didn't matter when. She'd read me the Bible for half an hour, the Old Testament in the main, tales of wrath and retribution, read cross-legged and naked from the foot of the bed, untouchable geography. Not surprisingly I began to look forward to my new Sunday schooling.

'I'm not sure we should go on like this,' she once teased, pressing the open book against her breasts. 'Are you sure you can concentrate properly knowing that you're going to fuck me afterwards?'

'Katie, I wish you wouldn't use that word.'

'What do you want to call it? Making love? Is that better?'

'Don't you think it might be?'

She shrugged her shoulders.

'Do you love me, Charles? Can you say that? Of course you can't. But you want me, don't you. That's the sin within you taking hold. That's religion working. Jacob told me about this writer, Graham Greene somebody? He and his mistress used to do it behind church altars. Did you know that?'

I did as a matter of fact, but said nothing, fearful that she was about to suggest something similar.

'Why indulge, then, knowing it's a sin?'

'Indulge!' She lunged forward, her arms around my neck. 'Only you could use a word like that. I *indulge*, Charles, because I'm human. I love the human part of me, the flesh and blood part of me, the weakness, the strength, that draws you inside. And for me, God knowing our sin is the same as your mother not knowing is for you. Don't you see?'

I pooh-poohed it, but I did see it. God knew, my mother didn't. It spiced the bed up no end.

The reception was held at Tommy's house, the bungalow where the new couple were to live just visible from the plate-glass window that fronted their open-plan living room. As for Nikolides, only a few representatives of his past life had shown up, the retired cashier who had sat behind the counter (and who, it was said, had broken the news to Nikolides of his first wife's desertion, and who had physically prevented him from pouring petrol over the premises and burning down the building with himself and Tommy in it) and another Greek, built and dressed like Nikolides, not related, who ran the pier café in Hastings. Most of the guests came from my mother's side, more than I expected or indeed wanted, all her old girl friends it appeared, women from the charity shop they all once worked in, Joanna somebody, who had been her long-standing bridge partner, a trio of stoic bosoms who used to take a table with her at cultural luncheons held over in Tonbridge every other month – a cross-section of her barely spoken-of womanly life outside the family, all excitedly pleased that my mother had done what none of them could or would do – found a new, and so different, a husband. Husband, was that the right word to describe Theo? Companion? Spouse? Soul mate? There was something of that here, wasn't there, the implication that Theo was reaching out to my mother in a way my father never had, an admission of past matrimonial deficiencies and neglected attributes, of a woman within, once dormant, now awakened. What they were, what old feelings Theo had aroused, what new ones he had instilled, were the subject of a silent commentary made up of looks, intimations and raised glasses. No one associated with my father had been invited, no one too closely linked with her married past, the couples they used to have round, the Rayworths, the Fergusons, Duncan's parents who still lived nearby and who at one stage they used to meet up with almost every other weekend; none of them. Why, because despite her ostensible happiness she was ashamed of what she had done, uncomfortable as to what she had traded in, in return for this new liberated life and the man who was about to provide it, with his lack of culture, his clumsy attempts at polite society, the undeniable coarseness of his flesh? Whatever she denied about the bedroom thing, there was no escaping the fact that she was going to be there, living cheek-by-jowl with him, seeing him, hearing him, conscious of his masculinity in all its base ways. Age hadn't reduced this male's potency. You just had to look at him to know that, the stocky, determined build, the squat shoulders, neck swollen like a bull's pizzle, hands shaped for holding an opponent fast. Perhaps she had recognized that any of her former friends would be as embarrassed by the prospect as was I.

Instead she'd invited Large, Large and Sophie, Sophie's

provenance, it seemed, no longer unsettling. For the months leading up to the wedding, I had been on the receiving end of manic bursts of Large energy as the idea began to take form. He was all over the place, dashing up to London, firing up prospective business partners, phoning me up at all hours to keep me informed of the latest developments. Some days I would be besieged by him. Others I would hear nothing at all. Some days I would be his bag-carrier, his fortune-teller, his guide to the ins and out of the district, others I would be left to my own devices, given time to follow my other clients, to field their enquiries, prepare their returns, dream up ways of minimizing their tax payments, but the truth was since Large's arrival they no longer held my attention, not Haydn Castle, not the embittered playwright, not anyone. There was no dynamic to them. I grew impatient, eager to be shot of them. And just when I thought he'd abandoned me, I'd hear his feet on the stairs and Large would bound into my office and chuck some fresh prospectus at me.

'Drop everything,' he would command. 'Let's bomb down to Deal. There's bound to be some run-down old guest house that's gone bust, bound to be. Opportunities, Charlie, opportunities. Don't sit there.'

'I'm busy, Clark,' I would protest. 'I can't just drop everything.'

'You sound like Nef. You'll be telling me it's the wrong time of the month next. Come on, Charlie, part those rippling thighs,' and off he'd drag me in his brand-new Land Cruiser, charging from one corner of Kent to the other, Large togged up in his best blue blazer and brown brogues, sat tight up against the wheel as if it was his energy alone that powered the engine as we swung into some weed-encrusted drive or barged in to yet another estate agent's office. Margate, Sandwich, out on the marshes, in towards Maidstone, we trawled them all, Large with a sheaf of prospectuses balanced on his lap, his mobile phone stuck on the dashboard, a wire trailing over the front seat to the fax machine bouncing on the back seat. He was restless, fired up, in a hurry.

My mother, too, had taken to Large. Ever since that first introduction it had been Clark this and Clark that, what a character, how she looked forward to his visits, how he made her laugh. To begin with it had seemed to me merely evidence of my mother's growing mental weakness (a decline I had imagined which would have made her more dependent on the home rather than less). Now it seemed to me to be indication of something a good deal more substantial, a directional change, a need to embrace something she had not been, a desire to enter into a rougher, cruder world, yet still belong to her own. Whatever her state of mind, one thing I knew for certain. She would never have found Large funny had my father been alive, never found him a character before she'd had her stroke. A disapproving sniff would have been as much as he would have merited. But now? Theo and Large, these seemed to be the men in her life now, rather than her husband and her son. Large had done what was expected of him, and greeted the news of her intended marriage and his peripatetic involvement in it with an exaggerated excitement that was positively American, charging into her room with a magnum of champagne and a huge box of chocolates, with the news that the six-month-notice requirement was to be waived – his very own contribution to the bottom drawer, as he so crudely put it. When the time came for her to leave, he'd given her a quite unnecessary send-off, hiring a horse and carriage to take her to the hotel where she was going to stay before the ceremony, and forcing everyone who could make it to stand in line on the entrance steps as she took her royal leave. For some reason, Katie had been tasked with giving her a farewell bunch of flowers. I was standing by my mother's side as she approached, Katie nervous. She didn't curtsy exactly, but inclined the head as she held them out, the livid bloom on her neck, a memento of the previous evening, peeking over the rim of her collar.

'It's been an inspiration to us, seeing you and Mr Nikolides getting together,' she said, stepping back, not looking once in my direction. 'It just shows what joy God's love can bring.'

My mother's smile was momentarily broken, but she recovered quickly enough and took the flowers with a grace that only those sure of their rank are able to muster. Katie walked with her to the carriage, my mother pointedly ignoring her proffered arm. Large draped a hand on my shoulder.

'I'm glad she's leaving. Guess what I'm going to do to her room?' It was eleven thirty. He had last night's drink on his breath.

'Divide it in half?'

He squeezed my neck. 'I'm putting Lilly in. She's getting it rent free, board and lodging in return for going back on the telly, the Golden Years adverts. She's going to become my Wimpy woman, my show house on legs. She's nearly seventy, Charlie, but you wouldn't know it. I mean, look at her. In six months' time she'll be a household name again. I've promoted her, did you know? We're on the move, kiddo. Sophie's dad's coming in for a bit too. Well, he's got to do something with his money. Katie looks a treat too, don't you think? She's looking at you. Go on, wave!'

I wasn't sure who he was referring to, Katie or my mother. Certainly both had turned to look at us. Katie was dressed in the new staff uniform, cream and green, which made her look like a courier in one of those old-fashioned tour companies, circa 1955. Monkton's itself was in the midst of its re-vamp, the residents moved from one room to another while new carpets were laid, new beds, new TV in every room, new curtains, fresh lick of paint, acres of heavy drapes, a newly shelved sitting room with books bought from a number of Kent libraries looking to reduce their stock.

I wiggled my fingers in an appropriately desultory fashion. My mother climbed inside the carriage. Katie disappeared back into the house, walking past us, eyes on the ground. That had been five days ago. I hadn't seen Katie since but I was due to meet her later that day, after I'd seen Mother and her new husband off on their honeymoon. I had promised Katie a short break of our own, to Brighton at last, and a hotel, not a boarding house, the Grand, the one the IRA had blown up when Mrs Thatcher had been staying for the party conference. I'd tried to tell Katie all about it but she'd shown no interest in what had happened at all. History, our history, England's, Britain's, didn't concern her one jot. The only story she was interested in was the one that had come down from on high.

We were off in a few hours, which was why I was sticking to one glass of champagne. But now, in came Large, bundling into the room like a fighter bouncing into the ring, blowing on his hands, sizing up the furniture and the acreage outside as he strode across, Sophie following in his wake, his ever-watchful trainer. He was dressed for the match too, a blue suit, a shade too bright, I thought, and a crimson bow tie, Sophie in some expensive tight cashmere that emphasized the plunderable wealth of her body.

'Clark,' my mother exclaimed. 'You've done me proud. A proper wedding outfit. Quite puts my son in the shade. And everybody else.'

He danced across, light on his feet, arms outstretched.

'Save you. Look at that. Who'd you steal it off, the Queen Mum? No wonder you've been snapped up again.'

He put his arms around her and almost lifted her off the ground. Red socks too, I noticed. Tommy and I stood to one side, beside the table of canapés.

'He should have gone on stage,' he said. For Tommy it was quite a remark.

'Where do you think he is now?' I replied.

Tommy gave a reluctant smile. We'd been forced to meet up a couple of times thanks to the forthcoming union. He'd been as against the idea as me, but for a different reason – the marriage would bring me closer into his orbit. Not that he ever said as much, but it was clear that was his principal objection. Lyn on the other hand had been positively enthusiastic. Starting out on a new marriage, Tommy's father wouldn't be such an overpowering presence in her own.

'You do realize we're related now,' I said, goading him a little. Tommy stuffed a cocktail sausage into his mouth.

'It doesn't change anything, Charles, if that's what you're thinking.'

'Tommy, I'm not expecting an invitation for Christmas lunch.'

'No? How do you work that one out?' In went another one. 'Dad always comes to us. You think he's going to leave your mother behind? And where Mummy goes . . .' Chewing only muffled the contempt. I rose to the bait.

'Actually, I may well have plans of my own. Go away somewhere.'

'Really?' He looked grateful, if surprised. 'Anywhere definite?'

'Texas,' I said, the image of Katie and her fringe-sleeved coat popping into mind. Tommy nearly choked.

'Are you mad? Why would you want to spend Christmas there?'

'Spend Christmas where?' My mother was eavesdropping again.

'Nowhere definite, Mum. Just a thought I had, somewhere abroad. You always said I should travel. Perhaps Sophie has some ideas. Have you met her properly yet?' I beckoned Sophie over. She clacked towards us, leg upon leg, the only woman in six–inch heels. She walked well, she always had. Stood well, walked well, dived perfectly into a lake of wet dreams. Tommy beat a retreat. He wasn't much pleased to see her here either.

'You remember Sophie, Mother.'

My mother looked her up and down. 'How could I not. You look marvellous, Sophie. Doesn't she, Charles? Almost too good to be true. And your parents,' she added, 'how are they? Your mother keeping well?'

'Very well, I think. She lives in Boston now, Mrs Pemberton.' She put her hand to her mouth. 'Oops, sorry. I should be calling you Mrs Nikolides, but it sounds so strange.'

'You'll get used to it. So, what's it like to be back on your old hunting ground? All those broken hearts only just mended.'

Sophie beamed and threaded her arm into mine. 'I love it! Just think, I can smash them to pieces, all over again!'

My mother failed to rise to the humour. 'And your father?' she persisted. 'Is he going to pop up one day, give us all a surprise?'

'I very much doubt it. He's enjoying himself far too much in California.' It was clear to us all what she was talking about. My mother batted it straight back.

'They're separated, then?'

''Fraid so.' It didn't bother her, she was saying.

'Is that why he went to California?'

'No.' Sophie laughed and spelt it out again. 'California was why she went to Boston. He became rather a naughty boy. Almost every afternoon.'

My mother savoured the information before speaking again.

'And I don't suppose he has any plans to come to England, then. Quite a different reception he'd get here.'

'Mother,' I warned.

'It's all right, Charles.' Sophie turned serious. Out went an understanding hand. 'Dad was very sorry for what happened, Mrs Pemberton. He thought very highly of your husband. We all did.' My mother nodded, her hands examining the folds of her dress.

'Do you see this gown I'm wearing? I last wore it when we took your parents as our guests on some business function in Leeds Castle. Your father lost one of his gold cufflinks. The catch must have come off when he and I were dancing. A very good dancer, your father. Knew how to lead, which very few men do these days. But he was put out, losing it, we could tell. And do you know what Alex did? He went and bought him a new pair from Asprey's. We were all such good friends when you and Charles were growing up. You went to dancing classes together, remember?'

Sophie flashed her teeth. 'I remember Charles refusing to dance with me.'

'Refusing to dance? You never told me this, Charles.'

'I refused everybody, Mother. It wasn't just Sophie.'

'I should hope not. Who did you dance with, then?'

'It was twenty years ago, I really . . .'

'He danced with Miss Oates, the dance mistress,' Sophie told her, her voice rising in glee.

'And why was that?'

'I'd have thought it was obvious.' I was becoming irritated. 'She was the only one who knew the proper steps.'

My mother shook her head. 'Sometimes, Sophie, I wonder if there wasn't some mix-up in the name tags back in the maternity ward. All those pretty young girls to dance with and he chose the dancing mistress. He didn't get that from his father, that's for sure.' She tapped Sophie on her arm. 'He let you swim in our lake, remember?'

'I'm sorry?' Sophie had become distracted. Lyn was pointing out to Large some feature outside.

'Alex,' my mother reminded her. 'He let you swim in our lake. For your dissertation or whatever you call it.'

Sophie's gaze dropped back to my mother. She was becoming slightly bored, a hint of condescension gathering about her.

'My sixth-form project. Yes, he was always there, rain or shine, helping me in and out of the boat, hands at the ready.' That registered well enough. My mother's face reddened.

'I'm sure your father must have asked him to keep an eye on you. It's very deep in places, the lake. We were all so very close. Or so we thought.' Her back tensed, anger and resentment flooding back. Perhaps inviting them hadn't been such a good idea after all. 'He never even called, you know. That's what hurt.'

'Mother,' I warned again. 'Not today.'

'When, then?' she snapped back.

Sophie stiffened. She was ready for it. Perhaps she wanted it, had learnt from Large. Exits and entrances. 'If you'd rather I left, Mrs Pemberton.'

'No. Forgive me.' My mother swallowed hard, regaining her equilibrium. 'Children aren't responsible for the actions of their parents. Perhaps if they were . . . I'm glad you're here, Sophie, truly glad. Alex always had a soft spot for you – we all did. Charles here especially, of course. And now you're back again with Clark. I'm not surprised. He's such fun, isn't he? I'm almost sorry to leave Monkton's. If he hadn't let me do the garden we'd have never . . .' She let her voice trail as she looked across the room. Theo was shadow-boxing with the twins, something which he was enjoying a good deal more than they

'Monkton's have done both you Pembertons proud.' Sophie's voice was of silken steel. 'First you and Mr Nikolides. Now Charles and that little cleaner that works there. Quite the little romance, by all accounts. No empty room is safe, I hear. What's her name, Charles?'

She drained her champagne, triumphant, her face daring mine. She packed the ammunition, now she'd used it. She knew what her name was. Large must have told her. And I thought we'd been the epitome of discretion.

'Katie.'

'Katie?' My mother was at a loss. 'My Katie? Miss Sourpuss?'

'That's the one! Though thanks to lover boy here, I don't think her . . . no, better not say that.' Sophie eased back against the windowsill, the swell of her breasts suddenly brazen, there to emphasize the sexual nature of her disclosure. She was revelling in my discomfort again, the same way she did with her legs that night above the chip shop.

My mother's lips moved around in agitation, as if she had a piece of gristle to contend with. 'You've been seeing my Katie?'

'Not seeing, exactly.'

'Charles! A mother's got to know.' Sophie leant into her, both pairs of eyes fixed on me. 'He waits for her in his car, tucked away in the lay-by, hoping no one will notice.' She laughed. 'They're all the same, Mrs Pemberton, once they've got that scent in their nostrils. You better watch out yourself. Now, where's that husband of mine?'

She left me with the wreckage. My mother picked at the sleeve of her dress.

'Is this true, Charles? You and Katie?'

'I wouldn't describe it as "me and Katie". We've been out once or twice, yes, but it's not as if we're serious. She's very religious, for a start.'

'She'll need to be, with a family like that. Katie Jinks! God in heaven.' She turned to look out of the window, fingers pressed to her lips.

'How long has this been going on?'

'Not long. A few weeks.'

'A few weeks. And she's been serving me in that little uniform of hers, never saying a word. Even had the nerve to spout religion at me.'

'What could she say? It was up to me, rather.'

'Yes, and you didn't say anything either. But that's you all over, isn't it, Charles.'

'Is it any wonder? I knew you'd be like this.'

'Like what?'

'Acting as if she's beneath me.'

'Where else should she be? She surely has nothing else to offer.'

'Mother, listen to yourself. Today you are marrying a man

from Greek peasant stock who can barely read and write, and you're lecturing me?'

'Are you saying I shouldn't have married him?' She turned, calling out. 'Theo. Charles is still wondering if you're suitable.'

She was trembling with indignation, but Theo took it as a joke. He was a little drunk. Not much, but enough to give the world he thought was his a glow.

'Me?' His ruffled the twins' heads and came over. 'Charles is right to think these things, Meredith. It is as a son should be.' He slapped me on the back. 'She looks wonderful, don't you think, Charles. I call her Meredith now, you understand. You have no objection?'

'It's her name.' I bristled. I stopped, aware of my own voice, how churlish I must have sounded. 'I'm sorry. It came out the wrong way. Of course I don't mind. It's good to hear it being used again.'

'And you, Charles, what am I going to call you?' He gripped me by the wrist, led me aside. 'There has been some bad blood between you and my Tommy, no?'

'A business misunderstanding, that's all, Mr Nikolides.'

'Theo,' he corrected. 'Your mother and me, we will bang your heads together, you and Tommy. But not today. Today I am married. I drink too much. I eat too much. I dance with your mother. She is built for dancing, don't you think? Such a figure for her age.'

We both turned to look at her again. I didn't think it my place to say what my mother was built for, nor his for that matter. My mother's build, her place in the world was something that I thought had been fixed many years before. She was standing, momentarily alone in the centre of the room, and I realized how wrong I had been. Sophie might have the figure, the flesh, the bloom of promise soaking her skin like perfume, but it was my mother who carried the room for all that. Not because it was simply her wedding day, but standing alone in that funny, old-fashioned dress it was as if she had swum into the centre of the stage transformed, my quiet, fussy mother now a radiant black swan, trim, alert, a sort of indomitable fierceness encased in sleek plumage. She had become. Out of her years of duty, of marriage and child-raising and subsequent ill-health, had finally emerged the woman she had always wanted to be. Everyone was looking at her. I turned back to say something conciliatory but Nikolides had already left me and was making his way towards her, clapping his hands to gain her attention.

'We dance,' he announced, holding his hand out.

'Theo,' she scolded, poking his foot with her stick. 'You know I can't dance any more.'

He shook his stubborn head. 'We dance,' he repeated. 'Come. Show them how.' He stretched out a hand. She took it, rubbed her fingers along the calloused edge. It surprised me, how familiar she was with it.

'What about you, Theo?' she questioned. 'Can you dance?'

'Can I dance? Tommy, put on a record.'

Of course he could dance. So could my mother, gammy leg or no. She came from the ballroom-dancing era, evenings spent in out-of-town hotel ballrooms, chandeliers and velvet drapes, candlelit tables ranged around a sprung floor, chatter and cigarette haze, my father driving them back, like the rest of the menfolk, three-quarters cut. It was what they did, what they had always done.

'She's got some spirit, your mum.'

Large was standing next to me. He'd dragged Tommy back over too. We stood in a line together.

'Sorry I was late, Tommy. I had a meeting. You know how it is. Not very polite of me, though, seeing as we're going to be neighbours.'

'Neighbours?' Tommy was looking at the couple on the floor, not concentrating on what Large was saying. Large pulled the sheaf of paper out of his inside pocket, tapped Tommy's shoulder.

'That veg shop one over from you. I talked them into selling. Thought I should tell you, a matter of courtesy.'

'Fletcher's? But Steve Tanner made enquiries only a month ago.'

'Yes, but Steve Tanner's a bit of a plodder, isn't he? I laid it on the line, Tommy. There's no future for them there. She could see that. Couldn't get rid of it quick enough.'

'What is there a future for, if it isn't a rude question?'

'Tell him, Charlie.'

Tommy turned to face me. Everything he had known about me draining from his eyes.

'Kitchens,' I said.

'Kitchens,' Large repeated. 'Custom-made. Everyone's on the up, Tommy, you must know that. Bet your punters don't want just ordinary plants any more, do they? They want palm trees and pampas grass and fig trees growing out of Grecian urns, everything laid out like they was lord of the manor. Appear richer than you really are, that's the word out now. Give it some oomph, even your underwear. There are people out there willing to spend thirty, forty grand on a kitchen these days. Thirty grand to grill a pair of kippers! You couldn't make it up. If they don't have it, they'll stick it on their mortgage or take out a loan, what's the difference. I've got this south-east exclusive, real craftsmanship, German-made, mostly. Island units, walnut wrap-arounds, worktops made of that stuff what everyone wants these days. What they call it, Charlie?'

'Asbestos?'

'Very funny. He means granite, Tommy. They're all crazy for a drop of the hard stuff. What you got in yours?'

'Not granite.'

'Trust me, you will have, One day Lyn will wake up, scratch her fanny, walk downstairs, take one look at her kitchen and say, "You know what? This has had it. What I need is a circo-therm fan oven and a beech-block breakfast bar. What I need is a nine-foot-high American fridge and a built-in wine cooler. What I need is granite."'

'Lyn's very fond of our kitchen. I made the units myself.'

'When was that, then?'

'About six years ago, when we moved in.'

Large smiled. 'She *was* very fond of them, Tommy. Now, she's looking into the Sunday supplements and thinking, "Christ, how much longer do I have to put up with this crap? Where's the four-speed extractor fan and pull-down power points? Where's the plinth lighting that should set off my quarry-tile floor? Where's the sheen, the shine, the evidence that I've arrived? Tommy, you fucking cheapskate, I need a new kitchen."' He tapped his lapel. 'And that's when you'll trot along to yours truly. Fair's fair. You do my garden. I'll do your kitchen. Look sharp, your dad's calling.'

Tommy hurried over. Large rubbed his mouth with the back of his hand. 'That told him.'

'I didn't know the sale had gone through.'

'It hasn't. I'm not going to buy it after all. Just wanted the prick to stew a while. She's as bad as he is, swanning about as if she owns the place.'

'She does own the place.'

'What, this house? All this bleached wood? Where are we, Stockholm?'

'But those papers . . . ?'

Large grinned. 'That's something else altogether.' He stared at me. 'You'll never guess what I've been and done.'

'Large, I thought we'd agreed.'

'Nothing to do with the business. I've bought your old gaff, Charlie, the lawns, the lake, the lot. Just right for me and Nef. We were over there this afternoon, measuring up. I'm going to convert that outbuilding into a duplex for Rhoda, put a bar and games room in the cellar and a Jacuzzi in the master bedroom, right next to the four-poster. You won't recognize the place when it's finished.'

Ten

Brighton was, well, Brighton, a little too intent on being Brighton. We checked in, took the lift to a well-appointed room round the side. Katie was thrilled, the size of the bed, the mini-bar, the complimentary soap and shampoos. She might have travelled to America, but she hadn't stayed in places like this before, that was obvious. She placed her bag carefully on the bed and started unpacking, quick, methodical movements, more attuned to making a caravan tidy than settling in to a four-star hotel, underwear in the top drawer, tops neatly folded underneath, an evening dress, more nightclub than decent restaurant, hung up on the hotel hangers. Next came the examination of the bathroom. I looked out of the window. If you craned your neck you could just see the sea.

'You didn't say nothing the whole journey,' she complained. I turned. She had the bathrobe round her. In it she seemed thinner than usual, whiter, more bone, more in need of . . . what? She also seemed, dare I say it, out of place.

'I never talk much when I'm driving,' I told her. 'Too busy watching out for the idiots on the road.'

'Too busy thinking about that bloody house.' She pushed the drawer shut and slung her arms around me.

'Shall we get some air?' I said. 'You need a bit of sun.'

'I need a bit of something else first.'

'Please, Katie.' I unwrapped her arms. 'I need a little time to wind down. You have no idea what that house meant to me. First the Merry Boys, or Rameses as we now have to call it, and now this. It's as if my whole life's being sold

off. God knows what he'll do to it. Gold-plated bath taps, probably.'

'What wrong with that? It's his house.' She broke open a
packet of biscuits, the wrapper falling to the floor.

'It was ours! Do you think my father would have sold it if
he hadn't needed to? They'd just put in a new greenhouse.
My mother was talking of getting a gardener in. You know who
she had asked, my as-of-six-hours-ago father-in-law. Tea and
cake in the kitchen, that was to be his reward, nothing about
handing herself over body and soul. She could have had the
converted flat, not Rhoda with her rings and her ubiquitous
cleavage.'

'Her what cleavage?'

'Ubiquitous, you know, always there, always on show.'

'So? It's her cleavage. I've got one. She's got one. I show
mine, she shows hers. What's the difference?'

'Decency, for one thing. Why would anyone want to do
that, show off their sixty-five-year-old breasts, if not some
sort of horrible statement about how you see the world, or
how you want the world to see you – all sex and daring and
never-ending show. Shouldn't one have gone beyond that a bit
by then?'

'Maybe she doesn't want to get old.'

'Not wanting to has got nothing to do with it. She is old.
Can't you be lively and fun and still be dignified? I'm sorry,
Katie. It just gets to me, the whole thing. Yes, all right, let
her show her cleavage if she wants to. I just wish she wasn't
showing it in my house. My father killed himself there. My
mother had a stroke because she was chucked out of it. I have
to drive past it and—'

'That's just it,' she cut in. 'You don't.' Her face had that
pale fierceness upon it again. 'You don't have to drive past it
ever again, not if you don't want to. You didn't have to drive
past it today. I might not have a car but I do know that you
don't have to go down Warwick Avenue to get to the main

road. Forget about it, Charles. Here we are in Brighton, my first time in a posh hotel, up for anything, and all you do is go on about where you once lived as a kid. It doesn't matter. It's over.'

'I know. It's just ... It was going to be my inheritance, Katie, bricks and mortar, cash, one or the other. He has no right to it.'

'And you do?' She gave a little jump of excitement. 'I'm not sure which one this is, greed or envy, one or the other, but you're caught in the thick of it. You covet that house, Charles. Even after what happened. You covet it.'

'Of course I bloody covet it. It's my house!'

'And it's eating into you, greed, envy, lust, you're all wound up, ready to kick off, I can just feel it. Don't covet that house, Charles, not now. Covet me. Isn't that that why you've brought me here, for that sort of greed, that sort of lust.' She pressed herself against me again. 'Have you seen the shower?'

'Something wrong with it?'

'It's the size of our front room, that's what wrong with it.' She untied the cord. 'We can have a wash afterwards. Before we hit the beach.'

She did her best, but I wasn't up to it. Large and Sophie would be in my old house, wandering in and out, the garden, the living room, my parents' bedroom, taking pleasure in their new life where they would. My mother would be on a plane with her new husband taking pleasure in hers. Perhaps she and Theo had already checked in. Perhaps they were in a hotel room like this one. Perhaps ...

'My father was here, you know,' I said, breaking free.

'What?' She was on the bed, disorientated.

'My father,' I repeated. 'The IRA bombing. I told you, remember.'

She didn't remember at all.

'Was this like, in the war, then?'

'Of course it wasn't. It was in the eighties. The Irish terrorists, IRA. Don't you remember the bombings in Birmingham and places, all the trials?'

She shook her head. How could she not know something like that?

'They planted a bomb to go off weeks before the party conference,' I explained. 'It went off two or three in the morning. My father had a room right at the back.'

'What, he'd come here for a dirty weekend like us?' She dug her fingers into me, trying to get the conversation back on the rails.

'Of course he hadn't. I told you. He was a delegate. The funny thing was he didn't hear it.'

'And they tried to blow him up?'

'Don't be ridiculous, Katie. They were trying to blow her up.'

'Who?'

'Who do you think? Mrs Thatcher!'

'Oh.'

It barely registered. She raised herself up on one elbow, staring at me.

'How many years ago was this?'

'Ten? Twelve?'

'And they didn't blow her up, right?'

'No. She was very lucky.'

'Right. And this is why you stopped, to tell me about a bomb that didn't go off.'

'It's history, Katie. What might have happened here could have changed the course of British history – if not the world's. I thought you might be interested.'

'Who says I'm not. It's just you chose a funny time to tell me.' She turned her face into the bed, puzzled, thwarted, uncertain.

'I'm finding all this a bit of a rush, Katie. I didn't come here, just to . . .' I took her far hand, eased her round. She looked lost. 'I wanted to do things with you, out in the open, not just here, just this. Back home we lock ourselves away all the time. Of course I want you, but I was hoping here we might behave differently, be more natural, more relaxed, more like any other couple.'

'Who usually come here to screw the weekend away.'

'Katie! You know what I mean.'

'Just teasing.' She jumped up, hopping across the floor, one leg caught in her underwear. 'That was a sweet thing to say. And you're right. We've got plenty of time. Let's go out. See what Brighton has to offer.'

We got dressed, went for a walk along the front. Brighton seemed to me rather like the Sophie I had just left, brazen, on show, everyone there to flaunt whatever it was they wanted, whether it be their bodies, their drinking, their age, the crowds high on a permanent sherbet-laced fizz, on the promenade, on the pier, even when crossing the road it seemed obligatory for men to act like young matadors, waving their shirts at the passing cars. Katie had a pink T-shirt with '*I know nothing*' written in silver, not a judicious epigram I thought as far as she was concerned. She linked her arm through mine. It was hot, unseasonably so.

'This is great,' she said, hugging me close. 'We've got a whole weekend of this. Just you and me. I bet you forgot to bring your cossie, didn't you?' She stopped and kissed me, a full-length, tiptoe affair. A first for me. My hands seemed superfluous. No one seemed to notice.

'Do you know what time of year it is? The sea will be freezing.''

'OK, scrap the beach. What can we do that's ours, that doesn't involve the hotel room?' She turned and started to walk backwards, her face impish.

'Just walking's nice.'

'Walking! I know.' She pulled at my arm, jumping up and down. 'Let's go into town and nick something. How about a shoe shop? Try a few pairs on, get them all relaxed, and when you find something nice and stylish that fits, we'll leg it.'

'Katie!'

'I used to do it all the time. Go up to London, on with a decent pair of clogs and run like fuck to the nearest church. They never look for you there. What do you say? Doesn't have to be a shoe shop.' She looked across the road, to the Lanes to where the shops lay, took my hand ready to lead me across the road. I had to hold fast.

'Katie,' I said. 'What on earth's got into you.'

She stopped, fizzy light in her eyes. 'I just want us to do something that's just us, that's all, a kind of bond, like that man and his woman having it off in all those churches. Doing something like that would keep you alive for months, just thinking about it. We could do that, if you want. Leave my knickers on the altar. There's bound to be one nearby.' She was half serious.

'You can't go around stealing things. It's wrong, it's against the law, the ten commandments.'

'That's the whole point. It puts you that much closer to God, don't you see, puts you right in His sights. You've got to get close to Him after that.'

'This is ridiculous. You can't sin just because God tells you not to. Sin for sinning's sake.'

'Can't we? Isn't that what we're here for, lots of unsanctified sex? And even that was enough for Graham what's-his-face. He needed to desecrate the altar. Stealing shoes? It's nothing!'

'I need a drink,' I said.

There was a pub overlooking the Parade. We sat by the window and drank a late afternoon lager, conversation at a low ebb. Later we walked into the old town, drinkers spilling out onto the pavement, heat in the narrow lanes. I found a restaurant I liked the look of, a little up-market, white napkin on the table, and a daily menu written up in chalk. I chose the braised oxtail, Katie the chicken. We'd eaten out before, of course, but nowhere quite as good, quite as formal. There was an awkwardness to the proceedings which neither of us could ignore. I couldn't help noticing that she held her knife like a pencil, and sprinkled her food with salt even before she'd tasted anything. On the table opposite another couple about the same age as us had noticed her too. The woman was choosing the wine. She was dressed simply, but knowingly, the cut understated, desirable. She was elegant, well bred. She could have gone to my old school. She could have been Sophie's best friend. They were having a good-natured argument over a film they'd both seen, every thrust and parry adding to their mutual attraction. 'Godard,' she was saying, 'simply doesn't hold up any more.' If anyone could have worn Katie's T-shirt . . . I hated myself for what I was feeling.

'What's your chicken like?' I asked her.

'Very nice.'

'And the wine? I chose it specially. It's a very good burgundy.'

'Actually, it's a bit too strong for me.'

The woman was trying not to listen.

'It's called depth, Katie. Let it hang in your mouth a while, try and appreciate the flavours coming out. It cost enough.'

Katie dropped her knife onto the plate.

'Perhaps we should have saved your money and gone back to the shopping mall. You were a good deal better company then.'

'Don't you like it here?'

'Not at the moment. I'm a complete wash-out as far as you're concerned. I can't even drink a glass of your precious wine properly. Are you going to be like this all weekend?'

The couple across looked across at each other, smirking. We were making their evening.

'I'm not some sort of seaside end-of-the-pier performer, Katie,' I hissed. 'If you want one of those, why don't you try one of your brother's friends. I'm sure they need saving just as much as me.' I pushed my plate away. 'We shouldn't have come. As soon as I heard about our house, I should have postponed it to another time.'

'Let's go back, then.'

'To my spacious two-room flat, you mean.'

'Why not? What's to keep you here? Not me, that's for sure.'

I paid up, the couple staring hard at their plates. Back in the hotel room I sat on the edge of the bed while she flung her clothes back in her bag. She held up the dress, tears in her eyes.

'I bought this special, Charles. Twenty quid it cost me. God must be really pissed off with me.'

She was crying. She'd come all this way, and for what? It had been deliberate, what I had done, what I was doing. Such a hard, unforgiving thing, knowing we were different.

'I don't know, Katie. Don't you ever get that feeling that you're behaving like a shit but you just can't stop yourself, you almost force it on everyone, regardless. I did want to come here with you, really I did. I could hardly say anything at my mother's do, for thinking about it, our first time away together. It's just something always comes over me, holding me back, trying to find fault, as if I want something that isn't there. Nothing's ever right, and yet, that's what I want it to be, more than anything. I wanted it to be right with you, Katie, this weekend, truly I did. But then . . . I shouldn't have driven past the house.'

'Charles, you silly.' Her voice had gone soft again. 'We don't have to go back if we don't want to. It's not as if the house is going to disappear if we do. You can't wish it away, whatever your feelings about it.'

'I realize that.'

'Whereas if we stay here . . .' She came and sat down, cross-legged beside me. 'Why don't we just go to bed, cuddle up, all cosy. You'll feel different in the morning, you see if you don't. Look.' She leant over, opened the drawer of the bedside table and pulled out the Bible. 'Tomorrow morning I'll give you a reading that'll make God wet his socks.'

'Katie.'

'Why not. If the preacher is willing . . .'

She bounced on the bed, happy. I felt a cloud lifting, a shadow passing. I patted her knee.

'You're right. It would be a shame to leave now. Tomorrow we'll have a lovely day. Promise.'

'We could steal something together. I'll steal something for you and you can steal something for me. Bring us closer, Charles. What do you say?'

'We'll see.'

We lay in each other's arms, close without intrusion. She brushed my forehead with her hand, her voice in Monkton mode.

'Poor Charles, losing his lovely home.'

I put a finger to her lips. 'Don't let's talk about it any more. You're right. It isn't mine now. It never was mine.'

'But it feels as if it is, that's it isn't it. The need to possess, it's so strong, so hungry. Sometimes it feels as if you'd do anything to feed it. Even steal, just so you can beg forgiveness.' She threaded her fingers through my hair. 'It must have been great, living in a house like that, all that space.'

'It was wonderful,' I boasted, enlivened, 'especially in the summer, the French windows open, my mother in the garden, planting and weeding, Dad in his study, playing his records, me swimming in the lake, playing badminton with school friends.'

'What about Clark. Did he ever come round?'

'We weren't really friends.'

'Not posh enough for you then,' she teased. 'Just like me.'

'It wasn't that. We simply didn't share the same interests.'

'Except that Sophie.'

'What do you mean?'

'You were sweet on her too.'

'How you know that?'

'Your mum. She used to go on and on about how you two was practically engaged until your dad lost all his money.'

I sat up.

'I was nothing of the sort. God, I only wish I—' I stopped, but not in time. Katie was up on her feet.

'Go on, finish it,' she shouted. 'Only wish you had been. Only wish you was married to her, not stuck here with me.'

'Katie. I didn't mean anything by it. I don't know if it's even true.'

'You said it, though, straight off the top. Here's me trying to be as nice to you as best I can and all you can do is chuck it back in my face.'

'Katie, don't be silly. Of course I'm glad I met you.'

'I bet you are. Some scraps off the table at least. You know what?' She threw the Bible at me. 'You can read it on your own from now on. I've had it with you.'

She picked up her bag, banged the door behind her.

I looked for her half-heartedly up and down the promenade, but the lamp-lit streets were not fashioned for forsaken men that night. I was out of place, an intruder, and besides, wherever she'd gone, I wasn't going to find her. I returned to the hotel, paid the bill, and drove home. That was it, then. Katie was right. It was Sophie I wanted. The house, the girl, the money, I wanted them all. They were meant for me, they were my birthright. This was my town, my parents' town, my mother's, my father's, Tommy's too. But Large? What right had he got to any of it?

It was late by the time I got back, tired but not at all sleepy. I'd talked to myself out loud on the way back, a kind of fury bouncing about in the back of the car and the words were still ringing in my head. I was relieved at Katie's departure. It would have happened anyway at some time or other. Mother was right. She wasn't for me. She'd served her purpose.

I parked at the bottom of the road and walked up, a walk I'd done thousands of times, past the walls I'd patted, the hedges I'd brushed my hands against, the little things you do approaching home. Once I had known what lay at the end of it – the light over the garage door, the unlocked side door, a sudden warmth tinged with the faint smell of turps from my mother's cleaned paintbrushes, the objects in the darkened kitchen through which I could move with ease. It was all there, ordained by my every movement, and yet, it had all vanished, the slate wiped dark. I was coming home an emptied man, the guts pulled out of me. I passed the other dwellings, remembering the neighbours I had known. Some were still living there, a continuity within their walls, others had moved away, but gone through choice, not scattered like us hither and thither from one world to the next because of . . . because of what? 'Events, dear boy, events,' wasn't that what Macmillan had said, describing the uncertainty of life in politics, but the observation applied to existence outside Westminster in equal measure. One moment my mother had been sitting down to Romney Marsh lamb, anticipating a summer of slow, methodical contentment, and the next her husband was swinging from a rope in her greenhouse and she turfed out on her ear and into a second-rate residential home, one side of her body half paralysed. And for why? No crime committed, no moral transgression, no outrage to God or greater humanity. What wrong had they sent out into the world that it should come back to devastate them so? What right had Large that he should go out into that same world and return to a town supine at his feet? Considering the terms and conditions demanded, I am surprised that we manage any semblance of morality at all. The policy simply doesn't hold up.

My shoes sounded on the gravel, inordinately loud. With

all the scaffolding up, the roof and side partly shrouded in canvas, the house had an uneasy, anaesthetized look, like a troubled patient strapped down on the gurney, waiting for the knife. There was radical surgery planned here, I could tell. I pushed open the wooden door that led into the back garden, pressing up on the catch as I had always done, anticipating the lift as the door swung free on its hinges. That hadn't changed yet. As I moved onto the veranda, the scents of the summer garden hit me, the old familiarity of it breaking over me like a sweat. It lay suspended above the ground as thick and familiar as the mist I used to see from my bedroom window in the morning. I stood there, my heart racing like a thief's. The moon was up. I could see quite clearly how the garden had been neglected these past few months. Ragged spiky shadows sprang up from the low, clipped hedge that separated the two lawns. The bay tree too had lost its lozenge-like shape, taken on new, distorted forms. I stepped out onto the lawn, the grass underneath me long and irregular, like a dog's uncombed coat. My father had been meticulous about that lawn, walking both up and down the same strip to ensure the same shade of green throughout, cut every other day, weather permitting, three notches up on the blades, first thing he'd do back home off the train, old corduroy trousers, old shoes, but with his city shirt still on, collar unbuttoned. We used to play cricket there, him and me, me bowling, him at the far end, trying to coax me onto the off stump. He did that for a while, when I was about ten. He still had hope for me then. 'You'll never be a batsman,' he said, 'you don't know how to walk out onto the pitch, make a stand, but you've the makings of a bowler.' He was right. I made the second eleven, played once for the first, when Archie Lawson took sick, Large captain in all but name, strolling out, bat over his shoulder, something Tommy, still the captain, had warned against, but Large had taken no notice, carrying it level to the ground, like the block of wood it was, as if it didn't matter. That wasn't all. 'See that!' Godly Miller exclaimed, jumping up out of his seat. 'He's wearing *cufflinks*,' and as he stood in the crease, looking round, brushing the hair out of his eyes, we saw that indeed he was, the first eleven shirt with the extra cufflink holes sewn in, he told us, by Rhoda. 'Tommy was going on about his bloody ring the other day,' Large announced later that night in the Merry Boys, celebrating his top score of seventy-three, 'so I thought if he can get away with it, why can't I? So I got Mum to do the honours, and she did, bless her, stayed up special so it would be ready. I told Godly, you show me in the rule book where it says I can't wear cufflinks. Anyway it didn't half put that bowler of theirs off his stroke. Even Charlie scored against him. How many was it Charlie, seven?'

I picked up a couple of the round stones that marked the narrow flowerbed running down the left-hand side and walked back out, not a flicker of hesitation. Rising above the hedge stood the Ark, my mother's silver ship of promise, my father's silent catafalque. The stones were round and heavy. I rubbed one against my trousers, feeling it cold and hard against my crotch, my fingers played out for the turn. My father and I had watched bowlers above all, enthralled by their ability to swing the pitch, to find the thread that led to the stump, to tempt the batsmen into losing the very thing he needed to keep at all costs, his guard. There had been a time when we used to go regularly to the ground at Canterbury, him and me, not saying much to each other, neither on the journeys there and back, nor during the matches, both of us hoping that what we saw, what we felt, would infuse the two of us with some sort of shared understanding, of what we were, male members of a family line. I'd once asked him why Mother never came. She liked Wimbledon enough, golf too. 'Watching cricket,' he'd replied, 'is like working soap into cracked leather. It keeps us supple, ready for the elements. Women don't understand. They think it's a matter of runs and LBWs, but it's not. It's absorbing a whole history, the affirmation of our destiny. Cricket is what an Englishman is all about. If they want to play on the golf course, I've no objection to that, football, tennis, anything, but this . . .' He pointed to the players strung out around the pitch. 'You can't have them playing cricket. I mean what would they rub the seam against, their *fanny*? Mark my words, Charles, money or women, either one will ruin it.'

I took a short run and sent the stone spinning high and hard, losing sight of it as it curled into the sky. It was a rocket launch, a missile moment, a pre-emptive strike, destruction into the dark. On the stone flew, into one of the roof's twelve glass panes. Three foot by two, those panes measured, strong thick glass with edges that had cut into my hands. We had slid them up into their metal grooves all that afternoon, my father, old Nikolides and me. Only Tommy, with only one good arm, had been idle, him and my mother watching us from below, watching the sails raised into her, as yet, unnamed ship. Now it had no cargo, no captain, no crew either. Just the breaker's yard.

The crack shot through the night, hard, followed by a clatter of jangling notes – emotions flooding out of me like flat champagne. This garden, this house, all of it, bundled out of my presence along with his dead body. This was my home, my mother's. He'd robbed us of it, my father, handed it over to the very people his own father had helped build a wall against. I lobbed the other stone, revelling in the discord that ripped a hole in the night. The core of a vandal's motivation is neither destruction, nor boredom; not even protest. Sound is the drug, the dissonance it makes, its cacophonous reach.

'If I'd known you was coming I'd have baked a cake.'

I whipped round. A match flared. Large was seated on a sun-lounger, his legs sticking out like a boy on a swing. A cigar hung in his fingers.

'Breaking into a chap's garden, smashing up his property. I should call the police.'

'Large, I . . .'

249

'Don't worry. My dad hated rozzers.' He laughed, a drinker's laugh. I could smell it on his breath too.

'I don't know what came over me.'

'I do.' He sucked on the flame, streams of smoke smothering the air. 'Remember that time you invited me in, when I was working for the council and you was going downtown,' he crooked his little finger, 'for coffee and biscuits? You could have taken me straight here, but you didn't. You led me through the whole effing ground floor to show off what you got, what we hadn't. Silver teapot on the kitchen table, all that crap behind them glass cabinets. You think I don't deserve this, where you was brought up. Want a beer?' He rolled a bottle out with his foot.

'Large.'

'On your way to see Sophie, wasn't you? Only she didn't show. Now why was that, you think?' He pursed his lips, wet sucks on the cigar. 'Lucky in love, that's me. And in broad daylight. I thought you were off somewhere this weekend?'

'It didn't work out.'

'So you came back, needing a bit more than a wank in the wash basin. I can relate to that. Have you been drinking?'

'I had a couple of whiskies down the pub just now.'

'Thought you might. Large ones, I bet. Good job I recognized you, otherwise . . .' He stretched out his free hand. A shotgun lay against the arm rest, barrel to the sky. He took hold of the stock, lifted the gun onto his knee.

'In parts of Texas I could shoot you now, no questions asked. I'm out on my patio, minding my own business, and in you charge, all spunked up. Doesn't matter that I know you, that you didn't mean me any harm. I could blow your head off just for being here, call the cops and be back here, cracking open another beer, before the sun's up.' He tapped the stock of the gun. 'Did you have trouble with the wildlife when you lived here, foxes and that?'

I shook my head.

'Must have been them others after you. Nef and I were going to have a cuddle right here under the stars tonight, sort of christen the place. Just got settled down when all this barking starts up, some bastard fox out on the razzle. Every time we thought he'd gone, he'd start up again, like we was disturbing *him*. Ruined everything. Sophie pissed off back to the farm, and I came back with the shotgun. Can't hear him now, though. I think you've scared him off.'

'Large, what can I say?'

'Nothing. I don't care about the greenhouse. I'm going to get Tommy to take it off my hands. We had a bit of chin-wag after you left. He's all right.'

'That's not what were you saying earlier.'

'He's a businessman, Charlie, like me. If a job's on offer, he'll take it, whatever who's paying thinks of him. He'll sort this fucking garden out.' He sensed me bridle. 'We're a young couple, Charlie, we want barbecues and somewhere to be a bit physical, tennis and what-not. All them special plants of your mum's, we've no call for them. We'd kill 'em without even meaning to. Tommy's going to dig them out, cost them against his work. I'm scrubbing the lot. More lawn, a few bushes, a nice bit of decking where we can have dinners and that, and that's it. Sacrilege, I know, but there it is. You want to trash the greenhouse too, it's fine by me. Here ... I got an idea.' He got up and walked towards me, the gun balanced over his shoulder.

'Is that thing loaded?'

'No, I thought I'd smack him over the head with it. Course it's fucking loaded. Walk behind me, Charlie, just in case.' He brushed past me.

'Large, you're not . . .'

I trotted after him, round to the other side of the hedge. The greenhouse stood there, tall and implacable, like a ghosted schooner, its dark elaborate rigging all in place. My futile missiles had accomplished nothing, torn a sail that's all. He started checking the gun.

'Large, you can't.'

'I'm not going to. You are.' He came up beside me.

'Look at it, standing there, like it doesn't know. It's like they were in cahoots. He let you down, your old man, you and your mum. He chickened out right here, on that bit of cross-bar, just when you needed him the most. You ever think that's what it was there for all along, that's why he bought it in the first place?'

His voice softer than I'd ever heard it. Tender almost. He handed me the gun.

'Don't you just fucking hate him for it. I would.' He hoisted the gun up on my shoulder, raised my arm up. 'That's it, Charlie. Go on. You know you want to.'

I hesitated.

'Go on. Right between the eyes.'

I looked at it. He was right. It had brought my mother and father back together, yet within two years it had carried off my father and broken my mother. I loathed the very sight of it. I squeezed the trigger.

The greenhouse exploded in a burst of dark tumbling light. I was thrown back, the gun leaping in my hands, my ears ringing with the blast. I felt a streak of blood running down my cheek. Large was laughing.

'Did you see it jump? I swear it fucking jumped.'

He grabbed the gun from me, dropping in two more cartridges.

'He's not dead yet, Charlie. Finish him off. Both barrels. It's what we have to do.'

I lifted the gun again. Through the hanging shards of glass the far side stood mostly unscathed. A thick sliver swaying in the centre crashed to the ground, a section of the roof slithering loose in its groove.

'Hold still, you bastard!'

Who said that? Me, Large? I fired again, taking the recoil better this time, though my cheek felt badly bruised. There was little now left but the frame. Large took the gun from me, broke it open, folded it over the crook of his arm. Cordite hung in the air.

'Nice shooting. But what the fuck am I going to tell Nef? She was going to grow her wacky baccy in there.'

'But you said . . .'

'I wasn't having her do that. We're respectable now. Dead lucky, you turning up.'

'So what will you tell her?'

'What happened. A couple of vandals wrecked the joint. That's what you are now, you and me, a couple of vandals.'

He slung his arm over me. For that one moment I had never felt more at home.

Eleven

That year properties fell to Large like ninepins, and on the relative cheap. Who else was looking to invest in empty piles rotting away on the depressed margins of the south-east coast? Two, three, four, in no time at all, by the coming of spring he had seven properties on the go, all with their insides lying out in front on the ground, plumbers and carpenters and decorators sauntering in, preparing them for what he liked to describe as 'the nugget touch'. Each one added to the portfolio only served to whet his appetite for more, his pockets bulging with details of other properties he'd found, bankruptcies, repossessions, vast crumbling edifices that he called 'the untouchables'. First on his books came the one-time barracks down in Deal, then a long-abandoned hotel on the outskirts of Hastings. Ramsgate fell next, then a surprisingly spacious alms house on the outskirts of Hythe. When I tried to warn him of the dangers of stretching himself too thin, he simply snorted with contempt.

'Where you been the last couple of years, Charlie? In a fucking monastery? Haven't you noticed nothing at all? The banks are stuffed with so much cash they can barely close their doors at night. They have to climb over piles of it just to get to the coffee machine. They're giving it away, Charlie. Mortgages, loans, it doesn't matter what you want it for, it's how much you can take off their hands that counts. That's all they're interested in. Walk in off the street, tell them how much you want and it's yours. One hundred thousand, two hundred, step this way, squire. Credit rating? Collateral?

Forget it. As long as you can wipe your own arse and hold a pen, come in and join the fun. It's party time. Like them lap-dancing clubs I used to go to, up in town. We want to see money push its muff in our face. Money's the floor show these days, and what's more, they give you money just to see it. Don't you know that? Remember that song? "One day older and deeper in debt"? They didn't know how lucky they were.'

Property after property. It was as easy as breaking eggs; grants, tax concessions, planning permission, they simply dropped into his hands. He was supplying a service, after all. Local councils were only too willing for him to take some of the worry off their hands, and if he made a profit while doing so, good luck to him. They wanted him to make a profit. They wanted him to convert the old into new. Access to roads, adequate drainage, whatever the building concern might be, their planning departments nodded them through. Lumley's, the contractor he hired for Monkton's, was, by the end of the following year, working almost exclusively for him, his work-force increased times ten, his vans criss-crossing the county, plaster to Large's dream. And Large, Large hared from build-ing site to building site, becoming what he always wanted, a force, someone to be reckoned with. Whenever I saw him, and I saw him almost every day, he seemed to have grown a little overnight, a little more solid, a little more planted, stuck in the Kentish soil, dominating the landscape, casting shadows, spreading roots, providing shelter.

'I'm putting something in here, Charlie,' he said once, 'something special. I'm making a mark, like your old man did. I'm the new broom, the new axe, clearing the dead wood out, chucking all the crap on the bonfire. You might not think it, but him and me have got a lot in common.' He caught my expression.

'That's right. He might have spoke better, had better quali-fications, but from what I've heard he was a bit of a maverick himself, not averse to the old two fingers when it suited. He liked looking at the women too, I know that much. I remember at school do's, he was always eyeing up the younger mums.'

'Was he?'

'Always. He came round to our house once. Bee Bee was there that day, surprise surprise. She was only fourteen but when she answered the door his eyes fair popped out.'

'My father came to your house?'

'Spring term. Something he wanted the old man to do, only Mum and he had gone out sudden. He said very sorry and left. Made Bee Bee's day, though, him staring at her like that, like she was straight out of Page Three.'

'I'm sure he didn't mean to.'

'I'm sure he bloody did. Fourteen, fifteen, that girl was at her peak.'

Lilly's role in the day-time advertising campaign proved something of an inspiration, a larger-than-life soap-opera star returning to the screen, her old-fashioned, fifties pin-up body seemingly intact, her voice still redolent with the vulgar husky lilt that had made her such a hit with men such as my father, who were besotted with the idea of the pert, common and slightly improper woman, as long as they or none of their friends were married to them. Lilly's reappearance as the Golden Years spokeswoman had been an event in itself. On millions of television screens throughout the south-east, and still the busty siren with her twenty-a-day lips and her sauce-laden eyes, she fixed her gaze upon her younger pensioners, telling them not to be so short-sighted, so head-in-sand, to make sure they prepared the ground. 'Remember,' she closed with, 'age matters. Your Golden Years are all you have left.'

Whether it was that phrase, her look or simply the idea, none of us, Large included, expected the response he got, the speed of it. Enquiries poured in; phone calls, letters, faxes, emails, people turning up on his office doorstep to make an appointment, wanting to look around Monkton's or any of the other properties. It was one of those things that had been waiting out there all the time. It just needed someone to cast the line and reel it in. I was surprised. Privately I had thought that the last thing people wanted to face up to was their own incarceration, their own dead-end future, but it wasn't writ like that. Any doubts Large might have had were blown away.

Within ten months of the start of the campaign he had near four hundred and fifty prospectors on his books, pragmatic men mostly, looking to buy security for their wives, over forty-five thousand pounds coming in every month, five hundred thousand pounds a year just for starters, with no overheads, no bills, 'no nothing', as Large would boast. No matter that I pointed out that they would come in in time. 'Time, what's time, Charlie? Even Einstein couldn't answer that. And what's more, you know what the profit is on every bed already occupied?' I knew that. Close on fifty per cent. His homes were filling up with a vengeance. It was easy to see why. They were good value. They looked right. They *felt* right. You'd want to stay there yourself.

He bought a couple of people-carriers, painted them cream and green. By the end of that year the Golden Years livery had spread across Kent, a Golden Years standing at the back of one of those oddly spacious streets in Ramsgate, a Golden Years overlooking the changeling sea off Deal, a Golden Years tucked away around the back of Hastings, a Golden Years looking out across the Medway, a Golden Years and three-acre apple orchard outside Sandwich and one with a walled garden on the outskirts of Hythe; not to mention our very own Monkton's. And Large, Large bestrode them all. He was proud of what he'd done. He had a right to be. He was doing something different.

Each rest home had a private dining room that a resident could hire, for lunch parties, dinner, drinks, card games, whatever they fancied. If you felt like baking a cake or cooking a special meal for someone, you could do that too, given the kitchen enough notice. That's the secret, Large had insisted.

'I'm going to let them do it themselves if they can, like Charlie's mum in Monkton's garden. They can do that as well, put a few plants out, grow a few lettuces, prune some roses if they want to. We'll supply the gloves and forks and what-not. We'll even buy the fucking plants. Tommy's best discount, of course.'

One of his most popular innovations was the mid-week National Lottery draw. Every home was bought a ticket by Large, the numbers pulled out of a hat the Sunday before. If they won, the whole home would share, residents and staff. It became a focal point, the Golden Years' Golden Hour, gathering round the TV in the recreation room, free glass of wine in hand, Large as often as not putting in an appearance in one, whipping up the excitement, expressing frustration, disappointment, sympathy as the numbers ran out. 'You look unhappy,' he would cry at the end, 'what about me? I've been counting on you to take me on a cruise. You're wearing me out, you lot. I need a rest.' Wearing him out, what a clever phrase to use, and how they loved the idea of that, wearing this thick, physical presence out, his swagger, his sweaty maleness, his energy, draining him to the last drop. They loved his visits. They loved him. He knew how to do it, talk to them, make them feel young again, flirt audaciously with the old girls, treat the men as if they were still players in the world, still had the nous and the sperm count. He'd visit each home once a month, walking round, chatting to everyone, hearing their worries, their complaints, the successes of their grandchildren, sitting down, taking their hands in his, serving up their food, muscling in on a game of cards, picking out a jigsaw piece, standing a round in the little bar every place had; he was brilliant at it. 'Clark is coming tomorrow,' the staff would tell them, his old name resurrected, newly fit for purpose, and there they'd be, waiting, sitting in their rooms or bunched together downstairs, hair done, make-up on, checking their watches for his arrival, and he, he rose to the occasion every time, bustling up the steps, glad-handing them all, treating each and every one as if they were the one he'd really come to visit. He remembered everything, their names, where they came from, what their children or grandchildren were doing. He'd pick up a photograph on the sideboard: 'Mark's at college, isn't he? Law, isn't it?' he'd say, or, 'Your Pam looks lovely in that wedding dress. Now where's a picture of you in yours?' and out it would come. He returned to the boy I'd known back at school, never forgetting a face, a name, the core of a person, all the while adding a little bit of himself into the mix. He was better than vitamins. There was one I remember, a Mrs Hooker, a keen follower of flat racing. He'd lay bets with her, Happy Lad running in the three-thirty at York, or Dingly Dell at Cheltenham, always a horse with a feel-good name, a pound to place, occasionally five, the sum wasn't important, the thrill it gave her was, that injection of playful risk into her bloodstream. He even took her to the point-to-point out at Charing, Sophie and Lilly Martin and Mrs Hooker sitting in his four-wheel-drive Merc, knocking back the champagne while he danced attendance. He liked being generous that way. He was making money. He wanted everyone to know it. Me included. As good news followed good news, and his balance sheet started to blossom, the phone would ring.

'Get your glad rags on, Charlie boy. You're going out tonight.'

How many times did I hear that phrase, how many times did I walk down the street, to find him waiting outside, his jacket slung around his shoulders, flicking his house keys through his fingers. We didn't talk about how that was going. He had the sense not to tell me, and I didn't ask. Apart from that unspoken territory I was a fully paid-up member of the entourage. Why not? I didn't see my mother much. Tommy never spoke to me, Katie rebuffed my every approach. What else was I to do? Besides, they were fun, and well, I'd developed a taste for them. They were captivating. They had made me feel odd, a little outside myself, but I'd liked being with them all the same. I was out on the inside.

That year we seemed to go from one to the other, Rameses at the weekends, the Five Maidens every Wednesday evening. The weekends were something of an endurance test, Friday to Saturday lock-ins in the Tomb, five-hour Sunday lunches, Rhoda ensconced in her motorized wheelchair in her place in the corner, while Bee Bee sat at the other end, perched on a high stool on the other side of the bar, dressed in black mesh tights, holding her cigarette over her shoulder, like a cut-price Princess Margaret. From there she would direct her coven, a collection of coarse, like-minded, heavy-drinking, cigarette-smoking, youngish women, hard beyond their years, who wore their cynicism as thickly as their make-up. They were the floor show, expected to dress up the flesh, match the men drink for drink (no problem there), find life a laugh, while doing exactly as they were told. Fridays was when Large's chums would descend, who'd spend the weekend in dazed bemusement, unable to get their heads around what Large was doing here anyway, away from the smoke. Jay and Bee Bee ran the place, the atmosphere febrile, teetering on the brink of depravity, the heavy smell of Bee Bee's perfume, the parade of cleavages, Jay in his tight white T-shirt wiping down the bar with a manic grin, the bar's unofficial bouncer, the odd-job man, even, when the girls were short, or just plain lazy, serving food with a starched napkin draped over a bulging, tattooed arm.

I'd been right. Large wasn't interested in the place much. He saw it as his own when he wanted it to be his own, and at other times, to get on with the job in hand – attracting the town's young and affluent. That doesn't mean to say it wasn't a success. It was, and for much of the week he would leave it alone. Come Friday though, two, two-thirty, the week's work over, he would appear, and move into the Tomb, the arbiter of who accompanied him and who did not. Friday afternoon would segue into Friday evening, the lock-in ending on Saturday morning with Large cooking up bacon and eggs (never served at any other time in the place) dressed in a striped apron and wielding an outsize iron slicer. After breakfast he'd go shooting, play a round of golf, perhaps go on a fishing trip Deal way, Large and his gang, telling jokes, drinking canned beer, creasing up, fooling around. They were not popular. None of them understood the difference between enjoyment and enthusiasm, or realized that it was possible to take pleasure in something without having to shout about it. No matter; they'd return in high or higher spirits, depending on the success of the expedition. Either way, it called for more drink, for tales to be told, for arguments as to comparative hand and eye coordination to ensue, discussions on sports and sportsmen, great cricketers, great rugby players (none of them cared for football very much) and of course great boxers. Who was the greatest, Rocky Marciano or Muhammad Ali? What about Randolph Turpin, Jack Dempsey? Large had photographs of old British boxers put up in the men's lavatories, Henry Cooper, Joe Bugner, Freddy Mills. Pride of place was a signed photograph of Brian London, who'd fought in the sixties. I remember standing once at the urinal one Saturday, when Large lurched up next to me, bits of crisp hanging from his wine-stained lips. I never liked standing next to him much. He always managed to produce twice as much volume as me.

'My old man knew them boxers,' he said, unbuttoning his fly. 'Joe Erskine, Dick Richardson, 'specially Brian. Said Brian might not have been the cleverest fighter around, but was the bravest. Dad went to Wembley to watch him fight Ali. Sixty-six I think it was. Ali was unbelievable, a fucking master class he gave him, but it took him three rounds to put Brian down. He was so proud, Dad said, to be British that night, the stubbornness London showed. He wasn't called the British Bulldog for nothing. Sometimes I think I should have done that, taken up boxing. It's a good feeling you know, winning medals.'

We stared at the picture, two bare fists held up beneath what looked like a suspiciously glass chin.

'He fought Floyd Paterson too for the world heavyweight a few years before,' Large continued, still in full flow. 'Lost that too. Still, Patterson got his comeuppance with Ali not long after. Ali didn't like him. Patterson used to call him Cassius Clay when he knew he wanted to be called Ali. Quite cruel Ali was, could have finished him off, quickly, but held him up, so he could batter him about a bit.'

I walked to the basin, turned on the tap.

'That reminds me,' I said, wondering why I had never asked him since he'd come back. 'You never did tell us. What did he say?'

His voice floated back over the running stream. 'What did who say?'

'That farmer's boy you beat in the sports centre. What did he say?'

'Oh, that. Should I tell you?' He turned, buttoning up his fly. 'He said, "Now I know where your mum gets her tits from." It was meant to put me off, see. Big mistake.'

While Rameses was Large at play, Wednesday evenings had an element of business about it, or rather commerce, There was any number of us, it depended on his mood; expansive, vexed, confidential, it fluctuated. There was Barry, an old mate from the City, and his wife, Charlene, who'd been a croupier, and had that pallid, see-nothing face to match. There was a friend of Sophie's, Eileen, an angular Bostonian who came over once a month to buy paintings for her wealthy clients, who boasted of having slept with Henry Kissinger two nights running. There were others; investment friends, some local businessman he'd met on a shoot, and as often as not, Lilly Martin, ever the old trouper. One thing was constant. We arrived at the restaurant late, deliberately so, booked for half eight, nine, not turning up until well past ten, fuelled by drinks in his office, or more likely at Rameses. No matter that we were late, Large was only doing what was expected of him. He was the new royalty, there to be indulged, and to arrive past the appointed hour, surrounded by his entourage, cocooned by an appreciation of his position, became the norm. The table was always waiting, untouched. Customers who turned up on Wednesdays and found only this table free, who promised to eat quickly and leave on time, were politely, firmly refused. This was Large's table, set in the restaurant's chancel, the white tablecloth, the ice bucket, the wine glasses he preferred, his chalice, his cross, the covering on his altar. Sometimes he'd bring his own food, a couple of lobsters he'd been given, a brace of pheasants he'd shot, some fish he'd caught, the restaurant could charge whatever they liked, he didn't mind. Sometimes he'd have Geoffrey Price, the owner, come and join us for coffee, and we'd stay there until the early morning, Geoffrey fetching out the prized Armagnac that was once the province of my father. After a while, Geoffrey, now known as Pricey, came to think this had become a custom, setting the Armagnac down before he had been invited, but Large didn't seem to mind. It lengthened the evening, and that's what he wanted; long, drink-laden dinners, four, five courses, three and a half hours minimum, jackets slung on the back of chairs, elbows on the table, Large expounding on his plans, holding forth, blowing cigar smoke into the air; the economy, the Prime Minister, the fate of the euro, what he wanted out of us. And I was one of them, Charlie Pemberton as I now was, seated next to indolent, indiscreet, Sophie forever listing Large's inadequacies, or nodding knowledgeably as Eileen told me how she discovered an ink drawing of Miró's; other times I'd be fascinated by Charlene's descriptions of her oil-sheikh gamblers or Barry's stories from the City. And I could tell a tale or two as well, Large's many exploits at school or the day my father the mayor stepped on an African dignitary's ceremonial robe and robbed him of his dignity. I knew about wine, I could talk intelligently about opera to Eileen (her father was a patron of the Met), and thanks to Jay's sales technique (Got rid of that Nissan yet? – Not yet – Why don't you let me find you a decent Continental motor? – Japanese cars are very reliable – So is All-Bran), I now owned a different make of car, a Saab, one very careful previous owner, only three thousand miles on the clock. Not that I usually drove there. We had the local taxi firm on tap, two, three cars, waiting outside for when we were ready.

The Golden Years Insurance Policy had its first claimant in its second year. A Mrs Pauline Hargreaves, six months' free board and lodging, and a ten per cent discounted bill there-after. It made the local paper, and one of the nationals, the way of things to come. Large was disappointed that his picture didn't make it. The next week, though, he passed the five hundred mark.

'Get your glad rags on, Charlie boy. You're going out.'

It was ten past four. Large closed up the office. I closed up mine. By five o'clock we were all at Rameses, Barry, Charlene, Jay, Sophie, Bee Bee, the girls, the boys, even Lilly Martin. We drank black velvet, champagne and Guinness, Lilly and Large arguing which should go first, the champagne or the Guinness. Lilly said the champagne should go first. Large insisted it should be the other way around. Only then did you get the proper lot of head.

'I don't want a lot of head,' Lilly argued.

'Not what you said yesterday afternoon.' Even Sophie smiled.

We tried it both ways. A pint with the champagne first, then a pint with the Guinness. I preferred it Lilly's way. In no time at all we were on the high seas, waves of fearsome energy crashing round. The drink combination seemed to go straight to different parts of the body, the Guinness to the spine and the nervous system, the champagne to the head. By nine we were all wildly unstable, lurching from room to room as the pub and its contents tipped up and down, Large the mad captain, drunk on success, striding up and down the deck, the star of the show, running through his repertoire. We had Norman Mailer, we had Tommy Cooper, we had the boy stood on the burning deck, we had little Norman Lamont and 'Today has been an extremely difficult and turbulent day', we had Ali again, doing the Ali shuffle, jabbing out 'What's my name, what's my name,' to a battered Ernie Terrell, and finally, balancing on an upturned beer crate, we had our one-time Prime Minister, John Major, delivering his infamous Mansion House speech in all his prim and proper, priggish certainty. 'All my adult life,' Large started, in that hectoring nasal delivery that Major had made his own, 'All my adult life I've seen British governments driven off their virtuous pursuit of low inflation by market problems or political pressures. I was under no illusions when I took Britain into the ERM. I said at the time that membership was no soft option . . . the soft option, the devaluer's option, the deflationary option, in my judgement that would be a betrayal of our future at this moment and I tell you categorically that is not the government's policy.' Large's voice rose to a crescendo of self serving indignation. 'No,' he shouted, adenoids in full flight, 'our policy is in no small measure to considerably fuck it up and blame it on the Germans.'

A roar went up. Jay began goose-stepping up and down the room à la Fawlty Towers. Bee Bee and her friends started limboing under the bar flap. Large jumped down and pushed his way through to where Sophie, Lilly and I were standing.

'Word perfect or what? Come on, I've had it with this lot. Charlie, Lilly? Let's get some nosh. I'll give Pricey a call. He'll squeeze us in.' He flipped his phone on. 'Pricey? The Prince of the Primus Stoves here. We need feeding. Four. Maybe five. Half an hour, all right? I know it's not Wednesday, but get us that table anyway. And Pricey. Get us a bottle of that Romany Conti what I like.' He snapped the phone shut. 'Little bleeder's wetting himself, the mark-up he slaps on. If he plonks himself down with the Armagnac tonight, I'm going to make him drink the whole fucking bottle himself.'

We piled into the taxi.

'What are we going to eat?' Large demanded. 'Something special?'

'What about boar?' Sophie suggested. 'I haven't had boar for years.'

'He won't have any fucking boar. He just is one.'

'Venison, he might have venison,' she countered. 'You like venison.'

'He doesn't hang it long enough. He's a bit of a tosser, old Pricey.'

'What about salmon en croute? He does a decent salmon.'

'It'll be farmed,' Large objected.

'What *do* you want, then?' Sophie was becoming exasperated. We'd all seen Large like this many times before, not knowing what he wanted, yet wanting it even more.

'I don't know, something I haven't had there before, something that will put him on the spot.'

'What about pancakes?' Lilly spoke quietly.

'Pancakes?'

'Yes.' She pulled on an earring. 'Start with pancakes and see where we go from there. He can stand and toss them by the table.'

'Pricey tossing pancakes.' Large banged a fist against the palm of his hand. 'I like that. He can wear a little dinky-doo apron, so he don't mess himself.'

Sophie started to giggle. 'Were you any good at tossing pancakes, Lilly?'

She shook her head. 'Film producers were my speciality.'

Even the driver laughed.

We stumbled out. Geoffrey Price was waiting by the door. The restaurant was full, Large's table empty, laid for four as asked, an unopened bottle standing in the centre. We sat down.

'This is a nice surprise,' Geoffrey said, hovering with napkins and mineral water. 'Will you be coming tomorrow too?'

'Have to ask the wife that, Pricey. Is that a stain on your trousers?

'Sorry?'

'Nothing. Just a trick of the light.' He rubbed his hands together. 'Now, the reason we have come here in such a God-awful hurry is that we need you to rustle us up some pancakes?'

'Pancakes?'

'You know, them flour and milk things. Crêpes, you probably call them. Lilly here has a craving for them. Let's have thirty. With a dose of that Grand Marnier. And I want you to do the tossing, Pricey. At the table. I bet you tossed a lot of pancakes in your time.'

Geoffrey Price clapped his hands.

'When it comes to pancakes . . .' He looked down, beaming. This was just what he liked, Large pushing the boat out.

'Not thirty, though,' he said, trying to take control 'There's four of you. It's got to be twenty-eight or thirty-two. Got to be.'

Large shook his head. 'Listen up, Geoffrey. Seven pancakes apiece is twenty-eight, I'll give you that, but what you're forgetting is the two extra that I get for being the greedy bastard what's paying. Which is why I said thirty, and not twenty-eight. Not your strong point, Pricey, the psychology of maths.'

'You've got me there.' Geoffrey was at his most placatory. He put his hand out, leant over the table. 'And I better take this away.' He took hold of the bottle. 'You can't possibly drink it with pancakes.'

The table stilled for a moment.

'How do you mean?' Large said, his face open, beguiling.

'For crêpes,' Geoffrey said gaily. 'It is far too sweet.'

'The wine's too sweet?'

Geoffrey raised his eyebrows. 'The dish is too sweet,' he explained.

'Well, make it less sweet. Scrub the booze. Lemon'll do the trick.'

Geoffrey shook his head. 'It's not appropriate, this wine, whatever you put on them.'

Large put his hand out, pressed the bottle back down. 'But I like this wine. I've probably drunk a bloody crate of it right here at this table. What's your problem?'

'They just don't go. It's a Grand Cru.'

'Exactly my point. An exceptional wine to go with your exceptional pancakes. I mean, you're not going to toss me thirty pieces of crapola, are you?'

Geoffrey shook his head like a dog shaking water. His voice took up the challenge. 'Clark, please, I know what I'm talking about.'

'And I don't?' Large looked around. 'Hear that, everyone. I don't know what I'm talking about.'

'Clark, trust me. You'll ruin it. This wine is in a different class altogether. I thought you'd understand that by now.'

If Geoffrey had not said that word, 'class', I think the stand-off would have eventually evaporated. Up to this point Large had been enjoying himself. The little darts of his eyes had told us that, reassured us that this was just a diversionary sport, something to get Pricey all worked up about. He'd be allowed to take his precious bottle away after the fun. But with that one word the game changed. Large put his hands behind his head.

'By now? You mean, you think by coming here for the last eighteen months you've *educated* me? That before coming here to this third-rate apology for haute cuisine I thought quenelles was some poncy French dance, or that a velouté was an Italian motor scooter rather than a roux moistened with chicken or veal stock?'

'Clark, I never thought any such thing.'

'No?' He tipped back on his chair. 'Do you want to know

what I think, Geoffrey? You think ten years ago I sat at a desk, punched in a few keys, followed the little coloured numbers on a screen and made it all up. You think I'm a London chuck-out who struck lucky. You think that all of us from the City are barrow-boys at heart, only it's currencies and arbitrage instead of cauliflowers and greens. You think it was easy, you prick.'

'Clark, please. You've got it all wrong.'

'No I haven't. You think every one of them things, everyone does, Tommy, Lyn, Charlie here, even Nef once, though she probably knows better by now. You don't like me. I know that, do you think I don't? You make fun of me behind my back, can't wait till I get my just deserts. That don't bother me neither. But ignorant? You put up against me, I'd fucking crucify you, any subject you like, kings, queens, current affairs, economics, rap music, long-range weather forecasts, the ship-ping industry, oil, steel, what shape EMI is in, who's building tankers, who's the President of Chad, what the drought's going to do to American grain production, who's looking to buy Chelsea, fish stocks in the North Sea, how the Internet is affecting greetings-card sales, *The Times*, the *Telegraph*, the *Financial Times*, I know it all. You know why? 'Cause that's what I had to do, 'cause if I didn't I was fucked, 'cause it's all part of the same of the same thing, everything all joined up, interconnected, every bit of it, quenelles, veloutés, wine—'

'Clark, please. I didn't mean to imply—'

'And you have the arse to tell me how I should drink this poxy bottle.' Large picked it up. He moved in his chair, shifting his shoulders like a fighter. There was no stopping him now.

'All I was trying to do was—'

'I know as much about wine as anyone in this room. More, probably. I went out with this bird from Christie's for two years. Did you know that, Pricey? Lady Annabel Hot-to-trot.' Pricey shook his head, vastly embarrassed. 'Double-barrelled name but the dirtiest cow in Debrett's. Filthy, she was. I'd give it to her from behind while she sloshed it out in front. You ever done that with one of your waitresses here, Pricey?'

'Clark, don't do this,' Sophie pleaded.

'It's all right, Nef. I'm just having a discussion with Geoffrey here, about the best way to savour a full-bodied burgundy. Well?' There was no reply. 'I haven't told anyone this before, because it's a bit intimate, but what I learnt from that experience was, I like it stirred up a bit. You follow me?'

Geoffrey was looking round. The restaurant had grown silent. The other diners were watching, all food, talk, suspended. 'Clark, please. The other guests.'

Large took no notice. 'I like it best after a good shaking. The better the vintage, the more it needs. I was thinking of patenting the idea, you know, inventing a wine vibrator for when there isn't a sommelier like you floating around, have an adjustable dial setting, you know, starting at a minor tremble on number one for a run-of-the-mill Chianti, all the way up to ten for a jack-hammer pounding for something like a 1975 Penfold.' He took hold of the bottle and handed it to him. 'Go on, Pricey. You have a go. Both hands.'

'Really, a wine of this magnitude . . .'

'Never mind a wine of this magnitude, just shake it about a bit, like you would a pair of maracas.'

'Clark, come on now. This has gone far enough.'

'Oh, I can take this a lot further than this, believe me. All the way up the hill and down again.'

Geoffrey took a breath, then tipped the bottle back and forth carefully. Large stopped his arm.

'Not like that. Like you was Schumacher up on the podium spunking bubbly over the birds, like you was a hero, Pricey, like we all looked up to you, wanted to be like you, successful like you, money and women and crêpe suzettes shooting out your arse, witty and worldly and not a wanker at all.'

'Clark, I can't.'

The man was nearly in tears. Large said nothing, just stared at him, without mercy. He was back in the ring again, implacable, cruel, ruthless in his conviction.

'Yes you can. You want to. You've always wanted to. All these ponces twirling and sniffing your wine like they know. What you'd like to do is to shove a plastic funnel down their gob and watch them choke on the stuff. A hundred and eighty quid a bottle? Makes you sick to your stomach. Do it now, Pricey. Lay it out flat, before I do you.' He leant forward, tapped his fork against his wine glass.

'Seconds out,' he said.

Geoffrey held the bottle out from his chest and began to shake it hard, his right hand gripped round the neck, his left over the body, his neck stretched, his teeth bared, eyes closed, his face rigid with fear and fury. It was almost as if we were witnessing a murder, a strangulation, a man who could take it no longer. You could see everything he hated about his life in those hands, on that face, the lifetime of insults and humiliations, the rage against subservience. He shook the bottle harder and harder, his hands tightening round it to such an extent I thought the glass would break apart, staining us all with his victim's blood. Large looked on calmly.

'That's a very good wrist action you have there, Pricey. No wonder your collar's so stiff.' He tipped his chair back on its two legs. 'OK that'll do. You can crack it open now.'

Geoffrey put the bottle on the table, pulled the corkscrew from his pocket. He was out of breath.

'Would you like to try it?' he said, his voice a thousand miles away.

'Just pour it out.'

The wine came out dark and muddy. Geoffrey's hand was shaking.

'Up to the top, Pricey. Watching you has put a thirst on me.'

We drank three bottles in all, but only the Romanée Conti shaken and only twelve pancakes at the table, two pancakes for me, two for Lilly, Sophie none at all, Large laying siege to the rest, half the wine too, cracking jokes, telling stories, his mouth, his hands, permanently engaged, eating, drinking, spluttering with laugher, the rest of us stilled, enthralled, exhausted by his performance. When the bill came, Large beckoned Geoffrey over.

'No Armagnac tonight?'

'I thought under the circumstances, you might not want . . .'

'What? A night out at the Five Maidens without Pricey gracing the table? What do you take me for? Get that Armagnac out pronto and grab a chair.'

And there we sat, the three of us watching Clark Rossiter and Geoffrey Price, Large acting as if nothing had happened, pouring Geoffrey measure after measure, his voice like an arm draped around Price's shoulder, coaxing, confidential, Price's upturned face optimistic and buoyant, surprised by the latest turn of the evening.

'Clark, I never meant to be disrespectful. I was only trying . . . it's such a great wine.'

'Tasted like shit though all stirred up.'

'Did it?' His eyes were full of tears.

'Course it did, you numpty. And that lot there,' he waved his arm at us, 'never said a word. Not even Charlie here, and he should know.'

'He's his father's son,' Price mumbled.

'He came a lot here, then, old man Pemberton?' Large asked, looking at me.

'Every week almost . . . He was one of my best customers, a gentleman of the old school.'

'All those business lunches.'

'I assumed so.' Price was looking at me now. There was a pause in the air.

'Bet he wasn't as much fun as me, though.'

'A different time, Clark, a different set of rules.'

'Bet he never lost his rag either. Brought up better than me.'

'Please, I wasn't trying to compare—' Large stopped him with his hand.

'This evening, Pricey. Forget what I said. It never happened.'

'If only I thought you meant that.' It was almost a lover's plea.

'I do mean it, Pricey. Don't you know that? We had black velvet before we came here, only Lilly here poured the champagne in first. Set me all out of balance. Good job it never happened, otherwise it would be all her fault.'

'Well, if it never happened . . .' Geoffrey reached over to where the bill lay on the side plate. 'There can be nothing to pay, can there.'

He tore it up, three, four, five times, and threw the shreds over the table. A scrap landed on Large's shoulders. He brushed it off.

'There's a logic to that, I suppose. The psychology of maths.'

Geoffrey Price seized on the phrase. 'The psychology of maths, exactly! The psychology of maths!'

We left as we arrived, Pricey standing by the door waving us goodbye.

Large never went there again. By the time the next week rolled around, he'd found somewhere else, a restaurant a little further out. That didn't matter. It was just an extra twenty minutes in the taxi, that was all. Who cared when it was three o'clock in the morning?

Twelve

For Golden Years, expenditure was gathering momentum. The upkeep of the properties, the managers he had to pay, the nursing staff, the cooks, the cleaners, the utilities bills, the cars, the insurance, money simply gushed through his fingers. On top of that he had new acquisitions to finance, investment in infrastructure to put in place, rising house prices to accommodate, escalating building costs. The once depressed southeast coast was beginning to attract interest. Artists, TV stars, media folk in general had discovered the attraction that years of depression brought. Properties were cheaper down here, houses by the sea, houses in the town, Georgian stand-alones, Victorian terraces, vicarages, you got a bigger bungalow for your buck, for a while at least. Towns that had survived on bread shops and butchers suddenly needed gourmet pantries, delicatessen counters, patisserie corners. Gentleman's outfitters were driven to the wall by purveyors of brightly coloured casual wear made ostensibly for the yachting fraternity. Folk were beginning to find that being offered six varieties of over-priced coffee to drink on a traffic-fumed pavement was something they had always aspired to, whatever the weather. We had been Sunday Supplemented.

Large's borrowings soared, but then so did his projections. Every time he went to the banks, to other investors, they rolled over, legs in the air. The more he asked for, the easier it came. Banks, investors, speculators wanted people like Large. They needed people like Large. Large was their future. They had to spend their money somehow. As everyone knew, the worst thing you could do to your money was to leave it idle, let it atrophy, lose its muscle. As an accountant, I wasn't wholly comfortable, floating this stitched-together Kon-Tiki enterprise out onto this sea of debt, but as Large never failed to point out, 'As long as there are lenders, Charlie, it's our Christian duty to borrow. The only time you have to worry is when the money runs out. But take a look around you. Does it *look* like it's going to run out?' It seemed churlish for me to point out that Lloyd's had said much the same thing to my father.

Like the majority of his breed, Large disliked paying tax. Tax was against natural justice. He was pre-First World War in that way. We had moved Golden Years Holdings to Guernsey, the usual stuff, nominal off-shore directors, Sophie and Large down as paid employees. Large's take on the move was much the same as the Merry Boys. As long as everything was running smoothly, he didn't want to know. He came to St Peter Port with me when we set it up, but even then he was more interested in being taken round the German Occupation ruins, snorkelling, speed-boating, drinking in the evening, than going through the paperwork. I could deal with Mr Nathan Edge. We sailed, rather than flew, on a power boat owned by a friend of his who'd made his money from garages. Large didn't like the look of those idiotic wasp-like planes that flew the regular commercial flights and I agreed. On subsequent trips, which I subsequently took every three or four months, I would take the Poole–St Malo ferry, small enough to be pleasant, large enough to be anonymous.

This was the good times, good times for the business, good times for Large and the flock of quad bikes he and his mates would burn around the lake on Sunday afternoon, good times for Sophie and her Eileen-led West End shopping expeditions, good times for the Merry Boys, good times for the builders, the electricians, the taxi drivers, the cooks and the waiters, good times for me, good times for you, good times for the whole town. It was probably good for Tommy too, but he wasn't in evidence the way he used to be. Tommy's gloss had gone, Lyn's too. Tommy was the past. Tommy was small time, the owner of one, albeit highly successful, shop. He still served behind the counter. Lyn was of the same provenance. Large was of the town and yet more than that. His nature was expansive, his eye took in more than the High Street. He encompassed and he expanded. Yes it was Large you would see strolling down the street, swanning in and out of the estate agents, shadow-boxing with the butcher's son, giving the V sign to some of Jay's dubious friends, treating the town as an arena, but it was also Large who now wrote to the council about the lack of lighting down by the church, Large who donated money to the local Scout hut, and Large who persuaded the headmaster of our old school to organize his sixth-formers to visit house-bound pensioners. There was even talk, he told me with a pride that was almost childlike in its simplicity, of asking him to stand for the council.

'You know what, Charlie. I'll be dining with dignitaries next. Just like your old man. I'm donating to the school, did you know that? A clock.'

'They already have a clock. Above the music school.'

'This is going over the new gymnasium. Kindly donated by Clark Rossiter, that's what it will say. Kindly donated. I'm thinking of giving them some sort of bursary, to send someone like me there, someone who's got the spark but not the education. The Rossiter Fellowship. We're in talks. They're thinking of making me a governor. Your old man was a governor, wasn't he.'

'For about twenty years.'

'He was one of the ones that my mum saw, before I was accepted.'

'Very likely. The governors always took a keen interest in the town. It's where they came from.'

'Exactly my point. I should know in a couple of months. If

276

I do get appointed, it'll put Tommy's nose out and no mistake. He's been trying to get on the board for years.'

I tried hard not to show my displeasure at Large's baring of his newly civic breast. My father's prophecy was taking hold sooner than he had imagined. And yet, why should I complain? I was doing as well out of it as anyone. My increased workload meant an increased fee. Income was good. Opportunities were opening up. The downstairs flat became free. I didn't even have to show the bank a surveyor's report. They advanced me the asking price plus an extra twenty-five per cent so I could do the place up. So do it up I did, tore the centre out, the ebony nude ushering you in this wide open space running front to back, a mother-of-pearl grandmother clock behind the door, an antique settee, high-backed, loose-cushioned, with matching armchairs arranged around the fireplace, an 1850 corner drinks cupboard, decent glass inside in the far wall, the complete works of Gibbon and Dickens in the bookcase recess, John Lewis heavy brocade curtains, two thousand pounds' worth of stereo and an antique French wood-burning stove where the gas fire had stood. It cost me a lot, that stove, but that was all right. I had money to burn.

At the new restaurant, an extra variant had been introduced, all-night poker in the private room at the back. It suited the times. We were all gamblers now. It didn't take place every week, but often enough for the boys to come down, play for seven hours before heading back to the City in a half-past five taxi. Apart from Barry's wife, Charlene, the women rarely played, Sophie never. She would always go home. I didn't join in either. I didn't think it appropriate, an accountant cavalier with risk, adept at masking whatever was in his head. Better to maintain a hesitant respectful presence where money was concerned.

That was why, that late June night, knowing that a poker game was in the offing, I'd driven over, deciding not to drink at all so as not to loosen my guard. Preparation is nine-tenths of any game. There was the usual mixed crowd, Barry and Charlene, another power duo I hadn't met before, a stuffed shirt from the council, Paul Langley the builder, quite a mate of Large's now, Steve Tanner the estate agent, a couple of girls that they had corralled. Unexpectedly, Eileen was there. I hadn't seen her for months. She gave me a little wave through the door as I handed my coat to the attendant. It struck me then that physically she was similar to Katie, a slightly harsh slim body, her manner too. Only the background was different. Usually Barry managed to sit next to Eileen, Barry on one side and whoever was the other single male apart from me on the other. This time though I engineered it so I sat next to her, me on her left, the stuffed shirt on her right. Eileen was in an expansive, sexual mood, a drinking mood too. She was dressed in bold green, boldly cut. Her pallid, angular demeanour set her apart from the others, an attraction in itself. She seemed pleased to see me, tipping wine into my glass the moment I sat down. I decided there and then to leave the car in the car park, take one of the taxis home, perhaps, if her body language was anything to go by, with her in it too. We talked wonderfully, Maria Callas' lovers, the shortcomings of CDs, a dinner Eileen's father once gave for Pavarotti, how extraordinary it was that both Gracie Fields and Dame Eva Turner were born within five miles of each other. She had never heard of Gracie Fields, nor indeed Rochdale. She didn't know that much about Dame Eva Turner either, which I found surprising. I excelled myself, a little bit of operatic history here, an amusing anecdote about Gracie and the Isle of Capri, even sang her a snatch of that dreadful song, 'Sally', to her evident delight. Large noticed it too, giving me a slight shake of the head, as if despairing of me. Well all right, I thought. Maybe I would have looked down on Katie. Doesn't what you're seeing now tell you why. No cheap perfume on her.

The dinner finished. It had been a good evening. Waiters came round to clear the table. A fresh tablecloth was laid, fresh brandy glasses put out, the humidor, another pot of coffee. They knew what was required.

'I'm off, then,' Sophie said. 'See you back at the ranch.' She slung her coat over her shoulders.

'Don't wait up,' Large shouted out after her. 'It's going to take me all night to clear this lot out.'

Sophie left. Eileen stood up, and turned into the large bay window at the back of the room which looked out at the illuminated garden beyond. I came up behind her. They had a sofa-swing on the terrace, I noticed.

'I was wondering if you might like to come back to my flat,' I said. 'I could play you that *Turandot* recording I was talking about.'

Eileen turned to me, her face set. 'I'm sorry?'

'I wondered whether you'd like to come back. I have an interesting collection.'

She gave a short, irritated laugh. 'You're asking me back to look at your etchings?'

'My records. My LPs.'

'Right. I forgot. The vinyl queen. Tell me, have I given you any indication that I would welcome such a suggestion?'

'Not in so many words, no.'

'Just because I tried to make a fist of a conversation with you and your Dame Edith Turner.'

'Eva,' I corrected her. 'Her name was Eva.'

'Couldn't have been paying that much attention then, could I?' She turned. 'Clark,' she called out. 'Set another place. I'm in.'

I picked up my jacket and went outside. Sophie was pacing up and down, looking at her watch.

'No taxi, can you believe it?'

'Have you phoned?'

'There's been some sort of accident on the motorway. They're all caught up in the tailback.' She rubbed her arms. 'I'm not standing here. I guess we'll have to go back in.'

'No.' The thought of another confrontation with Eileen with Large looking on was too much to bear. 'That's all right. My car's here. I'll drive you home.'

'You sure?'

'I shouldn't, but it'll be all right.'

We walked over. I held open the passenger door.

'Charlie,' she purred, 'no one's done that for me for a long time.'

She wriggled her bottom into the seat.

I got in, switched on the ignition.

'Nice car, Charlie. It's like an aeroplane in here. Do you know what all those little buttons do? You look like a man who might not be totally up on his buttons.'

'It took a while.' I started her up. 'The seat warms up, you know, in winter.'

'I thought they all did that, these days.' She snapped her seat belt on. 'You and Eileen seemed to be hitting it off rather well tonight. I thought perhaps the creak of bedsprings might be in the offing.'

'I'm not her type.'

'No? Whose type are you?'

I drove through the narrow country lanes. We saw a barn owl flying low alongside us, Sophie squealing in excitement. The light of the town drew near. We had to drive through the centre. At the first roundabout we hit the fluorescent lighting. We were the only car around. I was beginning to wish I hadn't offered.

'Do you still see that funny little thing from Monkton's?'

'You know I don't.'

'Large has promoted her, you know. She's practically running the place.'

'I didn't know.'

We passed the bus shelter, lit in an empty glare.

'Remember when you found me here?' Sophie tugged at her hair.

'The night Large walked out.'

She shook her head. 'He'd been gone a week by then. I was so wasted when you found me. No sleep, just vodka and cigarettes. You know what I thought when I got in your car? I thought you were going to whisk me off home.'

'I did whisk you home.'

'I mean your home, Charlie, smuggle me up the back stairs to your bedroom, Charles Pemberton, his blood up at last. You'd always been sweet on me, giving me little presents, holding the door open, hanging round when I went for a swim, pretending you were interested in my fish.'

'My fish, actually . . .'

'I kind of wanted you to, that night, wondering what I'd do if you pulled over, tried your luck. I still don't know. Missed an opportunity there.'

The car held hard round the corner, her body sliding into mine. I shifted myself away. I'd had way too much to drink.

'I was too fond of you to do something like that.'

'Fond of me!' She pushed herself back against the passenger door. 'What about wanting me, and to hell with the consequences.'

She touched my leg with her bare foot. She was mocking me with every inch of her flesh she could summon. We'd stopped at traffic lights. A police car was waiting on the other side of the crossroads, its snazzy lines, cut bold like my companion, ready to pounce. They were staring at us. It was two thirty in the morning.

'Have you got your seat belt on properly? I'm way over the limit here.'

'Don't look at them,' she said. 'Relax. We're perfectly sober, remember, a nice respectable young couple going home after a nice respectable evening. Strict observers of the drink-driving laws. Unlike our parents, who, as far as I can make out, drove around pissed *all* the time.' She nudged me with her foot again. 'You still haven't answered my question? Didn't it cross your mind at all, to pull over, see what happened?'

The lights turned. The road was blotchy. I let the clutch out, felt the car hiccup as the engine stalled. I twisted the ignition, once, twice, the engine racing as it caught. The police car hadn't moved. I lurched ahead, the wheels screeching.

'Jesus, Charlie, are you trying to get yourself done?' She turned to look. 'Christ, they're turning.' She twisted the mirror to get a better look. 'They're coming after you. Quick, put your foot down. Get out of here.'

'I'll get arrested.'

'You're going to get that anyway. You'll lose your licence! Quick, down the next turning, then first left. Come on, Charlie. Just do it!'

I swung right, pushing on the accelerator. The sides of the buildings slid into one another.

'Left,' she said. 'And turn off your lights.'

There was a line of meagre shops, their back ends facing onto the road: concrete driveways, parking lots, brick walls, colours bled pale in the lamp light. Sophie jabbed her arm at the windscreen.

'There, see! Turn right as you go in. There's space behind the wall.'

The car bounced over the concrete lip. I swung hard into a loading bay, Sophie squealing as I stamped on the brakes, a plastic dustbin bouncing up over the bonnet. I sat there, gripping the wheel, my breath coming in gasps. I'd never known such fear. Sophie giggled.

'I must be mad,' I said. 'They'll have got my number, anyway.'

'So? Once you get safely home, there's nothing they can do about it. We'd better lie low for a while, though. Turn off the engine.' She unclipped her seat belt, twisted round to lean against the door again. We waited. No whoop of a siren, no blur of blue light, no engine growl. We'd given them the slip.

'Where the bloody hell are we?' I said.

'The back of the chip shop. They didn't keep the bins out in our day. Too many rats.' She started to laugh again.

'Funny to think the room where it all started is just a few yards away. Probably hasn't changed, the same peeling wall-paper, the same smell of chip fat, the same rats on the stairs. Well, not the *same* rats, exactly. I don't know how long a rat lives, do you?'

'Five years?'

'That long. We were always seeing them, on the stairs, rooting around in the sacks. Once when we were fucking, a rat came into the room and sat down on the floor and watched us. Couldn't take his eyes off us. Couldn't take his eyes off *me*. It was so funny to see him, sitting back, twitching his whiskers, watching us hard at it. I had the better view. I was on top, see, doing most of the work as usual.' She nudged me with her foot. 'You still haven't answered my question.'

'What question?'

'The question that made you stall the car. Why didn't you try your luck that night? Didn't you want to?'

She put her head to one side, like a questioning dog. She had a smile on her face, all sex and smugness. I could see her lips and her white teeth and the steel of her bare shoulders. I knew I ought to push her out, but I hadn't the strength.

'You never gave me any reason to think that you felt that way for me.'

'What's reason got to do with anything? You've got to learn to take it, Charlie, take it while you can. I might have said no. But the state I was in, a one-night stand to get back at Large and my dad, why not? Dad got him that job, you know, in London.'

'I didn't know.'

'Got him the introduction, at least. Thought he'd get him

away from me that way. He did. For a while.' She placed her leg back on the seat.

'I didn't know,' I repeated.

'There's an awful lot you don't know, isn't there.' She tucked the flap of her skirt between her legs. I was fed up with being condescended to.

'I know a hell of a lot more than you credit me with.'

'Really?' She placed her foot on my knee, wriggled her toes. 'What do you know?'

'I know you're making fun of me.'

'I do that to all the men I fancy, Charlie.'

'Please. And don't call me Charlie. You know I hate it.'

'What if I asked Charlie to kiss me. Would he hate being called Charlie then?'

I stared at the blank wall. She patted the seat.

'Come on, Charlie, come and kiss me. Kiss me like you've always wanted to. Kiss me and I'll never call you Charles again.'

I didn't move. She nudged me again.

'Everything carries a price. This is mine. The sale of the century, don't you think?'

Charles looked. The sale of the century. He moved over, into a different world. How long he was there he doesn't know. He remembers pulling back, though.

'Don't look so startled, Charlie,' she mocked. 'Underwear is so over-rated, don't you think?'

*

I parked the car round the corner, on the waste ground by the sycamore that come autumn would soon start shedding its leaves across the lawn. Apart from the mowing, it was the only gardening job my father did with good grace, raking in the leaves, carrying them to one of the three compost heaps dotted round. She took me by the hand, and half ran down the drive, past where Rhoda's conversion was being built.

'Don't worry,' she whispered, 'he hasn't installed the old hag in there yet.'

It thrilled me to hear her describe Large's mother that way. I thought I was the only one who'd never liked her.

The old door opened to the old push, only it was Sophie's shoulder and hand rather than mine that gave it the needed impetus. Jesus, I thought, she's learnt that trick quickly. Was she as familiar with the rest of the house as that, the banister rail that shook as you held it on the way down, the light by the cellar which you had to press in as well as flick down, the handle on my parents' bedroom door that had to be pulled towards you before you could open it. My parents' bedroom. I had a feeling I would be seeing it soon enough. The kitchen door, too, gave in to her with a creak, though it opened onto a disquietingly different aspect, colder than before, the room more expansive, large ceramic tiles on the floor, an island unit of dark wood standing full square in the centre, like an altar, surrounded by the artefacts of worship; white cupboards with dark, fathomless granite tops beneath; an eye-level grill sunk into the wall, an air extractor above; a breakfast bar where the dresser had been, a six-foot-high wine rack (in the kitchen! I could hear my father's voice in anguish) and the corner where my mother's collection of antique teapots had once stood, a collection which had taken her over thirty years to assemble, was now occupied by a gigantic American refrigerator, in Chevrolet cherry red. Sophie pulled the chrome handle and pulled out a half-consumed bottle of champagne, a top-hat stopper stuck in the neck. She popped it with one hand and grabbed me by the hand again as it skittered across the floor. A quick, thoroughly shameless tour followed, Sophie half proud, half ashamed at what we saw, her body indecently close. The dimmed lighting that suddenly flooded the drawing room revealed a huge television screen on the wall where my grandfather's ham-fisted painting of Balmoral had once hung. Below three huge curved cream-leather settees encircled a glass top which stood on four ugly teak elephant legs. It was an odd height, too low for a dining table, too high for a coffee table. Magazines were scattered on it, *TV Times, GQ, Viz.*

'His trophy from Bangkok,' she said, swigging from the bottle. 'Apparently they would lie under and it and pay to watch girls shit. Can you believe it?'

Wine spilled down her front, streaks of cloth clinging to the swell of her breast. She touched the stain with her fingers, a naked stare in her eyes. Then it was upstairs, Sophie leading the way, me barely able to tell the difference between the present and the past, the heavy wooden panels on the way up still unpainted, the passageway still uncarpeted, but Sophie's bare legs and her bare feet in front of me. My nerves were hammering. I was scared, out of myself. At the door at which as a child I had been taught to knock, she gave the handle a pull and pushed it open. It had been a big room, my parents' bedroom, two long windows looking over the garden at the back, but now it seemed to have shrunk, despite the fact that there was barely anything in it, just a series of full-length mirrors on the wall to the left of the bed, and another massive television at the bed's foot. Behind the mirrors, she told me, running her finger along the glass, was a walk-in cupboard, unable she said to even account for *half* her clothes, a boast, under the circumstances, quite lost on me. The bed was ghastly, a mock leopard-skin cover, at least I assumed it was mock, and a console area to one side, a suggestion of activity rather than repose, its shape neither round nor rectangular, but a perversion of both, with pillows arranged round the edges, as if to emphasis the variety of libidinous opportunities afforded to the occupants. The sheets were a murky yellow, special tailored no doubt. I skirted round it to the window, expecting at least a semblance of familiarity there. There was a dark gaping hole where the croquet lawn should have been.

'What in God's name . . .'

Sophie flicked a switch on the console. Light broke across,

the void transformed into an as yet unfinished swimming pool. She came up behind me, took my hands, held them against her flanks, pressing herself close.

'It's going to be heated all the year round, so I can swim there whenever I want. Costs a fortune, apparently, but won't that be great?'

'I loathe swimming pools,' I told her. 'What's wrong with the lake?'

She pushed me away playfully. 'Nothing's wrong with the lake. But not in the winter, Charlie. In the summer, that's a different matter. Remember the last time I swam there?'

'Of course I remember.'

'Couldn't take your eyes off me, could you?' she said, tipping the bottle back to her mouth again, not taking her eyes off me.

'Who could have?'

'And now?' She dropped the bottle into a wastepaper basket by the bed and came close again. The last time I had been in this room, my mother had been packing her shawl.

'Charlie Pemberton. Who'd have thought it?' She kissed me, slowly, full and wet, her body almost liquid.

'I'm not sure I can do this,' I said. I was bloody sure I couldn't.

'Why? Is Charlie nervous?'

'Hugely.'

'You got to learn to take what's on offer. Grab it with both hands. That's if you want it enough.'

She crossed her arms and pulled her dress over her head. She stood before me. It was all there, in this room, everything I had ever wanted, Charles Pemberton, mastery of person, mastery of place.

'Are you just going to stand there all night?' she said. 'Or are you going to come here and let me fuck every last drop out of you.'

She pulled me down onto the bed. I surprised her, the

alacrity with which I took to it. I surprised myself. A while later we drew apart. I leant across, pulled the discarded champagne out of the basket and took a swig. It trickled down onto her chest. Mine too. That seemed about right.

'Well?' She had a sheen to her. She lay back, her breasts floating in the light. They were the most wonderful things I had ever seen.

'I'm exhausted.'

She touched my nose, pleased with herself. 'So, it was worth the wait, would you say.'

'Oh, Sophie . . .' I touched her head, traced the flow of her hair, the blood pulsing in her neck. 'But why me, why now? I still don't understand. You had everything, a career, a husband, a future. And yet you came back here, to this town. To me.'

'And Large.'

'And Large.'

'He's never told me I'm beautiful. Never. Do you know what a joy that is.'

'I've never told you that.'

'You think it, though. Everyone does. You've no idea, the burden of being beautiful. When I saw him that morning, standing outside with those fish and chips, it was such a relief. He saw through all that. I couldn't wait to get back.'

'Was California that bad.'

'California is just the worst place to be for someone like me. You're never allowed to forget it, not for a moment. It makes all the easy things easy and all the hard things well nigh impossible. Large is so different from all that, dirty fingernails, can't shave properly, doesn't give a toss. Fuck-you success, that's what he was, least that's what I thought.'

'He's not?'

'Not in the way I'd imagined. That flat in Canary Wharf he keeps on about? It must have been the smallest in the block. Oh, he was a success of sorts, but nothing spectacular.

That's what he'd always been to me. Spectacular. He's more small-minded than I thought. Do you know he gives me an allowance? Like I'm a fucking housekeeper.'

'I never put him down as being mean.'

'It's degrading, Charlie. He has three accounts and I'm allowed to share only one of them, where we pay all the house bills and stuff. I don't know where his money is. He's so funny about it.'

I said nothing.

'I'm his wife, for Christ's sake. He treats me like one of his manageresses.' She rolled alongside me, one hand stroking my stomach. 'That money on the bed. Do you believe that story of his?'

'No reason not to.'

'Tossing him off like that? I'm fucked if I would.'

'Perhaps he wouldn't have asked you.'

'I don't think she did it. Screwed on it, yes. But that? I think it's something he wishes he had done. Large and the ultimate money shot. He regrets not doing it. That's why he's always boasting about it.' She scooped champagne droplets onto her fingers. 'Fancy a shower? I've put in wonderful shower heads.'

I looked across the room, remembering.

'I thought he was going to put a Jacuzzi in here.'

'I talked him out of it. Told him he'd get pissed one night, fall in it and drown. He's bloody ruining this house. Do you know what I call it? The dog's dinner. I mean look at those mirrors. No taste at all.' Our eyes met in the glass. 'Though they do have their attractions.' She lay back, splayed one leg out.

'See?'

'Yes. I need to go to the loo.'

'Perhaps they had a mirror by the bed. Perhaps that was it. Touch me, Charlie.'

Charlie did as he was told.

'How many hands do you think have been there before you?'

'Sophie.'

'Doesn't it interest you at all? Large's, of course, and my ex's, Wallace. His hands were always very clean, they had to be in his line of work. Then there was Randle, and the basketball player and one of the writers in residence at Keele, eager to read me his short story, and now yours. Oh, I was forgetting Tommy. Tommy's were the first. I wonder if he ever thinks about them, his fingers lying at the bottom of the ocean, what they used to do.'

She raised herself up a little.

'What do you think? Is it pretty?'

'Not at all.'

'Ugly, then?'

'Not exactly, more like something from the deep. It doesn't mean to say it's not . . .'

'Attractive?'

'Mysterious.'

'And yet so common.'

'I suppose.'

'Only some are more common than others. Take Bee Bee's, for instance. Bee Bee's is very common indeed.' We both laughed.

'There was one more, of course,' she said, touching my hand with hers.

'One more what?'

'One more visitor to these shores. Can't you guess?'

'Sophie, I can't.'

'Go on. Someone linked to my studies.'

'A teacher?'

'A teacher!'

'I can't think. Duncan?'

She punched me in the arm. 'It begins with a D, though.'

'Sophie, I don't know any other D's.'

'Yes you do. We all know another D. The big D. Daddy.'

'Your father! Jesus Christ, Sophie. I'm sorry. I had no idea . . .'

'No.' She held my hand fast. 'Not my father, you idiot. Yours.'

Downstairs someone knocked into something, a table, an umbrella stand.

Sophie sat up.

'Who put that fucking thing there?' Large's voice was unmistakable.

I turned in panic. 'I thought you said . . . ?'

She put her hand to my mouth. 'Shh.'

She slipped out of bed and locked the door, then sprang back, giggling. I was petrified. We heard him coming up the stairs, his steps over-careful, a man full of drink.

'Nef?' The voice came on as he drew nearer. He turned the door handle. 'Nef? Are you awake?'

'I am now. Is that you, Large?'

'Course it's fucking me. Who else it's going to be? Have you locked the door again?'

'Looks like it, doesn't it. I thought you weren't coming back tonight.'

'They were playing like cunts, the lot of them. Fooling about, flicking pretzels at each other, waste of fucking time, Barry, Jay, Charlene. Eileen was no better. I though you said Charlie might be cracking her open tonight.'

'Apparently not.'

'Well someone should, tight little cow.' The door handle rattled again. 'Come on, Nef. I'm in the mood for a little Egyptian. I want to toot and cummoon.'

'You're pissed, that's what you are. Try again tomorrow, when you're sober.'

'Don't mess me about, Nef. Open up, there's a lamb chop.'

'A lamb to the slaughter, more like. I don't like it when you're like this, Large. You know I bruise easily.'

'Locking the door on me.' Resignation was creeping into his voice. 'Who you got in there, then?'

'Wouldn't you like to know?'

There was an effortless languor to her voice. She was smiling, unperturbed. Large banged on the door again.

'You're denying me my conjugal rights, woman?'

'Absolutely.'

'This wouldn't have gone down well in Akhenaten's day. He'd have drowned you in the bulrushes.'

'You can lay claim to them in the morning. Eight thirty sharp. I'll feel more like it then. Now go away and get some rest and let me scandalize this local.'

'Anyone I know?'

'Charlie, who else? We've been having it off ever since we left.'

'Having it off, eh? My, we are posh. Any good?'

'Marvellous.'

'Well, don't wear him out too much. He's got a heavy day tomorrow.' There was a pause. 'Come on, Nef. Let me in. There's a girl.'

'No. I told you.' Her voice was firm, almost indignant. I might as well not have been there. 'Go and sleep it off. We'll make love in the morning. You'll enjoy it more, anyway. You always feel extra-randy the morning after.'

We heard him stumble away; it sounded like into my old room at the far end of the corridor. She turned into me, her finger on my lips.

'He'll be dead to the world in five minutes,' she murmured, 'then you'd better go. You know the way out, I presume.'

'But my father.'

'I shouldn't have said,' she whispered. 'It was nothing.'

'But what happened? Did he . . .'

'No! It was a long time ago, Charlie, up by the lake, a girl in a summer dress, the older man with wandering hands. It happens all the time.'

She rolled away. I was astonished at her sangfroid. I sat on the edge of the bed, pulling at my clothes while she fussed with the pillows.

'Will I see you again?' I said.

'Of course. It's a small town.'

'You know what I mean. You could come to the flat, Thursday afternoons or something.'

'Charlie.' Her look became reproachful. 'Let's keep it simple, shall we? What happened tonight was tonight.'

'A night to remember.'

'That's what they said about the *Titanic*. Remember, no talk about it, that's all. Our little secret.'

'Who would I talk to?'

She ruffled my hair.

'That's my Charlie. Ever reliable. I bet you know lots of secrets.'

'A few.'

'Then here's another. That police car didn't turn round at all. You were in the clear. If you hadn't listened to me, you'd be safely tucked up in bed by now.' She pulled the duvet up to her chin, as if protecting herself from my gaze. I put my hand on where her stomach appeared to be.

'I don't want to be tucked up safely in bed. I'm fed up with being tucked up safely in bed. I want . . .' I pressed down, the stretch of her immense.

'Charlie. Please.'

'OK. I'm going. Look out of the window, though.'

I closed the door behind me, oddly emboldened. All the lights were on, the corridor, the stairs, the downstairs rooms. If Large chose to open my bedroom door now . . . I took the stairs swiftly, my hands running down the balustrade, every ridge, every smooth plateau as familiar as my mother's voice, chiding me for being late for school. Out through the kitchen, onto the veranda and there I was standing on the lip of the black hole where the croquet lawn had been. I looked up, my hands fishing with my fly, my flesh sticky and bloated. Sophie was standing at the window, a kimono wrapped around her. I could smell it all as I started to piss, her, me, the waste of an evening. I pissed long and hard, listening to the arc of it falling into nothing. Was there ever such a clamour? It seemed louder than the breaking glass, louder than the gunshots, the sheer persistence of it.

Then it stopped. At my parents' window, Sophie had gone. I was drained, the house, the garden had taken it all. Up by the lake a fox started barking. I walked to my car and drove home.

Back in my new flat I lit the stove, opened a bottle of my father's wine and watched the flames till dawn.

Thirteen

I waited a week before I rang her, went back to the flat midday to call, when I knew Large would not be at home. She greeted me as if nothing had happened. I could picture her standing in the drawing room, holding the phone, looking out through the window. How many times had I stood there, fielding calls for my mother, my father. Why, even the slight echo surrounding her was familiar.

'Charlie! How are you?'

'Cold.' I was heartened by her choice of name. It suggested an acknowledgement of the bargain we'd made. 'I thought I'd take the afternoon off, light the fire. You could come round. You haven't seen my new place.'

'Charlie. It wouldn't be a good idea.'

'It was last week.'

'Was it? I don't think those sorts of things are ever a *good* idea, Charlie. They just happen even though you know they shouldn't. I can't start meeting you in the afternoons as if you were a tennis coach.'

'Don't you want to see me at all?'

'I see you most Wednesdays, weekends too. Isn't that enough?'

'It's not the same.'

'Ah. You want me to be indiscreet again. Katie's no longer available, Eileen gave you the thumbs down. She couldn't wait to tell me. If she'd said yes, we would never have happened. I was just the rebound girl.' She was almost indignant.

'It was nothing like that and you know it. You made me

realize what I really wanted. It took me by surprise, how easily it came. It took you by surprise too.'

'Charlie. We went to bed together. We got away with it. Just. Let's leave it at that. We were all a little crazy that evening, but that's what it was, *one* crazy evening. It was never going to be two crazy evenings, or a series of them. Let's face it, you're not that crazy.'

'You sure about that?'

'We can only be what we are, Charlie.'

'And what are you, then? Married to a London chuck-out made good, before that a surgeon from the west coast, and before that the same London chuck-out made bad. None of them seem to have helped you find your bearings.'

'And you could?' The conversation was heading into dreamt-of areas. There was no going back now.

'This is the new Charles Pemberton speaking, his blood up at last. I want to take you away.'

'Everybody wants to take me away. I'm not a fucking trophy, you know.'

'Not sweep-you-off-your-feet take you away. Take you away, rationally, calmly, like I did that night I found you by the bus stop. You hoped I'd do something then, you said, but I wasn't ready then. I wouldn't be taking you away, Sophie. I'd be bringing you home. Leave him. Come with me.'

'As if I could. Where, come with you?'

'Wherever you wanted. There's a nice accountancy business in Winchester I saw advertised this month.'

'Winchester! Where the fuck's that? Hampshire!'

'Laugh it off if you want. I can give you what you daren't admit to wanting, stability, foundation, a fixed horizon. It sounds hopelessly old fashioned, I know, but you've lived all wrong, and you know it. That's why you left California, because you couldn't bear to see your father behaving like that. It disgusted you, though you pretend otherwise.'

'It's what they do, older men. Most of them are fathers, I guess. This one happened to be mine.'

'It can't have come as too much of a surprise. There's only one reason a man of his age goes to California.'

'It wasn't just the one, that was it. It was anyone under the age of thirty he could lay his hands on. It made me wonder, how he looked at me. I'm their age, for Christ's sake. I'd have to have dinner with them, meet them on the beach, hanging on his arm, falling out of their halter tops. He even got Wallace to see one professionally. Can you imagine it, my husband coming home, eating dinner, holding me in our bed, his fingers still warm from my father's lover's . . . OK, I jumped ship. What of it? It's what you have to do sometimes.'

'And you think I'm unable to take that risk, not crazy enough? Isn't what I'm doing now a disclaimer to that?'

'Disclaimer?' She was scornful. 'What are you Charlie, a lawyer?'

'Of sorts. Facts, figures, strengths, weaknesses, eking out the truth from my clients, representing their best interests, saving them from their own excesses. I do that for everyone. I could do that for you. You could study again. Go back to university. I could buy a boat. Wouldn't you like that?'

'Charlie.'

'You would, I know you would. When did you last study your fish, use your brain? The wine bar, the poker evenings, that ridiculous bedroom, it's all nonsense. Large isn't for you. He's the wrong sort. You know it. He'll never be right.'

'You're talking about class, I take it.'

'Call it whatever you want. It's written on your face every time he launches into one of his ungrammatical monologues, the way you tap your foot, lower your eyelids. I've seen you looking at me sometimes, when he's in full throttle, a slight raising of the eyebrows, only for me. It's entertaining enough,

297

but we're the only ones who can really see it, the brutal paucity of it all. You and me, Sophie, you and me. Come round now.'

'No.'

'Yes. I'll show you something, something huge.'

'Don't be disgusting.'

'Not that, something that will set you reeling.'

'What?'

'I can't say. A demonstration. Fire. Heat.'

'Charlie . . .'

'Charles. Call me Charles. Come round now. You won't regret it.'

'I can't.'

'Yes you can. We've got all afternoon, Sophie. You can say my name, and I can say yours. No Nefertiti, no Californian beach goddess. Just Sophie Marchand, the girl I've always known. I'll transform your life.'

Silence. I was hovering on greatness. The world was teetering on balance.

'Why am I listening to you?' Her voice was small, plaintive.

'Because I'm offering a way out.'

'From what?'

'From everything. From having to be who you are.'

'What about Large?' Her voice was quiet.

'What about him?'

'This is about him, isn't it, the town, the house, me. It's all about him. A fight for possession.'

'Not possession. Desire. Being possessed, lit by the fire of another. What gets burnt in the flame, that's possession.'

'Charles.'

'See. You're halfway there already. Quickly, don't hesitate. I'm five minutes away. I'll come and get you if you want, like I did before. Not my father's old car, though.' It was the wrong thing to say. The moment I said it, I knew, it was the wrong thing to say.

'No, no, no!' She was coming to her senses again, the ones

that had driven her across the Atlantic and back again. 'There's not a moat here, Charlie. I'm not some damsel in distress. I don't want to do this. Not to you, not to me and not to Large. Nor should you. He's saved us, Charlie, me from Silicon Valley, you from death by a thousand calculators. What were you before he came back? What was I? Hasn't he set you free? He has done me. Yes, there's a price to pay, but there always is. Yes, he's impossible. Yes, he's a bully, but God he's alive, drunk or sober he's alive, and you know what, if he didn't have a bean, he'd be alive too. Would you? Would I? We need people like Large. We couldn't survive without them, not any more. To use a phrase I'm sure you're familiar with, he's our main man. That's what gets you. If I'd married Tommy you wouldn't feel like this at all. Tommy's one of us. Tommy had a right to me, like the school had a right to me, like Keele had a right to me, yes, like your father had a right to me. Large, Large came in and stole it all. The school, me, this house. That's what gets to you. You've had me in your old home, in your parents' bedroom, now Large's house, now Large's bedroom but it isn't revenge enough. Well, no, Charlie. A thousand fucking times no. Fuck off, Charlie. Fuck off to hell.'

Months passed. I didn't see her at all. When I tried to ring, she'd hang up. I worked on the embittered playwright's returns. Haydn Castle was having problems with the man from the VAT. Cracks began to appear in the Golden Years Insurance Scheme.

Although he had put aside a small number of rooms for sudden demand, all the projections that he'd made had assured him that no significant take-up would happen for at least five years. There was a sudden cold spell in October, coupled with a severe bout of influenza, one of those new-strain varieties that periodically sweep across the land carrying hospitals and doctors' surgeries and healthy sixty-five-year-olds before them. The problem wasn't those who succumbed, they were safely six foot under or scattered over any number of Kentish crematorium gardens. It lay with their spouses (they were not the generation to have partners) who now, faced with any number of conundrums – family stresses, insecurity, loneliness, or sheer bloody-mindedness – decided to cash in their policies and log in early. That November, the second week to be exact, twelve policy holders made applications to exercise their Golden Years option. But Golden Years didn't have twelve rooms waiting. Golden Years didn't have even half that number. They had three, one at Monkton's, one down at Hastings, and one at Burmarsh. Large called me in a panic.

'I'm going to need some ready cash, Charlie. I'm going to have to book accommodation in rival homes until some of our own rooms come available. If they were halfway decent, they'd want to help me out, but they won't. They'll wring their hands and charge me double. It's a bastard, I know, but I can't see any way out.'

He was excitable, headstrong, risk-disposed. He'd do it in a moment, and fuck the money. I had to be at my most measured, speak like an avuncular, wood-panelled office.

'You don't want to give them that satisfaction, losses on tax concessions, early calls on investments notwithstanding. There must be another way. What about this new place at Cranbrook?'

He'd recently acquired another property, Burnham House, already in use, but severely run down. There had been some, possibly litigious, issues with the former owners, health and safety concerns, improper use of tranquillizers, endemic negligence, and though the price he'd offered was rock bottom, they had been glad to get shot of it, the council too. It hadn't looked good, what had been going on, on their patch.

'Have you seen it? It's a fucking shit hole. It would kill the brand stone dead. '

'You misunderstand me. You can't move your new Golden Years policy-holders there, but there's nothing to stop you transferring some of your ordinary residents from other homes there. Move them out, refurbish their old rooms and lo and behold Golden Years gets its first key-holder residents.'

'And the relatives of those we move will cry blue murder. The press'll hang me out to dry. With good cause too. They hate moving, oldies.'

'Then choose residents with no relatives. No relatives, and if you can find them, no visitors either. That way there'll be no one to raise objections on their behalf.'

'God, but you're a cold-hearted bastard. That's brilliant. I'll have Katie go through the files special. But I'll still have to tell them something, why they're being moved. I only need one to kick up a fuss, and the whole thing'll get blown wide open.'

I cleared my throat. It seemed obvious to me.

'Asbestos,' I said. 'Why don't you tell them their rooms aren't safe any more, that they have asbestos in the ceiling. Tell you're moving them for their own good. You don't want to, but you have no option.' He went quiet for a moment.

'Christ, Charlie, you're better than Wonder Woman. Asbestos, death-watch beetle, galloping scrapie, they won't like it, but that's life. It'll save me thousands.'

The conversation was over.

He moved them out a week later, done with an efficiency that would have done justice to Vichy France. He didn't use the people-carriers. He didn't want them talking together. He hired taxis instead, Jay and his mates scurrying round the county ferrying in their personal effects. It took a day and a half. At the end of the second morning, Large came stumbling into my office, faded jeans and a pale green folder under his arm.

'I need a fucking drink,' he said.

I went to the little drinks cabinet I had put in place, poured him a whisky. He sank back, chucking the file on my desk.

'Thank God that's over. It's been horrible, Charlie, horrible, I can't tell you how bad. We've only just finished.'

He knocked back the whisky, helped himself to another, rubbed his face with his hands.

'That's them, you know, the ones we moved.' He pointed to the file. 'I want you to give them each a little gift, Charlie, a bit of cash to make up for it, a hundred quid each. Hide it away somewhere, can you do that?'

I leafed through the files. Mrs Todd, Mrs Mulvane, George Henty, the names had all meant something to somebody once. They'd all had lives, lives with husbands and wives, children and work, colleagues and lovers. And this was the end for them, Patricia Beaumont, eighty-seven, Daisy Sutcliffe, seventy-four, Donald Coleman, seventy, Christina Palfrey, eighty-eight, Mrs Hooker, eighty-nine.

'Mrs Hooker?' I said. 'She's gone?' Large took the file from me.

'It's a bastard, isn't it. She didn't want to go; none of them did. They might not have had no relatives, but they had friends, playing cards, having a crafty fag in the smoking room. But what choice did I have? You know that old boy opposite Lilly, your mum's old room, Henry Glover. Held on to the bar of his bed like he was halfway up the Eiger, me and Katie trying to work his fingers loose. He was going on and on about Walter, what was going to happen to Walter, had I told Walter?'

'His son?'

'This fucking blackbird that he feeds every morning. Who would feed Walter when he came tomorrow morning and he wasn't there? He didn't want to leave him. He was crying his name out, "Walter, Walter." Broke my heart, him doing that, broke my fucking heart.' His eyes were brimming with tears, his voice wavering. 'I mean, it could have been my mum we was dragging away, could have been yours. When we finally got him to his feet and out the room, he sagged back in my arms, like all the life had gone out of him. I might as well have taken him out and shot him. I never want to see that again, not as long as I live.'

He got up, brought the bottle back over.

'Do you think we could catch this Walter of his, take him

down? No, you're probably right. Chances are he'll find another. I mean all he's got to do is to put his breadcrumbs out and bob's your uncle. All birds like breadcrumbs, don't they?' He pulled out a handkerchief, blew his nose. 'Bet you in a month's time he'll be so pleased with his new robin or whatever he won't remember Walter at all. But, Jesus, what he put me through this morning. But asbestos. That was a light-ning touch, Charlie. Don't know what I would have done without that.'

He looked exhausted. I didn't like to tell him that the income from Golden Years Holdings had been down for the third successive month.

He sighed.

'You deserve a lunch. So do I. I'll take you to the golf club. You wouldn't believe it, but we got another problem that needs sorting out too.'

We drove out. He'd been a member for over a year, crashed through the waiting list to the top of the queue. Outside golfers were playing in their shirtsleeves. It was warm for the time of year. As we sat down he beckoned over the girl in the black dress standing by the coffee machine. She came over, a differ-ent girl, the same breezy familiarity. I recognized it right away.

'Polly here's looking for a job up at Monkton's,' Large told me, smiling up at her. 'Seems we're too frisky for her here.'

'Mr Rossiter!' she scolded. She pulled on her skirt. 'Waiting on tables, it's not much, is it.'

Large nodded in approval. 'If you don't want it, you won't get it, not in this life. Well, what do you think, Charlie? She Golden Years material?'

I looked her in the face. This was how they did it, girls like Bee Bee and Polly. I ordered a sherry.

'I'm having lunch with our old headmaster,' Large said. 'Can you believe it?'

'Godly Miller?'

'The very same. He's retiring next year.' He sat back, a

glass of mineral water in his hand. Polly returned with my sherry. Too sweet.

'How's Sophie?' I asked.

'Never better.'

'Only we haven't seen her much the last few months. Not Wednesdays, nor the Merry Boys.'

'I know. She's getting to be a right stay-at-home. Think she could be getting broody?'

'I wouldn't know, Large.'

'It would make sense.' He looked across where Polly was standing, and lowered his voice. 'Between you and me, some days she's dead eager for it, won't let up until she's squeezed the last bit of toothpaste out the tube so to speak. Other times she's not interested at all. It's like she's trying to get herself pregnant, you know, her cycles and that, rather than just wanting a bit. Like it's an ends to a mean.' He looked a little hurt, genuinely puzzled.

'I'm no expert, but I thought that's what women were like about sex. Not so indiscriminately keen as men.'

He nodded. 'There's that, of course.' He thumbed his nose. 'Indiscriminately keen. That's a good one. I like that, Charlie. I wouldn't mind that on my grave. Here lies Clark Rossiter. Indiscriminately keen. Now, more importantly . . .'

Six months ago he'd bought a new property, Cranleigh Court in Margate. Paul Langley, the builder, had had his men in for weeks, but with very little to show for it. Large had turned up uninvited a week before, and not a builder in sight, just upended wheelbarrows and sacks of hardening plaster.

'They're playing us for Charlies, Charlie. I saw the bill they put in for that month. Apparently there were five men working there that day. All the time I was there I never saw a single one of them. Funny that. I want you to go through their accounts, every last penny. Get me some ammo. Give it to me pronto. Yesterday would be a good date to aim for. I'm meant to be seeing him in a couple of days. Game of golf, would you believe. If you could come up with something . . . We usually have a little wager. I might well lay a big one on him, then tell him what I know. See how his game is then.'

I went back to the office, fished out Lumley's books and took them home. I threw a few bundles of fuel into the stove, and spread them out, went through the bills and receipts one by one, itemizing all the materials that Langley had billed us for over the last six months, the hours they had claimed, the number of workers, the VAT. Of course it was fraudulent, or at least a good part of it was, something like an extra two hours added for every one worked, materials dribbling through their fingers like water, the whole thing wildly out of balance, almost improbable. The more I examined their invoices, the more it became obvious that as the months progressed from June to November, so did their audacity. What had taken three hours in July took fifteen in September; the average rate of plaster usage in June had tripled come October. Paul Langley and his associates had become careless, careless and greedy, to the extent that at one point he (or someone) had turned the figure 7 into 97 simply by squashing the extra digit where there was no room. What did they think, that no one would notice this slurry of scams? That I'd turn a blind eye? In fact they'd been right. No one had. What did we care how much it cost? It was all being paid for by the loans we were taking out, passing the debt on, from one institution to another. It wasn't the figures that had betrayed him, it was Lumley's attitude, the belief he shouldn't have to bother with the detail of his deception, that it was his right to thumb his nose at us. Had he been present when Large had turned up, had his men been scurrying up and down ladders, dropping a few sacks of plaster just to demonstrate the profligacy of their calling, nothing would have happened. But he didn't, and so . . . and so here I was, loading the shot for Large's musket.

By eight I had most of it nailed down. I could have rung him, gone round to his office in the morning, but the chance of seeing Sophie was too good to miss. She'd avoided me for too long. I walked round, chill in the air, my books tucked under my overcoat. Large answered the door.

'Charlie. What are you doing here. It's Thursday evening.'

'I've been going through the books, as you asked.' I pointed to them under my arm. 'I thought you should know right away. You were right.'

'Thought you might use it as an excuse to look at the old pile, see what the bastard's done to it, more like.'

'Not at all.'

'If you say so.' I could hear voices in the dining room, Sophie laughing. 'We're having dinner,' he explained. 'I wasn't meaning for you to come round right away.'

'I'd better go.'

'Bit late for that now. Come in, then. I'll show you around.'

I followed him down the corridor. In the drawing room, gone were the curved settees, in their place a pair of good comfortable sofas either side of the fireplace. The television had been relocated to a corner, and in its place was a picture of a nineteenth-century frigate battling against the elements. There was a decent bookcase in the alcove, by the wall what I took to be a drinks cabinet with a couple of decanters on the top, and in the corner a small round table studded with family photographs, pictures of Large's parents in loud summer clothes, one of the three of them riding in some vintage car, one of Large and Sophie at their wedding, a helicopter in the background, and that one of his father again, that I'd seen that afternoon, his father and the fish hanging on the hook. Of the stuff I had seen last time, only the glass table remained, on it two bottle of champagne, four flute glasses and a near-empty bowl of olives.

'Pass muster?' he said.

'It's very nice.'

'Bet you thought I'd have ruined it with mock Hollywood rubbish, humungous TVs, crap like that.'

'Not at all.'

'This table came from Bangkok, you know,' he said, scoffing one of the last olives. 'Them legs is teak.'

'Who are you talking to?' Sophie's voice came ringing through.

'Supersums,' he said and beckoned me through, dark red wallpaper, gilt wall brackets, a large round table.

There were just four places, Sophie in the far quarter, the empty chair for Large opposite, and in between them Tommy and Lyn, with what smelt like hot crab in front of them, little white rolls on the side plates, two bottles of white burgundy and two lit candles ranged in the centre. The women were dressed up, décolletage, pearls and painted nails, Tommy, like Large, in a white shirt and pressed jeans. Tommy would be wearing the better shoes, though.

'Behold the gatecrasher,' Large said, pushing me in. 'While the rest of us eat, drink and be merry, Charlie's idea of fun is to go through my accounts. That bastard Paul Lumley's been stitching me up, Tommy. How much for, Charlie?'

'I haven't worked out the exact figure yet.'

I stood there, not knowing where to look. Tommy hadn't even said hello. I'd had a birthday party here once, when I was ten, balloons on the gate outside, a bonfire and toffee apples in the garden after dark. Tommy had been there then, Sophie too, all of them, lemonade and chocolate cake and Colin the Clown, the only time any of them had ever been here. And now . . .

'Tommy never trusted him,' Lyn put in. 'You haven't had anything to do with him since that time with the extension, have you, darling.' She turned to Sophie. 'I hope you haven't been using him here.'

'Just to dig the fucking hole for the pool,' Large told her. 'I'm going to dig another fucking hole and bury him in it if this is true.'

'Large,' Sophie warned, 'not now. This is meant to be a

celebration.' She wagged her finger at me. 'I'm very cross with you, Charlie, coming here, spoiling our party.'

'I'm sorry. So, you've had some good news, Tommy?'

The two men looked at each other.

'Tommy and me are going into partnership,' Large explained. 'Fletcher's. I'm providing some of the capital and Tommy here the expertise. I mean, what do I know about running a shop.'

'A showroom,' Lyn corrected.

'Lyn is going to manage it, and Sophie, well she's got a pretty good idea of what people round here are looking for, up-market. She's doing your old house up beautiful, don't you think?'

'Is that what you have been doing all this time? We haven't seen you on Wednesdays for ages.' I held her gaze firm. Her eyes had never seemed wider.

'You know how it is. Things to do. Lyn and I spend all our time planning, don't we, Lyn. She's such a good organizer.' Lyn coughed, pleased with the compliment.

'You have the eye for it, though.'

'It?' I asked.

'Kitchens!' Large clapped me on the back. 'Like I said at your mum's wedding. The High Street's crying out for it. We'll be open in two months. Just in time for the New Year sales.'

Tommy dabbed at his mouth, before speaking to me directly. 'Rodney Wright will do the accounts, of course. Same as the garden centre.'

'It complements our business very well,' Lyn added, making light of it as best she could. 'Kitchens and gardens, well, they go together, don't they?'

'Like that crab and that Chablis,' Large offered. It was time for me to leave.

'Well.' I stood there, an intruder in my home, another helping of humiliation growing cold. 'Perhaps you could come round to my place, advise me on the decor there?'

It hung there for a moment, the question.

'I'm very busy at the moment, with Lyn and everything.'

'I know. Why don't you all come round? A little house-warming. I don't know why I didn't think of it before.'

They looked at me with pity.

'That would be lovely,' Lyn said. 'Wouldn't it, Tommy?'

'A house-warming,' Large repeated. 'We'd be up for that, wouldn't we, Nef. You got a garden now, isn't that right? Do it outdoors, a bonfire and a barbie, a complete winter warmer. I'll bring some fireworks. You, me, Tommy, Nef, the old gang, just like old times. No offence, Lyn.'

No offence was taken. It was all settled. A barbie. Fireworks. A bonfire.

I walked home. There was a ten-pound note caught in a hedge in the street down from me, barely a mark on it. I stuffed it in my pocket, wondering how long it had been there. It's amazing how unobservant people can be.

Fourteen

I didn't work well the next week. I just stared out of the window, looking at the empty office rooms opposite. One by one, all the things that had been the strands of me had been loosened, lying tangled in Large and Sophie's hands. That weekend I went over to Canterbury, made a tour of the second-hand bookshops. I was looking for something I could send her, another book on marine life, something that would encapsulate my steadfast feelings. Instead I found a gift for my mother. I hadn't seen her for months. I didn't like going there, walking past Tommy's house, the thought of him and Lyn passing comments, staring at me through their drawing-room window. But the discovery galvanized me. I drove back, Handel on the CD, parked my car next to Lyn's silver Audi and walked briskly down the pale gravel drive. My mother was standing at the kitchen window, peeling potatoes. She met me at the door, wiping her hands dry.

'Charles,' she said. 'What's wrong?'

'Nothing.' I gave her a kiss on the cheek. 'Thought I'd drop by, that's all. I haven't seen you in ages. Look, I've bought you a present. *The Secret Garden.* Your favourite book. A first edition.'

I gave her the book. She turned the pages, ran her fingers over the illustrations.

'It was never my favourite, Charles.'

'You always told me it was.'

'To read to a child, maybe. But not my favourite book. How could it be? Turgenev's *First Love*, that was my favourite, that and his short stories. Your father never read him once.' She snapped the book shut, examination over. I followed her back into the kitchen. It was more cramped than I remembered, meagre, not properly equipped. A lick of paint wouldn't have gone amiss.

'I'm surprised Tommy hasn't put one of his new kitchens in here, Mum. It's a bit primitive, isn't it?'

'New kitchens cost money, even if you are Tommy's mother-in-law.'

'Not even a dishwasher?'

'Theo doesn't approve of dishwashers. He's old-fashioned that way. He's old-fashioned about a lot of things.'

'But what about you? It's you who does the washing up, isn't it.'

'Theo does what Theo does. It's his bungalow, after all. Out of the way, I've got supper to cook.' She banged an enamel bowl down on the Formica top.

'Are you enjoying it? This married life.'

'What sort of question is that? It got me out of Monkton's, didn't it. He's a good man in many ways. Drinks too much, but then most men do. That's one thing he shares with your father. Do you drink too much? I think you probably do. You've put on weight, that's for sure.' She moved over to the fridge. The drag on her leg had grown slightly worse.

'I'm getting older, Mum.'

'Older and singler.'

'You can't be more single.'

'You think?' She pulled out a scrawny carcass, started cutting it up on the draining board by the sink. The knife seemed quite blunt. 'You don't see that Katie any more, then.'

'No, you were right.'

'Was I? There are times when a man shouldn't listen to his mother.' She shuffled across, brought out a bag of flour, scooped a couple of handfuls of white into the bowl, then tipped in the jointed carcass. She began turning the pieces in her fingers. Her hands were the same texture as the meat, thin and pink and stretched to the bone.

'Come away with me, Mum. Let's leave here.'

'What?'

'Come away with me. Leave it all behind. You and me. Anywhere you want.'

'What are you talking about, Charles?' She grabbed hold of the pepper mill, twisting its head with exaggerated vigour, her face set hard, intent, unable to look up.

'You're not happy here. I know you're not.'

'Since when has happiness got to do with anything. We get on with it, my generation. We don't run away like yours.' She emptied the contents of the bowl into a pie dish.

'Is that rabbit?'

'What if it is.'

'You don't like rabbit.'

'Theo does.' She straightened up, her face clean of emotion. 'Now let me get on, please. He likes to eat early.'

I left. Theo's supper. I wasn't invited there either.

*

The following week was the Friday of the house-warming. It had taken quite some persistence for the four of them to agree on a date, Tommy proving to be particularly obtuse. I went to some trouble, ordered real caviar from the fishmonger down at Hythe and wild smoked salmon for the canapés, and purchased half a dozen bottles of decent champagne. I had some wine held in reserve, but didn't expect to have to open it.

The day came. I left the office early. I had much to do. Changing into some old clothes I went out into the garden to build Large's bonfire. I was determined for it to live up to expectations. I took great care, digging out the base, layering it with shredded cardboard and firelighters, then laid upon them the bundles of fuel, brought out in carrier bags and stacked with some skill. The outer facing proper came next, a well-constructed pyramid made from the wood the builders had left behind, and which I had neglected to remove to the county tip. Perhaps I'd always known I'd have to build a bonfire eventually.

Inside the house, it wasn't cold but I screwed up the newspaper and lit the stove. I had grown to admire the wood-burner, the manner in which it dominated the room by its monstrous shape. It was an unsightly affair, squat and pot-bellied, with a prodigious appetite. A ferocious provider of heat, it sat four-square on its fat little legs demanding to be fed. It had been my constant companion these months. Sitting in front of its bulbous stomach, listening to its digestion with a bottle of my father's claret by my side, had proved to be some of my happiest hours. The damper fully opened, it simply ripped through fuel, inert one moment, incandescent the next; the damper shut down completely, it simmered like a pot of stew.

I bent down and touched it. Its belly was cold. I laid a couple of small logs on the firelighters and left them to catch. My guests were due in just under an hour. I got out the ice bucket, shoved the blinis in the oven, prepared the sour cream and horseradish, opened the tin of caviar and gave the room the once-over with the Dyson. Ice bucket washed and cleaned next, in with the ice and water, two bundles of twenties onto the logs, then out with the blinis to let them cool.

I polished the glasses, five elegant champagne flutes (a couple of tumblers in case Lyn or Tommy required something non-alcoholic), then started on the other canapés, buttering the water biscuits before spreading on the smoked salmon or fish pâté. I checked on the stove. It was running a little too fast. I lowered the damper, and then took out fifteen packets of twenties from the holdall under the bed and packed them in tight. They should last the evening. I closed the fire door carefully, sweeping up any telltale ash in the grate. It paid to be to be careful with ash.

The blinis had cooled. On went the sour-cream mix and then a teaspoon of caviar. I carried them into the living room, then brought in the smoked salmon, et cetera. One bottle of champagne into the bucket, and a jug of mango juice. I put the cocktail sausages and the garlic roast potatoes in the oven. I washed and changed. Everything was set.

They arrived all together, Sophie and Lyn in the vanguard, Large and Tommy bringing up the rear. It was bad manners, I thought, to turn up like that. It probably meant they'd all met up beforehand, agreeing on how long to stay, what to say, what *not* to say, had a drink together no doubt, to fortify themselves. I took Lyn's coat, and hung it over the banister. Sophie wasn't wearing a coat, just a tweed jacket, tight at the waist with beige corduroy trousers to match. Her collarless shirt was buttoned up to the neck. County chic.

'Well, here I am at last,' she said. She kissed me on the cheek, vodka breath tinged with peppermint.

'A welcome visitor to these shores,' I said, choosing my words carefully. She remembered. I returned the kiss, my hand placed carefully on her shoulder, her neck bare and close, recently bathed and perfumed. I thought of her standing in front of her mirror not an hour before, flesh-damp, her fingers buttoning up her blouse, protecting herself from the only one who knew her, raising her chin to fix that last button, the finality of her appearance, how she wished to be judged tonight.

I dropped my hand. Large was leant up on the doorpost, taking it all in. He stood aside, guided Tommy through, then stepped in himself, rubbing his hands, looking around.

'Well, this is nice,' he pronounced. 'Them stairs go up to your old flat, I take it. You got that as well?' He knew perfectly well I had. I'd shown him the plans.

'Yes. I knocked through the upstairs kitchen to make a much bigger bathroom.'

'Two floors, Charlie. Going up in the world. What's that?'

'It's a nude.'

'I can see that. She hasn't got any clothes on. Bit lively, isn't it, the first thing you see, opening the front door. What do you think, nugget?'

Sophie turned. It struck me that the nude's and Sophie's proportions were almost identical.

'She doesn't leave much to the imagination.'

'That's what I mean. It's not what you expect on a respectable street like this. I mean what sort of party are we letting ourselves in for? Here.' He took off his scarf and draped it over her. 'That's better. Now, what more depravity you got in store for us?'

We walked through. The four of them stood in the room, looking round dutifully. I poured out the champagne. Lyn stepped forward.

'It's lovely, Charles. Just what you need to come back to after a hard day's work. Cheers.' Everyone echoed her sentiment, even Tommy, albeit reluctantly.

'Very nice,' Large repeated. 'Real cosy, classy too. It has a good feel to it. Them armchairs, what are they, French? Proper antique anyway. And no telly.'

'I have one upstairs.' I handed out the blinis. If they noticed, no one was saying.

'We're thinking of having a television room, aren't we, Nef? Leave the drawing room for reading and that. Opposite the dining room.'

'My mother's painting room.'

'That's what it was! I knew I could smell something funny in there. Lasted all this time. It would make a good TV room, don't you think?'

'It's very light. Another blini?' He took three.

'Anyway, here's to your new home. You done yourself proud. What's the garden like?' They moved to the window. 'Bigger than I imagined. What do you think, Tommy?'

Tommy peered out, taking a reluctant interest. 'It needs a

little shaping,' he said. 'He should dig part of the lawn out, give himself a broader bed. Maybe raise the back up, give it some perspective.'

'You mean a terrace?' It was the first remark I'd directed to him since he'd arrived. He nodded back.

'It would take the eye somewhere.'

'Off that bloody nude back in the hall.'

'Large, shut up about the nude,' Sophie said. 'You're betraying your prejudices. '

'I don't hold with them, that's all, nudes. I don't have *Men Only* lying open on the coffee table, and I don't have oil paintings of naked women on the wall. I mean, what's the difference? They're still all in the buff. What am I meant to say to my mum when she pops over? "Look at the jugs on that, Mum"? That's why I like pictures of boats and stuff. I know what a woman looks like, thank you very much, so does she, but a frigate in full sail? I don't think so.'

Sophie sighed. 'They're done for different reasons, Large, your oil painting and your centre-page spread.'

'You sure about that? Ask yourself why it's a woman's body those artists painted all the time? Why not a man's? Why not a goat's, or a dog's for that matter. Still using the same skill, light and paint and skin and that. They don't want to paint a dog or a goat, that's the thing. Or anything else. They want to paint women with nothing on. You know why. 'Cause they like copping an eyeful, that's why. Simple as that. So thanks to Renoir and Rembrandt and all them others, painting nudes became what counts. Anyone who started painting dogs or donkeys for a living was looked down on, chocolate-box rubbish and all that, but they started drawing some good-looking bird with a great pair of bazooms and bingo, they were in the fucking Louvre.'

Sophie raised her eyes. 'Well, that's the history of Western art out of the way.'

'You don't think there's truth in that? I'm not saying they

weren't good at it, Nef, effing geniuses and all that. I'm saying they did it because tucked away in that smock of theirs they had something else besides a couple of stiff paint brushes. I mean that bird back in the hall, whoever she was, I bet it wasn't just his little hammer she saw going up and down.' He ran his finger round his collar. 'Bloody warm in here, isn't it? Just because you have a wood-burning stove, doesn't mean you have to have it on all the time.'

'I'll open a window. It took me hours to light.'

Large came over, stood over it. They matched each other rather well.

'You should have got one with glass in the doors,' he said. 'That way you could see the flames. Not much point in having a fire if you lock it away like a nun in a convent. You want to see a bit of leg when you're warming your hands. How much did it cost you?'

'Five hundred. I light it most evenings. I find it very relaxing.'

'Perhaps it's something we should be looking into Tommy, stoves.'

Tommy shrugged his shoulders. 'May I?' He took another blini and sat down, his left leg swinging over his right. His shoes were a dark green, with fancy stitching running round the side; not a mark on the leather sole. Large was wearing black tasselled loafers.

'Is this real caviar?' Tommy asked. At last.

'Russia's finest.'

'Goodness, Charles. There was no need for that.'

'Yes, there was.' I offered Sophie another. 'A night to remember, that's what I'm aiming for.' She shook her head, hardly daring to look at me. Lyn stretched out her hand and popped one straight in her mouth.

'You've never bought me real caviar, Tommy.' Tommy shrugged his shoulders again. Large was still staring out the window.

'Where's the barbie?'

'I never got round to it. I built the bonfire, though.'

'And I brought the fireworks. Only one, mind, but it's a big bastard. I'll go and get it.'

He marched back in, pleased as Punch. It stood about five foot tall, three foot of stick and two foot of bulging, testosterone-filled rocket. With his blue suit, the rocket resting on his shoulder, he looked like an off-duty keeper from the Tower of London. We followed him outside. There was a length of old drain leaning against the back wall, another residue of the building alterations. He walked to the end of the garden, dropped it to the ground.

'There's a box of matches on that little table,' I called out. 'Why don't you light the bonfire as well. It's all ready. See the newspaper sticking out?'

He knelt down, indifferent to the mud and leaves sticking on his trousers. It was a sight I'd never expected to see, Large contributing so willingly to such a conflagration. He struck the long-stemmed match, holding a protective hand around the flame as it curled around the edges of the paper.

'Has it taken?' I called out. He nodded, brushing his trousers down, looking pleased. We could hear a quiet crackling inside. It would take some time to re-emerge. He turned to the drain, lifting it high, driving it into the soft autumnal ground, working it into the soil so that it stood at an angle. It was my house-warming but you wouldn't have known it. He dropped the firework in.

'Probably won't take,' he said, walking back, wiping his hands against each other. We grouped together, waiting.

'Bloody Chinese,' he said.

The rocket ripped into the sky. We could hear the thrust of it as it shot into the dark, its fiery tail sucking us in with it. What were they thinking, my guests, Sophie, her hand shading her eyes, Tommy, his good hand in his pocket, Lyn, Large? The spouting flame spluttered, the rocket vanished. The sky hung still, huge and empty. The explosion came behind us. Lyn screamed, Sophie grabbed my arm, then let go. Spangled stars streamed down, stars bursting into other stars bursting into other stars, on and on it went, torrential surges of sudden hope abruptly expended. We were young once, soaring into the world like that, in awe of our potency, ferocious in our dreams. This small garden was where I had ended up. I'd wished for more, that was all; Sophie and Large, Tommy and Lyn, why not me?

There was a sudden rush of air. The bonfire stirred, the stack of wood shifting as its womb took life. Flames leapt forth, light on our faces, heat searing our skin. We stepped back. What could they see or know?

'There's a tenner in this grass,' Large said.

'What?' Lyn laughed.

'A tenner, lying in the grass. Look.' He bent down, scraped it loose. 'One of your efforts, Charlie?'

'I must have dropped it when building the bonfire.' I stuffed it in my pocket. 'Who's for sausages, roast potatoes? Sophie, would you help?'

We went into the kitchen. I opened the oven, pulled out the roasting tray.

'Smells lovely,' she said. I moved towards her.

'So do you.'

'Charlie.'

'Come round tomorrow. What's he doing? Going shooting? Fishing? Or is it the turn of the quad bikes?'

'God, I knew we shouldn't have come.' She snatched up the plate of sausages and hurried into the drawing room. I followed with the potatoes and champagne.

'Sophie . . .'

'No!' She wheeled round, sausages sliding off the plate onto the fitted carpet. 'Now look what you've made me do.'

She dropped to her knee, picking them up, burning her fingers. 'We can't eat these. Fuck it.' She opened the fire door, swept them in. Her hand was back on the handle when something caught her eye.

'What's that?'

She grabbed the tongs, poked about, pulling one of the packets out, stamping on the smouldering notes with her foot.

'They're banknotes! Twenty-pound banknotes! What on earth!'

She peered in. I was watching her face.

'It's full of them!'

'It is?'

'Money! You're burning money!' She jabbed the tongs in again, the banknotes flaring into life. Out in the garden Large and Tommy were finishing off the champagne. Lyn was holding out one hand to the heat. Sophie had dropped to one knee, peering inside. She couldn't work it out.

'Charlie, what's going on? Have you gone mad?'

'What do you think's going on?' I picked up the smouldering bundle. 'Let's put this back. We don't want to set light to the carpet. Don't worry, they're quite worthless now.' I chucked it back in. I thought she would try and stop me but she didn't. She was transfixed by the impossibility of what she was seeing, its defiance of known reason. She tried to claw back the world to normalcy.

'Is this some sort of trick? It's not real money, right?'

'It's real, all right.'

'Real money! You're burning real money?'

'Quite a lot of it over the past year. It starts off by being money, but it doesn't stay that way for long.'

'Charlie, this is crazy! What's got into you? ... This is madness! Madness!' She was up on her feet again, eyes huge, all composure gone. Once she had lain on the bed, languid, sure, mocking my lack of experience. Now she was breathing heavily, frightened, caught in the headlights, lost in a world she did not know, her years of ingrained poise redundant. I spoke from a deep quiet within me.

'You haven't asked whose money it is that I'm burning.'

'It's not yours?'

'Of course it's not mine. How could it be? Feeding this monster every night? I don't have that sort of cash.'

'Then whose? Not the—' She stopped, catching my knowing expression. 'You don't mean . . .'

She looked to the French window. We could hear his voice outside. He was telling a joke, Lyn protesting without conviction at the crudity, her laughter heightening Sophie's sense of displacement.

'Christ, Charlie, what do you think you're doing? Have you any idea what he'll do when he finds out? You're burning his money! Jesus fucking Christ, what am I going to do?'

Her voice was shaking. I took hold of her shoulders. Her body too. I hadn't meant for her to see it, and yet maybe I had, her or Lyn or even Large himself. How thrilling it had been, how blood-pumping heart-thumping thrilling it had been, handing out the canapés, flirting with the risk of discovery. How magnetic, how purposeful, how utterly compelling deliberate sin is. No wonder Katie wanted to steal shoes, or Sophie hustle me into my parents' old bedroom, watch debauchery unfold in the mirror. No wonder there's a Catholic Church. Perhaps the honchos at Lloyd's had felt the same, enticing men like my father into their syndicates, knowing all the time they were going to take them for every brass cent. Imagine the excitement when they dreamt that scheme up, or the placid expressions on their faces as they welcomed the dupes in to the inner sanctum, the riots of laughter they would have had to mask. What bottles must have been opened after the day's work had been completed, what glorious champagne must have been drunk. It must have tasted like the nectar of the gods.

'Do whatever you want,' I said. 'Come round tomorrow. I'll tell you everything.'

'There's more?' She broke away.

Lyn was standing in the doorway, eyes moving between the two of us, savouring the tension. 'Those sausages ready? The boys are getting hunger pains. Everything all right, Sophie?'

'Fine.' She brushed the lapel of her jacket. 'I dropped his fucking sausages.'

Lyn looked for evidence, not believing a word.

'She tripped on the carpet,' I explained. 'Banged her head on the hearth. She's all right now. Here, you two take this lot out. I'll follow.'

They went back out, Lyn whispering into Sophie's ear, Sophie shaking her head. I brushed the hearth clean, then rejoined them, armed with another bottle. The fire was in full flow now, aroused, inflamed, sighing with passion, enamoured of the night, its thick timbers groaning, twisting, sinking into the heat. We stood in a semicircle, not saying a word, Sophie slightly apart, her glass dangling empty in her hand. I wanted to grab all my furniture, all my books, my shameless nude, and pile it all on. The whole world was burning. Large broke the spell.

'I love a good bonfire,' he said. 'Makes me all tingly inside. It's so elemental isn't it, fire. Must have been great to be the first cave man to know how to do it, make a fire. I mean think of the street cred in that, the birds he must have pulled.'

'Here we go again.'

'No, think about it, Tommy. There's the rest of them, with their caves as cold as Christmas, with only a bit of woolly-mammoth skin to keep you warm, while his pad's got a blazing fire *and* what's more, something new in the kitchen department, the world's first hot bit of sausage.' He was thinking on his feet now, enjoying himself. 'For the first time in her life her tits aren't frozen solid and she can get her mouth round something warm and tasty that she can also bite off and chew. I mean who's going to pass on that?' Lyn was laughing. Tommy too.

'Have you ever danced round a bonfire naked, Lyn?'

'Large. Trust you.'

322

'Not now. I thought it was what students did, Guy Fawkes night, Halloween.'

'Not in agricultural college.'

'Was that where you was, then?'

'For a year.'

'I always thought it would be a waste, dancing round a bonfire in the nuddie. I mean, the fire's the thing to concentrate on, isn't it, looking into them changing colours moving with your thoughts. Like the sea. Only drier.'

I'd come up beside Sophie. I took her glass, filled it again. She couldn't take her eyes off me.

'He should look inside this one,' I told her quietly. 'There's twenty thousand in tenners there. I'll have to get some more out soon. Winter's coming on.'

She swivelled round, the sound coming from her mouth part whimper, part moan, her face hanging open, one hand to her lips, the other unconsciously kneading her breast. Fire in the belly, fire in the heart, fire in the house and garden, husband and friends standing close, oblivious to the turmoil raging inside her; honesty, trust, the town's equilibrium burning before their eyes.

'What's the matter, Nef? Are you all right?' Large was at her side. I offered him the bottle.

'I was just telling Nef my secret of the evening. I'll tell you if you like.'

'Charlie, no!'

'It's all right, Sophie. I've quite made up my mind.' I cleared my throat. 'I've got something to tell you all,' I announced. 'I'm thinking of leaving, going away. Thanks to your father, Tommy, my mother doesn't need me any more, if she ever did. I'm just an irritant to her now.'

Lyn gulped at her food, shaking her head. 'Charles, that's not true. She's often asking about you.'

'Precisely. If she saw me more often, she wouldn't have to. Anyway, she is not the only one who finds me in the way.'

'How do you mean?'

'I think you all wish I wasn't here.'

'Charlie.' The chorus was two-fold. Sophie and Tommy said nothing.

'It's not just that. I feel constrained. It's time for me to move.'

'Where to?' Tommy's voice was matter-of-fact.

'Well, if Clark will let me go, I'd like to go to Texas.'

'Texas!' Large's champagne spilled down his front. 'What have I got to do with Texas?'

'Texas or Winchester,' I said, directing the last name to Sophie.

'Well, make up your mind,' Large retorted. 'They're not exactly twinned, you know.'

'Why Texas?' Lyn questioned.

'Texas is not at all English.'

'And Winchester's the ten-gallon hat of the West Country, I suppose.' Large looked round for laughter. He didn't get any. Everyone was taken aback at what I had said.

'Winchester's *very* English,' I told them. 'There's the choice, you see. Different ways of living. Different opportunities.'

'You're a dark horse, Charlie. I always said he was a dark horse. Didn't I always say he was a dark horse, Nef?'

'Who cares what you said. You can't just run off like that.'

Large made to speak, but thought better of it. Her remark unsettled him. Tommy coughed.

'I wouldn't like to think you'd be leaving on my account, Charles. You're appreciated in this town, I recognize that. You have roots here. You would be a loss.'

'Too bloody right.' Large came up to me, stood alongside, put his arm around me, hugged me in. 'What's all this about? Unlucky in love, is that it?'

'Possibly.'

'Miffed at the kitchen thing with Tommy and me.'

'A mite.'

'Losing the Merry Boys. Feeling a bit left out all round.'

'You could say that.'

'Charlie! You're my main man! How many times do I have to say it. There's always someone who feels a little left out, and you know what, it's always someone like you. It's your nature that leaves you out, not us. That's who you are, and you know what, we all love you for it. Don't we, Nef?'

'Large, please. We're all getting over-excited here. It's early days yet. Nothing may come of it. Anyway, wouldn't I be doing what you and Tommy do all the time – take a risk, a gamble? Isn't that what we're expected to do these days? You lot know me probably better than anyone. What real risk have I ever really taken? I'm trying to act out of character here.' I stopped. There was a rigidity to the assembly. They didn't know who they were looking at any more. I'd said too much. 'Here endeth the lesson. Lyn looks cold. Shall we go back inside?'

I brought out another bottle, but there were no takers. The balloon had deflated. Sophie stood with her back to the stove, staring at the wall. Large stood by the French window, staring at her. Tommy sat down and wiped the mud from his shoes. Lyn went upstairs to examine my new bathroom. When she returned, Tommy got to his feet.

'Come on, Lyn, we got a busy day tomorrow,' he said. Large followed suit. He unwrapped his scarf from the nude's neck and wove it around Sophie's.

'We'll talk about this later, Charlie, OK.'

They left. I took a chair outside and sat with my best burgundy glass until the small hours, watching the fire rise and fall as the banknotes breathed their last, two thousand portraits of Her Majesty and Charles Dickens twisting and turning, setting fire to each other, curling in amongst themselves like a nest of scorpions or self-devouring snakes, dancing and writing to the fire's music before rising up into nothing – a rope trick courtesy of Chief Cashier Andrew Bailey and his employer the Bank of England.

'It's done now, Dad,' I told him. 'I got your money back. You can rest easy now.'

The fire secured, I went to bed. I tried to sleep, but couldn't. My bed seemed barely habitable any more. I was like the girl in 'The Princess and the Pea', the hard kernel of what I had said and done lying under me, pressing me to the bone.

At six I got up, ran a bath, shaved, went out to rake over the embers. I was in my dressing gown, making coffee, listening to the *Today Programme*, when the phone rang.

'Charlie. I'm in the Range Rover. Just to thank you for last night. We should come round more often. We had a very good evening when we got back home, if you see what I mean. A very good evening. I'll have to start going to the gym if she keeps that up.'

'Large, I've got to go. Someone's at the door. I'll call you back later.'

She was standing at the door. It was ten past seven. She pushed past me, walked into the drawing room, looking round nervously.

'I didn't sleep a wink thinking about it.' She flung her bag on a chair. 'Do you have any left? Come on, show me?'

She followed me up to my bedroom. I pulled out the hold-all from under the bed, opened it up. The money lay in tidy bundles. She gave another of those whimpers.

'I nearly had a heart attack when I saw what you were doing. Jesus, what an evening. I thought my insides were going to drop out. God, look at it!'

'You weren't meant to see it. But I'm glad you did.'

'Well, I'm not. How do you get it here?'

'I bring it back from Guernsey.'

'Your little trips! Jesus, you've got a nerve. But the guys there? Don't they notice?'

'What do they care as long as it's an authorized signature. They're trained to look away. It's a look-away world.'

She grabbed hold of the bag, tipped it out.

'Charlie Pemberton. Who'd have thought it. I've said that before, haven't I?' She put her hand on me, as if to steady herself. 'Is it fun, stealing from him? How much is there here?'

'Eight, ten thousand? I haven't spent a penny of it. Even my trips to Guernsey I pay for myself, even though they're on business. I'm not stealing.'

'Of course you are. It's not your money.'

'What, and you think it's his?' I laughed. 'You think Golden Years is kosher? It won't last five years, Sophie, don't you know that. How can it? You saw what happened a few months ago. It's a mirage built on nothing but people's gullibility. It can never, ever work. Large knows it, the investors know it, probably every bank that has lent money to them knows it, but what do they care? None of them will lose. When it collapses, as collapse it will, Large and all the others will walk away with a small fortune. Only he won't. Cashes to ashes. Lust to dust.'

She made to touch it, but couldn't. She breathed on her fingers as if she'd burnt herself.

'When do you plan to burn this lot?'

'Now, if you want. You'll be amazed how wonderful it feels, watching it burn, just to see it evaporate. I didn't tell Large last night, of course, but usually I keep the doors open. It's so liberating, destroying this thing we all strive for, talk about, steal and lie for, mortgages, school fees, credit cards, overdrafts, salaries, bonuses, all going up in smoke. I think of my father when I'm doing it, how he's up there, warming his hands, watching the ashes of his lost money rising up to heaven. We have a little ritual, him and me. He left me some wine, seventy-two bottles. I think he always meant to leave them to me, although he never admitted as much. So, every time I have one of my money-burning sessions, I drink his wine. No, correction, I drink his health.'

'Charles.' She had calmed down. 'I still don't understand why.'

'Because he's the future, and I hate everything about it.'

'He's not that bad.'

'He's worse than bad. You like him. I like him. He's attractive, he's clever, and funny and good-natured, but it's all done in the name of this. Remember him boasting about him and Tiffany? What they did on his first bonus? Look at it. Would you want to do that? I don't want to do that. I want you to lie naked in my arms as we watch it burn together. Which would be more erotic? Doing that or doing what he did? Which would mean more, making love on the nominal value of it or while all the rubbish, all the false promises and false dawns, melts into nothing. Let's burn it now. Lie in my arms, see what it feels like. Wouldn't you like to know?'

The phone rang again. Sophie picked the bundles as if she hadn't heard me, letting them fall through her fingers. I couldn't take my eyes off her.

'Charles?'

'Tommy?'

'Dad's dead.'

For a befuddled moment I didn't know who he was talking about.

'Dad?'

'My father, Charles. He died a couple of hours ago. It was all rather sudden.'

'Tommy, I'm so sorry. How did it happen?'

'We're not sure. I think you ought to come over, Charles. Your mother's very distressed. The doctor's seen her. Lyn's with her now. We're worried she might have another stroke.'

We were out of the house in two minutes. I was at Tommy's in five. My mother was sitting at the kitchen table, holding a mug of tea. It seemed strange that they hadn't put her somewhere more comfortable.

'Mum, are you all right?'

She looked at me her, face all screwed up, angry that I

had come, or angry that I had not come earlier, it was hard to tell.

'Tommy brought me here me. I've lost my slipper, look.'

The words slid out of the side of her mouth. She was in her dressing gown, the leg poking out, bony and bare. The hair on top of her head looked patchy and thin, unwashed, uncombed, neglected. I had never seen her look so old. I took her hand and led her through to the living room. I sat her down in one of the armchairs. There was a folded blanket set out on the sofa. I laid it across her knees.

'What happened, Mum?'

'It's my leg.'

She bent down, fiddled with the edge of her gown.

'I've lost my slipper.'

'We'll find it, don't worry. What happened? Where's your nightie.'

'Tommy carried me here. Dropped my slipper. He's got one arm, you know.'

'Yes. It's OK, Mum. What happened to Theo?'

She turned, her eyes suddenly big like a child's.

'Is my room at Monkton's free? I want to go back there. Did you keep it for me?'

'You can't keep those sorts of rooms, Mum. There's other people in need of them. What happened? What was it, did he have a heart attack?'

'You should have kept it. It was my room. He wasn't always very nice, Charles.' She put her hand to her mouth. Her breath was bad. 'Is he dead?'

'Theo? Yes. What happened, Mum?'

'I thought he must be, not moving like that. I hit him, Charles, but he wouldn't move.' She looked down. There was something I didn't understand here.

'Have you said anything to the police, Mum?'

'The police? Why should I? Tommy came over and got me out, carried me here. He's lost my slipper.'

'Yes. I'll find it in a minute. But this hitting Theo, Mum. I'm worried about it, what you might say. Why did you hit him?'

'I don't want to talk about it. Find me some clothes. Do something useful for a change.'

I ran down to the bungalow. There was a police car and an ambulance and a car with 'Doctor on Call' plastered on the windscreen. Tommy was standing in the hall talking to Dr Fawcett and a uniformed officer. He wasn't our doctor but he'd worked in the town about as long as I had.

'Can I go in?' I asked. 'Only my mother needs some warm clothes.'

A policewoman led me in. Nikolides was covered by a sheet, the soles of his feet poking out bare and white and of a grotesque size. His body seemed to fill the whole mattress. The room was much smaller than I had imagined, just the bed and two side tables, with a chest of drawers in one corner, a mirror and a hairbrush on the top. I opened a drawer, pulled out a blouse and a folded skirt.

'She'll need a jersey or two,' the policewoman advised me. 'Perhaps some thick stockings and underwear. The shock will have lowered her temperature. Shall I have a look?'

I went back in the hall. Dr Fawcett and Tommy stopped talking, embarrassed.

'Do you know what happened?' I asked. 'I can't get much sense out of my mother.' The two of them moved awkwardly, shuffling their weight.

'It looks like he had a massive heart attack,' Dr Fawcett said. 'He would have been dead in seconds.'

'Mum said something about her leg.'

'Yes.' Tommy stared at the floor. 'He was lying on her bad leg. She couldn't move. I had to ... roll him off. It's lucky I was out so early, or I wouldn't have heard her. He'd been dead for five or six hours, Dr Fawcett here thinks.'

He looked to the floor, unable to voice what we knew had taken place. I felt sick. I hurried back to the house, grateful for the cold morning air. My mother rifled through the clothes, throwing them one by one to the floor.

'Trust a man to bring the wrong things. Where's Katie? Have you called her yet?'

'Katie?'

'I always liked her. Call her, will you, with your mobile thing? You can do that for me, can't you?'

I walked out into the garden, called Monkton's, not knowing whether she'd be there. I was put through to her funny flat voice. She was overall manager now.

'Katie. It's me, Charles. Don't hang up. It's my mother. She's had a bit of a relapse. The man she married has died. Dreadful circumstances, just dreadful. I was wondering if you could come over. She's been asking for you.' I could hear the intake of breath.

'I didn't think she liked me.'

'Who knows what my mother likes. Will you come?' A moment's hesitation, the beat between heart and speech.

'Of course. Where are you? The flat?'

I told her where and went back inside. Lyn was still nowhere to be seen. My mother sat hunched up, everything squeezed out of her. I knelt down beside her.

'I'm here, Mum, it's all right.'

There was no response. I held her hand, stroked her hair, as she sat there, eyes blinking, searching for clues on my face. She was as light and brittle as an autumn leaf. I pulled a jersey over her, threaded her arms through. She started to cry. I held her to me, flesh and bone, thinking of us Pembertons, how we had broken loose from our moorings, how far we were away from all the safety we had known. Five or six hours. Theo, lying on top of her, for five or six hours. She pushed me away, reclaiming herself.

'Well, what now?'

'I haven't really thought it through yet, Mum.'

'I can't stay here.' Her voice was firm. 'Tommy's always

resented my presence.' She looked past me, her face brightening. I turned, expecting to see Katie.

Large was stood in the doorway.

'I just heard.' He dropped down on his knees. 'How are you, Mrs P?'

'Clark!' Her face was transformed, all simple smiles. She grasped his hand. I thought for an instant she was going to kiss it. 'I knew I could rely on you. Quite the best man at my wedding, you were. Charles has done nothing, of course. I suppose he imagines I'm going back to the bungalow, save him the bother. Well I'm not, not after what happened. My old room, is it ready?'

He patted her hand. 'We'll sort something out, don't you worry.' He pulled me aside. 'You taking her back to your place? Do want some help?'

I thought of the state of it, Sophie's shoe coming off as we bundled down the stairs, me running round looking for the car keys, slamming the door, radio on, curtains undrawn and the money lying scattered on the bed.

'You heard her. She wants to go back to Monkton's. Is it possible?'

He put his finger to his nose, went back out. I watched him as he walked up and down, phone clamped to his ear, talking, cajoling, insisting, free hand jabbing the morning air. I felt like telling him then. I knew I'd have to tell him soon. He came back, matter of fact.

'Katie says there's the room upstairs, used for storage,' he announced. 'It's never been done up proper. Don't worry. We'll fix it up later. It'll do for now.' He put his arm around me. 'Don't worry, Charlie. She's stronger than you think, your mum, has to be. Your old man topping himself, losing the house, the stroke, now this? She's a survivor, don't you know that?'

Large left. The morning eked by. An ambulance came to remove Theo's body. We could hear Tommy on the phone to

Greece. Lyn gave us something to eat, tomato soup and toast. My mother attacked it in short determined movements, like a winter-starved bird. By two o'clock the room was ready. I drove her over. Katie was waiting by the front entrance. She ran down the steps and opened the car door.

'Katie, there you are. I've been waiting for you.'

'Welcome back, Mrs Pemberton.'

'Pemberton. That's right.' She turned to me. 'See, Charles, Katie knows.'

I gave her a kiss. It had been over a year since we'd lain eyes on each other. Mum took her hand, let her guide her up the steps.

'I hear you and Charles are engaged, Katie. You were very naughty, keeping it from me all this time.'

'We didn't want to upset you, Mrs Pemberton.'

'Why should it upset me? It's about time someone sorted him out.'

We walked down the corridor, past her old bedroom. She didn't give the door a second glance. We took the stairs slowly, Katie on one side, me slightly behind on the other, first floor, second floor, third floor. I recognized the room straight away, the Polish man who'd died when Large had first shown me round. The room had hardly changed, bare furniture, thin curtains, the sense of eternal isolation. They had put some flowers on top of the old television.

'It's the best we could do right away,' Katie whispered. My mother didn't seem to notice the threadbare state of the room at all.

'That's dangerous,' she said, pointing to the flowers, 'water near electricity. And lilies. Never did like them. Such obvious gaudy things.' She prodded the mattress. 'Will it be a church wedding? Charles tells me you're very religious.'

'We haven't decided quite yet, Mrs Pemberton. Now come on, let's get you nice and comfy. Mr Rossiter has given me strict instructions.'

333

The name seemed to placate her. We put her to bed. She sank back onto the pillow.

'I'm tired, Charles. I need to rest. Why don't you come back tomorrow?'

'I've only just arrived, Mum.'

'Hovering around, asking me questions. I just want some peace and quiet. I'll be all right. Come back tomorrow. I'll be better then.'

We stood outside. Katie folded her arms. I took her in for the first time. She looked fuller, less pale; some of the anger erased. Life at Monkton's clearly suited her.

'So, we're getting married are we?' she said, head cocked to one side, her jocularity professional rather than intimate.

'Apparently. Where would you like to go for your honeymoon?'

'Not Brighton, that's for sure.' She smiled, but it was a smile of loss, distance. 'How are you, Charles?'

'I'm in a bit of a mess, if the truth be told. Do you still go to church?'

'Not as often as I should. Come on, you've got to sign a few things.'

She walked me downstairs, we did the paperwork.

'You've become quite the person here, Katie.'

'I like it here. It's good.'

I got up. On the step outside she hugged me. It was a cold winter morning, trees bare, the sunlight weak and thin. I felt as if all my summers had been blown away.

'Don't worry. We'll look after her.'

She whispered, 'God bless,' and kissed me on the cheek. I got back in my car.

*

Back in the house the radio was playing, consumer advice. I pulled back the curtains, killed the radio and walked up to the bedroom. The banknotes lay on the bed, cold, inert. I stuffed them into the holdall and shoved the lot back under the bed. My money-burning days were over. The phone rang again. I knew who it would be.

'Charles. Thank God you rang. How's your mother? You must come over. We need to talk.'

'Is he there?'

'He's gone out shooting.'

I washed and changed and drove over. Sophie was waiting by the door, grey sweater, dark skirt, more reserved than I had imagined.

'Sophie . . .'

'Not in here. Not a word in here, nothing. Let's go for a walk.'

On the terrace, the swing seat was strewn with items of clothing, a pair of trousers, a shirt, what looked like a man's underwear. The croquet lawn was still a large dirty hole in the ground.

'No further on?' I said, trying to break the silence.

'I've gone off the idea. We've got a lake. What do we need with a swimming pool?'

We crossed the old lawn and the rose garden. Through the gap in the tall hedge stood the Ark, a blackened hull, all trace of glass removed.

'Tommy didn't want it,' she said. 'Not after you did your number on it. Yes, Large told me all about that, didn't you know?'

'No.'

'He tells me everything.'

Up at the lake the water was still and cold. I hadn't been there for years, but it hadn't changed. The boat was moored up on the jetty, the landing stage slippery underfoot, streaks of unthawed silver following the grain of the wood. Mother used to sit and paint there in the afternoons. Across the grey flat of the water, the tufted island looked almost like a sanctuary. Large was sitting on the little wooden seat, looking out, the gun laid across the lap of his overcoat.

'I like it here,' he said. 'Makes you realize that nothing changes much, not the birds, not the fish, they're always the same even if they're different, still behave the same, do the same things. We're all the same, deep down, what we is, what we was.'

He turned, beckoned us onto it.

'Nef's going for a swim. Aren't you, nugget?'

'Sophie?' I questioned. She looked only at him.

'Don't you worry about her, Charlie. She knows what's what. Off with your togs, girl.'

Sophie undressed, the woollen jersey, the grey checked shirt, the black skirt. She stumbled slightly pulling off her tights. She straightened up, arms pressed hard across her chest, her face held on his, painfully beautiful. The wind blew her hair into her eyes. The plank underneath my feet was shaking.

'Take a good look, Charlie. This is the last time you'll ever see that again. Them goosebumps, Nef?' His voice was cracking. There were tears in his eyes. Sophie shook her head, dropped her arms to her side. Large wiped his cheek with the back of his hand.

'In you go, then. Charlie and I have got some talking to do. Nice clean dive, mind.'

Sophie turned on the balls of her feet, the fluidity of the movement balletic in its choreography. She lifted her arms parallel to the water, the supple length of her picture perfect. She stood motionless, head unwavering, legs straight, only the muscle in her buttocks twitching. All my young life I had imagined this scene, and here she was, as I had always wanted her, not reckless on a bed, not corrosive in my arms, but standing resolute, mistress of my lake, naked and faultless and almost within reach. She raised herself up on the tip of her toes, her heels pale as the bleached wood, the back of her legs taut, the curve of her right breast rising visibly as she breathed in deep, as she sprang up, the boarding shuddering as she plunged in. The water barely moved.

'Ain't she beautiful, Charlie. I've never said it before, but ain't she the fucking tops. That's why I went scuba-diving, so I could see her move like that. I don't give a fuck about coral.'

We waited for her to surface. Large shifted his feet. I thought of the reeds that would have been allowed to grow unfettered over the years. It was easy to imagine her caught in the tangle of them, her hair waving back and forth as she struggled to set herself free. I saw myself diving in, hauling her out, the two of them pathetically grateful. Then the water broke and she emerged, a distance away, gasping for breath.

'Why did you do it, Charlie? Screw my beautiful wife.'

I closed my eyes. This wasn't what I was expecting at all.

'When did she tell you?'

He shifted to face me. 'She didn't. I knew at your house-warming, and later that night, when we got home, like she was trying to make up for it. I don't blame her. What, with a family like that, dad fucking knot holes in the floor, mum as warm and tender as last year's pickled onion. It's what she's been used to all her life, selfishness, snobbery, deception, treachery, a family at fraud. For twenty years the only thing she knew was how to look down. What does she know of loyalty, blood ties, not to give a shit? That's what families are all about.'

I held my breath. This was the time. I chose the words carefully.

'And if I were family? Would the same go for me too? Would you not mind no matter what I'd done? Not just your wife, but other things, as close to home.'

He shifted the gun, looking back. Sophie had struck out into the lake's deep water, shoulders broad, arms slicing clean into the water.

'What are you trying to tell me, Charlie?'

'Don't you know?' His eyes flickered, the brain clicking through the possibilities. You could almost see the wheels clunk in. 'Yes, you do. It's just dawned on you, hasn't it, after all this time. I'll say it, then. I've been taking your money. Month after month after month, ever since Golden Years started in earnest, in fact. Those trips to Guernsey? The affable Mr Edge? I wasn't taking it out. I was bringing it back.'

He looked at me in a way he'd never done before, man to man, interested, almost detached. 'How much?'

'That's always the first question to ask, isn't it, Large, how much? Don't you want to know why?'

'What you done with it? Put it somewhere safe? Not Texas or Winchester, I bet. Far as I know we still have an extradition treaty with Winchester. Some poxy off-shore account in the Cayman Islands. Charlie Pemberton in a ra-ra skirt.'

'I've burnt it. All of it.'

'What do you mean, burnt it?'

'In the wood-burning stove. And the bonfire the other night. That's why you had the caviar and champagne. It was a celebration. I'd nearly reached the figure I was aiming for, five hundred and eighty thousand, six hundred and seventy-five pounds. The last big conflagration.'

He got it now. Theft appropriation of what was his. His voice was sullen, almost schoolboyish. 'I want it back.'

'Large, you're not listening to me. I've burnt it. It's not there. You can't get it back. You can't trace it to an off-shore account or recover it through the goods I've bought. I haven't bought any. There is no off-shore account. It's all gone.'

I looked to the lake. We could hardly see her now, just a faint disturbance in the water.

'Burnt it?'

'Yes, as much as I could. Large, she can't stay there for long. It's freezing.'

'Why? Why burn it?'

'Because I don't like what it does to people. There's too much of it. It swamps everything, drowns reason, hope, compassion. I was getting rid of some.'

He walked up to the edge of the jetty, head bent, scuffing his shoes. Sophie had come round the other side of the island, heading back towards us. And she thought the conversation was about her.

'What's it like, burning money?' Again, the detached interest.

'Exhilarating. It's extraordinary how quickly it disappears. One moment it's there, thousand of pounds in the stove, two hours later there's nothing. It's all gone.'

'All gone.' He started to laugh. 'It's like one of them Agatha Christies. The accountant did it.' Sophie was on her back now, trying to preserve her energy, glimpses of flesh, pink and grey. In the distance we could hear an ice-cream van playing its jingle.

'Ice-cream vans, in this weather. Never fails to amaze me. Worth investing in, you reckon?'

'Large, please. The water.'

'You're probably right. Dodgy characters, those ice-cream operatives. Them turf wars in Glasgow. Remember?' He cupped his hands together. 'Another turn round the block, Nef. We're having a private conversation here.' She turned and started out again. She was tiring fast. He turned to face me.

'Why'd you do it? 'Cause you thought you was better than me?'

'Were better than me,' I corrected him. He acknowledged my nerve.

'You said you was leaving a couple of nights ago? "If Clark will let me", you said. Is that what you thought? I'd let you'd get away with it?'

'I can't go anywhere now. Not after Mother.'

He nodded. 'That was bad. He was pestering her every

night, did you know that, boasting about it to Tommy. That wasn't right. Tommy should have done something about it. You should have done something about it.'

'I didn't know.'

'Course you didn't. Too busy burning my money to look after your mum. You're not fit to be a son, putting her through that. She should be with you, not in some poxy home.'

'She doesn't want to stay with me.'

'I wonder why.' His mind was jumping from one subject to another, Sophie, my mother, the money, and Charlie Pemberton in every one. He shifted the gun in his hand.

'You haven't asked me if this is loaded or not.'

'I'm sure I'll find out in due course.'

'Nerves of steel, eh, Charlie. So, what am I going to do? You tell me that.'

I thought for an instant that he might do it, that he might simply lift the gun to belly height and finish it, have me jerk back with the blast, flop onto the deck clutching my guts, roll me in the water with his tasselled foot and watch me go under. I could even imagine him waving me goodbye as the life bled out of me. Charlie Pemberton. His main man! It flickered in his mind too, how good it would be just to break the air with the righteous noise of it. I took out the greenhouse, after all, set the precedent. He could go to prison then, a proper prison with thieves and murderers, hold his head up high, be one of them. He could take up boxing again, be strong, make contacts. He'd be out in six years ready for the fray, one side of the law or the other, he could take his pick. Why not? Why not shoot me? Why not? And then he heard Sophie turning again and the moment passed, and he lowered the barrels a fraction of an inch and I realized there was nothing else he could do. It was either shoot me or nothing, and he'd just chosen nothing. I'd been brought back to the living.

The water burst beneath us. Sophie was clinging to the mooring post, her head lolling on her arm.

'Large. I can't go on. I'm going here.'

I ran to help her.

'Don't you fucking touch her!' He bent down, hauled her out, her body bloodless white, streaked with green. She fell on her knees, gasping.

'I'll go back if you want. Just give me a minute.'

'It's all right, Nef. It's done with now.' He wrapped his arms around her waist, lifted her to her feet, her head sagging. He rubbed his hands quickly over her body, her rubbery breasts, her quivering flanks, her skin squeaking with the friction. 'Here. Get this round you, nugget.' He wrapped his coat around her. She stood there, shaking, eyes on him alone. He turned back to me.

'I had a soft spot for you, Charlie, didn't you know that. Always did have, despite what your dad did to my family. You've set me back, I can't deny it, but it won't matter, not in the long run. You talk about your name. What's mine? I'm Clark, not fucking Large. I'm Clark, Clark Rossiter, kingpin of this town. It's my time now, my way of doing things that counts now, not yours. The thing is, you know that. You don't like to admit it, but you wish you could be like me, stick your fingers up at the world, make the rules up as you go along, screw the system and anything that takes your fancy. But you can't. You want rules and regulations, even if it's just to break them, but there aren't any rules any more, Charlie, there aren't any regulations. It's all up in the air. Warming your pimply arse is the closest people like you'll ever get to money like mine. He fucked my mother, do you know that, your dad? Fucked my mum. Dad knew, God bless him, broke his heart. That's what they must have been arguing about when he copped it. I'll never forgive your dad for that, the price Mum had to pay for getting me into that poxy school.'

'I didn't know.'

'Well, it wasn't something I wrote up in the school mag. OK. You stay. Nothing gets out. But you're having none of it

341

any more. This town is a closed book. You'll scrape a living here, long as your old mum lives, but that's it. When she dies, then you can fuck off to Winchester or wherever. Till then, be as a shadow, flitting in and out, moving through the parts no one sees or hears. Don't talk to me again. Don't talk to Tommy, Lyn, anybody within a five-mile radius of me. And don't talk to Nef. Never talk to Nef. Talk to her once more, even now, and by God I will shoot you and dump you in this fucking lake, then shoot your mum for good measure, God bless her. One more thing. Burn that last ten thousand and send me the ashes with that nude. I'm going to bury her in it, up to her neck, like a bit of modern sculpture. "Do you know what's keeping her fanny warm?" I'll say. "Ten thousand quid," and they'll laugh. I'll have made a statement. That's what art's about, isn't it, now. Money and statements. Now, piss off, leave us alone.'

I left them, locked in an embrace, wrapped in his coat. As I drove home, a clutch of boys were fooling around at the bus stop, kicking a football in amongst the crowd, disturbing those sitting, waiting for their rides out of town. They seemed to take pleasure in the disturbance, whooping and cheering as it bounced off another head. No one stopped them. Boys don't have anything any more, men neither. We're a lost tribe wandering about the desert of this life without a home, without a purpose. All we can do is bury our head in the sand and pity ourselves for the sorry state we have got ourselves into. In my father's day, and years after him too, right up to the late seventies possibly, it was still possible for a boy to look out on the map of man and see the signposts laid out for him, the hills he might have to climb, the obstacles he might have to overcome, but it would be there for him at the end, his place in the world, his function, his respect, the rewards too, or if not, sustain him through the monotony. Longevity, never a man's strong point, was seen not in his ability to keep alive (women could do that far better) but in his pack-mule capacity, his ability to wake up at six, board his train, get on his bike, clock in, day after day after day, work and work and work, and find some stability in it, some reward – a wife to wash his clothes, cook his food, open her legs when required and bear his children, and a job that could let him climb the property ladder, give him access to his inner material needs. It did not matter that the life was boring or unfulfilling, or that much of the time was spent in idleness. It was there, every day. Boredom was part of the deal, just as unfulfilment and disappointment were part of the deal, the price you paid for regular reward, for small incremental elevations, the slow climb to the futile end, the blank years of retirement. They were not stupid, my father's generation, nor were those before him. They knew the value of what they did, why they did it, why they allowed themselves to be ruled by its frustrations, its niggling pettiness, enlarging the small things in life so that the view of the larger things, courage, equality, freedom, did not drive them all mad. They knew what it was there for, but thank God it was there. Not any longer, pal. It's long gone. We don't have them any more, and by the way no one wants them, or rather no one thinks they want them. In fact we all want them, what they brought, but we can't have them. They're not there. Women can't have them either but then they never wanted them anyway. They can swim in and out of that world now as easily as fish. There is always the big other thing for them. They can always choose that, always. They might not want to, but (for a time) it's there. It gives them a reason, even if they never take it up. Men don't have a reason any more. No one wants us. Why should they? What can we do? We have no job, no home to go to. It's been taken away. Small wonder then that all that is left for us is to turn in upon ourselves, to clutch at the few things that give us meaning, hope. Money is one. Football another. Football with money does it big time. Football with money sends us in a frenzy of delirium. But football is made up by men like us now, not like men of my father's years. They have no idea who they are, where they are meant to go either.

343

Call it sport. There was sport to it once, where sport was the point. The point now? What is the point, exactly, of this beautiful game? See them on the pitch, biting each other, pulling at each other's shirts, kicking and scratching, flying tackles, jabs in the elbow, feigning injuries, bellowing obscenities at the ref: see them later, off the pitch, urinating in hotel plant pots, wrecking Indian takeaways, abusing shop owners, brawling in night clubs, gang-banging under-age groupies, punching unwilling women in the face; see them beating their wives, breaking their girlfriends' arms, standing outside their ghastly houses with their Doric columns and Lamborghinis, driving to each other's hideous celebrity-strewn weddings. Be worthless now, that's all you can be. The age of the bully is upon us.

I burnt the money as requested, sent him the ashes and the nude. Until my mother died I worked as best I could, though business dropped off so much I had to sell the house. My mother lasted in Monkton's another five years. Large never asked for a single penny. I would see him, of course, strutting about the town, driving in his Land Rover or sitting beside Sophie, talking on the phone as she drove him in her open-top Mercedes, glasses in her hair, or some days, standing on the street corner of Tommy's emporium, like a nineteen-twenties shopkeeper, the two of them chatting away, bosom buddies that they now were. He would outstrip Tommy eventually, but that brought no comfort to me. I had once imagined no town of mine would accept a character such as Large to their heart, that it would have done as that town in Oxfordshire had done all those years ago, built a wall to keep him out, but no. This time it, and all the other towns, had welcomed him, conspired with him, let him and all the other Larges loose upon the world, many better than he, cleverer, quicker, more ruthless, more plausible, more attractive – but all guided by the same desires, the same principles. Larges in the cities, Larges in the towns, Larges in the docks of Liverpool. Larges on our roads and streets, Larges in our Tudor mansions, our Yorkshire vicarages. Larges in our cricket teams and in our golf clubs, Larges in our pubs and restaurants, Larges with their wives and their children and their parents and their friends all infected with the same spirit, all seeking the purchase of life, to lever life up, to multiply life by ten, twenty, one hundred times, to inflate life to its very utmost, and in this great bubbling edifice eat and burrow and devour, until, like an infestation of woodworm, they consume the very edifice in which they live until it crumbles to dust. Yet who was I to say it was wrong. Who had been good here for all his faults? Who had shown fortitude, courage, belief? Who loved his family, embraced in all its shameless crudity, the fact of his inheritance, his life? Who had stolen from him? Not his chuck-out manageress, not ear-ringed tattooed Jay, not his City friends, but me. Who had strayed from the marriage bed? Not he, but a member of the town's aristocracy. Who had come to my rescue in an instant, thrown his arms around my poor distraught mother, carried her to care and safety? Who had pumped life back into this town, brought a brief shine back into Mrs Hooker's eyes? Who was more than honest, prepared to run with the world, right or wrong? Who was the hero here, who the villain?

So here I am in my modest new office in Winchester. It's a good place to start up a business, Winchester, a little firm dealing with local people, local issues, nothing extravagant, just Charles Pemberton, accountant, and the initials after my name. I rang Katie, told her I'd gone. She says she'll be praying for me. She's prayed for me before, but it didn't do me much good. Perhaps praying is not what's needed. Perhaps praying, worship, putting one's faith in something is the wrong thing to do entirely. Perhaps we should have no faith, not in science or money or religion, nothing at all. Perhaps we should just look ourselves in the eye, love our mother and father, feel for their sorrow, just as they must feel for ours, not knowing how terrible our lives may be, but knowing that our lives will come, have a beginning and an end, and what we do with them, is as faith, blind and trusting, leading us we know not where.